CREATION IN DEATH

CREATION IN DEATH

Nora Roberts
writing as J. D. Robb

ISIS
LARGE PRINT
Oxford

First published in Great Britain 2007
by
Piatkus Books
An imprint of Little, Brown Book Group

Published in Large Print 2011 by ISIS Publishing Ltd.,
7 Centremead, Osney Mead, Oxford OX2 0ES
by arrangement with
Little, Brown Book Group
An Hachette Livre UK Company

British Library Cataloguing in Publication Data
Robb, J. D., 1950–
    Creation in death.
    1. Dallas, Eve (Fictitious character) - - Fiction.
    2. Serial murder investigation - - New York (State)
    - - New York - - Fiction.
    3. Policewomen - - New York (State) - - New York
    - - Fiction.
    4. Detective and mystery stories.
    5. Large type books.
    I. Title
    813.6–dc22

ISBN 978–0–7531–8858–3 (hb)
ISBN 978–0–7531–8859–0 (pb)

Printed and bound in Great Britain by
T. J. International Ltd., Padstow, Cornwall

Ah! The clock is always slow;
It is later than you think.
— ROBERT W. SERVICE

And music pours on mortals
Her magnificent disdain
— RALPH WALDO EMERSON

PROLOGUE

For him, death was a vocation. Killing was not merely an act, nor a means to an end. It certainly was not an impulse of the moment or a path to gain and glory.

Death was, in and of itself, the all.

He considered himself a late bloomer, and often bemoaned the years before he'd found his raison d'être. All that time lost, all those opportunities missed. But still, he had bloomed, and was forever grateful that he had finally looked inside himself and seen what he was. What he was meant for.

He was a maestro in the art of death. The keeper of time. The bringer of destiny.

It had taken time, of course, and experimentation. His mentor's time had run out long before he himself had become the master. And even at his prime, his teacher had not envisioned the full scope, the full power. He was proud that he had learned, had not only honed his skills but had expanded them while perfecting his techniques.

He'd learned, and learned quickly, that he preferred women as his partners in the duet. In the grand opera he wrote, and rewrote, they outperformed the men.

His requirements were few, but very specific.

He didn't rape them. He'd experimented there, as well, but had found rape distasteful and demeaning to both parties.

There was nothing elegant about rape.

As with any vocation, any art that required great skill and concentration, he'd learned he required holidays — what he thought of as his dormant periods.

During them he would entertain himself as anyone might on a holiday. He would travel, explore, eat fine meals. He might ski or scuba dive, or simply sit under an umbrella on a lovely beach and while away the time reading and drinking mai tais.

He would plan, he would prepare, he would make arrangements.

By the time he went back to work, he was refreshed and eager.

As he was now, he thought as he readied his tools. More, so much more . . . with his latest dormant period had come the understanding of his own destiny. So he'd gone back to his roots. And there, where he had first seriously plied his trade, he would re-form and remake connections before the curtain came down.

It added so many interesting layers, he mused, as he tested the edge on an antique switchblade with a horn handle he'd purchased while touring Italy. He turned the steel blade to the light, admired it. Circa nineteen fifty-three, he thought.

It was a classic for a reason.

He enjoyed using tools from long ago, though he also employed more modern pieces. The laser, for instance — so very excellent for applying the element of heat.

There must be a variety — sharp, dull, cold, heat — a series of elements in various forms, in various cycles. It took a great deal of skill, and patience and concentration to spin those cycles out to the absolute zenith of his partner's aptitude.

Then, and only then, would he complete the project and know he'd done his best work.

This one had been an excellent choice. He could congratulate himself on that. For three days and four nights, she'd survived — and there was life in her yet. It was so satisfying.

He'd started out slowly, naturally. It was vital, absolutely vital, to build and build *and build* to that ultimate crescendo.

He knew, as a master of his craft knew such things, that they were approaching that peak.

"Music on," he ordered, then stood, eyes closed as he absorbed the opening strains of Puccini's *Madame Butterfly*.

He understood the central character's choice of death for love. Hadn't it been that choice, so many years before, that had sent him on this path?

He slipped the protective cover over his tailored white suit.

He turned. He looked at her.

Such a lovely thing, he thought now. He remembered, as he always did, her precursor. Her mother, he supposed.

The Eve of all the others.

All that pretty white skin covered with burns and bruises, with narrow slices and meticulous little punctures. They showed his restraint, his patience, his thoroughness.

Her face was untouched — as yet. He always saved the face for last. Her eyes were fixed on his — wide, but yes, a bit dull. She had experienced nearly all she was capable of experiencing. Well, the timing worked well. Very well, because he'd anticipated, he'd prepared.

He'd already secured the next.

He glanced, almost absently, at the second woman across the room, peacefully sleeping under the drug he'd administered. Perhaps tomorrow, he thought, they could begin.

But for now . . .

He approached his partner.

He never gagged his partners, believing they should be free to scream, to beg, to weep, even to curse him. To express all emotion.

"Please," she said. Only, "Please."

"Good morning! I hope you rested well. We have a lot of work to do today." He smiled as he laid the edge of the knife between her first and second ribs. "So let's get started, shall we?"

Her screams were like music.

CHAPTER
ONE

Every once in a while, Eve thought, life was really worth living. Here she was, stretched out in a double-wide sleep chair watching a vid. There was plenty of action in the vid — she liked watching stuff blow up — and the "plotline" meant she didn't have to actually think.

She could just watch.

She had popcorn, drowned in butter and salt, the fat cat stretched across her feet keeping them nice and warm. She had the next day off, which meant she could sleep until she woke up, then veg until she grew mold.

Best of all, she had Roarke cozied up in the chair beside her. And since her husband had complained after one handful that the popcorn was disgusting, she had the whole bowl to herself.

Really, it didn't get any better.

Then again, maybe it did — would — as she planned to nail her husband like an airjack when the vid was over. Her version of a double feature.

"Iced," she said after a midair collision of a tourist tram and an ad blimp. "Seriously iced."

"I thought this storyline would appeal to you."

"There *is* no storyline." She took another handful of popcorn. "That's what appeals to me. It's just some dialogue stitching explosions together."

"There was brief full-frontal nudity."

"Yeah, but that was for you, and those of your ilk." She flicked a glance up at him, as on screen pedestrians ran screaming from falling wreckage.

He was so damn gorgeous — in anyone's ilk. A face sculpted by talented gods on a really good day. Strong bones laying the excellent foundation under that Irish white skin, the mouth that made her think of poets, until he used it on her so she couldn't think at all. Those wild Celt's eyes that saw just who she was.

Then you topped it off with all that black silky hair, added that long, lean body, the sexy Irish accent, tossed in brains, wit, temper, and street smarts and you had yourself a hell of a package.

And he was all hers.

She intended to make really good use of what was hers for the next thirty-six hours or so.

On screen a street battle erupted among the rubble with hurled miniboomers and whooshing blasters. The hero — distinguished by the fact he'd kicked the most ass thus far — burst through the mêlée on the back of a jet-bike.

Obviously caught up, Roarke dug into the popcorn. Then immediately pulled his hand out again and scowled at his own fingers. "Why don't you just dump salt into melted butter and eat that?"

"The corn makes a nice vehicle for it. Aw, what's the matter? You get your pretty hands messy?"

6

He wiped his fingers down her face, smiled. "Clean now."

"Hey!" She laughed, set the bowl aside. It would be safe, she knew, as even Galahad, the cat, wouldn't eat it her way. She poked a finger hard into Roarke's ribs, rolled until she was on top of him.

Maybe they'd just have a sneak preview of tonight's second feature.

"Going to pay for that one, pal."

"How much?"

"It's going to be the installment plan. I figure we'll start with . . ." She lowered her mouth to his, nipped that excellent bottom lip. She felt his hand move over her. Lifting her head, she narrowed her eyes at him. "Are you feeling my ass or wiping the rest of the butter and salt off your fingers?"

"Two birds, one ass. About that first payment."

"The interest is going to be — ha-ha — stiff." She went for the mouth again, started to sink in.

And her communicator signaled.

"Goddamn it." She pulled up. "This is crap. I'm not on call."

"Why is it in your pocket?"

"Habit. Stupid. Damn it," she spurted as she dragged the communicator out, checked the display. "It's Whitney." Sighing, she shoved a hand through her hair. "I have to take it."

"Pause vid," Roarke ordered, then rubbed the butter off her cheek. "Lights on, seventy percent."

"Thanks." Eve clicked on. "Dallas."

"Lieutenant, report to East River Park, at Second Street and Avenue D, as primary."

"Commander —"

"I understand you were neither on duty nor on call," he interrupted. "Now you are."

The word *why* went through her head, but she was too well-trained to verbalize it. "Yes, sir. I'll contact Detective Peabody en route."

"I'll see you at Central."

He clicked off.

"Unusual," Roarke commented. He'd already turned off the vid. "For the commander to contact you personally, and to yank you in this way."

"Something hot," Eve replied and shoved the communicator back in her pocket. "I've got nothing hot open. Not that it would have him tagging me directly when I'm not on the roll. Sorry." She glanced over. "Screws vid night."

"It'll keep. But as my evening is now open, I believe I'll go with you. I know how to keep out of the way," he reminded her before she could object.

He did, she admitted. And since she knew he'd changed his own schedule, possibly postponing acquiring a small country or planetoid, it seemed only fair.

"Then let's get moving."

He knew how to stay out of the way when it suited him. He also knew how to observe. What Roarke saw when they arrived at the park were a number of black-and-whites, a small army of uniforms and crime scene techs.

The media people who had a nose for this sort of thing were there, firmly blocked by part of that army. The barricades had been erected, and like the media and the civilian gawkers, he would have to make his observations from behind them.

"If you get bored," Eve told him, "just take off. I'll make my own way back."

"I'm not easily bored."

He watched her now, observed her now. His cop. The wind kicked at her long black coat, one she'd need as this first day of March was proving as brutal as the rest of 2060 had been. She hooked her badge on her belt, though he wondered how anyone could mistake her for anything other than a cop, and one with authority.

Tall and rangy, she moved to the barricades in strong strides. Her hair, short and brown, fluttered a little in that same wind — a wind that carried the scent of the river.

He watched her face, the way those whiskey-colored eyes tracked, the way her mouth — that had been so soft and warm on his — firmed. The lights played over her face, shifting those angles and planes.

She looked back at him, very briefly. Then she moved on, moved through the barricades to do what, he supposed, she'd been born to do.

She strode through the uniforms and techs. Some recognized her; some simply recognized what Roarke had. Authority. When she was approached by one of the uniforms, she stopped, brushed her coat back to tap her badge.

"Sir. I was ordered to look out for you, to escort you. My partner and I were first on scene."

"Okay." She gave him a quick once-over. On the young side, cut as clean as a military band. His cheeks were pink from the cold. His voice said native New Yorker, heading toward Brooklyn. "What have we got?"

"Sir. I was ordered to let you see for yourself."

"That so?" She scanned the badge on his thick uniform coat. "All right, Newkirk, let's go see for myself."

She gauged the ground covered, studied the line of trees and shrubs. It appeared the scene was well secured, locked tight. Not only from the land side, she noted as she glimpsed the river. The water cops were out, barricading the riverbank.

She felt a cold line of anticipation up her spine. Whatever this was, it was major.

The lights the techs had set up washed white over the shadows. Through them, she saw Morris coming toward her. Major, she thought again, for the chief medical examiner to be called on scene. And she saw it in his face, the tightness of concern.

"Dallas. They said you were on scene."

"They didn't say you were."

"I was nearby, out with friends. A little blues club over on Bleecker."

Which explained the boots, she supposed. The black and silver pattern she assumed had once belonged to some reptile wasn't the sort of thing a man would normally sport on a crime scene. Not even the stylish Morris.

His long black coat blew back to reveal a cherry-red lining. Under it, he wore black pants, black turtleneck — extreme casual wear for him. His long, dark hair was slicked back into a tail, bound top and tip with silver bands.

"The commander called you in," she said.

"He did. I haven't touched the body yet — visual only. I was waiting for you."

She didn't ask why. She understood she was meant to form her own conclusions without any outside data. "With us, Newkirk," she ordered, and walked toward the lights.

It might have been a sheet of ice or snow. From a distance, it might appear to be. And from a distance, the body arranged on it might appear to be artful — a model for some edgy shoot.

But she knew what it was, even from a distance, and the line of cold up her spine took on teeth.

Her eyes met Morris's. But they said nothing.

It wasn't ice, or snow. She wasn't a model or a piece of art.

Eve took a can of Seal-It from her kit, set the kit down.

"You're still wearing your gloves," Morris told her. "That stuff's hell on gloves."

"Right." With her gaze steady on the body, she pulled the gloves off, stuffed them in her pocket. Sealed up. She hooked her recorder to her coat. "Record on." The techs would be running one, as would Morris. She'd have her own.

"Victim is female, Caucasian. Did you ID her?" she asked Morris.

"No."

"As yet unidentified. Mid-to late twenties, brown and blue. Small tat of a blue and yellow butterfly on left hip. The body is naked, posed on a white cloth, arms spread, palms up. There's a silver ring on the third finger of her left hand. Various visible wounds indicating torture. Lacerations, bruising, punctures, burns. Crosshatch of slash wounds on both wrists, probable cause of death." She looked at Morris.

"Yes. Probable."

"There's carving in the torso, reading eighty-five hours, twelve minutes, thirty-eight seconds."

Eve let out a long, long breath. "He's back."

"Yes," Morris agreed. "Yes, he is."

"Let's get an ID, TOD." She glanced around. "Could have brought her in through the park, or by water. Ground's rock hard, and it's a public park. We may get some footprints, but they won't do us much good."

She reached in her kit again, paused when Peabody hustled up. "Sorry it took me so long. Had to come crosstown and there was a jam on the subway. Hey, Morris!" Peabody, a red cap pulled low over her dark hair, rubbed her nose, looked at the body. "Oh, man. Someone put her through it."

In her sturdy winter boots, Peabody sidestepped for a better view. "The message. There's something about that. Dim bell." She tapped at her temple. "Something."

12

"Get her ID," Eve ordered, then turned to Newkirk. "What do you know?"

He'd been standing at attention, but went even stiffer, even straighter. "My partner and I were on patrol, and observed what appeared to be a robbery in progress. We pursued a male individual into the park. The suspect headed in an easterly direction. We were unable to apprehend, the suspect had a considerable lead. My partner and I split up, intending to cut off the suspect. At which time, I discovered the victim. I called for my partner, then notified Commander Whitney."

"Notifying the commander isn't procedure, Officer Newkirk."

"No, sir. I felt, in these circumstances, that the notification was not only warranted but necessary."

"Why?"

"Sir, I recognized the signature. Lieutenant, my father's on the job. Nine years ago he was part of a task force formed to investigate a series of torture murders." Newkirk's gaze shifted to the body, back to Eve's. "With this signature."

"Your father's Gil Newkirk?"

"Yes, sir, Lieutenant." His shoulders relaxed a fraction at her question. "I followed the case back then, as much as I could. Over the years since, particularly since I've been on the job, my father and I have discussed it. The way you do. So I recognized the signature. Sir, I felt, in this case, breaking standard and notifying the commander directly was correct."

"You'd be right. Good call, Officer. Stand by."

She turned to Peabody.

"Vic is ID'd as Sarifina York, age twenty-eight. Address is on West Twenty-first. Single. Employed at Starlight. That's a retro club in Chelsea."

Eve crouched down. "She wasn't killed here, and she wasn't wrapped in this cloth when she was brought here. He likes the stage clean. TOD, Morris."

"Eleven this morning."

"Eighty-five hours. So he took her sometime Monday, or earlier if he didn't start the clock. Historically, he starts on the first very shortly after he makes the snatch."

"Starting the clock when he begins to work on them," Morris confirmed.

"Oh, shit. Oh, crap, I remember this." Peabody sat back on her heels. Her cheeks were reddened by the wind, and her eyes had widened with memory. "The media tagged him The Groom."

"Because of the ring," Eve told her. "We let the ring leak."

"It was, like, ten years ago."

"Nine," Eve corrected. "Nine years, two weeks, and . . . three days since we found the first body."

"Copycat," Peabody suggested.

"No, this is him. The message, the time — we didn't let that leak to the media. We closed that data up tight. But we never closed the case. We never closed him. Four women in fifteen days. All brunettes, the youngest twenty-eight, the oldest thirty-three. All tortured, between a period of twenty-three and fifty-two hours."

Eve looked at the carving again. "He's gotten better at his work."

14

Morris nodded as he made his study. "It appears the more superficial wounds were inflicted first, as before. I'll confirm when I get her home."

"Ligature marks, ankles, wrists — just above the slashes." Eve lifted one of the hands. "She didn't just lie there and take it, not from the looks of this. He used drugs on the others."

"Yes, I'll check."

Eve remembered it all, every detail of it, and all the frustration and fury that rode with it. "He'll have washed her, washed her clean — hair and body — with high-end products. Wrapped her up, probably in plastic, for transport. We never got so much as a speck of lint off any of the others. Bag the ring, Peabody. You take her, Morris."

She straightened. "Officer Newkirk, I'm going to need a full and detailed written report, asap."

"Yes, sir."

"Who's your LT?"

"Grohman, sir. I'm out of the one-seven."

"Your father still there?"

"He is, yes, sir."

"Okay, Newkirk, get me that report. Peabody, check Missing Persons, see if the vic was reported. I need to contact the commander."

By the time she exited the park, the wind had died down. Small mercy. The crowd of gawkers had thinned out, but the media hounds were more dogged. The only way to control the situation, she knew, was to meet it head on.

"I won't answer questions." She had to shout to be heard over the questions already being hurled at her. "I will make a brief statement. And if you keep shouting at me, you won't get that either. Earlier this evening" — she continued through the shouts and the noise level dropped — "officers of the NYPSD discovered the body of a woman in East River Park."

"Has she been identified?"

"How was she killed?"

Eve simply stared holes into the reporters who attempted to break rank. "Did you guys just drop into the city out of a puffy cloud, or are you just running your mouths to hear your own voice? As anyone with half a brain knows, the woman's identity will not be given out until after notification of next of kin. Cause of death will be determined by the medical examiner. And anyone stupid enough to ask me if we have any leads is going to be blocked from receiving any ensuing data on this matter. Clear? Now stop wasting my time."

She stalked off, and was halfway to her own vehicle when she spotted Roarke leaning against the hood. She'd completely forgotten about him.

"Why aren't you home?"

"What? And miss the entertainment? Hello, Peabody."

"Hey." She managed to smile even though her cheeks felt like a couple of slabs of ice. "You've been here the whole time?"

"Nearly. I did wander off." He opened the car door, took out a couple of insulated takeout cups. "To get you presents."

16

"It's coffee," Peabody said, reverently. "It's hot coffee."

"Should thaw you out a bit. Bad?" he said to Eve.

"Very. Peabody, track down contact info on the vic's next of kin."

"York, Sarifina. On it."

"I'll get myself home," Roarke began, then stopped. "What was that name?"

"York," Eve repeated, "Sarifina." Something sank in her belly. "You're going to tell me you knew her."

"Late twenties, attractive brunette?" He leaned back against the car again when Eve nodded. "I hired her a few months ago to manage a club in Chelsea. I can't say I knew her other than I found her bright, energetic, capable. How did she die?"

Before she could answer, Peabody stepped back up. "Mother in Reno — that's Nevada — father in Hawaii. Bet it's warm there. She has a sister in the city. Murray Hill. And the Missing Person's data came through. The sister reported her missing yesterday."

"Let's take the vic's apartment first, then the club, then the next of kin."

Roarke laid a hand on Eve's arm. "You haven't told me how she died."

"Badly. This isn't the place for the details. I can arrange for transpo for you or —"

"I'm going with you. She was one of mine," he said before she could object. "I'm going with you."

She didn't argue. Not only would it waste time and energy, she understood. And since she had him, she'd use him.

"If an employee — especially one in a managerial position — didn't show for work a few days running, would you be notified?"

"Not necessarily." He did what he could to make himself comfortable in the back of the police issue. "And I certainly wouldn't know her schedule off the top of my head, but I will find out about that. If she missed work, it's likely someone covered for her, and — or — that her absence was reported to a supervisor in that particular arm of the Entertainment Division."

"I need a name on that."

"You'll have it."

"Reported missing yesterday. Whoever was assigned to that case would have, or damn well should have, interviewed coworkers at the club, neighbors, friends. We need to connect to that, Peabody."

"I'll run it down."

"Tell me," Roarke repeated, "how she died."

"Morris will determine cause of death."

"Eve."

She flipped a glance in the rearview mirror, met his eyes. "Okay, I can tell you how it went down or close to it. She was stalked. The killer would take all the time he needed to observe and note her habits, her routines, her mode of traveling, her vulnerabilities — i.e., when she would most likely be alone and accessible. When he was ready, he'd make the grab. Most likely off the street. He'd have his own vehicle for this purpose. He'd drug her and take her to his . . ."

They'd called it his workshop, Eve remembered.

". . . to the location he'd prepared, most likely a private home. Once there he would either keep her drugged until he was ready, or — if she was the first — he'd begin."

"The first?"

"That's right. And when he was ready, he'd start the clock. He'd remove her clothes; he would bind her. His preferred method of binding is rope — a good hemp. It chafes during struggle. He would use four methods of torture — physically, we can't speak to psychologically — which are heat, cold, sharp implements, and dull implements. He would employ these methods at increasing severity. He'd continue until, you could speculate, the victim no longer provides him with enough stimulation or pleasure or interest. Then he ends it by slitting their wrists and letting them bleed out. Postmortem, he carves into their torsos, the time — in hours, minutes, and seconds — they survived."

There was a long moment of absolute silence. "How long?" Roarke asked.

"She was strong. He washes them afterward. Scrubs them down using a high-end soap and shampoo. We think he wraps them in plastic, then transports them to a location he'd have already scouted out and selected. He lays them out there, on a clean white cloth. He puts a silver band on their ring finger, left hand."

"Aye." Roarke murmured it as he stared out the window. "I remember some of this. I've heard some of this."

"Between February eleventh and February twenty-sixth, 2051, he abducted, tortured, and killed four

19

women in this manner. Then he stopped. Just stopped. Into the wind, into the fucking ether. I'd hoped into Hell."

Roarke understood now why she'd been called in, off the roll, by the commander. "You worked these murders."

"With Feeney. He was primary. I was a detective, just made second grade, and we worked it. We had a task force by the second murder. And we never got him."

Four women, Eve thought, who had never gotten justice.

"He's surfaced again, here and there," she continued. "Two weeks, two and a half — four or five women. Then he goes under. A year, a year and a half. Now he's come back to New York, where we think he started. Back to where he started, and this time, we'll finish it."

In his well-appointed living room, with the split of champagne he traditionally opened to celebrate the end of a successful project, the man the media had long ago dubbed The Groom settled down in front of his entertainment screen.

It was too early, he knew, most likely too early for any reports. It would be morning before his latest creation was discovered. But he couldn't resist checking.

A few moments, just to see, he told himself, then he'd enjoy his champagne with some music. Puccini, perhaps, in honor of . . . he had to pause and think before he remembered her name. Sarifina, yes. Such a lovely name. Puccini for Sarifina. He really believed she'd responded to Puccini best.

He surfed the channels, and was rewarded almost immediately. Delighted, he sat up, crossed his ankles, and prepared to listen to his latest reviews.

Identification is not being released in order for the woman's next of kin to be notified. While there is no confirmation at this time that the woman was murdered, the participation of Lieutenant Eve Dallas on the scene indicates foul play is being considered.

He applauded, lightly, when Eve's face came on screen. "There you are," he said. "Hello, again! So nice, so very nice to see old friends. And this time, this time we're going to get to know each other so very much better."

He lifted his glass, held it out in a toast. "I know you're going to be my very finest work."

CHAPTER
TWO

Sarifina's apartment was urban hip. Strong colors dominated in paint and fabric, with glossy black as counterpoint in tables, shelves. Sleek and vibrant, Eve thought. And low-maintenance, which made her think of a woman who didn't have the time or the inclination to fuss.

Her bed was made, covered with a stoplight-red spread and boldly patterned pillows. In the closet was a collection of vintage gowns. Sleek again, simple, and still vibrant in color. Shoes Eve thought might be vintage as well were in clear protective boxes.

She took care of what was hers.

"Is this the sort of gear she'd wear at the club?" Eve asked Roarke.

"Yes, exactly. It's retro — 1940s theme. She'd be expected to mingle, to recognize and greet regulars, to table hop. And to look the part."

"Guess she would have. Some more up-to-date street clothes, two business-type suits. We'll tag her electronics," she added glancing at the bedside 'link. "See if he contacted her. Not his usual style, but things change. Tag her 'links, her comp. Did she have an office at the club?"

"Yes."

"We'll tag the e-stuff there, too." She pulled open a drawer on the little desk under the window. "No date book, no planner, no pocket 'link. She would have had them on her. Big-ass purse in the closet, and one of those — what do you call them — city bags. Go with the suit and the street clothes. A few evening bags. We'll see if the sister knows what's missing."

"A pint of soy milk in the fridge," Peabody reported as she entered. "Expired Wednesday. Some leftover Chinese, which by my gauge has been in there near to a week. Found a memo cube."

Peabody held it up. "Shopping list — market stuff and a few other things. Also a fridge photo of her and a guy, but it wasn't on the fridge. It was facedown in the kitchen drawer, which says recently ex-boyfriend to me."

"All right, let's bag and tag." Eve glanced at her wrist unit. It was nearly one in the morning. If they started to knock on doors and woke up neighbors at this hour, it would only piss people off.

Pissed people were less willing to talk to cops.

"We'll hit the club next."

With Roarke's fondness for old vids, particularly the moody black-and-whites produced in the middle of the last century, Eve knew something about the fashions and music, the cadence of the 1940s. At least as depicted in the Hollywood of that day.

Walking into Starlight at two in the morning, she felt she now also knew what it might be like to take a spin in a time machine.

The club was a wide and sparkling space divided into three levels. Each was accessed by a short set of wide, white stairs. And each, even at this hour, was filled with people who sat at white-clothed tables or silver-cushioned booths.

The waitstaff, men in formal white suits, women in short, full-skirted black dresses, moved from table to table serving drinks from trays. The patrons were decked out in black tie, retro suits, sleek gowns of the type that had been in Sarifina's closet, or elaborate and frothy ones.

Elegance and sophistication were the bywords, and Eve was mildly surprised to see tables of people in their twenties, straight through to those who had, no doubt, celebrated their centennial.

Music pumped out from the band on the glossy black stage. Or maybe "orchestra" was the term, she thought, as there were at least twenty of them with strings, horns, a piano, drums. And the swinging beat had couples massing over what was the centerpiece of the club. The dance floor.

Black and silver, the large pattern of squares gleamed and sparkled under the shimmering lights of slowly revolving mirror balls.

"This is, like, ultimately uptown," Peabody commented. "Extreme."

"Everything old is new again," Roarke said, scanning the club. "You'll want the assistant manager here, a Zela Wood."

"You have all your employees' names at the tips of your fingers?" Eve asked.

"No, actually. I looked up the file. Name, schedule, ID photo. And . . ." He zeroed in. "Ah, yes, that would be Zela."

Eve followed his direction. The striking woman wore pale gold that glowed against skin the color of good, strong coffee. Her hair was worn in long, loose waves that tumbled around her shoulders, down her back. She covered a lot of ground quickly, Eve noted, and still managed to glide as if she had all the time in the world.

It was obvious she'd seen and recognized the big boss as her eyes — nearly the same color as her dress — were fixed on him. Her fingers skimmed the silver rail as she climbed the steps toward him.

"Ms. Wood."

"How lovely." She offered him a hand and a dazzling smile. "I'll have a table arranged right away for you and your party."

"We don't want a table." Eve drew Zela's eyes to hers. "Let's see your office."

"Of course," Zela said without missing a beat. "If you'll just come with me."

"My wife," Roarke said and got an automatic scowl from Eve, "Lieutenant Dallas, and her partner, Detective Peabody. We need to talk, Zela."

"Yes, all right." Her voice remained as smooth as the cream that might be poured in that strong, black coffee. But worry came into her eyes.

She led the way past the coat check, the silver doors of rest rooms, then used a code to access a private elevator.

Moments later, they stepped out into the twenty-first century.

The room was simply and efficiently furnished, and reflected business. All business. Wall screens displayed the club, various areas — which included the kitchen, wine cellar, and liquor storage area. The desk held a multi-link, a computer, and a tray of disc files.

"Can I offer you anything to drink?" Zela began.

"No, thanks. You know Sarifina York?"

"Yes, of course." The worry deepened. "Is something wrong?"

"When did you last see her?"

"Monday. We have our Monday teas geared toward our older patrons. Sarifina runs those, she has such a knack for it. She's on from one to seven on Mondays, and I take the evening shift. She left about eight, a little before eight, I think. I asked because she didn't show on Wednesday."

Zela glanced at Roarke, pushed at her hair. "Tuesdays are her night off, but she didn't come in Wednesday. I covered. I just thought . . ."

Zela began to fiddle with the necklace she wore, running her fingers over the sparkling, clear stones. "She had a breakup with the man she's been seeing, and she was down about it. I thought they might have picked things up again."

"Has she missed work without notice before?" Eve asked.

"No."

"Are you saying that to cover?"

"No. No. Sari's never missed." Now Zela's gaze latched onto Roarke's face. "Never missed, and that's why I covered for her initially. She loves working here, and she's wonderful at her job."

"I understand and appreciate that you'd cover a night for a friend and coworker, Zela," Roarke told her.

"Thank you. When she didn't show Thursday, and I couldn't reach her, well, I'm not sure if I was annoyed or worried. A combination of both, really, so I contacted her sister. Sari had her sister listed as contact person. I didn't contact your office, sir. I didn't want to get her in trouble."

Zela's breath trembled as she drew it in. "But she is in trouble, isn't she? You're here because she's in trouble."

It was going to be a kick in the face, Eve knew. It was always a kick in the face. "I'm sorry to tell you, but Sarifina is dead."

"She's . . . what? What did you say?"

"You should sit down, Zela." Taking her arm, Roarke nudged her gently into a chair.

"You said . . . she's dead? There was an accident? How . . ." Those pale gold eyes gleamed with wet and shock.

"She was murdered. I'm sorry. You were friends?"

"Oh, God. Oh, God. When? How? I don't understand."

"We're looking into that, Ms. Wood." Eve let her gaze drift briefly to Roarke as he walked to a wall panel, and opening it chose a bottle of brandy from the selection of liquors. "Can you tell me if anyone bothered her or seemed unusually interested in her?"

"No. No. I mean, a lot of people were interested in her. She's the sort of person who interests people. I don't understand."

"Did she complain about anyone bothering her, or making her uncomfortable?"

"No."

"Drink a bit of this." Roarke pressed a glass of brandy into Zela's hand.

"Has anyone come in, asking questions about her?"

"Just tonight, a few hours ago, a police detective. He said, he told me that Sari's sister had reported her missing. And I thought . . ." Tears spilled now. "I honestly thought Sari's sister was overreacting. I was a little worried, a little, because I thought she'd gone back to the ex, and he'd talked her into blowing off this job. That was the problem," Zela continued as she rubbed a tear from her cheek. "He didn't like her working here because it took up most of her nights."

Now those damp eyes widened. "Did he hurt her? Oh, my God."

"Did he strike you as the type who would?"

"No. No, no. A whiner, that's what I thought. Passive-aggressive, and kind of a jerk. I'd never have believed he'd hurt her. Not like this."

"We have no reason to believe he has, at this time. Can you give me his name, his address?"

"Yes. All right."

"Would you still have your security discs from Monday?"

"Yes. Yes, we keep them for a week."

"I'm going to need those. I'll take the discs from last Saturday and Sunday as well. On Monday, did she leave alone?"

"I didn't see her leave. What I mean is, I came in here at about quarter to eight, and she was just putting on her coat. I said something like, 'So you can't get enough of this place?' and she laughed. Just wanted to finish up some paperwork. We talked for a few minutes, just shop talk mostly. She said she'd see me Wednesday, and I said . . . I said, 'Have a good day off.' Then she went out of the office, and I sat down to do a quick check on the late reservations. And I assumed, she'd gone straight out. She never mentioned being with anyone."

"All right. I'd appreciate it if you could get me those discs, and that information on the man she'd been seeing."

"Yes." Zela got to her feet. "Is there something I can do? I don't know what I should do. Her sister? Should I contact her sister?"

"We'll be taking care of that."

When there was a knock on the door in the middle of the night, most people knew, in the gut, it wasn't going to be good news.

When Jaycee York opened her door, Eve could already see the dread. Even as she stared into Eve's eyes, before a word was spoken, Eve saw grief rise up through that dread.

"Sari. Oh, no. Oh, no."

"Ms. York, may we come in?"

"You found her. But . . ."

"We should go inside, Ms. York." Peabody took Jaycee's arm, eased her around. "We should go sit down."

"It's going to be bad. It's going to be very, very bad. Will you please say it quickly? Would you please tell me fast?"

"Your sister's dead, Ms. York." With her hand still on Jaycee's arm, Peabody felt the shudder. "We're very sorry for your loss."

"I knew, I think. I knew as soon as they called from the club. I knew something awful had happened to her."

Peabody guided Jaycee to a chair in the living area. Lots of clutter, Eve noted, the kind that shouted a family lived there. There were photographs of young boys, of a laughing man, of the victim.

There were several colorful throws, a lot of big floor pillows that looked as if they'd had a great deal of use.

"Is your husband at home, Ms. York?" Eve asked. "Would you like us to get him for you?"

"He's not . . . Clint took the boys to Arizona. To . . . to Sedona. A week. It's a school camp." Jaycee looked around the room as if expecting to see them. "They went to camp, and I didn't. I didn't want to camp, and I had work. And wouldn't it be nice, I thought, wouldn't it be nice to have a week at home by myself. I didn't call them. I didn't tell them because they'd worry. Why worry them when everything's going to be fine? I kept telling myself everything was going to be fine.

30

"But it's not. It's not."

She covered her face with her hands and began to weep.

Eve put her at a decade older than her sister. Her hair was short and blond, her devastated eyes a summer blue.

"I called the police." She sobbed out the words. "When they said she hadn't come into work, I called the police. I went to her apartment, but she wasn't there, so I called. And they said to file a report. A missing person's report."

She closed her eyes. "What happened to Sari? What happened to my sister?"

There was an ottoman in front of the chair. Eve sat on it so they would be face to face. "I'm sorry. She was murdered."

The splotchy color weeping painted in her cheeks died away to shock-white. "They said — I heard — they said there was a woman found tonight, in East River Park. Identification withheld, they said, until notification of next of kin. I'm next of kin."

Jaycee pressed a hand to her lips. "I thought, 'No, no, that's not Sari. Sari doesn't live on the East Side.' But I kept waiting for someone to knock on the door. And you did."

"You were close, you and your sister."

"I . . . I can't. I can't."

"I'm going to get you some water, Ms. York." Peabody touched a hand to Jaycee's shoulder. "Is it all right if I go into the kitchen and get you some water?"

Jaycee only nodded as she stared at Eve. "She was my babydoll. My mother died when I was little, and a few years later, my father remarried. They had Sari. Sarifina. She was so pretty, like a doll. I loved her."

"Would she have told you if anyone was bothering her? If she was disturbed or uneasy about anything?"

"Yes. We talked all the time. She loved her job. She was so good at it, and it made her so happy. But it was a problem for Cal. The man she'd been seeing for the last few months. The fact that she worked at night and couldn't spend that time with him. She was angry and hurt that he'd given her an ultimatum. That she had to quit her job or he'd break things off. So they broke up. She was better off."

"Because?"

"He isn't good enough for her. That's not just sister talk." She paused, took the water Peabody offered her. "Thank you. Thanks. He just wasn't good enough — selfish streak, and he didn't like the fact she was making more money that he was. She knew it, recognized it, and was ready to move on. Still, she was sad about it. Sari doesn't like to lose. You don't think . . . Do you think Cal hurt her?"

"Do you?"

"No." Jaycee drank, breathed carefully, took another small sip. "I wouldn't have thought it. It never crossed my mind. Why would he? He didn't love her," Jaycee said dully. "And he was much too interested in himself to get worked up enough to . . . I need to see her. I need to see Sari."

"We'll arrange for that. When did you see her last?"

"Last Sunday afternoon. Before Clint and the boys left. She came by to say good-bye. She was so full of life, of energy. We made plans to shop on Saturday — tomorrow. My guys aren't coming home until Sunday, they're taking a play day before they come home. Sari and I are going shopping, and out for lunch. Oh, God. Oh, God. How did she die? How did my baby die?"

"We're still investigating, Ms. York. As soon as I can give you details, I will." She would not, Eve thought, tell this poor woman, not while there was no one to lean on, what had happened to her sister. "We can contact your husband. You want him and your sons home now?"

"Yes. Yes, I want them to come home. I want them home."

"Meanwhile is there someone we can call, a neighbor, a friend, to stay with you?"

"I don't know. I don't . . ."

"Ms. York." Peabody spoke gently. "You don't have to be alone now. Let us call a friend to come be with you."

"Lib. Could you call Lib? She'll come."

When they were outside, Roarke took a long breath. "I often wonder how you do what you do, standing over death, looking so unflinchingly into the minds of those who bring it. But I think of all you do, taking what's been done to those left behind, feeling — as you'd have to — their pain — is more wrenching than all the rest of it."

He brushed his hand over Eve's. "You didn't tell her what happened to her sister. You're giving her time to get through the first of the pain."

"I don't know if I did her any favors. It's going to break her to pieces. Might've been better to do it now when she's already broken."

"You did it right," Peabody said. "She's got her friend, but she'll need her family. They're going to need each other to get through that end of it."

"Well. We'll go see what Morris can tell us. Listen." She turned to Roarke. "I'll get in touch as soon as I can."

"I'd like to go with you."

"It's already, what, after four in the morning. You don't want to go to the morgue."

"A moment," he murmured to Peabody, and taking Eve's hand drew her aside. "I'd like to see this through. I'd like you to let me."

"I can tell you whatever we get from Morris, and you can grab some sleep. But," she continued before he could speak, "that's not the same thing. I want you to tell me you don't feel responsible for this."

He looked back toward the sister's apartment, thought of the grief that lived there now. "She's not dead because I hired her. I'm not quite that egotistical. All the same, I want to see it through."

"Okay. You drive. We're going to need to make a stop on the way. I need to talk to Feeney."

He'd been her trainer, her teacher, her partner. He was, though neither of them spoke of it, the man who stood as her father in the ways that mattered.

He had plucked her out of the pack when she'd still been in uniform, and made her his. She'd never asked

Feeney what he'd seen that persuaded him to take on a green uniform. She'd only known that by doing so, he'd made all the difference.

She'd have been a good cop without him. She'd have made detective through her own need, dedication, and aptitude. And maybe, eventually, she'd have held the rank she held now.

But she wouldn't have been the same cop without him.

When he'd earned his bars, he'd requested EDD. E-work had always been his specialty, and his passion, so his request for the Electronic Detective Division was a natural.

She remembered she'd been just a little annoyed he'd moved out of Homicide. And for the first few months, she'd missed him, seeing him, working with him, talking to him every day, like she might've missed her own hand.

She could've left this for morning — at least a decent hour of the morning. But she knew, had their positions been reversed, she'd want this knock on the door.

She'd have been damn pissed if she didn't get the knock.

When he answered his face was sleep rumpled, making it more lived-in than usual. His hair, a gingery scrubbing brush mixed with silver, was standing straight out. As if the air around him had been suddenly ionized.

And while he might've been wearing a tattered robe in the surprising color choice of purple, his eyes were all cop.

"Who died?"

"Need to talk to you about that," Eve told him. "But more how than who."

"Well." He scratched his jaw, and Eve could hear the rasp of his fingers on the night's growth of beard. "Better come on in. Wife's asleep. Let's go on in the kitchen. Need coffee."

It was a homey place. Lived in, Eve thought, like Jaycee's had been, if you added another decade or two. Feeney's kids had grown up, and there were grandkids now. Eve was never quite sure of the number. But there was a good-sized eating area off the kitchen, with a long table to accommodate the lot of them at family dinners.

Feeney brought in coffee, scuffing along in slippers Eve would bet a month's pay were a Christmas gift.

On the middle of the table was a strangely shaped vase in streaky colors of red and orange. Mrs. Feeney's work, Eve determined. The wife had a penchant for hobbies and crafts, and was always making things. Often unidentifiable things.

"Caught a case," Eve began. "Vic is female, brunette, late twenties, found naked in East River Park."

"Yeah, I caught the report on screen."

"Found nude. She'd been tortured. Burns, bruising, cuts, punctures. Her wrists were slashed."

"Fuck."

Yeah, he had it already, Eve noted. "Vic was wearing a silver band on the third finger of her left hand."

"How long?" Feeney demanded. "How long did she last? What was the time he carved into her?"

"Eighty-five hours, twelve minutes, thirty-eight seconds."

"Fuck," he said again. "Motherfucker." Feeney's hand balled into a fist to rap, light and steady, on the table. "He's not walking again, Dallas. He's not walking away from us again. He'll have number two already."

"Yeah." Eve nodded. "I figure he's got number two."

Feeney braced his elbows on the table, scooped his fingers through his hair. "We've got to go through everything we had nine years back, what data there is on him from the other times he went to work. Put a task force together now, at the get. We don't wait for the second body to show up. You get anything from the scene?"

"So far, just the body, the ring, the sheet. I'll get you a copy of the records. Right now, I'm heading to the morgue to see what Morris can tell us. You're going to need to get dressed, unless you're wearing purple terry cloth to work these days."

He glanced down, shook his head. "If you saw the one the wife got me for Christmas, you'd understand why I'm still wearing this one." He pushed to his feet. "Look, you go on, and I'll meet you at the morgue. Going to need my own ride anyway."

"All right."

"Dallas."

In that moment, Roarke realized neither he nor Peabody existed. They simply weren't a part of the reality between the other two.

"We have to find what we missed," Feeney said to Eve. "What everybody's missed. There's always something. One piece, one step, one thought. We can't miss it this time."

"We won't."

Roarke had been to the morgue before. He wondered if the white tiles through the tunnels of the place were meant to replace natural light. Or if they had merely been chosen as an acceptance of the stark.

There were echoes throughout as well — the repeat and repeat of bootsteps as they walked. More silence, he supposed, as the staff would be on graveyard shift. So to speak.

It was still shy of dawn, and he could see the long night was wearing on Peabody a bit, with a heaviness under her dark eyes. But not on Eve, not yet. The fatigue would rush up and choke her — it always did. But for now she was running on duty and purpose, and an underlying anger he wasn't sure she recognized as vital fuel.

Eve paused outside the double doors of an autopsy room. "Do you need to see her?" she asked him.

"I do. I want to be of some help in this, and if I'm to be of any help, I need to understand. I've seen death before."

"Not like this." She pushed through.

Morris was inside. He'd changed, she noted, into gray sweats and black and silver skids she imagined he kept on the premises for working out. He sat, and continued to sit for a moment, in a steel chair drinking something thick and brown out of a tall glass.

"Ah, company. Protein smoothy?"

"So absolutely not," Eve said.

"Tastes marginally better than it looks. And does its job. Roarke, good to see you, even though."

"And you."

"Vic worked for Roarke," Eve said.

"I'm very sorry."

"I barely knew her. But . . ."

"Yes, but . . ." Morris set the smoothy aside before he pushed to his feet. "I regret that we'll all come to know her quite well now."

"She managed one of Roarke's clubs. The Starlight down in Chelsea?"

"Is that yours?" Morris smiled a little. "I took a friend there a few weeks ago. It's an entertaining trip back to an intriguing time."

"Feeney's on his way in."

Morris shifted his gaze to Eve. "I see. It was the three of us over the first of them the last time. Do you remember?"

"Yeah, I remember."

"Her name was Corrine, Corrine Dagby."

"Age twenty-nine," Eve confirmed. "Sold shoes in a boutique downtown. Liked to party. She lasted twenty-six hours, ten minutes, fifty-eight seconds."

Morris nodded. "Do you remember what you said when we stood here then?"

"No, not exactly."

"I do. You said: 'He'll want more than that.' And you were right. We learned he wanted more than that. Should we wait for Feeney?"

"He'll catch up."

"All right." Morris crossed the room.

Roarke looked over, then he stepped over.

He'd seen death, bloody, vicious, violent, useless, and terrible death. But he saw, once more, Eve was right.

He'd never seen the likes of this.

CHAPTER
THREE

So many wounds, he thought, and all washed clean. Somehow it might have been less horrid if there had been blood. Blood would be proof, wouldn't it, that life had once been there.

But this . . . this woman he remembered as vital and brimming with energy looked like some poor doll, mangled and sliced by a vicious child.

"Tidy work," Eve stated, and had Roarke's gaze whipping toward her.

He started to speak, to let loose some of the horror he felt. But he saw her face, saw the anger was closer to the surface now however calm her voice. Saw, too, the pity. She had such pity inside her he often wondered how she could bear the weight of it.

So he said nothing.

"He's very methodical." Morris engaged the computer before offering Eve microgoggles. "You see these wounds on the limbs? Long, thin, shallow."

"Scalpel maybe, or the tip of a sharp blade." Though the wounds were displayed, optimized, on screen, Eve leaned down to study them through the goggles. "Precise, too. Either she was drugged or he had her restrained in such a way she couldn't struggle enough to make a difference."

"Which gets your vote?" Morris asked.

"Restraints. What's the fun if she's out of it, can't feel fully? Burns are small along here." Eve turned the victim's left arm. "Here in the bend of the elbow, precise again, but the skin's charred some at the edges. Flame? Not a laser, but live fire?"

"I would agree. Some of the other burns look like laser to me. And there, on the inner thigh where it's mottled? Extreme cold."

"Yeah. The bruising — no laceration, no scraping. Smooth implement."

"Sap." Roarke studied the bruising himself. "An old-fashioned sap would bruise like that. Leather's effective if you can afford the cost. Filled with ordinary sand, it does its job."

"Again, agree. And we have the punctures," Morris continued. "Which are in circular patterns here, here, here." The screen flashed with close-ups of the back of the right hand, the heel of the left foot, the left buttocks. "Twenty minute punctures, in this precise pattern."

"Like needles," Eve mused. "Some kind of tool . . . He could . . ." She curved her right hand, laid it on the heel of the body, pressed. "That's new. We don't have this wound pattern on record."

"He's an inventive bastard," Peabody added. "Morris, can I get a bottle of water?"

"Help yourself."

"You need air," Eve said without looking at her, "go get some."

"Just the water."

"This pattern might be new," Eve continued, "but the rest is consistent. More creative, maybe, a little more patient. You do what you do long enough, you get better at it. Longer, deeper wounds along the rib cage, over the breasts. Wider burn areas, deeper bruising up the calves.

"Increases the pain, gradually. Wants it to last. Cuts and burns on her face. No bruising there. Sap her and she might lose consciousness. Don't want that."

The doors swished open. Feeney walked in, came straight to the table. He looked down. "Ah, hell," was all he said.

"We've got one new wound type. Circular pattern of punctures. See what you think of it."

Eve bent close to the ruined face, her eyes behind the goggles unflinching. "No bruising here that would indicate he gagged her — or not tightly. Nothing that would mar the skin. He has to have a place, a very, very private place. So she can scream. Tox back?"

"Yes, just before you came. There were small traces of a standard sedative in her bloodstream. Barely registered. She'd have been awake and aware at TOD."

"Same MO. Puts her to sleep when he's busy with other business."

"There were traces, too, of water and protein in her system. The lab will confirm, but . . ."

"He likes to give them enough nutrients to keep them going," Feeney said.

Eve nodded. "I remember. Then ends it this way." She lifted the victim's hand, turned the wrist up. "Crosshatches, but not too deep. She'll bleed out, but it'll take time. Adds to his clock."

"I expect, given the prior blood loss, trauma, two hours. Three at the most. She would have lost consciousness before the end of it."

"Any trace of what he used to wash her down?"

"Yes. In the scalp wounds, and the punctures under the nails. I sent it to the lab."

"Send over some skin scrapings, some hair. I want to see what kind of water. City water? Suburbs?"

"I'll take care of it."

"He'll be starting on the second." Feeney looked at Eve as she took off the goggles. "Probably has the third picked out."

"Yeah. I'm going to see the commander. For now, you tag a couple of your best men. I want them running and analyzing data as we get it, running probabilities. First on scene was Gil Newkirk's son."

"Son of a bitch."

"Yeah, you reach out to Newkirk, senior? He's out of the one-seven, so's his kid. I'm bringing the son in on the uniform end of the task force, if his lieutenant doesn't have a problem with it."

"Who's the LT?"

"Grohman."

"I know him," Feeney told her. "I'll handle it."

"Good." Eve checked the time, calculated. "Peabody, book us a conference room, and I want it for the duration. They give you any lip about it, toss them to

44

Whitney. We'll meet there for the first briefing at oh-nine-hundred."

As they headed out, Eve shot a look at Roarke. "I take it you want to stick for the briefing."

"You trust correctly."

"I'm going to need to clear that with Whitney."

"All right."

"Take the wheel. I'll see what I can do."

She put the call through, unsurprised to find Whitney already at his desk. "Sir, we're heading into Central now from the morgue. We're booking a conference room."

"Locked in A," Peabody said from the backseat.

"Conference room A," Eve relayed. "And I'm scheduling the first briefing at oh-nine-hundred."

"I'll be there. So will Chief Tibble."

"Yes, sir. I've brought in Captain Feeney as we worked together on the previous investigation. I've asked him for two additional e-men to run data. I would like to put Officer Newkirk on the uniform part of the task force as he was first on scene, and is the son of an officer who was involved in the previous investigation."

"I'll clear that for you."

"Sir, Feeney's on that. I want four additional men. Baxter, Trueheart, Jenkinson, and Powell. I'll reassign whatever caseloads they're currently carrying. I need them clear for this."

"It's your call, Lieutenant, but Trueheart's an aide, not a detective, and doesn't have extensive experience."

"He's tireless, sir, and has an excellent eye. Baxter's given him some seasoning."

"I'll trust your judgment."

"Thank you. I'll need Dr. Mira to review and possibly update the profile, and could make use of an expert consultant, civilian."

Whitney said nothing for five long seconds. "You want to bring Roarke in on this, Dallas?"

"The victim was an employee. The connection can clear some roads in the investigation and interviews. In addition, Commander, he has access to better equipment than the NYPSD. We may have use for it."

"Again, your call, your judgment."

"Yes, sir."

Dawn was breaking as Roarke swung into the garage at Central. "We're in the house, sir. I'll be set up by nine hundred."

"I'll contact Dr. Mira and the chief."

Eve sat for a moment when Roarke pulled into her slot. In the back, Peabody snored in quiet, almost ladylike snorts. "You know something about torture," she said at length.

"I do, yes."

"And you know people who know people."

"True."

"That's what I want you to think about. And if you have a contact that can add to the data, I want you to use it. He has tools, and he has a workshop. It would be well set up, well equipped. I think he'd have e-toys, too. Monitor the vic's pulse rate, maybe brain wave patterns. Cameras, audio. It seems to me he'd want to watch, and you can't watch and work. Not when you're that focused."

"Whatever you need from me."

She nodded, then turned and shoved Peabody's knee.

"Huh? What?" Peabody jerked upright, blinked. "I was thinking."

"Yeah, I always drool and snore when I'm lost in thought."

"Drool?" Mortified, Peabody wiped at her mouth. "I wasn't drooling."

"You've got one hour in the crib."

"No, I'm okay." Peabody climbed out, blinked her eyes wide as if to show she was alert. "Just nodded off for a minute."

"An hour." Eve strode toward the elevator. "Take it, then report to the conference room. I'll need you to help me set up."

"You don't have to get pissed just because I dropped out for a couple minutes."

"If I was pissed I'd be kicking your ass instead of giving you an hour down. And you don't want to argue with me when I'm jonesing for coffee. Take the hour. You're going to need it."

When the doors opened, Eve stepped off with Roarke, then turned, jabbed a finger at Peabody's sulky face. "That hour starts now."

Roarke waited until the doors closed. "You could use an hour yourself."

"I could use coffee more."

"And food."

She slid her eyes up to his. "If you start nagging me about eating and sleeping, I'm booting you off my team."

"If I didn't nag you about eating and sleeping, you'd do precious little of either. What's in your office AutoChef?"

"Coffee," she said, and yearned for it.

"I'll meet you there shortly." When he turned and headed in the opposite direction, she only scowled after him.

Still, if he was off doing whatever, it would be easier for her to write her initial report, call in the members of her team.

She passed through the bullpen. It was nearly change of shift. In her office, she went straight for the coffee, then stood where she was and drank the first half of the first cup.

There hadn't been real coffee to wake up her blood the first time around, she remembered. Instead of a cramped office, she'd had a cramped desk in the bullpen. She hadn't been in charge then; Feeney had. She knew that was weighing on him, knew he was remembering all the steps, all the fizzled leads, the dead ends. All the bodies.

It needed to be remembered. It all needed to be remembered, so it didn't happen again.

She sat at her desk, shot out transmissions to Baxter and to Jenkinson, with orders for them to notify their respective aides and partners, and report.

She mercilessly dumped their caseloads on other detectives.

There would, she knew, be some extensive bitching and moaning in the bullpen, very shortly.

She ordered up the cold-case files from nine years before — including Mira's initial profile — sent out the request for the files and reports on the other cases, yet unsolved, that matched the MO.

She contacted the lab and pushed for any and all results, left a clipped voice mail for the chief lab tech, Dick Berenski.

And with a second cup of coffee on her desk, began to write her report.

She was fine-tuning it when Roarke came in. He set an insulated bowl on her desk, handed her a toss-away spoon. "Eat."

Cautious, Eve pried up the lid of the bowl and peeked. "Damn it. If you were going to go to the trouble to get food, why did you get oatmeal?"

"Because it's good for you." He sat in her single visitor chair with his own bowl. "Are you aware that the Eatery here serves nothing that could be considered remotely palatable?"

"The eggs aren't that bad. If you put a lot of salt on them."

Roarke simply angled his head. "You put a lot of salt on everything, but it doesn't make it palatable."

Because it was there, she spooned up some oatmeal. It would fill the hole. "Cop food's what you get around here." She ate, frowned. As oatmeal went, it wasn't completely disgusting. "And this isn't cop food."

"No. I got it from the deli around the corner."

For a moment, her face rivaled Peabody's for full sulk. "They have bagels there, and danishes."

"So they do." He smiled at her. "You'll do better with the oatmeal."

Maybe, she thought, but she wouldn't be as happy about it. "I want to say something before this really gets started. If you feel, at any time, you want to step out, you step out."

"I won't, but understood."

She took another spoonful of oatmeal, then swiveled in her chair so they were face-to-face. "Understand, too, that if I feel your involvement is doing more harm — on a personal level — than it's adding to the investigation, I'll have to cut you loose."

"Personally or professionally?"

"Roarke."

He set his bowl aside to get up and program coffee for himself. She could attempt to cut him loose, he thought, but they both knew she wouldn't shake him off the line. And that, he acknowledged, would be a problem indeed.

"Our personal life has, and will, weather the bumps and bruises it takes when we work together, or more accurately, when I contribute to your work."

"This one's different."

"Yes, I understand that as well." He turned with his coffee, met her eyes. "You couldn't stop him once before."

"Didn't stop him," Eve corrected.

"You'd think that, and so it's personal. However much you try to keep it otherwise, it's personal. It's harder for you, and it may be harder for us. But things have changed in nine years, a great many things."

"I didn't have anybody pushing oatmeal on me nine years ago."

"There." His lips curved. "That's one."

"It's unlikely we'll save the second one, Roarke. Barring a miracle, we won't save her."

"And so, you're already afraid you won't save the next. I know how that weighs on you, and eats at you, and pushes you. You have someone who understands you, who loves you, and who has considerable resources."

He crossed over, just to touch a hand to her face. "*His* pattern may have changed little in all this time, Eve. But *yours* has. And I believe, completely, that it will stop here. You'll stop it."

"I need to believe that, too. Okay, then." She took one more spoonful of oatmeal. "Peabody's crib time's up. I need to finish this report, have copies made for the team. I've ordered copies of the old reports, and put in requests for files from other murders attributed to him. Find Peabody, tell her I need her to pick up the cold files, and then the two of you can start setting up. I need another ten minutes here."

"All right. But unless you have something other than the usual drudge around here in that conference room, I'm taking coffee with me."

True to her word, Eve walked into the conference room ten minutes later. Behind her, a pair of uniforms hauled in a second board. She carted a boxful of file copies.

"I want the current case up first," she told Peabody. "Then we'll have our history lesson." She pulled the files out, set them on the conference table. "I generated stills of the scene and the body. Use the second board for those."

"On it."

She walked over to a white data board on the wall and began to print.

Her printing always surprised Roarke. It was so precise, so perfect, while her handwriting tended toward scrawl. He saw she was printing out the victim's name, and the timeline from the moment she'd been reported leaving the club, through her death, and the discovery of her body.

After drawing a line down the center of the wide board, she began printing out the others, beginning with Corrine Dagby.

Not just data, Roarke thought. A kind of memorial to the dead. They were not to be forgotten. More, he thought, she wrote them out for herself because she stood for all of them now.

Feeney walked in. "The kid's cleared for this. The Newkirk kid." His gaze moved to the board, stayed there. "His old man's going to dig out his own notes from before. Said he'll put in any OT you want, or take his own personal time on this."

"Good."

"I pulled in McNab and Callendar. McNab knows your rhythm and won't bitch about the drone work. Callendar's good. She doesn't miss details."

"I've got Baxter, Trueheart, Jenkinson, and Powell."

"Powell?"

"Transferred in from the six-five about three months ago. Got twenty years in. Chips away at a case until he gets to the bones. I've got Harris and Darnell in uniform. They're solid. But I'm giving Newkirk the lead there. He was first on scene and he knows the previous investigation."

"If he's like his old man, he's a solid cop."

"Yeah, I'm thinking. Tibble, Whitney, and Mira should be on their way down."

She stepped back from the board. "I'm going to brief on the current first. Do you want to brief on the prior investigation?"

Feeney shook his head. "You take it. Might help me see it from a different angle." He pulled a book out of his pocket, handed it to her. "My original notes. I made a copy for myself."

She knew he wasn't only passing her his notebook, but passing her the command as well. The gesture had something tightening just under her heart. "Is this how you want it?"

"It's the way it is. The way it's supposed to be." He turned away as cops began to come into the room.

She snagged one of the uniforms, ordered him to distribute the files, then studied the boards Peabody and Roarke had set up.

All those faces, she thought. All that pain.

What did she look like, the one he had now? What was her name? Was anyone looking for her?

How long would she last?

When Whitney walked in with Mira, Eve started over. It struck her what a contrast they made. The big-shouldered man with the dark skin, the years of command etched on his face, and the woman, so quietly lovely in the elegant pale pink suit.

"Lieutenant. The chief is on his way."

"Yes, sir. The full team's assembled and present. Dr. Mira, there are copies of your original profile in each packet, but if there's anything you want to add verbally, feel free."

"I'd like to reread the original murder books."

"I'll make them available. Sir, do you wish to speak?"

"Lead it off, Dallas." He stepped to the side as Tibble entered.

The chief of police was a tall man and — Eve always thought — a contained one. Not an easy man to read, but she doubted he'd have climbed the ranks as he had if he'd been otherwise. He played politics — a necessary evil — but to her mind he found a way so that the department came out on top.

Dark skin, dark eyes, dark suit — part of his presence, she decided. Along with a strong voice, and a strong will.

"Chief Tibble."

"Lieutenant. I apologize if I delayed the briefing."

"No, sir, we're on schedule. If you're ready now."

He only nodded, then moved to the back of the room. He didn't sit, but stood. An observer.

Eve gave Peabody a nod, then walked to the front of the room. Behind her, the wall screen flashed on.

"Sarifina York," Eve began. "Age twenty-eight at TOD."

She was putting the victim first, Roarke realized. Putting that image, that name into the mind of every cop in the room. So that every cop in the room would think of her, remember her as they were buried in routine, in data, in the long hours and the frustrations.

Just as they would remember what had been done to her as those next images came up.

She went through them all, every victim. The names, the faces, the ages, the images of their suffering and death. It took a long time, but there were no interruptions, no signs of restlessness.

"We believe all of these women, twenty-three women, were abducted, tortured, and murdered by one individual. We believe there are likely more than these twenty-three who have not been connected or reported, whose bodies may not have been found or who were not killed in the same manner. Earlier victims, we believe, before Corrine Dagby, when he decided on his particular method."

She paused, just a moment, to insure, Roarke understood, that all eyes, all attention focused on the image of that first victim.

"The method deviates very little from vic to vic, as you'll see in your copy of the case file from nine years ago. Copies of case files, in full, from murders attributed to the unsub will be forthcoming."

Her eyes scanned the room, and Roarke thought, saw everything.

"His methodology is, initially, typical of a serial. We believe he stalks and selects his victims — all within a certain age group, race, gender, and coloring — learning their routines, habits. He knows where they live, where they work, where they shop, who they sleep with."

She paused again, shifting. Roarke saw the light slanting through the privacy screens on the window glint on her sidearm.

"Twenty-three women, known. They were specific targets. No connection was found between any of the victims other than age and basic appearance. None of the victims ever reported a stalker, never mentioned to a friend, coworker, relative that she had been approached or troubled. In each case, the victim left a location and was not seen again until her body was discovered.

"He must have private transportation of some kind, and using it takes the victim to a preplanned location. It, too, must be private as he takes — as with Sarifina York — several days to kill them. In all prior investigations, it was learned through time lines and forensics that he always selects and abducts his second victim before finishing with the first, and so selects and abducts the third before killing the second."

She outlined the investigator's on-scene reports, the ME's reports, taking them through the process of the torture, the method of death.

Roarke heard the e-cop, Callendar, breathe out a soft "Jesus," as Eve outlined the specifics.

56

"Here, he may deviate slightly," Eve continued, "adjusting his method to suit the specific victim. According to Dr. Mira's profile, this is tailored to the victim's stamina, tolerance for pain, will to live. He's careful, he's methodical, patient. Most likely a mature male of high intelligence. He lives alone, and has some steady method of income. Probably upper bracket. Though he selects females, there is no evidence he abuses them sexually."

"Small blessing," Callendar murmured, and if Eve heard she gave no sign.

"Sex, the control and power gained from them doesn't interest him. They aren't sexual beings. By carving the time spent on them into their torsos — postmortem — he labels them. The ring he puts on them is another kind of branding.

"It's ownership." She glanced at Mira for confirmation.

"Yes," Mira agreed, and the lovely woman with the soft waves of sable hair spoke in her calm voice. "The killings are a ritual, though not specifically ritualistic in the standard sense. They are *his* ritual, from the selection and the stalking, through the abduction and the torture, the attention to detail, which includes the time elapsed, to the way he tends to them after death. The use of the rings indicates an intimacy and a proprietary interest. They belong to him. Most likely they represent a female who was important to him."

"He washes them, body, hair," Eve continued. "While this removes most trace evidence, we were able to determine the brand of soap and shampoo on

57

previous vics. It's high end, indicating their presentation matters to him."

"Yes," Mira agreed when Eve glanced at her again. "Very much."

"It matters, as does the dumping method. He lays them on a white sheet, habitually leaving them in a park or green area. Legs together, as you see — again, not a sexual pose — but arms spread."

"A kind of opening," Mira commented. "Or embrace. Even acceptance of what was done."

"While he follows the traditional path of the signature serial killer to this point, he then deviates. Full timeline up, Peabody," Eve ordered, then turned when it flashed on screen. "He does not escalate in violence, the time between killings doesn't appreciatively narrow. He spends two to three weeks at his work, then he stops. In a year, or two, he cycles again, in another location. His signature has been identified in New York, in Wales, in Florida, in Romania, in Bolivia, and now again in New York.

"Twenty-three women, nine years, four countries. The arrogant son of a bitch is back here, and here's where it stops."

And here, Roarke noted, was the fierceness she'd held back during the relaying of data, of names and methods and evidence. Here was the hint of the anger, of the avenger.

"Right now, there's a woman between the ages of twenty-eight and thirty-three. She has brown hair, light skin, a medium to slender build, and she's already been taken. We find him. We get her back.

"I'm going to give you your individual assignments. If you have any questions, any problems, wait until I'm done. But I'm going to tell you one more thing. We're going to nail him. We're going to nail him here, in New York, with a case so tight he'll feel it choking him every hour of every day of every year he spends in a cage."

Not just anger, Roarke noted, but pride. And she was pushing that anger and pride into them so they'd work until they dropped.

She was magnificent.

"He doesn't walk, run, fly, or crawl out of this city," Eve told them. "He doesn't slither out in court because one of us gave his lawyer an opening the size of a flea's ass.

"He pays, we're going to make goddamn sure he pays for every one of these twenty-three women."

CHAPTER
FOUR

As Eve wrapped up, Tibble walked to the front of the room. Automatically, she stopped, stepped to the side to give him the floor.

"This team will have the full resources of the NYPSD at its disposal. Any necessary overtime will be cleared. If the primary determines more manpower is needed, and the commander agrees, that manpower will be assigned. All leave, other than hardship and medical, is canceled for this team until this case is closed."

He paused, gauging the reactions, and obviously satisfied with them, continued. "I have every confidence that each and every member of this team will work his or her respective ass off until this son of a bitch is identified, apprehended, and locked in a cage for the rest of his unnatural life. You're not only the ones who'll stop him, but who'll build a case that will lock that cage. I don't want any fuckups here, and trust Lieutenant Dallas to flay you bloody if you come close to fucking up."

Since he looked directly at her as he made the statement, Eve simply nodded. "Yes, sir."

"The media will pounce like wolves. A Code Blue status has been considered, and rejected. The public requires protection and should be made aware that a specific type of female is being targeted. However, they will be made aware by one voice, and one voice only, which represents this task force, and, in fact, this department. Lieutenant Dallas will be that voice. Understood?" he said, looking directly at her again.

"Yes, sir," she said, with considerably less enthusiasm.

"The rest of you will not comment, will not engage reporters, will not so much as give them the current time and temperature should they ask. You will refer them to the lieutenant. There will be no leaks unless they are departmentally sanctioned leaks. If there are, and the source of that leak is discovered — and it damn well will be — that individual can expect to be transferred to Records in the Bowery.

"Shut him down. Shut him down hard, clean, and fast. Lieutenant."

"Sir. All right, you all know your primary assignments. Let's get to work."

Tibble signaled to Eve as feet and chairs shuffled. "Media conference, noon." He held up a finger as if anticipating her reaction. "You'll make a statement — short, to the point. You'll answer questions for five minutes. No longer. These things are necessary, Lieutenant."

"Understood, sir. Chief, we held back the numbers carved into the victims in the previous investigations."

"Continue to do so. Copy me on all reports, requests, and requisitions." He looked over at the boards, at the faces. "What does he see when he looks at them?" Tibble asked.

"Potential." Eve spoke without thinking.

"Potential?" Tibble repeated, shifting his gaze to hers.

"Yes, sir, that's what I think he sees. Respectfully, sir, I need to get started."

"Yes. Yes. Dismissed."

She walked over to Feeney. "This space work okay for the e-end of things?"

"It'll do. We're bringing down the equipment we need. It'll be set up inside of thirty. He comes back, he comes back here, you gotta wonder does he use the same place he did before? Does he have a place? Maybe even lives here when he's not working."

"Private home, untenanted warehouse. Lots of that in the city, the outlying boroughs," Eve speculated. "Bastard could be working across the river in Jersey, then using New York as a dump site. But if it is the same place — and he strikes me as a creature of habit, right? — then it narrows it some. We check ownership of buildings that fit the bill for ones in the same name for the last nine years. Ten," she corrected. "Give him some prep time."

"Narrows it some." Feeney pulled on his nose. "Like looking for an ant hill in the desert. We'll work it."

"You okay with taking the Missing Persons search?"

He blew out a breath, dipped his hands into his saggy pockets. "Are you going to ask me if I'm okay with every assignment or step in this?"

Eve moved her shoulders, and her hands found her own pockets. "It feels weird."

"I've run the e-end of your cases and ops before this."

"It's not like that, Feeney." She waited until their eyes locked, until she was certain they understood each other. "We both know this one's different. So if it bugs you, I want to know."

He glanced around the room as uniforms and team members carried in equipment and tables. Then cocked his head, gesturing Eve to a corner of the room with him.

"It bugs me, but not like you mean. It burns my ass that we didn't get this guy, that he slipped out and on my watch."

"I worked it with you, and we had a team on it. It's on all of us."

His eyes, baggy as a hound's, met hers. "You know better. You know how it is."

She did, of course she did. He'd taught her the responsibility and weight of command. "Yeah." She dragged a hand through her hair. "Yeah, I know."

"This time it's on you. You're going to take some hits because we both know there's going to be another name, another face on the board before we get him. You'll live with that; can't do anything else but live with it. It bugs me," he repeated. "It would bug me a hell of a lot more if anyone else was standing as primary on this. We clear?"

"Yeah, we're clear."

"I'll start the Missing Person's run." He cocked his head toward Roarke. "Our civilian would be a good one to handle the real estate search."

"He would. Why don't you get him on that? I'm going to swing over to the lab, bribe and/or threaten Dickhead to push on reports." She glanced over, saw that Roarke was already working with McNab to set up data and communication centers. "I'm just going to have a word with the civilian first."

She crossed to Roarke, tapped his shoulder. He'd tied his hair back as he often did before getting down to serious e-business, and still wore the sweater and jeans he'd put on — had it only been that morning? — when they'd left the house for the crime scene.

She realized he looked more like a member of the team than the emperor of the business world.

"Need a minute," she told him, then stepped a few feet away.

"What can I do for you, Lieutenant?"

"Feeney's got work for you. He'll fill you in. I'm heading out with Peabody. I just want . . . look, don't go buying stuff."

He lifted his eyebrows, and the amusement showed clearly on his face. "Such as?"

"E-toys, new furniture, catered lunches, dancing girls. Whatever," she said with a distracted wave of her hand. "You're not here to supply the NYPSD."

"What if I get hungry, then feel the urge to dance?"

"Suppress it." She gave him a little poke in the chest that he interpreted — correctly — as both affection and warning. "And don't expect me to kiss you good-bye, hello, and like that when we're on the clock. It makes us look —"

"Married?" At her stony stare he grinned. "Very well, Lieutenant, I'll try my best to suppress all my urges."

Fat chance of that, she thought, but had to be satisfied. "Peabody," she called out, "with me."

On the way out, Peabody hit Vending for a Diet Pepsi for herself, a regular tube for Eve. "Gotta keep the caffeine pumping. I've never been on something like this, not when you catch a case and a few hours later you've got a task force, a war room, and a pep talk from the chief."

"We work the case."

"Well, it's this case, and the ones from nine years ago, and even the ones between that went down elsewhere. That's a lot of balls in the air."

"It's all one," Eve said as they got into the car. "One case with a lot of pieces."

"Arms," Peabody said after a minute. "It's more like arms. It's like an octopus."

"The case is an octopus."

"It's got all these tentacles, all these arms, but there's only one head. You get the head, you get it all."

"Okay," Eve decided, "that's not bad. The case is an octopus."

"And say, okay, maybe you can't get to the head, not at first, but you get a good hold on one of those tentacles, then —"

"I get it, Peabody." Because she now had an image of a giant octopus swimming in her head, Eve was relieved when her dash 'link signaled. "Dallas."

"So, what's up?"

"Nadine." Eve let her glance shift down to the screen where Nadine Furst, a very hot property in media circles, beamed out at her.

"Media conference, you as the department's spokesperson — I know you love that one."

"I'm primary."

"I got that." On screen, Nadine's cat eyes were sharp and searching. "But what gives this one enough juice? A dead woman in the park, identity yet to be given."

"We'll give her name at the conference."

"Give me a hint. Celebrity?"

"No hints."

"Come on, be a pal."

The trouble was, they were pals. Moreover, Nadine could be trusted. And at the moment, Nadine had plenty of juice of her own. She could, Eve mused, be useful.

"You're going to want to come to the media conference, Nadine."

"I've got a conflict. Just —"

"You're going to want to be there, and when it wraps, you're going to want to find your way to my office."

"Offering me a one-on-one after a media announcement takes off the shine, Dallas."

"You're not getting a one-on-one. Just you, just me. No camera. You're going to want to do this, Nadine."

"I'll be there."

"That was smart," Peabody said when Eve clicked off. "That was really smart. Bring her in, bargain, and get her resources and contacts."

"She'll keep a lid on what I ask her to keep a lid on," Eve agreed. "And she's the perfect funnel for any departmentally sanctioned leaks." She parked, rolled her shoulders. "Let's go harass Dickhead."

Dick Berenski had earned his nickname. Not only did he have a head like an egg covered with slick black hair, his personality was oilier than a tin of sardines. He was slippery, sleazy, and not just open to bribes — he expected them.

But despite being a dickhead, he ran a top-flight lab and knew his business as well as he knew the exact location of the dimples on the ass of this month's centerfold.

Eve strode in, moving by the long white counters and stations, the clear-walled cubes. She spotted Berenski scooting back and forth on his stool in front of his counter, tapping his spider-leg fingers on keyboards or tapping them to screens.

For a dickhead, she thought, he was hell at multitasking.

"Where's my report?" she demanded.

He didn't bother to look up. "Back up, Dallas. You want it fast or you want it right?"

"I want it fast and right. Don't fuck with me on this one . . . Dick."

"I said, 'Back up.'"

She narrowed her eyes because when he swung around on the stool, there was fury on his face. Not his usual reaction to anything.

"You think I'm screwing with this?" he snapped out. "You think I'm jerking off here?"

"Wouldn't be the first time."

"This isn't the first time either, is it?"

She flipped back through her memory. "You weren't chief nine years back."

"Senior tech. I did the skin and hair on those four vics. Harte took the bows for it, but I did the work. Goddamn it."

Harte, Eve remembered, had also had a nickname: Blowharte.

"So you did the work. Applause, applause. I need an analysis of *this* vic's hair and skin."

"I did the work," he repeated, bitterly now. "I analyzed and researched and identified what was barely any trace. I gave you the damn brand names of the soap, the shampoo. You're the one who didn't catch the bastard."

"You did your job, I didn't do mine?" She leaned down, nose-to-nose. "*You'd* better back up, Dick."

"Ah, excuse me. Don't clock the referee." Courageously — from her point of view — Peabody eased between the chief tech and the primary. "Everyone who was involved nine years ago feels this one more now."

"How would you know?" Dick rounded on Peabody. "You were in some Free Ager commune sitting in a circle chanting at the frigging moon nine years ago."

"Hey."

"That's it." Eve kept her voice low, and the tone stinging. "You can't handle this one, Berenski, I'll request another tech."

"I'm chief here. This isn't your shop. I say who works what." Then he held up his hand. "Just back off a minute, back off a minute. Goddamn it."

Because it wasn't his usual style, Eve kept silent while he stared down at his own long, mobile fingers.

"Some of them stick with you, you know? They stick in your gut. Other shit comes in and you work that, and it seems like you put it away. Then it comes back and kicks you in the balls."

He drew a breath, looked up at Eve. It wasn't just fury, she saw now, but the bitter frustration that on the job could push perilously close to grief.

"You know how when it stopped, just stopped cold, everybody figured he got dead, or he got tossed in a cage for something else? We didn't get him, and that was a bitch, but it stopped." Berenski heaved out a breath. "But it didn't. He didn't get dead or tossed in a cage. He was just bopping around Planet Earth having his high old time. Now he's back on my desk, and it pisses me off."

"I'm serving as President of the Pissed-off Club. I'll take your application for membership under advisement."

He snorted out a laugh, and the crisis passed.

"I got the results. I was just rerunning the data. Triple check. It's not the same brands as before."

"The old brands still available?"

"Yeah, yeah, here's the thing. He used shea butter soap with olive and palm oils, oils of rose and chamomile on the four prior vics. Handmade soap, imported from France. Brand name L'Essence or however the frogs say that. Cake style, about fifteen bucks a pop nine years back. Shampoo, same manufacturer, same name, caviar and fennel extracts."

"They put caviar in shampoo?" Peabody demanded. "What a waste."

"Just fish eggs, and disgusting if you ask me. Tech in Wales was good enough to work the trace, got the same deal as me. Same for Florida. They didn't get anything in Romania or in Bolivia. But now he's switched brands."

"To?"

"Okay, what we got is still handmade soap, got your shea butter — cocoa butter addition, olive oil, and oil from grapefruit and apricot. Specifically — and this took a little finessing — your pink grapefruit. It's made in Italy, exclusively, and get this, it's going to run you fifty smacks a bar."

"So he upgraded."

"Yeah, that's the thing. I took a look at the internet site, check these out." He brought the images of the soaps up. Each was a deep almost jewel-like color, with various flowers or herbs studding the edges. "Only one store in the city carries them. The shampoo's from the same place. White truffle oil, running one-fifty for an eight-ounce bottle."

He sniffed, he snorted. "I wouldn't pay that for a bottle of prime liquor."

"You don't have to pay," Eve said absently. "You get your booze in bribes."

"Yeah, but just the same."

Pricey, exclusive products. Prestige, Eve thought. The best of the best? "What's the outlet in the city?"

"Place called Scentual. Got a store midtown on Madison and Fifty-third, and one down in the West Village on Christopher."

"Good. How about the sheet?"

"Irish linen, thread count of seven hundred. That's another change. First time he used Egyptian cotton, five hundred thread count. Manufacturer's in Ireland and Scotland. Buncha outlets around. Your higher-end department stores and bedding places carry the brand. Fáilte."

He massacred the Irish, Eve knew, as she'd heard the word before.

"Okay, send copies to me, to Whitney, to Tibble, and to Feeney. You finish with the water?"

"Still working it. At a guess, and I mean guess, it's city water, but filtered. May be out of the tap, but with a filtration system that purifies. We got good water in New York. This guy, I'm thinking, is a fanatic for pure."

"For something. Okay, thanks. Peabody, let's go shopping."

"Hot dog!"

"Dallas." Berenski swiveled on his stool again. "Bring me something more this time. Get me something."

"Working on it."

She hit the downtown boutique first, and was assaulted with fragrance the moment they walked in. Like falling into some big-ass bouquet, Eve thought.

The clerks all wore strong colors. To mirror the products, Eve supposed, and the products were displayed as if they were priceless pieces of art in a small, intimate museum.

There were a number of customers, browsing, buying, which, given the price tag on a bar of soap, made Eve wonder what the hell was wrong with them.

She and Peabody were approached by a blonde who must have hit six-two in her heeled boots. The boots, like the skinny skirt and rib-bruising jacket, were the color of unripe bananas.

"Welcome to Scentual. How can I help you today?"

"Information." Eve pulled out her badge.

"Of what sort?"

"Soap with cocoa and shea butter, olive oil, pink grapefruit —"

"From our citrus line. Yes, please, this way."

"I don't want the soap, I want your customer list for sales of that soap, and for the truffle oil shampoo. Customers who purchased both products."

"That's a little difficult as —"

"I'll make it easy. Customer data or warrant for same, which will tie up the shop for a number of hours. Maybe days."

The blonde cleared her throat. "You should probably speak to the manager."

"Fine."

She glanced around as the blonde hurried off, and saw Peabody sniffing at minute slivers of soap that were set out as samples. "Cut it out."

"I'll never be able to afford so much as a scraping of this kind of thing. I'm just smelling. I like this one — gardenia. Old-fashioned, but sexy. 'Female,' as my guy would say. Did you see the bottles? The bath oil?"

Her dazzled eyes tracked along the jewel-toned and delicate pastels of fancy bottles in display shelves. "They're so mag."

"So you pay a couple hundred for packaging for stuff that eventually goes down the drain. Anything in a bottle costs that much, I want to be able to drink it."

She turned back as another woman came over, this one petite and redheaded in a sapphire suit. "I'm Chessie, the manager. There's a problem?"

"Not for me. I need your customer list for purchases of two specific products as said products are related to a police investigation."

"So I understand. Could I see some identification, please?"

Eve pulled out her badge again. Chessie took it, studied it, then lifted her gaze to Eve's. "Lieutenant Dallas?"

"That's right."

"I'll be happy to help you in any way I can. The specific products?"

Eve told her, nodded as the woman asked for a moment, then watched her walk away. "Peabody —" When she looked around, her partner was testing out an elf-sized sample bottle of body cream on her hands.

"It's like silk," Peabody said, reverently. "Like liquid silk. I've got a cousin who makes soaps and body creams and all, and they're really nice. But this . . ."

"Stop rubbing stuff all over yourself. I have to ride with you, and you're going to make the ride smell like some big, creepy meadow."

"Meadows are pastoral."

"Exactly. Creepy. He could've bought the stuff here," she said, thinking out loud. "Or at the midtown store, off the Net. Hell, he could've bought the stuff in Italy or wherever the hell else it's sold and brought it with him. But it's something."

Chessie came back with some printouts. "We haven't had any sales — cash or credit — of both products at the same time. Nor has our Madison Avenue store. I contacted them. As a precaution, I've generated all the sales for each product, from each of our stores. Obviously, we don't have customer names for the cash sales. I went back thirty days. I can go back further if that would be helpful."

"This should do for now. Thanks." Eve took the printouts. "Did you get a memo about me?"

"Yes, certainly. Is there anything more I can do for you?"

"Not right now."

"If she got the 'Cooperate with Lieutenant Dallas' memo, Roarke owns that place," Peabody said when they were back on the street. "You can *swim* in that bath oil if you want. How come you —"

"Hold on." She flipped out her 'link, contacted Roarke.

"Lieutenant."

"Do you manufacture bedding — sheets and linens — under the brand name Fáilte?"

"I do. Why?"

"I'll let you know." She ended transmission. "I'm not buying coincidence here, Peabody."

"Oh. Just caught up. First vic worked for him, was washed down in products from a store he owns, was laid out on a sheet he manufactures. No, I'm not buying that today either, thanks. But I don't know what the hell it means."

"Let's go. You drive." Eve pulled out her 'link again, and tagged Feeney. "Missing persons, add in a new piece of data. Look for a woman who's employed by Roarke. Don't say anything to him as yet. Just look for anyone reported missing in the last few days who fits our vic profile and who works for one of Roarke's interests in the city."

"Got that. I've got three potentials from MP from the tristate. Give me a minute on this. Aren't you due at the media blather?"

"I'm on my way there."

"Okay, okay," he grumbled, "takes time. He's got a lot of layers on some of his . . . son of a bitch. Rossi, Gia, age thirty-one, works as a personal trainer and instructor at BodyWorks, a subsidiary of Health Conscience, which is a division of Roarke Enterprises. She was reported missing last night."

"Take one of the uniforms, get to her place of employment, her residence, talk to the person who reported her missing, to —"

"I know the drill, Dallas."

"Right. Move on it, Feeney." She clicked off. "Goddamn media."

"You have to tell him, Dallas. You've got to tell Roarke about this."

"I know, I know. I've got to get through this media crap first, and *think*. I have to think. Roarke will deal. He'll have to deal with it."

She'd think about that part later. At the moment, she could only think that it might be too late for Gia Rossi. She could only wonder what might have been done to her already.

He cleansed her to *Falstaff*. It always put him in a happy mood — this music, this little chore. His partner needed to be absolutely clean before the work began. He particularly enjoyed washing her hair — all that lovely brown hair.

He enjoyed the scents, of course — that hint of citrus, the feminine fragrance mixed with the smell of her fear.

She wept as he washed her, blubbered a bit, which concerned him just a little. He preferred the screams, the curses, the prayers, the pleas, to incoherent weeping.

But it was early days yet, he thought.

The water he hosed her off with was icy, which turned the weeping to harsh gasps and small shrieks. That was better.

"Well now, that was refreshing, wasn't it? Bracing. You have excellent muscle tone, I must say. A strong, healthy body makes such a difference."

She was shivering now, violently, her teeth chattering, her lips pale blue. It might be interesting, he decided, to follow up the cold with heat.

"Please," she choked out when he turned away to study his tools. "What do you want? What do you want?"

76

"Everything you can give me," he replied. He chose his smallest torch, flicked on the flame, then narrowed it to the point of a pin.

When he turned, when her eyes wheeled toward that flame, she rewarded him with those wild, wild screams.

"Let's get started, shall we?"

He moved to the base of the table, smiled in delight at the high, elegant arch of her feet.

CHAPTER
FIVE

She hated media conferences, but nearly always hated the media liaison more. It was suggested, by same, that Eve might prep for fifteen minutes with the media coach, and make use of the provided enhancements in order to present a more pleasant image on screen.

"Murder isn't pleasant," Eve snapped back as she strode toward the main doors of Cop Central.

"No, of course not." The liaison jogged to keep up. "But we're going to avoid words like murder. The prepared statement —"

"Isn't going to be tasty when I stuff it down your throat. I'm not your mouthpiece, and this isn't a political spin."

"No, but there are ways to be informative and tactful."

"Tact's just bullshit with spit polish over it."

Eve pushed through the doors. Tibble had opted for the steps of Central not only to show the sturdy symbol of the building, but, Eve guessed, to insure the briefing would remain short.

The March wind wasn't being tactful.

She stepped up to the podium, and waited for the noise level to drop off. She picked Nadine out immediately. The bright red coat stood out like a beacon.

"I have a statement, then I'll take a few brief questions. The body of a twenty-eight-year-old woman identified as Sarifina York was found early this morning in East River Park. It has been determined that Ms. York was most likely abducted last Monday evening, held against her will for several days. The method in which she was murdered and the evidence gathered so far indicates Ms. York was killed by the same individual who took the lives of four women in a fifteen-day period in this city, nine years ago."

That caused an eruption, and she ignored it. She stood still and silent while questions and demands were hurled out. Stood still and silent until they ceased.

"The NYPSD has authorized and formed a task force. Its soul purpose will be to investigate this crime, and to apprehend and incarcerate the perpetrator. We will use every resource, every man-hour, and all the experience at our disposal to do so. Questions."

They flew like missiles. But the fact that there were so many allowed her to cherry pick.

"How was she killed?" Eve repeated. "Ms. York was tortured over a period of days, and died as a result of blood loss. No, we do not have any suspects at this time, and yes, we are, and will continue to follow any and all leads."

She fielded a few more, grateful her time was nearly up. She noted Nadine tossed out no questions, and had in fact moved out of the pack to talk on her 'link.

"You said she was tortured," someone called out. "Can you give us details?"

"I neither can nor will. Those details are confidential to this investigation. If they weren't, I wouldn't give them to you so you could broadcast her suffering and cause yet more pain for her family and friends. Her life was taken. And that's more than enough for outrage."

She stepped back, turned, and walked through the doors of Central.

It would take Nadine a few minutes to get up to Homicide and charm her way through any potential roadblocks to Eve's office.

Besides, Eve thought, she could wait. Just wait.

First, Eve needed to speak to Roarke.

She caught the scent as soon as she stepped into the conference room, and much preferred it to the olfactory bombardment at Scentual.

Somebody, she thought, brought in gyros.

She made her way over to Roarke's workstation, noted he'd gone for the cold-cut sub. He paused in his work long enough to pick up half the sub, hand it to her. "Eat something."

She peered between the slabs of roll. "What is it?"

"No substance in nature, I can promise you. That's why I said eat *something*."

More to please him than out of appetite, she took a bite. "I need to talk to you."

"If you're after some answers on this chore you gave me, you won't get any as yet. There are, literally, countless homes, private residences, warehouses, and other potential structures in New York, the boroughs, into New Jersey, that have been owned by the same person or persons or organization for the last decade."

"How are you handling it?"

"Dividing into sections — quadrants, you could say. Subdividing by types of structure, then by types of ownership. It's bloody tedious work."

"You asked for it."

"So I did." Watching her, he picked up a bottle of water, drank.

"There's something else. The lab's identified the soap and shampoo used to wash down the vic."

"Quick work."

"Yeah, Dickhead's got his teeth in it. He worked the case before."

"Ah."

"He uses extremely high-end products. Very exclusive. Only one outlet in New York, two locations. It's yours."

"Mine?" He sat back, eyes cold and hard on her face. "And so was the sheet he used."

"That's right." Now, simply because it was there and so was she, Eve took another bite of mystery-meat sub. "Someone less cynical might think coincidence, particularly since you manufacture or own big, fat chunks of everything."

"But you and I aren't less cynical."

"No, and so I tagged Feeney and put you into the Missing Persons search he was running. You're not going to like it."

"Who is she?"

"Gia Rossi." She picked up his water, took a gulp. "She's a trainer and instructor at Body Works. Do you know her?"

"No." He pressed his fingers to his eyes a moment, then dropped them. "No, I don't believe so. Were there any of these connects, any of these overlaps in the previous investigation to me or mine?"

"No, not that I know of, and I started a check on the way back. He changed the products with this one. If you're part of the reason, we need to figure out why. A competitor maybe, a former employee. We need to work that angle."

"When did he take the second one?"

"She was reported missing yesterday. I don't have the details yet — Feeney's on it. I've got to go pull another chain now, but we're going to dig into this. I know this is a kick in the ass, but it's also a mistake. His mistake. There was nothing connecting the victims in any of the other cases. Now there is."

"Yes. Now there is."

"I'm sorry, I have to go do this."

"Go on. I'll stick with this for now."

She didn't kiss him, though part of her wanted to, just to give comfort. Instead she laid her hand over his, squeezed gently. Then left him.

She started back toward her office and crossed paths with Baxter. "Got nothing," he told her. "Reinterviewed the sister, went to the club, talked to the vic's neighbors. Big zero."

"Ex?"

"Out of town for the weekend. Neighbor said he went snowboarding out in Colorado."

"Why would anybody deliberately jump and flop around in the snow, on a mountain?" she wondered.

"Beats me. I like summer sports, where the women are very, very scantily clad. Snow and ice? No skin."

"You're such a pig, Baxter."

"And proud of it. Do you want me to run down the ex? The neighbor thought he knew where the guy was staying. He'll be back tomorrow night."

"We'll hit him once he gets back. Check with Jenkinson. See how far he and Powell have gotten going down the list of people interviewed in the other cases. You and Trueheart can help them run through it. Media's out with this now, which means by tomorrow we'll be buried in looney leads. We'll have to follow up on them, so let's clear this first plate today."

Nadine was waiting, sitting in the visitor's chair, legs crossed, examining her nails as she talked on her headset.

"You have to reschedule or cancel," she said. "No. No. We agreed in writing when I took this that if and when I had something hot, something I felt it was necessary to pursue personally, it would take precedence over everything else. That was the deal."

She looked over at Eve, rolled her clever green eyes. "That's what assistants are for, and assistants to assistants. And as far as the piece, the reporter can reschedule. I know. I'm a goddamn reporter."

She yanked off the headset.

"Heavy is the price of fame," Eve said.

"Tell me, but I wear it so very well. Can I have coffee?"

Obligingly, Eve moved to the AutoChef. Her own system kept begging to sag. Coffee would put it back on alert. Nadine sat, saying nothing.

She did wear fame well, Eve supposed. The streaky and stylish hair, the sharp features, the camera-ready suit. But Eve knew: Though Nadine might have her own show, though *Now's* ratings were reputedly higher than a souped-up chemi-head, the woman was exactly what she'd claimed — a goddamn reporter.

"Who were you talking to during the briefing?"

"Who do you think?" Nadine countered.

Eve turned, offered the coffee. "Your research people to give you the pertinent details of the case from nine years ago."

Nadine smiled, sipped. "Look who's wearing her thinking cap today."

"Some of the details on that investigation leaked."

"Some," Nadine agreed and the smile faded. "Some of the details on how the victims were tortured. I imagine there was a lot more, a lot worse, that didn't leak."

"There was more. There was worse."

"You worked it."

"Feeney was primary, I was his partner."

"I wasn't in New York nine years ago. I was fighting my way out of a second-rate network affiliate in South Philly. But I remember this case. I remember these murders. I bullied my way into doing a series of reports on them. That's part of what got me out of South Philly hell."

"Small world."

Nadine nodded, sipped more coffee. "What do you want?"

"You've got that research department at your fingertips now, being you're a big shot." Eve eased a hip down on the corner of her desk. "I want everything, anything you can dig up on the murders. All the murders. Here, Europe, Florida, South America."

Nadine blinked. "What? Where?"

"I'm going to explain it all to you, off the record, then you can put your researchers and your own honed skills on the scent. He's already got the second one, Nadine."

"Oh, God."

"Can't help her. Odds are slim we'll track him fast enough to save her. I need to know everything I can know. Maybe we can save the one he's hunting now."

"Let me think." Closing her eyes, Nadine sat back. She drank more coffee. "I've got a couple of smart people I can bully and bribe to keep the work and the results off the radar. I'm pretty damn smart myself, so that's three." Nodding, she sat up again. "You know I'd do this because I believe a life is worth more than a story. Marginally," she said with a smile. "I'd do it because you and I are friends who also happen to respect each other to play it straight. No payback required."

"I know that. Just like you know I'm going to pay you back."

Nadine cocked a brow. "Being pretty damn smart, I'm not going to say no. A one-on-one exclusive with you."

"After he's bagged, not before."

"Deal. A live appearance on *Now*."

"Don't push it."

Nadine laughed. "By any member of your team you choose — with portions of that exclusive — and did I mention extensive — interview by you to run during the show. Recorded prior."

Eve thought it through. "I can work with that."

"Okay. To get details, I need details." Nadine pulled out her recorder, cocked her head. "All right?"

"All right."

There was something unnerving on some visceral level about working in a cop shop. It was an interesting experience, Roarke thought, but very, very strange for someone with his . . . colorful background.

He'd worked *with* cops — in addition to his own — a number of times now, had had cops in his home professionally and socially. But working in a war room in the core of Cop Central for the best part of a day, well, that was a different kettle.

They came and went, he noted. Clipping into the room, clipping out again, communicating for the most part in that cop speak that was oddly formal, as clipped as their footsteps and somehow colorful all at the same time.

He was flanked by McNab whom he had great fondness for, and the dark, curvy, and sloe-eyed

Callendar. They might sit, or stand and walk — almost dance — around as they worked. Slogging through data, searching for just one vital byte. Busy bees in their busy hive.

As for colorful, well, excepting their captain, it appeared the e-division went for the flashy. McNab with his bright yellow jeans, the turquoise shirt with what appeared to be flying turtles winging across it. He had his long blond hair sleeked back in a tail and secured with a thick yellow band. On either side of his thin, pretty face, his earlobes were weighted down with a complex series of hoops and studs.

Roarke wondered why, honestly, anyone would wish to have that many holes punched into his flesh.

But the boy had a way about him, and was damn clever at this job.

The girl, for she looked barely twenty, was an unknown. She had burnt honey skin, masses and masses of black curly hair pinned in a multitude of hanks with a neon rainbow of clips. Silver hoops he could have punched his fists through hung at her ears. She wore baggy, multipocketed pants in bleeding colors of lavender and pink with a snug green sweater that exclaimed E-GODS! across her rather impressive breasts.

She had long, emerald-colored nails, and when she went to manual they clicked against the keys like mad castanets.

She, like McNab, appeared to be tireless — brightly wrapped bundles of energy barely contained so that something on them constantly jiggled or bounced. A foot, a head, shoulders, ass.

Fascinating.

"Yo, Blondie-Boy," she called out and McNab glanced over his shoulder.

"You talking to me, D-Cup?"

"You're up. Liquid."

"Can do. You want?" he said to Roarke. "Something to drink."

"Yes, thanks."

"Buzz or no buzz?"

It took Roarke a moment to translate, and in that moment he felt very old. "Could use the buzz."

"On it." As McNab bounced out of the room, Callendar sent Roarke a quick and pretty smile.

"So, you're like absolutely packed, right? Doing the backstroke in the megawealth. What's that like?"

"Satisfying," he decided.

"Betcha." With a push of her feet, she sent her chair skidding over so she could see his screen. "Wow. Multitudinous data with simo searches and cross. You got secondary recog going, too?"

This, he could easily translate. "I do. Checking like names, anagrams, cross dates. Lay it down for a spread, go deep for ancestry and other potential connects."

"Smart. McNab said you were frosty in there. Serious mining." She looked back at her own station. "All around."

She slid back to her work, and jiggling her shoulders to some internal tune, went back to the task at hand.

Amused, he turned back to his own work, then stopped when Eve and Feeney came in.

Gia Rossi, he thought, as the name, the idea of her that he'd made himself set aside, pushed once again into the forefront of his mind.

His eyes met Eve's, so he pushed back from the work to walk to her.

"We need to update the team regarding Rossi," Eve said. "Those in the field will be briefed via 'link. We need to factor your connection in."

"Understood."

"Okay, then."

Peabody came in, sent Roarke a quiet, sympathetic look. She crossed over to insert a new data disc.

"We have an update," Eve announced, and the clacking, the bouncing, the voices, and shuffling ceased. "We have reason to believe a woman reported as missing since Thursday night was abducted by our unsub. Rossi, Gia."

Peabody ordered the image and data on screen. "Age thirty-one, brown and brown, height five feet, five inches, one hundred and twenty-two pounds. She was last seen leaving her place of employment, a fitness center called Body Works on West Forty-sixth. Captain Feeney."

"Rossi's ex-husband," Feeney began, "one Riley, Jaymes, notified the police at oh-eight-hundred Friday morning. Per procedure, she wasn't formally listed as missing until the twenty-four-hour time limit had passed. The subject did not return home as expected on Thursday night where she was scheduled to meet her ex who, according to his statement, was there to drop off the dog they had joint custody of."

There were a few of the expected smirks at this, and Feeney just eyeballed the smirkers until they faded away.

"Neighbors confirm the arrangement. Nor was Riley able to reach her via her pocket 'link. We've confirmed that he did, in fact, attempt to ascertain her whereabouts by contacting her coworkers, her friends. The statements given to the responding officer and to me have been corroborated. He is not considered involved in her disappearance.

"Habitually the subject exited the building on Forty-sixth and walked west to Broadway, then north to the Forty-ninth Street subway. We'll canvass for witnesses in that area. Transit Authority security discs do not show the subject entering that station on Thursday evening, nor has her Metro pass been used since Thursday morning. Witnesses do verify the subject left the building at approximately seventeen-thirty on the night in question. She was wearing a black coat, black sweatpants, a gray sweatshirt with the BodyWorks logo, and a gray watch cap."

He stepped back, looked at Eve. "Lieutenant."

"The subject fits the established pattern. Probability runs exceed ninety-six percent that she was taken and is being held by the unsub. Her disappearance and other information gathered today add another element to the pattern. Both York and Rossi were employed by an arm of Roarke Enterprises. Given the breadth of that organization, that factor alone scores low on the probability scale for a connect. However, the soap and shampoo identified by brand by the lab has been determined to be manufactured and sold through subsidiaries of that organization, as was the sheet used with York."

Roarke felt the eyes on him, and the speculation. Accepted them.

"The probability is high," Eve continued, "that there's a connection on some level between the unsub and Roarke Enterprises. To this point, no connection, no central point has ever been determined. Now we have one, and we're going to use it. The hair and body products are extreme high-end and have limited outlets. He bought them somewhere. McNab, find out where."

"On it."

"Callendar, take the sheet, cross-reference purchases with McNab's data. Roarke."

"Lieutenant."

"Employee lists. Find and pull out individuals who fit the pattern and work or live in the city. He takes them from the city. He will, in all likelihood, move on number three within a matter of days. We need names."

"You'll have them."

"Jenkinson, I want a full and detailed report from you and Powell by nineteen hundred. Baxter, the same from you and Trueheart. I'll be available twenty-four/ seven, and expect to be notified immediately should any new data come to light. We'll brief again at oh-eight-hundred. That's it."

She pulled off her headset. "Peabody."

"Yes, sir."

"Log and copy, then go home and get some sleep. Feeney, can you look over the e-work to date, send me a basic rundown?"

"Can and will," Feeney confirmed.

"Roarke, go ahead and log and copy what you've got so far, then shoot additionals to my unit here and at home. When you're done, I need you in my office."

Eve walked out, contacting Mira's office on the way. "Put me through to her," she ordered Mira's overprotective admin. "Don't give me any crap."

"Right away."

"Eve." Mira's face swam on, and instantly her eyes registered concern. "You look exhausted."

"Second wind blew out, I'm waiting for the third to blow in. I need a sit-down with you."

"Yes, I know. I'll clear any time that works for you."

"I want to say now, but I need that wind before I start digging through the psychology of this. And there's more data that needs to be factored in from your end. Peabody's sending you a copy of the update right about now."

"Tomorrow, then."

"After the eight-o'clock briefing."

"I'll come to you. Get some sleep, Eve."

"I'm going to factor that in, somewhere."

She went into her office, programmed more coffee, and considered popping one of the departmentally approved energy pills. But they always made her jittery.

She drank, standing at her narrow office window, looking out at her slice of the city. Commuter trams were crisscrossing the sky, lights beaming against the growing dark.

Time to go home, time to have dinner and kick back, watch a little screen.

Below, the street was thick with traffic, with people thinking just the same as those who chugged along above their heads.

And somewhere out there was a man who really enjoyed his work. He wasn't thinking about kicking back.

Did he take a dinner break? she wondered. Have a nice, hearty meal before he went back to the business at hand? When had he started on Gia Rossi? When did he start the clock?

Forty-seven hours missing, Eve thought. But he wouldn't start it ticking until he got down to it. Number two always started after number one was finished.

She didn't hear Roarke come in, he had a skill for silence. But she sensed him. "Maybe we'll get lucky," she said. "Maybe he won't start on her until tomorrow. We've got another angle to work this time, so we could get lucky."

"She's gone. You know it."

Eve turned. He looked angry, she thought, which was probably a good thing, and just a little worn around the edges, which was a rare one. "I don't know it until I'm standing over her body. That's the way I'm dealing with it. We're going home. We can work from home."

He closed the door behind him. "I looked her up. She's worked for me for nearly four years. Her parents are divorced. She has a younger brother, a half brother, a stepsister. She went to college in Baltimore, where her mother and younger brother still live. Her employee evaluations have been, consistently, excellent. She was given a raise three weeks ago."

"You know this isn't your fault."

"Fault?" He could be faulted for a great deal, he knew and accepted that. But not for this. "No. But somewhere in it, I may very well be the reason these particular women die at this particular time."

"Reason has nothing to do with it. You're no good to me if you screw yourself up with misplaced guilt. You do that, you're out."

"You can't push me out," he countered, with considerable heat. "With or without your bleeding task force, your sodding procedure, I'm bloody well in this."

"Fine. Waste time pissing on me then." She grabbed her coat. "That's helpful."

She started to shove by him, but he grabbed her arm, swung her around. For an instant the rage was carved into his face. Then he yanked her against him, banded his arms around her.

"I have to piss on someone. You're handy."

"Maybe." She let herself relax against him. "Okay, maybe. But you have to think in a clear line with this. I need your brain, as well as your resources. It's another advantage we didn't have nine years ago."

"Knowing you're right doesn't make it easier to swallow. I've got to get out of this place," he said as he eased back. "That's God's shining truth. I can only breathe in cop for so long without choking."

"Hey."

He tapped his finger on her chin. "Excepting one."

She hauled up the file bag she wanted to take with her. "Let's go."

She drove primarily because she knew the battle uptown would keep her awake. A hot shower, she thought, something quick and solid in her stomach, and she'd be good to go for a few more hours.

"Summerset would be useful," Roarke considered.

"As what, a hockey stick?"

"The employee files, Eve. He can run those, generate a list of women who fit this pattern who work for me. It would free my time up for other things."

"All right, as long as he understands he answers to me. And that I get to debase him and ream him out as is often necessary with those under my command. And adds some entertainment to my day."

"Because you're so good at it."

"Yeah, I've got a knack." She scanned the army of vehicles heading north, the throngs of pedestrians hustling along on the sidewalk, the glides, or bullying their way on the crosswalks. "Nobody notices things — other people. Sure, if somebody jumps out of a building and lands on their head, it gives them a moment's pause, but they don't click to a woman being forced into a car or a van or Christ knows unless she puts up one hell of a stink about it. Mostly, they just keep their heads down and keep going."

"Cynicism is another of your finely tuned skills. It's not always so, not with everyone."

She shrugged. "No, not always. He's slick about it, or has some cover, something people don't register. If she kicked up enough fuss, yeah, somebody would notice. They might not do anything about it, but they'd notice. So no overt struggle on the street. One of the working theories is he drugs them somehow rather than overpowers them.

"Quick jab," she added. "Wraps an arm around her. 'Hey, Sari, how you doing?' Just a guy walking along with some zoned-out woman, helping her into his ride. Ride would need to be close to wherever he picks her up. Going to hit lots and garages tomorrow."

When she drove through the gates of home, she couldn't remember ever being more grateful to see the jut and spread of the gorgeous house, to see the lights in the windows.

"Going to grab a shower, grab something to eat in my office."

"You're going to grab some sleep," he corrected. "You're burnt, Eve."

No question she was, but it annoyed her to have it pointed out. "I got some left."

"Bollocks. You haven't slept in more than thirty-six hours. Neither have I, come to that. We both need some sleep."

"I'll take a couple hours after I set up a board here, review some notes."

Rather than argue — he was too bloody tired to bother — he said nothing. He'd just dump her into bed bodily, and he imagined once she was horizontal for thirty seconds, she'd be unconscious.

She parked in front of the house, grabbed her file bag.

She knew Summerset would be in the foyer, and he didn't disappoint. "Fill your personal cadaver in," Eve said before Summerset could speak. "I'm hitting the showers before I get started on this."

She headed straight up, neglecting to take off her coat and sling it over the newel as was her habit. And which, she knew, irritated Summerset's bony ass. Once she was out of sight, she rubbed at her gritty eyes, and allowed the yawn that had been barely suppressed to escape.

The shower was going to feel like a miracle.

She dumped the bag in the bedroom, shrugged out of her coat. As she hit the release on her weapon harness, her gaze landed on the bed. Maybe five minutes down, she considered. Five off her feet, then she could shower without risking drowning herself.

Tossing the harness aside, she climbed the platform where the bed spread like the silk clouds of heaven. She slid onto it, stretching out across it, facedown.

And beat Roarke's guess by being out in ten seconds flat.

He came in five minutes later, saw her on the bed, with the cat slung across her ass. "Well, then," Roarke addressed Galahad. "At least we won't have to fight about it. But for Christ's sake, couldn't she have pulled off her boots? How can she sleep well like that?"

He pulled them off himself — and she didn't stir a bit — pulled off his own. Then he simply stretched out beside her, draped an arm around her waist.

He dropped out nearly as quickly as she had.

CHAPTER
SIX

In the dream there was a white sheet over the dark ground, and the ruined body that lay on it. Bitter with cold, dawn carved its first light, etching the eastern spires into sharpened silhouettes.

She stood with her hands in the pockets of a black peacoat, a black watch cap pulled low on her forehead.

The body lay between her and a big black clock with a big white face. The seconds ticked away on it, and every strike was like thunder that sent the air to quaking.

And in the dream Feeney stood beside her. The harsh crime scene lights washed over them and what they studied. There was no silver in his hair to glint in those lights, and the lines in his face didn't ride so deep.

I trained you for this, so you could see what needs
to be seen, and find what's under it.

She crouched down, opened her kit.

She doesn't look peaceful, Eve thought, as people so often said about the repose of the dead. They really never do.

But death isn't sleep. It's something else again.

The body opened its eyes.

I'm Corrine Dagby. I was twenty-nine. I was born in Danville, Illinois, and came to New York to be an actress. So I waited tables because that's what we do. I had a boyfriend, and he'll cry when you tell him I'm dead. So will the others, my family, my friends. I bought new shoes the day before he took me. I'll never wear them now. He hurt me, he just kept hurting me until I was dead.

Didn't you hear me screaming?

She stood in the morgue, and Morris's bloody hand held a scalpel. His hair was shorter, worn in a neat and tidy queue at the nape of his neck. Over the body, he looked at Eve.

She used to be healthy, and had a pretty face until he ruined her. She sang in the shower and danced in the street. We all do until we come here. And in the end, we all come here.

In the corner, the big clock ticked the time so every second echoed.

They won't come if it stops, she thought. Not if I stop it. They'll sing in the shower and dance in the street, they'll eat cupcakes and ride the train if I stop it.

But you haven't. Corrine opened her eyes again. *Do you see?*

The faces and bodies changed, one melding into the next while the clock hammered the time. Hammered until her head pounded with it, until she pressed her hands to her ears to block it out.

Faster, faster, the faces flashed and merged while the seconds raced. So many voices, all the voices calling, coalescing into one, and the one cried out.

Can't you hear us screaming?

She woke with a gasp, with that awful cry echoing in her head. The light was dim, warm with the fire simmering low in the hearth. The cat butted against her shoulder as if telling her, "Wake up, for God's sake."

"Yeah, I'm up. I'm awake. Jesus." She rolled over, stared up at the ceiling as she got her breath back. With one hand she scratched Galahad between the ears, and checked the time on her wrist unit. "Oh, crap."

She'd been out nearly three hours. Shoving off sleep, Eve pressed the heels of her hands to her eyes and began to push off the bed. She heard it then, the sizzle and pulse of the shower.

She laid a hand on the spread beside her, felt his warmth lingering there. So they'd both slept, she realized. Good for them.

Stripping as she went, she headed for the shower.

She wanted to wash away the fatigue, the grit, the ugliness of the past twenty-four hours. She wanted the beat of the water to push away the vague headache she'd woken with, and flood out the remnants of the dream.

Then, when she stepped to the wide opening of the glass that enclosed the generous shower, she knew she wanted more.

She wanted him.

He was facing away from her, his hands braced on the glass, letting the water from the multiple jets beat over him. His hair was seal-sleek with wet, his skin gleaming with it. Long back, she mused, a taut, bitable ass, and all those tough, toned muscles.

100

He hadn't been up for long, she thought, and was likely as worn down as she.

The water would be too cold, she knew. But she'd fix that.

They'd fix each other.

She slipped in, wrapped her arms around his waist, pressed her body to his back. Nipped lightly at his shoulder. "Look what I found. Better than the toy surprise in the cereal box. Increase water temp to one hundred and one degrees."

"Must you boil us?"

"I must. Anyway, you won't notice in a minute." To prove it, she glided her hands down, found him. "See?"

"Is this how you behave with all the members of your task force?"

"They only wish."

He turned, caught her face in his hands. "And look how my wishes come true." He kissed her softly, brow, cheeks, lips. "I thought you might sleep a bit more."

"I already took more than I meant to." She pressed to him again, laying her head on his shoulder as the water flooded them. "This is better than sleep."

As the steam began to rise she tipped her head back. She found his mouth with hers, soft again, soft so they could both sink deep.

His fingers skimmed up into her hair, combing through the sleek cap of it as he murmured something that tasted sweet against her lips. Even through the sweetness she recognized need.

Yes, they would fix each other.

She tore her lips from his to press them to his throat, to feel his pulse beat while her hands stroked up his back. As he held her, as he turned her so the water sluiced over them, more than the day washed away.

Now his hands moved over her, creamy with soap, gliding over skin that all but hummed at the pleasure. Again he turned her, drew her back against him. And those hands circled her breasts, slid over them while his mouth sampled the side of her throat, her shoulder.

She moaned once, lifted an arm to hook around him, and quivered as his hands circled down.

He could feel her giving, opening, awaiting. The way her body moved, the way her breath caught. He could hear it in the quick cry that escaped her when he slipped his hands between her legs to cup her. How she trembled, her arm tightened when he used his fingers to tease and to pleasure. And the shock of her release when he dipped them into that hot, wet velvet.

"Take more." He had to give more.

Her trembles went to shudders, her breath to sobbing.

Her surrender, to him, to herself, aroused him beyond imagining. And the fatigue and sorrow that sleep and shower hadn't washed away drowned in his love for her.

He spun her around, pressed her back against the wall. Her breath was short, but her eyes stayed on his.

"You take more now," she told him.

Gripping her hips, he fought for control, to hold the moment. And so slipped slowly inside her.

Steam smoked around them; the water streamed. They watched each other, moved together.

More than pleasure, he thought. Somehow even more than love. At a time they each needed it most, they gave each other that essential human gift of hope.

Even as her breath caught, caught again, he saw her smile. Undone, he captured those curved lips. Surrounded by her, drowning in her, he let himself take the pleasure, take the love. Take the hope.

"Well, that set me up." Eve stretched her neck after she dragged on her old and favored NYPSD sweatshirt. "Sleep and shower sex. I ought to make the combo required for the team."

"I'm afraid I don't have the time to sleep and play in the shower with Peabody and Callendar. Even for the good of the team."

"Ha-ha. Funny." She sat on the arm of the sofa in the sitting area to pull on thick socks. "I'll just keep you as my personal energy booster. Gotta get back to it."

"Food," Roarke said.

"Yeah, I figured on —"

"I know what you figured on." He took her hand to walk out of the bedroom with her. "But disappointment is what you're doomed for as it's not going to be pizza."

"I think you have prejudice against the pie."

"I have no pie prejudice. However, I insist on another element to your energy boost. In addition to sleep and shower sex, we're having steak."

"Red meat's hard to argue with, but I'm having fries with it."

"Mmm-hmm."

She knew that *mmm-hmm*. It meant vegetables. She also knew that fussing over getting decent food into her would keep his mind off what was happening to Gia Rossi.

She let him order up whatever he considered proper nutrition while she fed the cat. The vegetables turned out to be some sort of medley he called *niçoise*. At least they had the crunch going for them.

She read over her detectives' reports while they ate. "People remember the details," she said. "Such as they were. The people who were close to the prior vics remember the details."

"I imagine so. For them — each of them," Roarke commented, "it was likely a once-in-a-lifetime shock and loss."

"If they're lucky. But even so, they don't tell us anything new. No new people in their lives, no comments or complaints about being bothered or worried. Each one had a basic routine — with some variations, sure. But each walked to and from work or transportation at basically the same time frame every day. No viable witnesses came forward claiming they saw them with anyone at the time they disappeared."

"Viable."

She shrugged, ate a fry. "You get the loonies and the attention-grabbers. Nothing panned. Still you check them out, every one. End up wasting time following false leads. People are a pain in the ass."

"You said you were going to check lots and garages. I assume you did then as well."

"Yeah. Watched hours of security vids, questioned dozens of attendants, droid and human, checked ticket records. We got nothing. Which means he could've used street parking, an unsecured lot, or just got lucky."

Roarke lifted his eyebrows as he ate. "Four times lucky?"

"Yeah, exactly. I don't think it was luck. He's not lucky, he's precise and prepared."

"Did you consider he might use an official vehicle? A black-and-white, a city official, a cab?"

"Yeah, we pushed that angle, and got nowhere. And we'll push it again. I've got Newkirk sifting through the records, looking for any private purchase of that kind of ride. They go up for auction a couple times a year. Checking the stolen vehicles records. I've got McNab searching the city and transportation employee records to see what we see there. We'll cross all that with the other case files. Even if he changed his name and appearance, prints are required on all ID for that kind of thing. Nothing's popped yet."

"What about medical equipment and supplies? He drugs them, restrains them, and certainly must have some equipment to deal with the blood."

"Went there, going there again. Countless clinics, hospitals, health care centers, doctors, MTs. Doctors and MTs and aides and so on who lost their licenses. Toss in funeral parlors and bereavement centers, even body sculpting salons. You've got hours and hours of leg and drone work."

"Yes. Yes, you would. You're covering every possible area."

"Maybe. We worked it for weeks, even after the murders stopped. Then Feeney and I worked it weeks more, every time we could squeeze it in. No sleep and shower sex and steak in those days."

She pushed up to pace a little. Maybe by looking back she'd see something she hadn't seen before. "We'd work around the clock sometimes, pushing and prodding at this on our own time. Sitting over a beer at three in the morning in some cop bar, talking it through all over again. And I know damn well, he'd go home, pick through it. I did."

She glanced back at Roarke, sitting at her desk with the remnants of the meal they had shared, with data on death on her comp screen, on the wall screen. "Mrs. Feeney, she's one of the ones who gets it. She understands the cop, the job, the life. Probably why she has all those weird hobbies."

"To keep her from sitting, worrying, wondering when it's three in the morning and he hasn't come home."

"Yeah. Sucks for you guys."

He smiled a little. "We manage."

"He loves her a lot. You know how he'll talk in that long-suffering way about 'the wife.' He'd be lost without her. I know how that is. I know how he's working this right now while she's probably knitting a small compact car. How he's seeing all those faces, the ones from then, the ones from now."

Can't you hear us screaming?

"And he knows it's on him."

"How can you say that?" Roarke demanded. "He did everything that could be done."

"No, because there's always something else. You missed it, or you didn't look at it from just the right angle, or ask just the right question at exactly the right time. And maybe someone else would have. Doesn't make them better or mean they worked harder at it. It just means they . . ." She lifted a hand, swiveled it like a door. "Means they turned something, opened something, and you didn't. He was in command, so it's on him."

"And now it's on you?"

"Now it's on me. And that hurts him because, well, he brought me up. As far as being a cop goes, he brought me up. I didn't want to bring him into this," she said and sat again. "And I couldn't leave him out."

"He's tough and he's hardheaded," Roarke reminded her. "Just like the cop he brought up. He'll handle it, Eve."

"Yeah." She sighed, looked back at the wall screen. "How does he pick them? We know, this time, part of his requirement is that they work for you in some capacity. He's so fucking smart he had to figure we'd click to that. So he wants us to know that much. He gives us the information he wants us to have. The type he prefers, how long he worked on them. He doesn't mind if we know what products he used to clean them up. But this time, he's given us a little more. Here's a new piece, what do you make of that?"

She looked back at Roarke. "Does he know you? Personally, professionally? Has he done business with you? Did you buy him out, and maybe he didn't want to be bought out? Did you underbid him on some contract? Did you fire him, or overlook him for promotion? Nothing's random with him, so his choice here is deliberate."

He'd inched all those same questions through his mind, turning them over from every angle. "If he works for me, I can find out. The travel," Roarke said. "Whether it was business-related or personal time, I can search files for employees who were sent to the locations of the other murders in that time period, or who took personal leave."

"How many employees would you figure you have?"

His lips curved again. "I honestly couldn't say."

"Exactly. But using Mira's profile — and we'll have an updated one tomorrow — we can cut that back considerably."

Following the usual arrangement when he dealt with the meal, Eve rose to clear the dishes. "I'll run a probability, but I think there's a low percentage he works for you. He doesn't strike me as a disgruntled employee."

"Agreed. I can check the same information on major competitors and subcontractors. Using my private equipment."

She said nothing at first, just carted the dishes into the kitchen, loaded them into the machine. His private office, with its unregistered equipment, would allow him to evade CompuGuard and the privacy laws.

Whatever he found, she couldn't use it in court, couldn't reveal where she'd gotten the data. Illegal means, she thought, crossing the line. Such maneuvers gave a defense attorney that flea-ass opening.

Can't you hear us screaming?

She walked back into the office. "Run it."

"All right. It'll take considerable time."

"Then you'd better get started."

Alone, she began to set up her murder board while her computer read off the progress reports from her team.

Board's too small, she thought. Too small to hold all the faces, all the data. All the death.

"Lieutenant."

"Computer pause," she ordered, then turned to Summerset. "What? I'm working."

"As I can see. Roarke asked I bring you this data." He held out a disc. "The employee search he asked I run."

"Good." She took it, walked over to put it on her desk. Glanced back. "You still here? Go away."

Ignoring her, he stood in his funereal black suit, his back stiff as a poker. "I remember this. I remember the media reports on these women. But there was nothing about these numbers carved into them."

"Civilians don't need to know everything."

"He takes great care in how he forms them, each number, each letter so precise. I've seen this before."

Her eyes sharpened. "What do you mean?"

"Not this, not exactly this, but something similar. During the Urban Wars."

"The torture methods?"

"No, no. Though, of course, there was plenty of that. Torture's a classic means of eliciting information or dealing out punishment. Though it's rarely so . . . tidy as this."

"Tell me something I don't know."

He looked over at her. "You're too young to have experienced the Urbans, or to remember the dregs of them that settled in some parts of Europe after they ended here. In any case, there were elements there, too, that civilians — so to speak — didn't need to know."

He had her full attention now. "Such as?"

"When I served as a medic, the injured and the dead would be brought in. Sometimes in piles, in pieces. We'd hold the dead, or those who succumbed to their injuries — for family members if such existed, and if the body could be identified. Or for burial or cremation. Those who didn't have identification, or were beyond being identified, would be listed by number until disposal. We kept logs, listing them by any description possible, any personal effects, the location where they'd been killed, and so on. And we would write the number on them, and the date of their death, or as close as we could come to it."

"Was that SOP?"

"It was what we did when I worked in London. There were other methods in other areas, and in some of the worst areas only mass burials and cremations without any record."

She walked back over to the board, studied the carving. It wasn't the same, she thought. But it was an angle.

"He knows their names," she said. "The name's not an issue. But the data's important. It has to be recorded. The data's what identifies them. The time is what names them for him. I need another board."

"Excuse me?"

"I need another board. I don't have enough room with one. We got anything around here that'll work?"

"I imagine I can find what you need."

"Good. Go do that."

When he left, she went to her desk, added the Urban Wars data to her notes, then continued to jot down her speculations.

Soldier, medic, doctor. Maybe someone who lost a family member or lover . . . No, no, she didn't like that one. Why would he torture and desecrate the symbol, you could say, of anyone who'd mattered to him? Then again, if a loved one had been tortured, killed, identified in that manner, this just might be payback or some twisted re-creation.

Maybe he'd been tortured, survived it. Tortured by a female with brown hair, within the age span.

Or maybe he'd been the torturer.

She rose, paced. Then why wait decades to re-create? Did some event trigger it? Or had he been experimenting all along, until he found the method that suited him?

And maybe he was just a fucking lunatic.

But the Urbans were an angle, yes they were. Mira's profile had indicated he was mature, even nine years back. Male, likely Caucasian, she remembered, between the ages of thirty-five and sixty.

So go high-end, and yeah, he could've seen some of the wars as a young man.

She sat again and, adding in new speculations, ran probabilities.

While they ran, she plugged in the disc Summerset had brought in. "Computer, display results, wall screen two."

Acknowledged. Working . . .

As they began to scroll, her jaw simply dropped. "Well, Jesus. Jesus." There were hundreds of names. Maybe hundreds of hundreds.

She couldn't complain that Summerset wasn't efficient. The names were grouped according to where they worked, where they lived. Apparently, there were just one hell of a lot of women with brown hair between twenty-eight and thirty-three who worked in some capacity for Roarke Enterprises.

"Talk about a big, honking octopus."

She was going to need a whole bunch of coffee.

Roarke's private office was streamlined and spacious, with a dazzling view of the city through privacy screens. The wide U-shaped console commanded equipment as sophisticated and extensive as any the government could claim.

He should know, he held several government contracts.

And he knew, however artful the equipment, successful hacking depended on the operator's skill. And patience.

He ran his own employee files first. However numerous they were, it was still a simple matter. As was the search he implemented to locate any male employees who worked or had worked for him who had traveled to the other murder locations or taken personal leave during that time frame.

As it ran he generated a list of major competitors. He would, subsequently, search through those companies he didn't consider genuine competition. But he'd start at the top.

Any company, organization, or individual who was, in actuality, competitive would have — as he did — layers and layers of security on their internal files. And each would need to be peeled back with considerable care.

He sat at the console where the controls shimmered or flashed like jewels. His sleeves were pushed up, his hair tied back.

He started with companies with offices or interests in one or more of the locations.

And began to peel.

As he worked, he talked to himself, to the machines, to the layers that tried to foil him. As time passed, his curses became more Irish, his accent more pronounced, and layers melted away.

He took a break for coffee and to scan the results of his initial search.

He had no employee who fit all the requirements. But, he noted, there were some who'd been in at least two of the locations or on leave during the time of the murders.

They'd be worth a closer look.

He shifted back and forth between tasks, to keep himself sharp. He wormed his way through security blocks, picked his way through data. Ordered search, cross match, analysis so his equipment hummed in a dozen voices.

At some point he got up for yet another pot of coffee, and glanced at the time.

4.16a.m.

Cursing, he sat back, scrubbed his hands over his face. Hardly a wonder he was losing his edge. And Eve, he knew, would be asleep at her desk. If she'd decided to call it a night, she would have come by to check his progress first.

Instead, she'd work herself into the ground, and as he was doing exactly the same, he had no room to fight with her about it.

Nearly half-four, he thought. Gia Rossi might already be dead, or praying to all the gods death would come soon.

Roarke closed his eyes a moment, and though he knew the guilt was useless, let it run through him. He was too tired for the anger.

"Copy document C to disc, save all data. Ah, continue current run, copy and save when complete. Operator will be off-line."

Acknowledged.

Before he left, he put in a call to Dublin.

"Good morning to you, Brian."

His old mate's wide face creased with a surprised smile. "Well now, if it isn't the man himself. Which side of the pond would you be on?"

"The Yank side. It's a bit early on your side of it for me to be calling a publican. I hope I didn't wake you."

"You didn't, no. I'm just having my tea. How is our Lieutenant Darling?"

"She's well, thanks. Would you be alone there?"

"I would be, more's the pity. I've no enchanting woman to warm the sheets with me at the moment, as you do."

"I'm sorry for that. Brian, I'm looking for a torturer."

"Is that so?" Only the mildest surprise showed in Brian's eyes. "And are you too delicate these days to be after taking care of such matters yourself?"

"I was always too delicate for this, and so were you. He's done over twenty women in the last decade, late twenties, early thirties, all of them. And all of them with brown hair, light skin. The last was found only yesterday. She worked for me."

"Ah," Brian said. "Well."

"Another is missing — that's part of his method — and she was mine as well."

Brian sucked air through his nose. "Were you diddling with them, on the side, like?"

"No. He'd be older than we are, that's how they're profiling him. At least a decade older if not more. He's very skilled. He travels. He must have enough of the ready to afford a place, a private place, to do this work. If he's a professional, he takes this busman's holiday every year or two. There's no sex involved. No rape. He takes, binds, tortures, kills, cleanses. And he times how long each lasts under it."

"I haven't heard of anyone like this. Nasty business." Brian pulled on his ear. "I can make some inquiries, tap a few shoulders."

"I'd be grateful if you would."

"I'll be in touch if and when," Brian told him. "Meanwhile, give Lieutenant Darling a sweet kiss from me, and tell her I'm only waiting for her to throw your worthless ass aside and come into my waiting embrace."

"I'll be sure to do that."

After he'd ended the transmission, Roarke took the discs he'd generated and, with the machines still humming, left the office.

He found Eve where he'd expected to. Her head was on her desk, pillowed on her forearm. He noted the murder boards, the pair of them, the discs, the handwritten notes, the comp-generated ones.

The half cup of coffee, not quite cold — and the cat curled in her sleep chair.

He moved to Eve, lifted her out of the chair. She muttered some complaint, stirred, and shifted.

"What?"

"Bed," he said as he carried her toward the elevator.

"Time is it? Jeez." She rubbed at her eyes. "I must've conked."

"Not for long, your coffee was still warm. We need to shut down, both of us."

"Briefing at eight." Her voice slurred with fatigue. "Need to be up by six. Need to organize first. I didn't —"

"Fine, fine." He stepped out of the elevator into the bedroom. "Go back to sleep, six will come soon enough."

"You get anything?"

"Still running." He set her on the bed, seeing no reason she couldn't sleep in her sweats. Apparently neither did she as she crawled under the duvet as she was.

"Is there any data I can use? Anything I can work in?"

"We'll see in the morning." He stripped off his shirt, his pants, slid into bed with her.

"If there's any —"

"Quiet." He drew her against him, brushed her lips with his. "Sleep."

He heard her sigh once — it might've been annoyance. But by the time the sigh was done, she was under.

CHAPTER
SEVEN

It was so unusual for him not to be up before her that Eve just stared into the Celtic blue eyes when he woke her by stroking her hair.

"You think of something?"

"Apparently, I inevitably think of something when I'm in bed with my wife."

"Being a man — and you — you probably think of sex when you're crossing the street."

"And aren't you lucky that's true?" He kissed the tip of her nose. "But thinking's as far as we'll get this morning. You wanted to be up at six."

"Oh, yeah. Shit. Okay." She rolled onto her back and willed her body clock to accept morning. "Can't you invent something that pours coffee into the system just by the power of mind?"

"I'll get right on that."

She climbed out of bed, stumbled her way over to the AutoChef. "I'm going to go down, swim a few laps. I think that'll wake me up and work out the kinks."

"Good idea. I'll do the same. Give me some of that."

She thought, crankily, he could easily get his own damn coffee, but she passed the mug to him, along with a scowl. "No water polo."

118

"If that's a euphemism for pool sex, you're safe. All I want's a swim." He passed her back the coffee.

They rode down together, she bleary-eyed, him thoughtful.

The pool house was lush with plants, sparkling with blue water. Tropical blooms scented the warm, moist air. She would have liked to indulge herself with a strong twenty-minute swim, followed by more coffee and a soak in the bubbling curve of the hot tub.

And hell, since he was there, maybe just one quick match of water polo.

But it wasn't the time for indulgence. She dove in, surfaced, then pushed off in a full-out freestyle. The dullness in her brain and body began to fade with the effort, the cool water, the simple repetition.

After ten minutes, she felt loose again, reasonably alert. She might have thought wistfully about lounging for just a couple of minutes in the hot, jetting water of the hot tub, but acknowledged the comfort of it might put her back to sleep.

Instead, she pulled on a robe. "Do you want to go downtown with me, or work from here?"

He considered as he scooped back his dripping hair. "I think I'll stick with the unregistered, at least for the time being. If I manage to finish or find anything, I'll contact you or just come down on my own."

"Works." She crossed to the elevator with him. "Any progress?"

"Considerable, but as of four a.m., nothing really useful."

"Is that when we finished up?"

"A bit later, actually. And darling Eve, you haven't had enough rest." He touched her cheek. "You get so pale."

"I'm okay."

"And did you find anything useful?"

"I'm not sure yet."

She told him about Summerset's observation while they readied for the day.

"So you think it's possible he was in one of the medical centers, in some capacity, during the Urbans."

"It's a thought. I did some research," she added as she strapped on her weapon harness. "Not a whole lot of detail about it, that I've found so far anyway. But there were other facilities that used that same basic method. A handful here in New York."

"Where he started this."

"I'm thinking," she agreed with a nod. "Something here in particular that matters. He starts here, he comes back here. There's a wide, wide world out there and he's used some of it. But now he repeats location."

"Not just location. You and Feeney. Morris, Whitney, Mira. There are others as well."

"Yeah, and I'm mulling on that. More usually if a repeat killer has a thing about cops, he likes to thumb his nose at us. Send us messages, leave cryptic clues so he can feel superior. We're not getting that. But I'm mulling it."

She took one last, life-affirming glug of coffee. "I've got to get started, or I won't have myself lined up for the briefing."

"Oh, I'm to tell you Brian's waiting for you with open arms when you're done with me."

"Huh? Brian? Irish Brian?"

"That would be the one. I contacted him, asked him to look for torturers. He has connections," Roarke continued. "And knows how to ferret out information."

"Huh." It struck her she'd married a man with a lot of unusual associates. Came in handy now and then. "Okay. I'll see you later."

He moved to her, ran a hand over her hair again. "Take care of my cop."

"That's the plan." She met his lips with hers, stepped back. "I'll be in touch."

In briefing the team, Eve had everyone give their own orals on progress or lack of same. She listened to theories, arguments for or against, ideas for approaching different angles, or for pursuing old ones from a new perspective.

"If the Urbans are an angle," Baxter put in, "and we look at it like this fucker was a medical, or he got his torture training back then, we could be looking for a guy pushing eighty, or better. That gives him a half-century or more on his vics. How's a guy starting to creak pull this off?"

"Horny Dog's missing the fact that a lot of guys past middle age keep up." Jenkinson pointed a finger at Baxter. "Eighty's the new sixty."

"Sick Bastard has a point," Baxter acknowledged. "And as a borderline creaker himself, he's got some insight on it. But I'm saying it takes some muscle and agility to bag a thirty-year-old woman — especially since he goes for the physically tuned ones — off the street."

"He could've been a kid during the Urbans." As if in apology for speaking out, Trueheart cleared his throat. "Not that eighty's old, but —"

"You shave yet, Baby Face?" Jenkinson asked.

"While it's sad and true that Officer Baby Face doesn't have as much hair on his chin as Sick Bastard does in his ears, there were a lot of kids kicked around, orphaned, beat to shit during the Urbans. Or so I hear," Baxter added with a wide grin for Jenkinson. "Before my time."

She accepted the bullshit and insults cops tossed around with other cops. She let it go for another few minutes. And when she deemed all current data had been relayed, all ideas explored and the stress relieved, she handed out the day's assignments and dismissed.

"Peabody, locate York's ex. We need to have a word. I'm taking Mira into my office for a few minutes. Doctor?"

"So many avenues," Mira commented as they started out.

"One of them will lead us to him." Eventually, Eve thought.

"His consistency is both his advantage and disadvantage. It'll be a step on the avenue that leads you to him. His inflexibility is going to undermine him at some point."

"Inflexibility."

"His refusal to deviate," Mira confirmed. "Or his inability to deviate from a set pattern allows you to know a great deal about him. So you can anticipate."

"I anticipated he'd have taken number two. That isn't helping Gia Rossi."

Mira shook her head. "That's not relevant. You couldn't have helped Rossi as she was already taken before you knew, or could know, he was back in business."

"That's what it is?" Eve led the way to her office, gestured toward the visitor's chair while she sat on the corner of her desk. "Business."

"His pattern is businesslike, a kind of perfected routine. Or ritual, as I said before. He's very proud of his work, which is why he shares it. Displays it, but only when it's completed."

"When he's finished with them, he wants to show them off, wants to claim them. That's why he arranges them on a white sheet. That's the ring he puts on them. I get that. During the Urbans — if we head down that avenue — bodies were laid out, piled up, stacked up, depending on the facilities. And covered. Sheet, drop cloth, plastic, whatever was available. Usually, their clothes, shoes, personal effects were taken. Mostly these were recycled to other people. It's 'waste not and want not' in wartime. So he takes their clothes, their personal effects, but he reverses, leaving them uncovered."

"Pride. I believe, to him, they're beautiful. In death, they're beautiful to him." Mira shifted, crossed her legs. She'd pinned her hair up into a soft roll at the nape of her neck, and wore a pale, pale yellow suit that seemed to whisper a promise of spring. "His choice of victim type indicates, as I said in the briefing, some prior connection with a woman of this basic age and coloring. She symbolizes something to him. Mother, lover, sister, unattained love."

"Unattained."

"He couldn't control this person, couldn't make her see him as he wanted to be seen, not in her life or in her death. Now he does, again and again."

"He doesn't rape or molest them sexually. If it was a lover, wouldn't he see her as sexual?"

"Love, not lover. Women are Madonnas or whores to him, so he fears and respects them."

"Punishes and kills the whore," Eve considered, "and creates the Madonna, who he cleanses and displays."

"Yes. It's their womanhood, not their sexuality, he's obsessed with. He may be impotent. In fact, I believe we'll find this to be the case when you catch him. But sex isn't important to him. It doesn't drive him or, again if impotent, he would mutilate the genitals or sexually abuse them with objects. This hasn't been the case in any of the victims.

"It's possible he gains sexual release or satisfaction from their pain," Mira added. "But it's secondary, we could say a by-product. It's the pain that drives him, and the endurance of the subject, and the result. The death."

Eve pushed up, wandered to the AutoChef, absently programmed coffee for both of them. "You said 'businesslike,' and I don't disagree. But it seems like a kind of science to me. Regular and specific experiments. Artful science, I guess."

"We don't disagree." Mira accepted the coffee. "He's focused and he's dedicated. Control — his own, and his ability to control others — is vital to him. His ability to step away, to step outside of the active work for long periods, indicates great control and willpower. I don't believe, even with this, it's possible for him to maintain personal or intimate relationships for any length of time. Most certainly not with women. Business relationships? I believe he could maintain those to some extent. He must have income. He invests in his victims."

"The high-end products, the silver rings. The travel to select them from different locations. The cost of obtaining or maintaining the place where he works on them."

"Yes, and given the nature of the products, he's used to a certain level of lifestyle. Cleansing them is part of the ritual, yes, but he could do so with more ordinary means. More mainstream products."

"Nothing but the best," Eve agreed. "But it also leads me down the avenue that he may be a competitor of Roarke's, or an employee in a top-level position."

"Both would be logical." Mira drank her coffee, quietly pleased Eve remembered how she preferred it. "He's chosen to make this connection. Just as he chose to come back to New York to work at this time. But there was a connection for him to make, Eve."

She set her cup aside now, and her gaze was sober when she looked at Eve. "There was you. These women are, in a sense, Roarke's. You are his in every sense."

Testing the idea, Eve frowned. "So he opts for this specific pattern because of me? I wasn't primary on the initial investigation."

"You were a female on the initial investigation, a brunette. Too young at that time to meet his requirements. You aren't now."

"You're looking at me as a target?"

"I am. Yes, I am."

"Huh." Drinking coffee, Eve considered it more carefully. Mira's theories weren't to be casually dismissed. "Usually goes for long hair."

"There have been exceptions."

"Yeah, yeah, a couple of them. He's been smart. This wouldn't be smart." Eve tipped the angle of it in her mind, shifted the pattern. "It's a lot tougher to take down a cop than it is a civilian."

"You would be a great prize, from his viewpoint. It would be a challenge, and a coup. And if he knows anything about you, which I promise you he does, he would be assured you would endure a long time."

"Tough to stalk me. First, I'd click to it. Second, I don't have regular routines, not like the others. They clocked in and out at fairly uniform times, had regular haunts. I don't."

"Which, again, would add to the challenge," Mira argued, "and his ultimate satisfaction. You're considering that he may have added Roarke as an element because he's in competition with him. That may very well be true. But what he does isn't payback, not on a conscious level. Everything he does is for a specific purpose. I believe, in this, you're a specific purpose."

"It'd be helpful."

"Yes." Mira sighed. "I imagined you'd see it that way."

Eyes narrowed, Eve tipped the angle again, explored the fresh pattern. "If we go with this, and I could find a way to bait him in — to nudge him into making a move on me before he grabs another one — we could shut him down. Shut him down, take him out."

"You won't bait him." Watching Eve, Mira picked up her coffee. "I can promise you he has his timetable already set. The only variable in it is the length of time his victims last. He has the third selected. Unless he planned only three — which would be less than he's ever taken before — the next won't be you."

"Then we have to find her first. Let's keep your theory between us, just for now. I want to think about it."

"I want you to think about it," Mira said as she got to her feet. "As a member of this team, as a profiler, and as someone who cares a great deal about you, I want you to think about it very carefully."

"I will."

"This is a hard one for you, for Feeney. For me, the commander. We've been here before, and in a very real sense, we failed. Failing again —"

"Isn't an option," Eve finished. "Do me a favor. I know it's a tough process, but take a look at the list Summerset generated. The female employees. Just see if any of them strike you as more his type. We can't put eyes on all those women, but if there's a way to whittle it down . . ."

"I'll start on that right away."

"I've got to get going."

"Yes." Mira passed her empty cup to Eve, brushed her fingers lightly over the back of Eve's hand. "Don't just think carefully. Be careful."

Even as Mira left, Eve's desk 'link beeped. Scanning the readout, she picked up. "Nadine."

"Dallas. Any word on Rossi?"

"We're looking. If you're interrupting my day looking for an update —"

"Actually, I'm interrupting mine to give you one. One of my eager little researchers plucked out an interesting nugget. From Romania."

Automatically Eve pulled up on her computer screen what she had on the Romanian investigation. "I should have the full case files from that investigation later today. What have you got?"

"Tessa Bolvak, a Romany — gypsy? Had her own show on screen. Psychic hour — or twenty minutes, to be accurate."

"You're interrupting both of our days with a psychic?"

"A renowned one in Romanian circles during the time in question. She was a regularly consulted sensitive, often consulting for the police."

"Those wacky Romanians."

"Other police authorities make use of sensitives," Nadine reminded her. "You did, not that long ago."

"Yeah, and look how well that worked out for everybody."

"However," Nadine continued, "we're not here to debate that issue. The amazing Tessa — as both she and her producers recognized the value of a big, juicy case — ran a special on the murders there, and her part in the investigation. She claimed your guy was a master of death, and its servant."

"Oh, jeez."

"*And*. That death sought him, provided for him. A pale man," Nadine said, shifting to read off her own comp screen. "A black soul. Death is housed in him as he is housed in it. Music soars as the blood runs. It plays for her — diva and divine — who sang for him. He seeks them out, flowers for his bouquet, his bouquet for her altar."

"Nadine, give me a —"

"Wait, wait. A pale man," she continued, "who bears the tree of life and lives by death. Tessa got a lot of play out of the program."

"Did I mention wacky Romanians?"

"And here's more wacky for you. Two days after the program aired, her body was found — throat slit — floating in the Danube."

"Too bad she didn't see that one coming."

"Ha. The authorities deemed it a robbery-homicide. Her jewelry and purse were never found. But I wonder if those in charge of such things over there lack my sense of irony or your innate cynicism."

"How come you get the irony?" Eve complained. "I've got plenty of irony. Maybe, maybe she's so busy looking through the crystal ball she doesn't notice some guy who wants her baubles."

Just a little too much coincidence, Eve mused, to pass the bullshit barrier. "And maybe our guy took her

129

out because something in the overdone woo-woo speak hit a little too close."

"It occurred to me," Nadine agreed. "Doesn't fit his pattern, but —"

"He doesn't give her the . . . status, we'll say, he affords his chosen victims. She just annoyed him, so he took her out. You got a copy of the program she did?"

"I do."

"Send me a copy. I'll reach out to Romania again, see if they'll get me the juice on her case. You got anything else?"

"A lot of screaming tabloid headlines, screen and print. My busy bees will pick through them, see if there's anything worth looking at twice."

"Let me know."

When she clicked off, Eve noted down: Pale man. Music. Tree of life. Death house.

Then she went to snag Peabody.

"I think it's getting warmer." Peabody hunched her shoulders and tried to lever her body so the wild March wind didn't blow straight into her marrow.

"Are you standing on the same side of the equator as I am?"

"No, really. I think it's a couple of degrees up from yesterday. And seeing as it's March, it's practically April. So it's almost summer if you think about it."

"The frigid wind has obviously damaged your brain." Eve pulled out her badge for the security scanner on Cal Marshall's building. "That being the case, I need to rethink the fact that I was about to tell you to take the lead on this guy."

"No! I can do it. It's freezing, okay. The wind's so freaking cold it's drilling right through my corneas into my retinas. But it hasn't yet entered the brain."

When they were cleared, Peabody stepped in, yanked off her earflap cap. "Do I have hat hair? You can't effectively interview with hat hair."

"You have hair. Be satisfied with that."

"Hat hair," Peabody muttered, raking her hands through it, shaking her head, fluffing and pushing as they got in the elevator.

"Stop! Stop being a girl. Jesus, that's annoying. If I had a partner without tits, there would be no hair obsessing."

"Baxter would combat hat hair before an interview."

Because it was inarguably true, Eve only scowled. "He doesn't count."

"And there's Miniki. He —"

"Keep it up, and I'll tie you down and shave you bald. You won't ever suffer the pain and embarrassment of hat hair again."

Eve strode out of the elevator, followed the numbers to Cal Marshall's apartment.

"Do I still take the lead?" Peabody asked, meekly.

Eve sent her a withering look, then knocked. When the door opened, she shifted slightly to the side so that Peabody had the front ground.

"Mr. Marshall? I'm Detective Peabody. We spoke earlier. This is my partner, Lieutenant Dallas. May we come in?"

131

"Yeah. Sure. Yeah."

He was blond, tanned, fit, with eyes the blue of an arctic lake. They looked a little hollow now, a little dull, and his voice held the same tone. "About Sari. It's about Sari."

"Why don't we sit down?"

"What? Yeah, we should sit."

Through an open door, Eve spotted the bed — made — with a large duffle tossed on it. There was a snowboard tipped against the wall. In the living area, a heavy ski coat was draped over a chair, the lift pass still clipped on it.

On the molded black table in front of the dark blue gel sofa were several empty bottles of beer.

Came in, Eve mused, tossed down his gear, checked his 'link messages. Got the word. Sat here and drank most of the night.

"I heard. I got home and heard —" He rubbed at his eyes. "Um, Bale — he heard from Zela. She works with Sari at the club. She told him . . . he told me."

"It must've been a shock," Peabody said. "That was the first you heard of her death? You didn't have your pocket 'link, or see any reports while you were gone?"

"I shut down my 'link. Just wanted to board. It was all about boarding. Me and Bale went out to Colorado. Incommunicado Colorado. Big joke," he said. "Shuttled back last night. Bale, he's closer to the station, got home first. Zela left him a message. Zela talked to him. He called. I got home, and he . . ."

"You and Sarifina were involved."

132

"We were . . . we were together until a couple of weeks ago." He scrubbed both hands over his face. "A couple of weeks . . . We broke up."

"Why did you break up?"

"She was always too busy. She was always . . ." He trailed off, lifted his gaze to Peabody's. "I wanted more, okay? I wanted her more available, more interested in what I wanted to do when I wanted to do it. It wasn't working out, not the way I wanted it. So I said I was done with it. With her."

"You argued."

"Yeah. We both got pretty harsh. She said I was selfish, immature, self-involved. I said something like, 'Right back at you.' Shit, shit, shit. She's dead. Bale said . . . I was snowboarding and trashing her to Bale. And she was dead. You think I hurt her? I wanted to hurt her. Here," he said, thumping a fist to his heart. "I wanted her to feel crappy that I flipped her, you know? I wanted her to be lonely and miserable while I found somebody — lots of somebodies — who knew how to have a good time. Christ."

He dropped his head in his hands. "Oh, my Christ."

"We don't think you hurt her, Mr. Marshall. Before you broke up, did she stay here with you?"

"Less and less. Things were disintegrating. We barely saw each other. Once or twice a week maybe."

"Did she ever mention anyone bothering her? Anyone that made her uncomfortable?"

"We weren't doing a lot of talking lately." He said it quietly while he looked down at his hands. "I don't remember her saying anything like that. She liked the old guys who came into the club. Especially the old guys. Smooth, she said. They got smooth with age, like whiskey or something. Some hit on her now and then, and she got a kick out of it. At least I didn't get twisted about that. I thought it was funny."

"Anyone specifically?"

"I don't know. I didn't pay much attention. I'm not into that retro crap. Bored me senseless, you know? She looked good though, when she dressed up for work? Man, she looked good."

"Not much of a well to pump there," Peabody commented as they rode down.

"I don't know. She liked older men, older men liked her. It's high probability the killer is an older man."

"And?"

"I bet he chatted her up somewhere along the line. A week or two before he grabbed her, he makes contact in the club. That'd be a big thrill for him, having a conversation, maybe a dance with his intended victim. A good way to get another sense of her, a gauge, a rhythm."

"Yeah." Peabody hissed in her breath as they started outside. "And . . . If he did, and she saw him later — on the street, wherever he made the grab, she'd be friendly, at ease. It's Mr. Smooth from Starlight."

"So, if he made contact with her . . . maybe he made contact with Gia Rossi."

"The fitness center."

"Place to start."

He knew how to blend. He knew how to make himself inconspicuous, so that eyes passed over him without notice. It was a skill he put to good use during the research phase of any project.

He used it now as he watched her — Eve Dallas — stride out of the apartment building, down the street. Ground-eating strides. Loose and busy. Strong.

He very much approved of strong women — physically and mentally.

She'd been strong. The Eve of all the others. The mother. She'd been very strong, he remembered, but he believed this Eve — this last Eve — would be stronger than any who had come before.

Not time for you yet, he thought as he watched her, watched the way she moved. Not quite time for this Eve. But when it was, oh . . .

He believed she would be his finest work to date. A new level of excellence. And the pinnacle of all he'd accomplished.

But for now, there was another who required his attention.

He really should get home to her.

The manager of BodyWorks was a six-foot Asian with a body like molded steel. He went by the name of Pi. He wore a black skin-suit and a small, trim goatee.

"Like I told the other cops, it was just another day. Gia had her classes, her clients. I gave them the client list. Do you need —"

"No, they have it. Thanks for cooperating."

He dropped down into a chair in his office, a glass box that allowed him to view all the areas on that level of the center. Outside it, people pumped, sweated, trotted, flexed, and twisted.

"We're pals, you know? I can't get through the idea something may have happened to her. But I'm telling you, she can take care of herself. That's what I think. She's tough."

"Anybody ask for her specifically in the last few weeks?" Eve asked him.

"Yeah, like I told the other guys. She'd get referrals from clients. Word of mouth. She's good at what she does, gets results, but doesn't drill sergeant the client into it."

"How about older guys, say over sixty?"

"Sure. Sure. Fitness isn't just for kids, you know. She has some clients like that, and we get them in for classes. She runs a tai chi class twice a week, a yoga class every other morning geared for the over-sixty group. Twice a week she has classes geared for the centennials."

"She pick up anybody new in any of those in the last few weeks?"

"Like I told the others, if you're a member you don't have to sign up for any of the classes. You just come in, take whichever you want."

"How about anybody who joined in, say, the last thirty days. Male, over fifty, let's say."

"I can get you that. But you don't have to have joined at this location. If you hold a membership from any of our clubs — that's global — you just key in."

"You have a record of who's keyed in? You keep track of how your members use the facilities, how often they use them, who pays the fee for a trainer?"

"Sure. Sure. That kind of data goes straight to the main offices. But I can —"

"I can get that," Eve told him. "No problem. Did she take outside clients?"

"That's against policy," he began.

"We're not worried about policy, Pi. She's not going to get jammed up if she pulled in some extra on the side. We want to find her."

"Yeah, well, maybe she did." He puffed out his cheeks, blew out the air. "Somebody's willing to pay you stiff for going to their house for an hour a couple times a week, it's hard to flip it. We're pals, but I'm management. She knows I know, and like that, but we don't talk about it. Not really."

"How about a sense, since you were pals, if she took on a private client recently?"

He puffed out his cheeks again. "She sprang for Knicks tickets — courtside. We're going to the game next week. My birthday. Son of a bitch." He smoothed his hands over his shaved head. "Pretty much out of her range. She joked, said she'd hit a little jackpot. I figured she'd gotten a side fee, a couple of them maybe."

"When did she get the tickets?"

"A few weeks ago. Look, you need to find her, okay? You just need to find her."

CHAPTER
EIGHT

Outside, Eve walked the route Gia habitually took to the subway. The woman was a New Yorker, Eve mused. Which meant she'd move along at a brisk pace, and though her radar would be on, she'd be inside her own thoughts.

Might be a window-shopper, Eve thought. Might stop and study a display, even go inside a shop. But . . .

"Baxter and Trueheart checked out the stores and markets along the route," she said to Peabody. "Nobody remembers seeing her that day. Some clerks recognized her picture. Previous visits. But not on the day she poofed."

"She didn't make it to the station."

"No. Maybe she wasn't going to the station." Eve turned, sidestepping toward the buildings as New York bustled by. "Had extra dough, enough for a pair of courtsides. She takes an outside client. Maybe the client's address is within walking distance. Or he provided cab fare or transportation."

And considering this, she factored in Baxter's point about the potential age difference, and the fact that Gia Rossi had been a trainer, in peak physical condition.

"Maybe she walked right into it. Maybe she walked right into his nest."

"He doesn't grab her. He just opens the door."

"Slick," Eve said softly. "Yeah, that would be slick. Contact Newkirk. I want him and the other uniforms canvassing this area. All directions, five blocks." Eve headed toward the car. "I want her picture shown to every clerk, waitperson, sidewalk sleeper, doorman, and droid. Get McNab," she added as she climbed behind the wheel. "I want him to send her picture to every cab company and private transpo service. Bus companies, air trams. Hit them all. Then the Transit Authority. Check the run for that night on other stations. She didn't use her pass, but maybe she took a ride anyway."

Peabody was already relaying to Newkirk.

"She went to him," Eve said before she swung out into traffic. "That's what I think. She went right to him."

Following the hunch, she contacted Zela at home.

"Yes?" Obviously half asleep, Zela stifled a yawn. "Lieutenant? What —"

"Did Sarifina ever give private lessons?"

"Private lessons? I'm sorry, I'm a little foggy."

"Dance lessons. Did she ever give private dance lessons?"

"Now and again, sure. People want to be able to do the moves for special occasions. Weddings, bar or bat mitzvahs, reunions. That sort of thing."

"At the club, or at the client's home?"

"Generally at the club. Mornings when we're closed."

"Generally," Eve pressed, "but there were exceptions."

"Give me a second." Zela moved as she spoke, and Eve heard the beep of an AutoChef. "I worked until nearly three last night, then took a pill. I haven't been sleeping well since . . . I need to clear my head."

"Zela." Impatience ground through Eve's voice. "I need to know if Sarifina went to clients' homes."

"Every once in a while, particularly for the older clients. Or the kids. Sometimes parents want their kids to learn. Or an older couple wants to swing it a little — for an occasion, or a cruise. But usually, we do that sort of thing here, through the club."

"Had she taken on any personal clients in the last few weeks?"

"Just let me think, okay? Let me think." Zela gulped down what Eve assumed was coffee. "She may have. She was an easy touch, you know? Liked to do favors for people. We didn't check that kind of thing off with each other all the time. But if it was through the club, I mean if she was going to instruct someone here, she'd have noted in down. The club gets a cut of the fee, and Sari was religious about keeping good records on that."

"No cut if she went to them?"

"Well, that's a gray area. Like I said, she liked to do favors. She might go give someone an hour or two, cutting her rate, doing it off the books. On her own time, before or after work, on her day off. What's the harm?"

What's the harm? Eve thought as she clicked off.

140

"We figured he grabbed them off the street. But they went to him. These two, at least, my money says they went right to him. How'd they get there?"

"York's image has been out since yesterday. Weekend, though," Peabody added. "If she took a cab, the driver might not have paid any attention, or might not have seen the reports on her yet."

"No. No. We have to run it down, but that would be sloppy, and he isn't sloppy. Why take a chance like that? Leave a record, a possible wit? Cab driver dumps the vic right at his door? Doesn't play."

"Well, the same thing applies to private transpo."

"Not if he's providing it. Personally. We check anyway, we check all the transits. All the pickups in the area the vics were last seen."

Man hours, wasted hours, Eve thought. And still it had to be done. "He's not going to chance something like that. Lures them in, that's what he does. Nice, harmless guy, nice older gentleman who wants to learn to tango, wants to get fit. There's a nice, sweet fee for the personal service. Provides transportation for them."

"Nobody sees them on the street because they're not on the street that long." Peabody nodded as the theory solidified for her. "They come out of work, get into a waiting vehicle. Nobody's going to notice. But . . ."

"But?"

"How can he be sure they're not going to tell somebody? What I mean is, neither of these women seems stupid. How could he be sure they're not going to tell a friend, a coworker, they've got this private gig. Here's where I'm going to be, and with whom."

Eve pulled over in front of Gia Rossi's apartment building, then just sat, tapping her fingers on the wheel. "Good point. We know they didn't tell anyone, or anyone who's passed on that information. So the why, the how can he be sure. Gotta play the percentages." She got out, drawing her master to deal with the door. "First he's going to give them a bogus name and address. Now, if they're smart, or concerned in any way, they're going to check that out, make sure it's legit. Not hard to pull that off if you've got enough money and know-how. But that's another area for EDD to look into."

They stepped inside the three-story walk-up, where Rossi's apartment was on ground level. "Next, think of his profile. Intelligent, mature, controlled."

She used the master again to break the seal Baxter had activated, and uncode the locks. "We know he travels, so we're looking at someone who's likely sophisticated, and I'm just going to bet charming. He *knows* his victims."

When they stepped in, Eve paused to look around the cramped living area. Big wall screen, she noted, small couch, a couple of chairs, tables holding decorative bits and pieces. Tossed socks, shoes — mostly of the athletic variety. The electronics had already been taken in.

"Knows what they like," she continued, "what appeals to them. Plays that. Gets familiar with them face-to-face, dropping into their respective clubs, chatting them up. But not too much, not so anyone pays particular attention. He blends, and he blends. Mr. Smooth, Mr. Nice Guy, Mr. Harmless."

142

She walked over to the window, studied the street, the sidewalk, the neighboring buildings. "He gains their trust. Maybe he talks about his wife or his daughter, something that paints a picture in their heads. Normality. Takes time, sure, but he likes to take time. Then he brings up the private work — or smarter, he maneuvers them into mentioning it or suggesting it."

She turned, walked into the tiny, equally cramped bedroom. "Then he's got them. She's got privacy screens, but they're old and cheap. Right equipment, you could watch her in here. You know when she gets up, how long it takes her to get ready for work, what time she leaves, her route. Bet you keep it all documented. Scientific, that's what it is. I wonder how many he's picked, watched, documented, and rejected. How many women are alive because they didn't quite fit his precise requirements."

"Creepy."

"Yeah." Dipping her hands into her pockets, Eve rocked back on her heels. "Maybe he's always worked this way, or worked this way before. The prior personal contact, the maneuvering the target to go to him. We'll go back over the old cases with that angle. And we'll look at the projected targets in this one with that in mind."

"Dallas? What are we looking for here? I mean, here in her place."

"Her. Gia Rossi. He knows the pieces of her, or thinks he does. Let's see what we find."

It was what they didn't find that added weight to Eve's theory. However cramped and messy the living space,

Gia Rossi kept her exercise and music discs meticulously organized.

"Two slots empty in her workout disc tree, three empty in her music disc tree. The way she's got them alphabetized, I'm guessing cardio and yoga on the fitness end. We'll check the personal effects Baxter took from her gym locker."

"She's got a lot of personal equipment. Hand weights, ankle and wrist weights, mats, medicine balls, running track." Peabody gestured inside the closet that Rossi had outfitted for equipment storage. "I'm guessing some's missing. Lightest and heaviest ankle weights, light and heavy resistance ropes."

"Light for him, heavy for her. Takes some basic equipment, some music, the demo vids. You ever work with a PT?"

"No." Peabody flexed her butt muscles, wondering if that was the way to reduce the square footage of her ass. "You?"

"No, but I'm betting a good one would outline a program for a client — something specifically created for his body type, age, weight, goals, and so on. If she did it here, EDD can find it. Let's go."

Roarke walked into a war room full of chatter of both the human and electronic varieties. Cops on 'links, on headsets, on comps. Cops sitting, pacing, dancing.

But his cop was nowhere to be seen.

He crossed paths with McNab, who was outfitted in silver jeans and a casual Sunday sweatshirt of searing orange. "Is the lieutenant in the house?"

144

"In the field. Heading in, though. Working some fresh angles. You want?"

"I want."

Tapping the toes of his silver airboots, McNab swiveled in his chair. "Just covered all public and private transpo with pictures of York and Rossi. Dallas is working the idea that our guy provided transpo."

"And they just hopped in?"

"Yeah. Need liquid. Walk and talk."

McNab filled Roarke in as he headed out to Vending, debated his choices, and opted for an orange fizzy — perhaps to match his shirt.

"A home lesson or consultation," Roarke mused. "Interesting, and it would eliminate the risk of any sort of public abduction. Still, the method has its own risks and problems."

"Yeah, what if they change their minds, don't show, decide to bring a pal along. Lots of possibles." He sucked in fizzy. "But she wants it worked, so we work it. She said if you popped in, you should take a look at your employee list with this angle in mind. Women who fit the parameters who might do a house call on the side."

"Yes, I can do that."

"Lots of possibles," McNab repeated, "considering all the pies you've got fingers in. Anything moving on the real estate angle?"

"Nothing that stands out from the crowd, no."

"Sometimes you've got to toss it up, you know. Let it fall in a different pattern. You keep working it, it gets so it's just data. Maybe I could take that for a while while you work the new business."

"Fresh eyes. Yes, that's a good idea."

"Icy, then . . . Hey, here come our ladies. Just looking at them gives you the *uh*, doesn't it?" McNab gave the sound a push that was unmistakably sexual as he grinned down the long corridor where Peabody got off the glide with Eve.

Then he shot Roarke a quick look. "I mean the *uh* me for mine, you for yours. It's not like I get the *uh* for the lieutenant, for which she would kick my ass, then leave you to turn what was left of it into bloody dust. Which She-Body would then grind into the earth before she set it on fire. I was just saying."

"I know what you were saying." McNab could, invariably, entertain him. "And I couldn't agree more, with everything including the bloody dust. They are compelling women. Lieutenant," Roarke said as her long stride brought her to him.

"So glad you two have time for fizzy breaks."

"Sir. I've been bringing Roarke up to date, and relaying your orders."

"Looked like slurping and ogling to me."

"Ah . . . those may have been minor factors, but neither overshadowed the update or relay. Vic's images are broadcasted, Lieutenant. I set up another line for responses from those sources. We've been fielding tips and inquiries on the investigations, and I figured if we got something out of this, we didn't want it to get bogged down in the general dump."

"Good. That's good thinking. I want you to pass off whatever you're doing and take Rossi's equipment. Her comp. I'm looking for personalized fitness programs. Find me one that matches our unsub."

"On that."

"Feeney?"

"Roving mode," McNab told her. "Gives a look and a buzz to whatever everyone's working. Tightens it up or opens it out. He was playing the medical equipment angle when I came out to get — when I stepped out to update Roarke."

"Tell him I need somebody to go down to Body Works. Rossi used a couple of comps there routinely. The manager's been contacted and is cooperating. Get them brought in and gone through. Same search."

"Yes, sir."

"Roarke, with me."

Roarke fell into step beside her. "Formidable."

"What?"

"You. I'd used compelling, but formidable suits as well. Very sexy."

"Don't say 'sexy' on the job."

"You just did."

Okay, she admitted, he made her laugh. Which was obviously the point and intent. And it did relieve some of the tension at the base of her skull. "Got your smarty pants on, I see."

She moved into the bullpen, stopped her forward motion when one of the men called her name. "Got a DB in a flop off Avenue D," he began. "Licensed companion over there . . ."

He jerked his head toward the skinny woman in a bloody shirt seated at his desk. "She says the guy

147

wanted to party, the party was had. He refused to pay the bill and popped her two good ones when she objected to getting stiffed. Pulled out her sticker, which she claims he ran into. Six times."

"Clumsy of him."

"Yeah. Thing is, Lieutenant, she called it in. Didn't try to rabbit, and she's sticking to the story. Claims he laughed like a looney bird every time the knife went in. Got a couple of wits saw them make the deal, another who heard them yelling in the flop. You can see she's got herself a pretty good shiner working there."

"Yeah. Got priors?"

"Couple little bumps, nothing violent. Had her LC ticket for three years."

"And the DB?"

"Oh, he had a nice long sheet. Assaults, assaults with deadlies, illegals — possession and intent. Just got out of the cage for an attempted robbery — beat hell out of a clerk at a twenty-four/seven. On the Zeus."

Eve studied the LC. The woman looked more annoyed than worried. And her face was sporting a sick rainbow of bruises. "Guy on Zeus could run into a knife multiple times. Wait for the tox screen on the DB, run her through again, see if she stands on the story, then put her in holding."

"Guy was juiced up, a lime green PD's going to get a self-defense. Could slap her for the sticker, as it was over legal limit."

"What's the point?"

"Yeah, that's what I was thinking. Wanted to run it by you first."

"She ask for a PD or a rep?"

"Not yet. Pissed is what she is." He nodded over to her desk. "Knows the incident means an automatic thirty-day suspension of her license. So she's out the fee and a month's work, got a fist in the face, and ruined what she says is a new shirt."

"That's the life. Get the tox, wrap it up. Reach out to Illegals on the DB if anything looks shaky," Eve added. "Somebody over there probably has a take on him."

She walked into her office, shut the door.

"She'll walk," Roarke commented.

"Likely. Smart not to run, to come in voluntarily. Less smart to party with a guy on Zeus, if that was the case. And if she's worked that sector for a couple, three years, she'd know if he was pumped."

"A girl's got to make a living."

"That's what they tell me. So, anything from the unregistered?"

"Nothing that gels, not at this point. I have Summerset running more searches and crosses. He knows what to look for, and how to find it."

Her brows drew together. "Am I going to have to be grateful to him?"

"I'll take care of that."

"Good." She pulled off her coat, went for coffee. "Did McNab actually give you an update?"

"He did, yes. I'll go through the employee list, cull out any who might take a home appointment or consultation. Do you think now this has been his pattern all along?"

"I don't know, can't say." Eve rubbed at her eyes, then scratched her head furiously as if to wake up the brain under her scalp. "But we're talking more than twenty women. How likely is it that not one of them ever told anyone where they were going? Bogus name, sure, but if they had the location in advance, made this appointment, how likely is it none of them told anyone, or left any sort of record of the appointment?"

"Low. Yes, I see. But . . . There may have been more than the twenty. And I see you've considered that as well," he added when he studied her face. "He picked them, made the arrangements, and if he sensed or learned they'd mentioned it, he'd simply follow through with the cover. Take his fucking dance lesson."

"Yeah, I think he could pull that off. And I think he could grab or lure them later in his schedule. So we go back over the prior cases, find out if any of the vics took a house call in the week or two before they were killed. He's focused," Eve continued, "careful enough to make sure he's clear, but focused. I can see him postponing the grab, or switching vics. If so, it's something we didn't have before. A mistake we missed."

Roarke drank his coffee. The office seemed ridiculously confining to him all at once. The piss-poor light barely seeping through her excuse for a window, the tight box formed by the walls.

"Haven't you ever considered asking for a bigger office?"

"What for?"

"A little breathing room might be a plus."

"I can breathe fine. You can't take this in, Roarke."

150

"And how would you suggest I avoid that?" he demanded. "I'm his springboard, aren't I? There's a woman dead because she worked for me. Another who, even now, is being tortured. It's too late for Gia Rossi."

"It's not too late until it's too late." Still, she knew she owed him the straight line, and that he had to be able to deal with it. "The probability is low that we'll find her in time. It's not impossible, but at this point, it's not likely."

"And the next, she'd already be in his sights."

"He'd have stalked her, selected her, worked her by now. But we've got more time there. He's not infallible, and there's only one of him. I've put the best I've got on this. It ends here."

Her eyes went flat, cop flat. "It's going to end here. But you're no good to me if you can't set the emotional connection aside."

"Well, I can't. But I can use it. I can do what I need to do."

"Okay."

"Which includes getting right pissed from time to time."

"Fine. But get this in your head. The responsibility for this is his. Totally, completely, absolutely. No portion of it's yours. He owns it. If his mother used him as her butt monkey when he was a kid, he still owns it. He made the choice. If his father, uncle, aunt, cousin from Toledo kicked his ass every Tuesday, it's still his. You and I know that. We know about the choice. We know, whenever we take a life, whatever the

151

circumstances, whatever the reasons, it's still our choice. Right or wrong, we own it."

Roarke considered his coffee, set it aside. And his eyes met hers. "I love you, for so many reasons."

"Maybe you can give me a few of them later."

"I'll give you one now. That unfailing moral center of yours. So very solid and true." He laid his hands on her shoulders, drew her in. Kissed her softly. "And then there's the sex."

"Figured you'd work that in."

"As often as humanly possible. Well then." He gave her shoulders a rub, stepped back. "There's one thing I can do now, and that's order in lunch for the team. Don't," he continued, lifting a warning finger, "give me any lip."

"I thought you like my lip — the set of them. Look, I don't want you to —"

"I was thinking pizza."

Her eyes slitted; she huffed out a breath. "That's hitting below the belt, pal."

"I know your every weakness, Lieutenant. And this one's topped with pepperoni."

"Just don't make a habit of it. The food. They'll get greedy."

"I think your team's steady enough to handle a few slices. I'll take care of it, and start on the employee list."

When he left, she closed the door behind him. She wanted to work in the quiet for a while, with minimal interruption. To think and theorize before she went back to the noise and pressures of the war room.

She brought up the files on the first investigation.

She knew these women. Their names, their faces, where they'd come from, where they'd lived, where they'd worked or studied.

A diverse group, in all but general appearance. And now she would look for one more point of origin.

Corrine, would-be actress working as a waitress, who'd squeezed in acting, dance, and vocal lessons when she could afford them. He could have played her, yes, he could have in several ways. Come to this location to audition for a part — what hungry young actress wouldn't bite? Or come to this address on this date and time to help serve at a party. Pick up some extra cash. Possibilities.

She went down the list of names. A secretary, a grad student working on her master's in foreign studies, a clerk in a gift shop who dabbled in pottery.

Following the string, she began to make calls, questioning people she'd interviewed nine years before.

There was a quick knock, then Peabody stuck her head in. She had a slice of pizza, half eaten, in her hand. "Pizza's here. They're pouncing on it like wolves. You'd better get out there if you want any."

"Minute."

Peabody took another bite. "You got something?"

"Maybe. Maybe." Eve wished the scent of pizza wasn't so damn distracting. "I'll bring it in. Get whoever's in the field on a headset. I want to brief everyone at once."

"You got it."

"Get the vics from the first investigation up on screen, with data."

Eve gathered her notes, her discs, then tagged Mira. "I need you in the war room."

"Ten minutes."

"Sooner," Eve said and clicked off.

When Eve strode into the war room, she noted that two pizzas had been demolished along with most of a third. After setting down her notes, she marched over, grabbed a slice.

"Got Jenkinson, Powell, Newkirk, and Harris on the line," Peabody told her. "Everyone else is here."

"Mira's on her way. I want her take on this." Even as Eve bit in, Feeney was coming toward her.

"You've got something. I can see it."

"Might. A possible link, possible method. I'm going to lay it out as soon as Mira's in the room." She glanced over, then handily caught the tube of Pepsi that Roarke tossed her. "Progress?" she asked him.

"I have fifty-six most possible, given their vocations or avocations. Still coming."

"Okay. Peabody, get the screen up, backed with the disc I brought in." She nodded when Mira came in. After taking a long sip, Eve put on the headset.

"Listen up, people. I need your full attention. If you can't eat pizza and think —"

"You got pizza?" was Jenkinson's complaint in her ear.

"We're working on a new theory," Eve said, and began to lay it out.

CHAPTER
NINE

"One of Corrine Dagby's coworkers at the time of her death remembers — or more accurately thinks she remembers — the vic mentioning she was up for a part in a play. Off-off Broadway. If she spoke of this to anyone else, family, friends, other students in her classes, they don't recall.

"Melissa Congress, second vic, secretarial position. Last seen leaving a club Lower West, well lubricated. This remains, most probably, a grab. A moment of opportunity. She was, however, known to complain with some consistency about her level of employment, her pay, her hours. There remains a possibility that she was approached about interviewing for another position and therefore knew or recognized her abductor.

"Anise Waters," Eve continued. "Grad student at Columbia. Fluent in Mandarin Chinese and Russian, and working on a master's in political science. She sometimes supplemented her income by tutoring, most usually on campus. Last seen leaving the university's main library. Wits stated that she took a pass on joining a group for drinks, claiming she had work. As she was a serious and dedicated student, it was assumed she was heading home to study. She didn't mention, to

155

anyone's recollection, an outside tutoring job. The language discs she checked out from the library were never recovered. The vic did have a scheduled tutoring job, on campus, the next day. It was assumed she'd checked out the discs for that purpose.

"Last, Joley Weitz. Last seen leaving Arts A Fact, a shop where she was employed, at approximately seventeen hundred. The vic did pottery, and had sold a few pieces she had on consignment at her place of employment. Her employer stated that the vic mentioned she had an important stop to make before she got ready for a date with a new boyfriend. The boyfriend was identified and cleared. As the vic had a dress on hold at a boutique she frequented, it was thought picking that item up for her date was her stop. She never reached the boutique, if indeed that was her intended destination."

She waited a moment, let it soak. "New theory. The vics were approached by the unsub at some time. York gave dance instruction, Rossi moonlights as a personal trainer off-site. It's a reasonable assumption all or most of these women were offered a private job, and went to their killer. I've begun examining the other cases, outside of New York, and believe this possibility extends. We have an assistant chef, a photographer, a nurse, a decorator, a data cruncher, a freelance writer, two health care aides, two artists, a clerk in a nursery — plants, the owner of a small flower shop, a librarian, a hair and skin consultant, a hotel maid. A music instructor, an herbalist, a caterer's assistant.

"No link but physical appearance was ever found between these women. But if we factor in this possibility. An opportunity to head the kitchen for a private dinner party, to do a photo shoot, private nursing care, write an article, so on."

"Why didn't anyone know they were going off for a private job, an audition?" Baxter asked.

"Good question. Some of them are likely grabs, as we assumed all along. It's also possible he took the time once they were inside the location to engage them in casual conversation, determine if they had told anyone. In some cases, outside jobs would be against their rules of employment. Cop moonlights as a security guard, a bouncer, a body guard, he keeps it to himself. Dr. Mira? Any thoughts on this?"

"It could be another form of control and enjoyment. Inviting his victims in, having them willingly enter, would be yet more proof to him of his superiority over them. It may indeed be another part of the ritual he's created. The lack of violence on the bodies — and by that I mean the fact there's no evidence he used his fists, his hands to strike, to throttle, that there is no sexual molestation — indicates he isn't physical in that way. The violence is through implements and tools. A method such as you're theorizing would fall within the structure of his profile."

"I like it," Baxter commented. "Makes more sense to me, if he's hitting on sixty or over, he'd use deception instead of force to bag them."

"Agreed," Eve said. "If this holds, it indicates he's aware they're physically stronger than he is, or might

157

be," Eve put in. "All these women were in good physical shape, a number of them in exceptional physical shape. He targets young, strong women. We believe he isn't young, maybe he isn't particularly strong."

"Which may be one of the reasons he needs to subdue, humiliate, and control them." Mira nodded. "Yes, by luring them into a location he has secured, he's dominated them intellectually, and then he proceeds to dominate them physically up to and including the point of their death. He not only masters them, but makes them other than they were. And by doing so, makes them his own."

"What does that tell us?" Eve scanned the room. "It tells us one thing we didn't know about him before."

"He's a coward," Peabody said, and gave Eve a quick, inner glow of pride.

"Exactly. He doesn't, as we believed, confront his victims, doesn't risk a public struggle, even with the aid of a drug. He uses guile and lies, the lure of money or advancement or the achievement of a personal goal. He has to know them well enough to use what works, or has the greatest potential of working. He may have spent more time observing and stalking each vic than we previously supposed. And the more time he spent, the more chance there is that someone, somewhere, saw him with one or more of the victims."

"We've been shooting blanks there," Baxter reminded her.

"We go back, interview again, and ask about men the vics spent time with at work, who may have taken one of their classes or talked about doing so. A month ago, two months ago. He wouldn't have been back since he abducted them. He's done with them; he's moved on from that stage. Who used to hang out at these locations, or frequent them who hasn't been there in the last week for York, the last three days for Rossi.

"McNab, dig into Rossi's comps, find me a new outside client. Roarke, names, addys, place of employment on everyone on your list who feels like she fits. Feeney, keep at the Urban War angle. Body identification, comments, commentaries, names of medics officially assigned, of volunteers where you can find them. I want photos, horror stories, war stories, editorials, every scrap you can dig up. Baxter, you and Trueheart hit the street. Jenkinson, you and Powell stay out there, find somebody whose memory can be jogged.

"Write it up, Peabody."

"Yes, sir."

She started out, and Feeney caught up with her. "Need a minute," he said.

"Sure. Got something?"

"Your office."

With an easy shrug, she kept going. "Heading back there. I want to go through the cases between the first and this one more carefully, start calling names on the original interview lists. We just need one break, one goddamn crack, and we can bust it. I know it."

He said nothing as they wound through the bullpen, into her office. "Want coffee?" she asked, then frowned as he closed the door. "Problem?"

"How come you didn't come to me with this?"

"With what?"

"This new theory."

"Well, I —" Sincerely baffled, she shook her head. "I just did."

"Bullshit. What you did was come out as primary, as team leader, you briefed and assigned. You didn't run this by me. My case, you remember? It's my case you were using out there."

"It just popped. Something York's boyfriend said clicked on a new angle for me. I started working it and —"

"*You* started working it," he interrupted. "Going back over my case. A case where I was primary. I was in charge. I made the calls."

Because the muscles in her belly were starting to twist, Eve took a long, steady breath. "Yeah, like I'm going to go back over the others. They're all part of the same whole, and if this is an opening —"

"One I didn't see?" His tired, baggy eyes were hard and bright now. "A call I didn't make while the bodies were piling up?"

"No. Jesus, Feeney. Nobody's saying that or thinking that. It just turned for me. You're the one who taught me when it turns for you, you push. I'm pushing."

"So." He nodded slowly. "You remember who taught you anyway. Who made a cop out of you."

Now her throat was drying up on her. "I remember. I was there, Feeney, from the beginning when you pulled me out of uniform. And I was there for this case. Right there, and it didn't turn for us."

160

"You owe me the respect of cluing me in when you're going to pick my work apart. Instead you roll this out, roll it over me, and you push me off on some bullshit Urban Wars research. I lived and breathed this case, day and night."

"I know it. I —"

"You don't know how many times I've dug it out since and lived and breathed it again," he interrupted furiously. "So now you figure it's turned for you and you can rip my work to pieces without so much as a heads-up."

"That wasn't my intent or my purpose. The investigation is my priority —"

"It's fucking well mine."

"Is it?" Temper and distress bubbled a nasty stew in her belly. "Fine, then, because I handled this the best I know how — fast. The faster we work it, the better Rossi's chances are, and right now they're about as good as a snowball's in hell. Your work wasn't the issue. Her life is."

"Don't tell me about her life." He jabbed his finger in the air toward her. "Or York's, or Dagby's, or Congress's, Waters's, or Weitz's. You think you're the only one who knows their names?" Bitterness crackled in his tone. "Who carries the weight of them around? Don't you stand there and lecture me about your priorities. *Lieutenant*."

"You've made your viewpoint and your feelings on this matter clear. *Captain*. Now, as primary, I'm telling you, you need to back off. You need to take a break."

"Fuck that."

"Take an hour in the crib, or go home and crash until you can shake this off."

"Or what? You'll boot me off the investigation?"

"Don't bring it down to that," she said quietly. "Don't put either of us there."

"You put us here. You better think about that." He stormed out, slamming the door hard enough to make the glass shudder.

Eve's breath whistled out as she braced a hand on her desk, as she lowered herself into her chair. Her legs felt like water, her gut like a storm inside a violent sea.

They'd had words before. It wasn't possible to know someone, work with someone, especially under circumstances that were so often tense and harsh, and not have words. But these had been so biting and vicious, she felt as if her skin was flayed from them.

She wanted water — just a gallon or two — to ease the burning of her throat, but didn't think she was steady enough to get up and get it.

So she sat until she got her wind back, until the tremor in her hands ceased. And with a headache raging from the base of her skull up to her crown, she called up the next file, prepared to make the next call.

She stuck with it for two hours solid, with translators when necessary. Needing air, she rose, muscled her window open. And just stood, breathing in the cold. A couple more hours, she thought. In a couple more, she'd finish with this step, run more probabilities, write up the report.

Organizing data and hunches, statements and hearsay, writing it all down in clear, factual language always helped you see it better, feel it better.

Feeney had taught her that, too.

Goddamn it.

When her communicator signaled, she wanted to ignore it. Just let it beep while she stood, breathing in the cold.

But she pulled it out. "Dallas."

"I think I've got something." The excitement in McNab's voice cut through the fog in her brain.

"On my way."

When she walked into the war room, she could almost see the ripple of energy and could see Feeney wasn't there.

"Her home unit," McNab began.

"Fell into your lap, Blondie," Callendar commented.

"Was retrieved due to my exceptional e-skills, Tits."

The way they grinned at each other spoke of teamwork and giddy pride.

"Save it," Eve ordered. "What've you got?"

"I'll put it on the wall screen. I found it under 'Gravy.' I'd been picking through docs labeled 'PT,' 'PP,' 'Instruction,' and well, anyway. I hit the more obvious, figuring gravy was like nutrition or, I dunno, recipes. What she means is extra — the gravy."

"Private clients."

"Yeah, like she couldn't have doc'd it that way? So, she's had a bunch. Works with someone until they don't want anymore, or does monthly follow-ups. Before she starts she does this basic analysis — sort of like a proposal, I think. Tons of them in there. But this one . . ."

McNab tapped one of his fingers on the comp screen. "She created sixteen days ago, and she's finessed and updated it here and there since. Up to the night before she poofed. She made a disc copy of it, which isn't anywhere in her files."

"Took it with her," Eve concluded as she studied the wall screen. "Took the proposal to the client. TED."

"His name, or the name he gave her. She has all her private clients listed by first name on the individualized programs she worked up."

"Height, weight, body type, measurements, age." Eve felt a little giddy herself. "Medical history, at least as he gave it to her. Goals, suggested equipment and training programs, nutrition program. Thorough. Boys and girls," Eve announced. "We've got our first description. Unsub is five feet, six and a quarter inches, at a weight of a hundred and sixty-three pounds. A little paunchy, aren't you, you son of a bitch? Age seventy-one. Carries some weight around the middle, according to these measurements."

She kept her eyes on the screen. "Peabody, contact all officers in the field, relay this description. McNab, go through the comps from Body Works, find us Ted. Callendar, do a search on York's electronics for this name, for any instruction program she might have written that includes body type, age. Anything that coordinates or adds to this data."

She turned. "Roarke, give me anything you've got. You and I will start contacting the women on your list, find out if they've been contacted or approached by anyone requesting a home visit. Uniforms, back to canvass, making inquiries about a man of this description. Baxter, Trueheart, you're back to the club, back to the fitness center. Jog somebody's memory. I need a station, a d and c. We've got a hole. Let's pull this bastard out of it."

He sighed as he stepped back from his worktable. "You're a disappointment to me Gia. I had such high hopes for you."

He'd hoped the rousing chorus from *Aida* would snap her back, at least a bit, but she simply lay there, eyes open and fixed.

Not dead — her heart still beat, her lungs still worked. Catatonic. Which was, he admitted as he moved over to wash and sterilize his tools, interesting. He could slice and burn, gouge and snip without any reaction from her.

And that was the problem, of course. This was a partnership, and his current partner was very much absent from the performance.

"We'll try again later," he assured her. "I hate to see you fail this way. Physically you're one of the best of all my girls, but it appears you lack the mental and emotional wherewithal."

He glanced at the clock. "Only twenty-six hours. Yes, that's quite a step back. I don't believe you'll be breaking Sarifina's record."

He replaced his tools, walked back to the table where his partner lay, bleeding from the fresh cuts, her torso mottled with bruising, cross-hatched with thin slices.

165

"I'll just leave the music on for you. See if it reaches inside that head of yours." He tapped her temple. "We'll see what we see, dear. But I'm expecting a guest shortly. Now, I don't want you to think of her as a replacement, or even a successor."

He leaned down, kissed her as yet unmarred cheek as kindly as a father might kiss a child. "You just rest awhile, then we'll try again."

It was time — time, time, time — to go upstairs. To cleanse and change. Later he would brew the tea, and set out the pretty cookies. Company was coming.

Company was such a treat!

He unlocked the laboratory door, relocked it behind him. In his office, he glanced at the wall screen, tsked at the image of Gia as she lay comatose. He was afraid he would have to end things very soon.

In his spotless white suit he sat at his desk to enter the most current data. She was simply not responding to any stimuli, he mused as he noted down her vital signs, the methods and music used in the last thirty minutes of their session. He'd believed the dry ice would bring her back, or the laser, the needles, the drugs he'd managed to secure.

But it was time to admit, to accept. Gia's clock was running down.

Ah, well.

When his log was completed, he made his way through the basement labyrinth, past the storage drawers that were no longer in use, past the old work area where his grandfather had forged his art once upon a time.

166

Family traditions, he thought, were the bedrock of a civilized society. He eschewed the elevator for the stairs. Gia had been quite right, he thought. He would benefit from more regular exercise.

He'd let himself go just a little, he admitted as he patted his plump belly, during his last dormant stage. The wine, the food, the quiet contemplation, and of course, the medication. When this work period was finished, he would take a trip to a spa, concentrate on his physical and mental health. That would be just the ticket.

Perhaps he would travel off planet this time. He'd yet to explore anything beyond his own terra firma. It might be amusing, and certainly beneficial, to spend some time in Roarke's extra-planetary playground, the Olympus Resort.

Doing so would be a kind of delicious topping after he'd completed his current goal.

Eve Dallas, Lieutenant, NYPSD. She would not disappoint as Gia had, he was sure. Still a few kinks to work out in securing her, he admitted. Yes, yes, that was true. But he would find the way.

He unlocked the steel-core basement door using code and key, stepped into the spacious and spotless kitchen. Relocked it.

He would spend some quality time the next day studying the data he'd accumulated on his final Eve. She wasn't as predictable as the ones he usually selected. But then again, that was one of the elements that would make her so special.

He was looking forward to getting reacquainted with her, after so many years.

He moved through the lovely old house, glancing around to make certain all was in order. Past the formal dining room, where he always took his meals, and the library, where he would often sit and read or simply listen to music.

The parlor, his favorite, where he had a pretty little fire burning in the rose granite hearth, and Asian lilies, blushed with pink, rising glamorously out of a wide crystal vase.

There was a grand piano in the corner, and he could still see her there, creating, re-creating such beautiful music. He could see her trying to teach his unfortunately stubby fingers to master the keys.

He'd never mastered them, nor had his voice ever mastered the demands and beauty of the notes, but his love for music was deep and true.

The double doors across from the parlor were closed, were locked. As he'd kept them for many years now. Such business as had been done there was carried on in other places.

His home was his home. And hers, he thought. It would always be hers.

He went up the curve of stairs. He still used the room he'd had as a boy. He couldn't bring himself to use the bedroom where his parents had slept. Where she had slept.

He kept it preserved. He kept it perfect, as she had once been.

Pausing, he studied her portrait, one painted while she had glowed, simply glowed, with the bloom of youth and vibrancy. She wore white — he believed she

168

should always have worn it. For purity. If only she'd remained pure.

The gown swept down her body, that slim and strong body, and the glittery necklace, her symbol of life, lay around her neck. Swept up, her hair was like a crown, and indeed the very first time he'd seen her he'd thought her a princess.

She smiled down at him, so sweetly, so kindly, so lovingly.

Death had been his gift to her, he thought. And death was his homage to her through all the daughters he lay at her feet.

He kissed the silver ring he wore on his finger, one that matched the ring he'd had painted onto the portrait. Symbols of their eternal bond.

He removed his suit. Put the jacket, the vest, the trousers, the shirt in the bin for cleaning. He showered, he always showered. Baths could be relaxing, might be soothing, but how unsanitary was it to lounge in your own dirt?

He scrubbed vigorously, using various brushes on his body, his nails, his feet, his hair. They, too, would be sanitized, then replaced monthly.

He used a drying tube. Towels were, in his opinion, as unsanitary as bathwater.

He cleaned his teeth, applied deodorant, creams.

In his robe he went back to the bedroom to peruse his closet. A dozen white suits, shirts ranged on one side. But he never greeted company in his work clothes.

He chose a dark gray suit, matching it with a pale gray shirt, a tone-on-tone gray tie. He dressed meticulously, carefully brushed his snow-white hair before adding the trim little beard and mustache.

Then he replaced the necklace — her necklace — that he'd removed before his shower.

The symbol of a tree with many branches gleamed in gold. The tree of life.

Satisfied with his appearance, he traveled down to the kitchen, moved through it to the garage where he kept his black sedan. It was a pleasant drive across town, with Verdi playing quietly.

He parked, as arranged, in a small, ill-tended lot three blocks from Your Affair, where his potential partner worked. If she was timely, she would be walking his way right now, she would be thinking about the opportunity he'd put in her hands.

Her steps would be quick, and she would be wearing the dark blue coat, the multicolored scarf.

He left the car, strolling in the direction of the store. He'd found her there, in the bakery section, and had been struck immediately by her looks, her grace, her skill.

Two months had passed since that first sighting. Soon, all the time, the work, the care he'd put into this selection would bear fruit.

He saw her from a block away, slowed his pace. He carried the two small shopping bags from nearby stores he'd brought along with him. He would be, to anyone glancing his way, just a man doing a little casual Sunday shopping.

No one noticed, no one paid any mind. He smiled when she saw him, lifted his hand in a wave.

170

"Ms. Greenfeld. I'd hoped to make it down and escort you all the way. I'm so sorry to make you walk so far in the cold."

"It's fine." She tossed back the pretty brown hair she wore nearly to her shoulders. "It's so nice of you to pick me up. I could have taken a cab, or the subway."

"Nonsense." He didn't touch her as they walked, in fact moved aside as a pedestrian, chattering on a pocket 'link, clipped between them. "Here you are, giving me your time on a Sunday afternoon." He gestured toward the lot. "And this gave me an opportunity to do a little shopping."

He opened the car door for her, and estimated they'd been together no more than three minutes on the street.

When he got in, he started the car, smiled. "You smell of vanilla and cinnamon."

"Occupational hazard."

"It's lovely."

"I'm looking forward to meeting your grand-daughter."

"She's very excited. Wedding plans." He laughed, shook his head, the indulgent grandfather. "Nothing but wedding plans these days. We both appreciate you meeting with us, on the QT, we'll say. My darling is very choosy. No wedding planners, no coordinators. Has to do it all herself. No companies, no organizations."

"A woman who knows her own mind."

"Indeed. And when I saw some of your work, I knew she'd want to meet with you. Even though you worked at Your Affair, and she refuses to so much as go through the doors." With a little laugh, he shook his head. "Over a year now since she had trouble with the manager. But that's my girl. Her mother, God rest her, was the same. Stubborn and headstrong."

"I know Frieda can be temperamental. If she found out I was doing a proposal like this on the side, she'd wig. So, well, keeping this between us is best for everyone."

"It certainly is."

When he pulled off the street, she gaped at the house. "What a beautiful home! Is it yours? I mean, do you own the whole building?"

"Yes, indeed. It's been in the family for generations. I wanted us to meet here, particularly, so you could see it, the wedding and reception venue."

He turned off the engine and led the way into the house. "Let me take you into the parlor — you can make yourself at home."

"It's gorgeous, Mr. Gaines."

"Thank you. Please, call me Edward. I hope I can call you Ariel."

"Yes, please."

"Here, let me have your coat."

He hung her things in the foyer closet. He would, of course, dispose of the coat, the scarf, her clothing. But he enjoyed this part of the pretense.

He stepped back into the parlor, sighed. "I see my granddaughter isn't here yet. She's rarely prompt. I'm just going to make us some tea. Be at home."

"Thanks."

In the kitchen, he switched his security screen to the parlor, so he could watch her as he prepared.

He had house droids, of course, and replaced their memory drives routinely. But for the most part he preferred doing for himself.

He selected Earl Grey, and his grandmother's Meissen tea set. He brewed it as he'd been taught — heating the pot, boiling the water fully, measuring precisely.

Using tongs, he added the precious and pricey sugar cubes to the bowl. She would add sugar, he knew. He'd observed her adding the revolting chemical sweetener to her tea. She would think the cubes a treat, and never notice they were spiked with the tranq until it was already swimming in her system.

After setting a lacy doily on a plate, he arranged the thin, frosted cookies he'd bought especially for this little tête-à-tête. And on the tray he set a single pink rose in a pale green bud vase.

Perfect.

He carried the tea tray — with the three cups to maintain the granddaughter fantasy — into the parlor where Ariel wandered, looking at some of his treasures.

"I love this room. Will you use this for the wedding?"

"We will. It's my favorite room in the house, so welcoming." He set the tray down between the two wing chairs that faced the fire. "We'll have some tea while we wait for the bride. Oh, these cookies are some of her favorites. I thought it might be nice if you re-created them for the reception."

173

"I'm sure I can." Ariel sat, angling herself so she could face him. "I brought a disc with images of some of the cakes I've done, and some I've assisted in making."

"Excellent." He smiled, held up the sugar bowl. "One lump or two?"

"I'll live dangerously, and go for two."

"Perfect." He sat back, nibbling on a cookie while she chattered about her plans and ideas. While her eyes began to droop, her voice began to slur.

He dusted the crumbs from his fingers when she tried to push out of the chair. "Something's wrong," she managed. "Something's wrong with me."

"No." He sighed and sipped his tea when she slumped into unconsciousness. "Everything's just as it should be."

174

CHAPTER
TEN

In order to work without going mad, Roarke erected a mental wall of silence. He simply put himself behind that wall and filtered out the ringing, the clacking, the voices, and electronic beeps and buzzes.

Initially, he'd taken the names A through M, with Eve working on the second half of the alphabet. How could he possibly employ so many brunettes with names beginning with A? Aaronson, Abbott, Abercrombie, Abrams, and down to Azula.

It hadn't taken long before it had been monumentally clear two people weren't enough to handle the contacts.

Eve pulled in more cops, and the noise level increased exponentially.

He tried not to think about the time dripping away while he sat, contacting employees he didn't even know, had never met, would unlikely ever meet. Women who depended on him for their livelihoods, who performed tasks he, or someone else who worked for him, created and assigned to them.

Each contact took time. A housekeeper at a hotel wasn't accustomed to receiving a call at home, at work, on her pocket 'link from the owner of that hotel. From the man in the suit, in the towering office. Each call was tedious, repetitious, and he was forced to admit, annoyingly *clerical*.

Routine, Eve would have called it, and he wondered how she could stand the sheer volume of monotony.

"Yo, Irish." Callendar broke through Roarke's wall, poking him in the arm. "You need to get up, move around, pour in some fuel."

"Sorry?" For a moment, her voice was nothing more than a buzz within the buzz. "What?"

"This kind of work, the energy bottoms if you don't keep it pumped. Take a break, get something to power up from Vending. Use a headset for a while."

"I'm not even through the bloody B's."

"Long haul." She nodded, offered him a soy chip from the open bag at her station. "Take it from me, move around some. Blood ends up in your ass this way, not that yours isn't prime. But you want to get the blood back up in your head or your brain's going to stall."

She was right, he knew it himself. And still there was a part of him that wanted to snarl at her to mind her own and let him be. Instead he pushed back from the station. "Want something from Vending, then?"

"Surprise me, as long as it's wet and bubbly."

It did feel good to be on his feet, to move, to step away from the work and the noise.

When he walked out, he noted cops breezing along, others in confabs in front of vending machines. A man, laughing wildly, was quick-marched along by a couple of burly uniforms. He didn't rate even a glance from the others in the corridors.

176

The place smelled of very bad coffee, he thought, old sweat, and someone's overly powerful and very cheap perfume.

Christ Jesus, he could've used a single gulp of fresh air.

He selected a jumbo fizzy for Callendar, then just stood, staring at his choices. There was absolutely nothing there he wanted. He bought a water, then took out his 'link and made a call.

When he turned, he saw Mira walking toward him. There, he decided, was the closest thing to fresh air he was likely to experience inside the cop maze of Central.

"I didn't realize you were still here," he said.

"I went home, couldn't settle. I sent Dennis off to have dinner with our daughter, and came back to do some paperwork." She glanced down at the enormous fizzy in his hand, smiled a little. "That doesn't strike me as your usual choice of beverage."

"It's for one of the e-cops."

"Ah. This is difficult for you."

"Bloody tedious. I'd sooner sweat a year running an airjack than work a week as a cop."

"That, yes, not at all the natural order for you. But I meant being used this way, and not knowing why, or by whom."

"It's maddening," he admitted. "I was thinking a bit ago that I don't know the bulk of these women we're trying to contact. They're just cogs in the wheel, aren't they?"

"If that's all they were to you, you wouldn't be here. I could tell you that you're responsible for none of what's happened, or may happen to someone else. But you know that already. Feeling it, that's a different matter."

"It is," he agreed. "That it is. What I want is a target, and there isn't one. Yet."

"You're used to having the controls, and taking the actions, or certainly directing them." She touched a sympathetic hand to his arm. "Which is exactly what you're doing now, though it may seem otherwise. And that's why I'm here, too. Hoping Eve will give me some job to do."

"Want a fizzy?"

She laughed. "No, but thanks."

They walked in together, then separated as Roarke went back to his station and Mira crossed to Eve.

"Give me an assignment," Mira said. "Anything."

"We're contacting these women." Eve explained the list, the approach, then gave Mira a list of names.

Wearing black-tie, he settled into his box in the Grand Tier of the Metropolitan Opera House. He richly anticipated the performance of *Rigoletto*. His newest partner was secured and sleeping. As for Gia . . . well, he didn't want to spoil his evening dwelling on that disappointment.

He would end that project tomorrow, and he would move on.

But tonight was for the music, the voices, the lights, and the drama. He knew he would take all of that home with him, relive it, re-experience it while he sipped a brandy in front of the fire.

Tomorrow, he would stop the clock.

But now, he would sit, tingling with pleasure, while the orchestra tuned up.

He ordered a freaking deli, was all Eve could think when the food began to roll in. There were trays and trays of meats, bread, cheese, side salads, sweets. Added to it, she saw two huge bags — distinctly gold — of the coffee (real coffee) he produced.

She caught his eye, and hers was distinctly hairy. He only shook his head.

"No lip," he said.

She pushed her way through the schoolyard rush to his station. "A word."

She moved out of the room, and when he joined her the din from the war room was a clear indicator no one else objected to the possibility of corned beef on rye.

"Listen, I went along with the pizza parlor, but —"

"I have to do something," he interrupted. "It's little enough, but at least it's something. It's positive. It's tangible."

"Cops can spring for their own eats, and if I clear an order in, I've got a budget. There are procedures."

He turned away from her, turned back again with frustration simply rolling off of him. "Christ Jesus, we're buried in shagging procedures already. Why would you possibly care if I buy some fucking sandwiches?"

She stopped herself when she felt the teeth of her own temper in her throat. "Because it's tangible." She

179

pressed her fingers into her eyes, rubbed hard. "It's something to kick at."

"Can't you take an hour? Look at me. Look at me," he repeated, laying his hands on her shoulders. "You're exhausted. You need an hour to stretch out, to turn off."

"Not going to happen, and by the way, you're not looking so perky yourself."

"I feel like my brain's been used as a punching bag. It's not the time, or even the lack of sleep so much. It's the unholy tedium."

That made her frown — and put her back up again, a little. "You've done cop work before."

"Bits and pieces it comes clear to me now, and that with some challenge and a clear end goal."

"Challenge? Like risking your life and getting bloody."

Calmer, he circled his head on his neck and wondered how many years it might take to get the last of the kinks out. "A lot more appealing, sad to say, than sitting in front of a screen or on a 'link for hours on end."

"Yeah. I know just what you mean. But this is part of it, a big part of it. It's not all land to air chases and busting in doors. Listen, you can take an hour in the crib. Probably should. I'll clear it."

He flicked a finger along the dent in her chin. "Not only does that sound extremely unappealing, but if you're on, I'm on. That's the new rule until we've finished this."

Arguing took energy she didn't have to spare. "Okay. All right."

"Something else is wrong." He put a hand under her chin, left it there even when she winced and tried to knock it off. "Shows what happens when your brain's used as a punching bag that I didn't see it before. What is it?"

"I figure having some murdering bastard who slipped by us before back torturing and killing women under our noses is pretty much enough."

"No, something else in there." It was the "slipped by us" that clicked for him. "Where's Feeney?"

For an answer, she shifted, and kicked the vending machine so viciously it sent off its security alarm.

Warning! Warning! Vandalizing or damaging this unit is a crime, and punishable by a maximum of thirty days incarceration and a fine not to exceed one thousand dollars per offense. Warning! Warning!

"All right, then," Roarke said mildly, and taking her arm, pulled her down the corridor. "Let's just take this to your office before we're both arrested for attempting to steal fizzies."

"I don't have time to —"

"I think making time is in everyone's best interest."

He took her straight through, so the scatter of cops on weekend evening shift barely glanced over.

Inside her office, he closed the door, leaned back against it while she kicked her desk. "When you're done abusing inanimate objects, tell me what happened."

"I screwed up, that's what happened. Fuck, fuck, and shit. I messed up."

"How?"

"What would it have taken me? Ten minutes? Five? Five minutes to give him the rundown before the briefing. But I didn't think of it, never crossed my mind." Obviously at wit's end, she fisted her hands on either side of her head and squeezed in. "What the hell's wrong with me that it never crossed my mind?"

"Once more," Roarke suggested, "with clarity."

"Feeney, I didn't feed him the new data, tell him about the new angle we'd work. That the suspect had contacted the target, lured her to him rather than doing the grab on the street. The way we'd worked the first case. Damn it!"

Her desk took another slam with her boot. "I just lumped him in with everyone else, didn't take into account that he'd led the first investigation. All I had to do was pull him aside, tell him, 'Hey, we've got something fresh.' Give him a little time to take it in."

"He didn't react well, I take it?"

"Who could blame him?" she tossed back. Her tired eyes were dark with regret. "Jumped on me with both feet. And what do I do? I get my back up, that's what I do. Can't just say, hey, I'm sorry, I got caught up in the roll and didn't think it through. No, can't say that. Oh well, shit!"

She covered her face a moment, heeled away the tears that got away from her. "This isn't good."

"Baby, you're so tired."

"So the fuck what? So I'm tired, that's the job, that's the way it is. Tired means nothing. I bitch slapped him, Roarke. I told him to take a break, to go home. Why

182

didn't I just knock him down and rub his face in it while I was at it?"

"Did he need a break, Eve?"

"That's not the point."

"It certainly is."

Now she sighed. "Just because it was the right call doesn't mean it was right. He said I didn't respect him, and that's not true. That's so far from any truth, but I didn't show him respect. I told you before, the other one was on him — that's command. All I did by handling it this way was add to that weight."

"Sit down. Oh, for Christ's sake, sit for five minutes." He strode over, all but lifted her bodily into her chair. "I know something about command, and it's often not pretty, nor comfortable, and very often it's not fair. But someone had to make the calls, the decisions. Maybe you didn't account for his feelings, and you can regret that if it helps you. But the simple fact is, you had a great deal more on your mind than coddling Feeney."

"It's not coddling."

"And he had a great deal on his, and obviously needed to vent some of the pressure," Roarke continued as if she hadn't spoken. "Which he did, quite handily, I'd say, on you. Now you're both feeling sorry for yourselves."

Her mouth dropped open in sheer shock for two seconds, then twisted into a snarl. "Bite me."

"I hope to have the energy for that at some point in the near future. You told him to go home because you understood, even if you were angry and hurt, you understood he needed to step away for a time. He went

183

because he understood, even being angry and hurt, that he needed to. So, mission accomplished, and I imagine sometime tomorrow, you'll both clean up the fallout and forget it. Correct?"

She sniffled, scowled. "Well, if you want to be all insightful and reasonable about it."

"He loves you."

"Oh, jeez."

Roarke had to laugh. "And you love him. If you were just cops to each other, it might still be a bit tricky. Add love, and it's a very thorny path the two of you walk when you're entrenched in something like this."

From where she sat she could still kick her desk. She did so, but lightly this time. "You sound like Mira 101."

"I'll take that as a compliment. Any better?"

"I don't know. Maybe." She pressed her hands to her temples. "My head's killing me."

He merely reached into his pocket, took out a tiny case. Thumbing it open, he held it out to her. She frowned down at the little blue pills. Standard blocker, she knew, just as she knew he'd nag her to take one if she balked — which would only make the headache worse. Or he'd just force one down her throat, which was a humiliation she didn't want to risk so close on the heels of pity tears.

She took one, popped it.

"There's a good girl."

"I repeat: Bite me."

He pulled her up, pulled her in. Nipped her bottom lip. "Just a preview of things to come."

184

Since it was there, she touched his face. "You looked a little worn and down before, too."

"I was feeling that way. Worn and down." He rested his brow on hers a moment. "Let's go have a sandwich and some decent coffee."

McNab signaled the minute they walked back in. "Getting some beeps here."

"Wipe the mustard off your face, Detective."

"Oh, sorry." He swiped at it with the back of his hands. "Started the Ted search at the branch where Rossi works," he began. "Got guys that fit the height and weight, but not the age, fit the age, but not otherwise. Fanned out to other branches. This Pi's being really trim about it. But still nothing that really rings the bell. So I moved out to the boroughs."

"Bottom-line it, McNab."

"Okay, I've got a few — nobody named Ted — but a few who fall into the description you may want to have checked out. But they don't fit the profile. We got married guys, with kids, grandkids, and no property like we're thinking listed under their name or names of family members I've dug up so far."

"And those are my beeps."

"No. I started thinking, hey, let's try the locales of the other murders. Hit Florida first, and got us a beep."

He called the data on screen. "Membership in the name of Edward Nave. DOB June 8, 1989 — down on the age — and the membership required a workup, so we've got his height — down with that — weight — a few pounds lighter, but you gotta figure on some flux.

185

Oh, and Peabody says that Ted's a nickname for Edward, so —"

"Address."

"Yeah, that's a problem. Address is bogus. He lists a Florida addy that would have him setting up in Miami's Grand Opera House. I checked it out."

"Bring up his ID."

"Okay." McNab pulled at his heavily decorated ear. "Problem number two. I can give you a fistful of Edward Naves, but none of their ID data matches the membership data."

"Copy me on them anyway. We'll run them down. How long has he held the membership? When did he pick it up in Florida?"

"Five years. About three months before the first murder there. It's him, Dallas." Conviction pushed through McNab's voice, hardened his face. "Gotta go with the gut on it, but he's covered it."

"We're going to uncover it." She looked at Roarke. "This franchise in Europe?"

"It is."

"Start searching the memberships in the other target cities. Maybe, just maybe, this was one of his trolling tools."

She started to go to her own station. She'd dig into Florida again, she decided, see if she could find any connection between the fitness center and any of the victims there. A member, one of the staff, cleaning crew.

"Eve." Mira stood up, and the look in her eyes had Eve's stomach sinking. "I've been trying to contact an

Ariel Greenfeld. She's a baker at a place called Your Affair downtown. She doesn't answer the 'link numbers listed on her information. I've just spoken with her emergency contact, a neighbor. Greenfeld hasn't been back to her apartment since she left for work this morning."

"Get me the address." She started to tell Peabody to get moving, then stopped. She'd made a mistake with Feeney, there was no point in giving out another personal slap. "Roarke and I will check it out. Unless notified, all team members are to go the hell home by twenty-three hundred or hit the crib. Report back at oh-eight-hundred for first briefing. Anything, absolutely anything pops meanwhile, I'm the first to know."

As they headed toward Ariel's apartment, Eve glanced at Roarke. His face was unreadable, but she understood it. Guilt, worry, questions.

"What's Your Affair?"

"An event shop. Ah . . . upscale, everything you might need under one roof. A variety of specialty boutiques — attire, floral and planting, bakery, catering, decor, event planners. It was something I thought of when we were dealing with our wedding. Why go to all these places, all these people, if you can go to one location and find effectively everything you'd need. And if you want something else, there are consultants who'll find that something else for you."

Eve thought she might actually shop in a place like that. If she fell out of a three-story window, cracked her head on the sidewalk, and suffered severe brain damage. But she said, "Handy."

"So I thought, yes. It's doing quite well. She's worked there eight months. Ariel Greenfeld."

"And right now, she could be boinking some guy she picked up in a bar."

He turned his head to look at her. "You don't think that. I should contact her supervisor, find out what time she left work."

"Let's wait on that. Let's check out her place, talk to her neighbor. Look, do you know why I'm keeping the team on another two hours? She might not be the one. We pull off, push everything into this, maybe somebody else gets taken. First, we get a clearer view of the situation."

"Yes, a clearer view. How's the headache?"

"Sulking behind the blocker. I know it's there, but it's pretty easy to ignore."

When they'd parked, he laid a hand over hers. "Where are your gloves?"

"Somewhere. Else."

He kept her hand in his, opened the glove box. And took out the spare pair he'd bought her on a recent shopping trip. "Wear these. It's cold."

She pulled them on, and was grateful for them as they hiked a block to the apartment building. "You never got that sandwich," she pointed out.

"Neither did you."

"At least I didn't shell out hundreds of dollars and not even end up with a pickle chip or a splat of veggie hash."

"I've never understood the appeal of anything referred to as 'hash.'" Appreciating her, he draped an arm over her shoulders as they walked.

Rather than wait to be buzzed in, she used her master on the front entrance door.

Decent building, she noted. What she thought of as solid working class. Tenants with steady employment and middle-class income. Tidy entranceway, standard security cams, single elevator.

"Third floor," she requested. "She could walk to work from here, if she didn't mind a good hike. Catch the subway and save five blocks in crappy weather or if she's running late. Bakers, they start early, right? What time does the store open?"

"Seven-thirty for the bakery, the café. Ten to six for most of the retail, with extended hours to eight on Saturdays. But yes, I'd think the bakery section would start work before opening hours."

"Couple hours maybe. So if she had to be there by six . . ." She trailed off as they reached the third floor. "Neighbor's 305."

She walked to it, had just lifted a fist to knock when the door opened. The man who answered was late-twenties, sporting spikey hair of streaked black and bronze. He wore a baggy sweater and old jeans, and an expression of barely controlled worry.

"Hey, heard the elevator. You the cops?"

"Lieutenant Dallas." Eve held up her badge. "Erik Pastor?"

"Yeah, come on in. Ari's not home yet. I've been calling people, to see if anybody's seen her."

"When did you see her last?"

"This morning. Early this morning. She came in to bring me a couple of muffins. We went out last night, a group of us. Ari went home before midnight, because she had to be at work at six this morning. And she figured — correctly — I'd be hungover."

He lowered to the arm of the couch. The area reflected the debris of a man who'd spent the bulk of the day nursing a long night. Soy chips, soft-drink tubes, a bottle of blockers, a blanket, a couple of pillows were scattered around.

"I only made it as far as the couch," he continued. "So I heard her come in, groaned at her. She razzed me a little, and said she'd see me later. If I wasn't dead, she'd pick up a few things on her way home and fix me some dinner. Has something happened to her? They wouldn't tell me anything on the 'link."

"You're tight? You and Ariel?"

"Yeah. Not, you know, that way. We're friends. We hang."

"Could she be out with someone she's more than friendly with?"

"There's a couple of guys — casual, nothing serious. I checked with them, hell, with every damn body. Plus, she'd have told me." His voice shook a little, telling Eve he was struggling with that control. "If she says she's going to come back and fix dinner, that's what she does. I was starting to worry before you guys called."

"What time did she get off work today?"

"Ah . . . give me a minute. Four? Yeah, I think four. It's her long Sunday, so it's four. Usually she heads

190

straight back. Short Sundays she might do some shopping, or some of us would meet up for lunch or something."

"We'd like to look in her apartment."

"Okay, sure. She wouldn't mind. I'll get the key. We've got keys to each other's places."

"Did she say anything about having an appointment today? About meeting someone?"

"No. Or, God, I don't know. I had my head buried under the pillow and was praying for a quick, merciful death when she popped in this morning. I didn't pay attention." He dug a set of keys out of a drawer. "I don't understand why she's not answering her pocket 'link. I don't understand why you're asking all these questions."

"Let's take a look at her place," Eve suggested. "Go from there."

It smelled of cookies, Eve realized. Though the kitchen was small, it was organized and equipped by someone who knew what they were doing.

"Some women buy earrings or shoes," Erik said. "Ari, she buys ingredients and baking tools. There's a specialty shop in the meatpacking district called Baker's Dozen? She'll have an orgasm just walking in there."

"Is there anything missing that would normally be here if she was just going to work?"

"Uh, I don't know. I don't think so. Should I look around?"

"Why don't you?"

While he did, Eve studied the little computer on a table just outside the kitchen. Couldn't touch it, she thought, not until there was an official report.

Bending the line of probable cause.

"He might be on there," Roarke murmured. "Something to do with this might be on there."

"And she could walk in the door in the next thirty seconds, and I'd have invaded her privacy, illegally."

"Bollocks to that." He started to move past Eve to open the computer himself.

"Wait, damn it. Just wait."

"Her shoes." Erik stepped out of the bedroom, his face radiating both confusion and concern.

"What about them?"

"Her good black shoes aren't here. She wears skids to work. She walks. It's eight blocks, two of them crosstown, and she's on her feet all day. Her work skids aren't here, either. She'd take a change if she was going somewhere after. She'd take other shoes."

His face cleared. "She took her good black shoes. She must've had a date or something, just forgot to tell me, or I was so out of it . . . That's all it is. She hooked up with somebody after work."

Eve turned back to Roarke. "Open it."

CHAPTER
ELEVEN

Eve relayed the new data to the team at Central, and ordered Ariel's electronics picked up. Riding on the fresh spurt of adrenaline, she turned to Roarke.

"We've got a jump on him."

Roarke continued to study the little screen with its images of wedding cakes and cost projections. "From the glass-half-empty side, it seems he's gotten the jump on us."

"That's wrong thinking. We're moving on a lead we didn't have before this investigation. And we're moving in the right direction. Otherwise, we wouldn't have known, not for hours — potentially days — that Greenfeld was missing. We wouldn't know how he pulled her in."

"And how does that help her, Eve?"

"Everything we know gives her a better chance of making it through. We know he's had her about five hours. We have to assume he's frequented the store where she worked, and contacted her by some method. Five hours, Roarke," she repeated. "He hasn't done anything to her yet. Probably has her sedated. He won't start on her until he's . . ."

He looked up then, eyes frigid. "Until he's finished with Gia Rossi. Until he's done cutting and carving on her."

"That's right." No way to soften it, Eve thought. No point in trying. "And until we find Rossi's body, she's alive. Until we find her body, she's got a chance. Now, with this, she has a better one. We canvass, we check parking lots, we check public transpo. We talk to her coworkers, her other friends. We have his age, his body type. We didn't have any of that twenty-four hours ago."

She stepped to him, touched his arm. "Make a copy of that program, will you? We'll work this from home. Maybe something will shake loose on the search Summerset's been running, or on the real estate angle. Something's going to click into place."

"All right. But neither of us is working on this until we've stepped back for a couple hours. I mean it, Eve," he said before she could protest. "You ordered your team to take some downtime for good reason."

"I could use a shower," she said after a moment. "An hour. Compromise." She held up a hand, held him off. "You've got to admit it beats fighting about it for half that downtime."

"Agreed." He copied the data, handed her the disc.

Since she didn't consider the drive home part of the break, she let Roarke take the wheel and shuffled through her notes, the timelines, the names, the statements.

He'd taken the third target sooner than projected, Eve mused. Two reasons she could think of for that.

Either the earlier snatch suited his personal schedule or the target's. Or Gia Rossi wasn't holding up well.

She could already be dead — a possibility Eve saw no reason to share with Roarke.

Hours, she thought. If the contact had been made hours sooner, they would have found Ariel Greenfeld before he had her. The right question, the right time. Not only would the woman have been safe, but they'd have had solid data on the suspect.

Off at four, she noted. Planned to make dinner for her neighbor. So, she'd planned to be home from this outside appointment in two or three hours, most likely.

"How long would you budget for a meeting?" Eve asked. "For going over a proposal for wedding cakes and desserts, that sort of thing?"

"From her end?" Roarke considered. "She put together a lot of images, a number of variations of style and type, flavors. A great deal of trouble. I'd guess she'd prepared for a couple of hours. If she assumed — correctly — that many people take every detail of a wedding very seriously, she would have been prepared to give the potential client all the time he needed or wanted."

"Okay, let's say two, so that makes it eighteen hundred not including travel time. She tells the guy across the hall she's going to pick up a few things on the way home to make — actually cook — a meal. That's got to take some time. The shopping part, the cooking part. Probably, what, an hour?"

"Your guess." Roarke shrugged. "Summerset would know better."

"Yeah, well, until we consult His Boniness, I'm figuring an hour. Which puts it at nineteen hundred, again without travel. Late night Saturday, long day Sunday, early to work on Monday. I don't figure she was prepping a late meal."

"And what does that tell you?"

"It tells me that, most likely, as far as she knew, she wasn't going that far for this meeting. Not across the river into Jersey, probably not across the bridge into Brooklyn or Queens. Too much bridge-and-tunnel traffic. Probability is higher he's in Manhattan. Narrows the search."

Eve shifted. "She's tossing a meal together for a friend, not planning a fancy deal for a lover. Just a pal, one she's hoping she can share this good news with if she copped the job. Picking up a few things on the way home. That says she planned to get herself home. Public transportation or on foot. So she can stop by the market. Decent chance he's downtown, at least not above midtown."

She sat back. "Focus there to start. Fan out, sure, but we start there, focus there."

She worked the problem the rest of the way home, adding in factors, playing with angles. Urban Wars, body ID method, Lower West or East Side clinics.

He almost certainly had some sort of transportation, but it would also serve if he could stalk any or all of his victims on foot.

People tended to shop and frequent restaurants in their comfort-zone. The soap and shampoo — downtown store was very likely the source unless he

196

web-shopped or brought it into New York with him. Starlight was in Chelsea, the bakery downtown, the first dumping spot in this round on the Lower East. Gia Rossi worked midtown.

Maybe he wasn't traveling far from home this time around.

Maybe.

She plugged her knowns and unknowns into her PPC, intending to transfer the information to her desk unit and run probabilities.

"I want whatever Summerset's worked up on disc and on my unit," she began as they drove through the gates. "We can get his take on the timing as far as shopping/cooking, but I want to check out what markets and stores Greenfeld most usually frequented. And other specialty places below Fiftieth. The way her neighbor talked, she'd have gotten a charge out of wandering some new food place. We'll interview the others she went out with Saturday night. Maybe she let something slip about her Sunday plans."

They got out on opposite sides of the car, but Roarke put a hand on her arm when they reached the base of the steps of home. "You never thought there was a chance for Rossi."

"I never said that, and there's always a chance."

"Slim to none. It didn't stop you pushing — hard and in every way you could push, but you knew her chances were all but nil, and on some level accepted it."

"Listen —"

"No, don't misunderstand me. That's not a criticism. It's a small, personal revelation that came to me on the way home. Watching you work, listening to you even when you weren't speaking. Your mind says volumes. You don't feel the same way about Ariel Greenfeld."

He slid his hand down her arm until he found hers, linked fingers. "You believe there's a real chance now. Not only in finding him, stopping him. That you have to believe every minute or you'd never be able to do what you do. But you believe you'll find him, stop him before it's too late for this woman, and because of it Gia Rossi's chances have gone up from slim to none to slim. It has to energize you, and at the same time, it must weigh all the heavier. They have a chance. You're their chance."

"We," Eve corrected. "Everyone working the case is their chance. And we'd better not let her down."

She expected Summerset to materialize in the foyer and intended to have Roarke take point with him. But the minute they stepped in, she heard laughter in the parlor, and the bubbling sound of it was unmistakable.

"Mavis is here."

"There's your hour of downtime." Roarke slipped Eve's coat from her shoulders. "Difficult to find a more entertaining or distracting way to rest the brain cells than a portion of Mavis Freestone."

It was tough to argue the point. But when Eve stepped to the parlor doorway, she saw Mavis had brought Trina along. If that wasn't scary enough, they'd hauled the baby out for the evening.

Most terrifying, at the moment, the infant Belle was being held by Summerset, and having her chin chucked by his skeletal fingers.

198

"I'm traumatized," Eve stated. "He's not supposed to smile like that. It's against the laws of man and nature."

"Don't be such a hard-ass." Roarke gave her a little poke in the ribs. "Ladies," he said in normal tones, and had the group looking over.

"Hey!" Mavis's already glowing face brightened. "You're back! We were about to head out, but Belle wanted another Summerset smoochie."

Which, to Eve's mind, confirmed the innate oddity of babies and kids.

Mavis bounced over, sending the short, flirty skirt she wore swirling over polka-dot tights. The skirt was candy pink, the tights pink on brilliant blue. She'd gone for the blue in her hair, too, Eve noted, in a few wild streaks against silvery blond.

She grabbed one of Roarke's hands, one of Eve's, and pulled them into the room. "Leonardo had to shoot out to New L.A. for a client, so Trina and Belle and I had a total girl day. Ended it with some Summerset time. Look who's here, Belle. Look who came to see you."

With little choice Eve looked down at the baby still tucked in Summerset's arms. Most, Eve supposed, would say the kid looked like a doll. But to Eve's way of thinking, dolls were just creepy.

The fact was, the baby was a knockout — if you discounted the drool — pink, pretty, and plump. A lacy white ribbon was tied around her hair, as if she'd been wrapped like a gift. The dark blue eyes were lively, maybe a little too lively. They made Eve wonder just

199

what went on inside the brain of a human the size of a teacup poodle.

She wore some sort of outfit with feet and a kind of sweater deal over it that may have been trimmed in actual fur. Over it all there was a bib — due, Eve supposed, to drool — that proclaimed:

MY DADDY IS ICED!

"Cute," Eve said and would have stepped back, but Roarke blocked her as he studied the baby over Eve's shoulder.

"I think gorgeous is more accurate. What nice work you do, Mavis."

"Thanks." The former street urchin and current music vid sensation stared down at her daughter with sparkling eyes of unearthly blue. "Sometimes I look at her and just can't believe she came out of me."

"Do you have to bring up that part of it?" Eve asked and made Mavis laugh again.

"Maybe we could hang a little while more, unless you're too tired. You guys look pretty whipped."

"Could use a treatment," Trina commented.

"Stay away from me." Eve jabbed a finger in the consultant's direction.

"We could use a meal." Roarke smiled at their guests. "Why don't you join us?"

"Summerset already fed us until we popped, but we could stick, keep you company. It's off knowing our big daddy won't be home when we get there, isn't it, Bellarama?"

"I'll prepare something right away."

Eve saw Summerset shift and — anticipating — was quick and cowardly. She sidestepped, hip-bumped Roarke, leaving him in the line of fire.

She loved her man, would unquestionably risk her life for his. But when it came to babies, he could sink. She was swimming.

His arms came out instinctively, as a man's might when something fragile or potentially explosive was about to be dropped into them. "I don't . . . I should . . . Oh, well then," he muttered as Summerset deftly made the transfer.

"Is there anything in particular you'd like?" The faintest wisp of a smile touched Summerset's lips as Roarke's eyes burned a hole through him. "For supper?"

"Something quick," Roarke managed. He'd once diffused a bomb with seconds to spare, and had felt less panic.

"I was hoping to see you." Mavis beamed at him, then dropped into a chair, leaving Roarke standing on what felt like very unsteady ground. "Just about dropped all the belly weight now, and got the full-steam from the docs. I've got a boat of new material, so I thought I could get in the studio, rock it out, cut some vids."

"Yes. That sounds . . . all right."

"Mag. I figured to bring Belle in with me. She's completely about music. If it doesn't work, Leonardo and I'll figure something."

"Doesn't want a nanny," Trina commented.

"Not yet anyway. I just want her to be all mine right now. Mine and her daddy's. But I've got the itch to get back to work, so I want to see if I can do it on my own."

"I'm sure you'll do fine." Roarke glanced down at the baby and saw Belle's eyes were drooping. As if the thick, dark lashes were too heavy for the delicate lids to hold. "She's going to sleep." His own lips curved as what he held went from being mildly terrifying to quietly sweet. "Worn out from all the partying, are you now? Is there something I should do?"

"You're doing it," Mavis told him. "But we'll put her down. There's a monitor in her travel bed." Mavis rose. "Receiver right here." She tapped a flamingo-shaped pin just above her right ear. "Just lay her right in here. If she wakes up a little, you just pat her belly for a minute. She conks."

It was something like a small, portable sleep chair, Roarke noted, well padded in Mavis's — or Belle's, he supposed — signature rainbow hue. Though setting her down in it seemed fairly straightforward, he actually felt sweat pool at the base of his spine.

When she was down, and he straightened, the relief and satisfaction was very nearly orgasmic.

Mavis crouched, fussed with the blanket. "She'll be fine right here, won't you, my baby girl?"

"The cat. Isn't there something about cats and babies?"

Mavis smiled up at Roarke. "I think it's bogus, but anyway, Galahad's scared of her. He took one look and

202

lit. If he comes snooping around her, I'll hear it. I can actually hear her breathing through the receiver."

After giving the blanket one last fiddle, Mavis stood. "You should eat in the dining room like we did. There's a nice fire in there, too. You'll relax more. You guys really do look wrung. We won't stay long."

"We're taking an hour down." Now that all danger of being expected to hold the baby had passed, Eve moved back to Roarke. "Let's go eat."

They settled in the dining room where the fire roared and a dozen candles were lit. To give Summerset his due, he'd managed quick and tasty. There were thin slices of roast chicken in some sort of fragrant sauce, fancy potatoes, and something that might have been squash but was prepared so it wasn't really objectionable.

He served Trina a glass of wine, and Mavis something rose-colored and frothy with a plate of thin cookies and fancy chocolates.

"I come around here too often, I'll be back to belly weight." Mavis picked up a chocolate. "Nursing makes me nearly as hungry as pregnancy did."

"No breast milk at the table," Eve warned her. "So to speak."

"I sort of carry it everywhere." But Mavis grinned. "You can talk about the case. You're going to think about it anyway. We heard about it on screen. I remember when this guy was around before. I was on the grift then. All the girls on the street were scared all the time."

"You were too young for him then."

"Maybe, but it was scary. Trina and I both went way far from brunette last night during our hair party. Just, you know, in case."

Eve eyed Mavis's silver and blue streaks, then Trina's flame red tower of curls. "Yeah, you're not his type."

"Glad to hear. How's it going, anyway? Everything's dire on screen."

"We've got some buttons to push."

"I was doing hair at Channel Seventy-five yesterday." Trina studied the cookies narrowly, picked one. "On-air reporter was trying to make my celeb, you know? Spouting and such. He gave her some gory on the case to impress her, and said the police were stymied."

"Reporters are mostly assholes."

"Lot of them say the same about cops." Trina smiled. "I think it's pretty much fifty-fifty. Anyway, it was the buzz in the salon yesterday, and we had the chairs full of women ditching their brunette."

Eve forked up some chicken. "You're still working the salon route?" she considered. "I thought you were on Nadine's show, and working private."

"You get private through the salon if you know how to play it. Plus, Roarke set me up pretty."

"To what?"

"Trina manages the salon section of Bliss, the downtown spa," Roarke explained. "An excellent choice on my part."

"You got that." Trina toasted him. "Business is up seven percent since I took over."

"Your operators take private?" Eve asked her.

"It's against policy." Trina wiggled her dramatic eyebrows at Roarke as she sipped her wine. "Private means they don't come in, the salon and spa don't get the business. And they don't drop impulse dough. But let's get real. A customer asks — they're called consultants, by the way — to do a house gig, they're not going to say no unless they don't want the job."

"I'm looking for a man about seventy, short, pudgy."

"We get that type, sure. Policy is to tactfully steer the pudge part into our spa or the body sculpting section. Barring, we talk up the fitness centers, and —"

"I'm talking specifically," Eve interrupted. "A man of that basic type coming in, feeling out one of the consultants for a private. Within the last, let's say, two months."

"Lotta room, Dallas," Trina said. "We get a lot of traffic, and being manager, most of the consultants aren't going to mention a private to me, unless it's sanctioned."

"Sanctioned how?"

"Like we send teams or a solo in for special occasions, and the salon takes the big cut."

"Long shot," Eve muttered.

"But come to think of it, I had somebody like that. I guess."

Eve set down her fork. "You guess or you had one?"

"Look, like I said, we get a lot of traffic. People tap me for private most every day. What's the big . . . Oh, hey, hey!" Her wine sloshed toward the rim as she hastily set the glass down. "Is this the guy? Is this the fucking guy? Holy shit storm."

"Just tell me what you remember."

"Okay, Jesus, let me clear the decks." Trina closed her eyes, sucked air through her nose several times. "This guy . . . walk-in. Manicure, I'm thinking. Don't remember who had him. I'm thinking it was a Saturday afternoon, and we're busting on Saturday afternoons. He waited a long time for the nail job, wandered over into the retail section. I think. I was busy. I just remember catching sight of him a few times. Then I took my break, went into the bar for a smoothie. Maybe a fizzy. No, it was a smoothie."

"Trina, I don't care what you had to drink."

"I'm getting the picture." Her eyes flashed open. "You want the picture, I need to get it first. So it was a smoothie. A banana-almond smoothie. We make killers. And he comes up, real polite. 'Excuse me, Miss,' like that. He noticed I was in charge, and since he'd had to wait awhile he'd noticed, too, how skilled I was."

She smiled to herself. "So I didn't tell him to flip, that I was on a break. He wanted to know how to arrange an at-home appointment. Not for him, though, not for him, wait a minute."

Frowning, she picked up her wine, sipped again while Eve struggled not to just leap up and pound the rest of the details out of her.

"His wife? Yeah, yeah, yeah, at-home for his wife. She wasn't well, and how he thought it would make her feel better to have her hair done, maybe a facial, a mani, pedi, like that. A package treatment."

"Trina —"

206

"Wait a damn minute. Let me get a fix on it. I'm telling him how we arrange this, the fees, and so on, and he's wondering if I'd consider doing this on my day off. So I wouldn't have to rush back to work, but could give his wife as much time as she wanted. Whenever it suited me. He even showed me a picture of the wife. He'd be happy to pay whatever I think appropriate."

"Did he give you an address?"

"You keep interrupting." Obviously annoyed, Trina opened her eyes again. "No. I said how I'd need to check my book. So I did, taking my time, thinking it over. Even the older guys can be stringing you, you know? I was booked up for a while. I think I gave him a couple possible dates. A couple of weeks down the road. He said he'd check the dates out with his wife's nurse, see which she thought would work best. He asked if I had a card, so he could contact me. I gave him one. And that was it."

"He didn't get back to you?"

"Nope. I thought maybe I saw him about a week later. Somewhere. Where was it? Oh, yeah, in this bar where I was having drinks with this guy I was thinking of doing. But I figured, nah. Not the kind of joint you see a suit with a sick wife."

"He give you a name?"

"Maybe. I don't remember. If I can pin down the mani he got, we'd have it on the books. First name anyhow. Is this the guy?"

Don't rush it, Eve thought. Dot the *i*'s. "What color was your hair?"

"You gotta be kidding. It was, like, a month ago. Yeah, a month, like the first Saturday in February, because I remember thinking if we did business like that through the month, I was going to ask for a raise. We did, I did. And hey, thanks again," she said to Roarke.

"Caramel Mocha," Mavis murmured. "With Starfish highlights."

"Yeah?" Trina turned to her. "You sure?"

"You did me Starfish with Candyland tips." Mavis's hand trembled a little as she reached for her glass. "I've got a memory for this stuff. Oh, wow. Oh, wow. I think I feel a little sick."

"You? I'm the one he was planning to torture and kill. I think I feel . . ." Trina pressed a hand to her belly, then squinted out of slitted eyes. "Pissed. That's what I feel. That son of a bitch. Sick wife? Pay me whatever. He was going to *kill* me." She picked up her wine, guzzled it. "Why didn't he?"

"You changed it." Mavis took slow, deep breaths. "You didn't stick with that shade even a week. You went straight to Wild Raven with Snow Cap streaks."

"Just back up," Eve demanded. "This mocha bit? Does that translate to brunette?"

"On a basic level," Trina confirmed. "Of course, the way I work it's way beyond anything basic."

"Can you describe him?"

"Yeah, yeah, I think. But he was wearing a hair enhancer."

"Meaning wig?"

"A good one, too, but you're talking to the expert. Hey, hey, that's why I didn't think it was him in the bar. He wasn't. I mean he was, the hair enhancer wasn't. At least not the same one. I didn't get a close or long enough look to tell if it was hair or enhancer."

"I want you to describe him. I want you to give me every detail you can remember about him. Appearance, voice, body type, gestures, any distinguishing marks. Everything. Tomorrow morning, you'll work with a police artist."

"Really? No shit? I'm like an eyewitness. Frosty."

"Let's take this up to my office. Think. Get him in your head."

She pulled out her 'link. "Peabody. I need you to contact Yancy. I want him ready to work with a witness tomorrow. Seven sharp."

"Is that *morning*?" Trina demanded.

"Stow it." Eve simply shot out a finger. "Got that, Peabody?"

"Got it. Is that . . . Is that Trina?"

"Yeah. She's our wit. Small freaking world. I want Yancy, Peabody. I'm taking down her description now, and I'll relay it to the team. Tell McNab I want him and the e-geeks ready to run with the description, then with the image as soon as Yancy's got one."

She was walking as she talked, moving briskly out of the dining room, through the corridor, the foyer, up the stairs. As orders and instructions rolled out of her, Trina glanced over at Roarke.

"She's a little scary when she's on the scent."

"She can be a lot scarier. You go up. I'll be along."
He turned back, brushed a hand over Mavis's shoulder.
"Why don't you and Belle and Trina plan to stay here
tonight?"

"Really? It's okay?"

"Absolutely. I'll have Summerset take care of
whatever you think you'll need."

"Thanks. Boy. Thanks. I know it's silly. Nobody's
going to bother us, but . . ."

"We'll all feel better, under the circumstances, if
you're tucked in here. Why don't you get in touch with
Leonardo, let him know?"

"Okay. Good. Thanks. Roarke?"

"Hmmm?"

"If Trina hadn't changed her hair . . ."

"I know." He kissed the top of her head now. "We're
all very glad mocha didn't suit her."

CHAPTER
TWELVE

Eve went straight to her desk, pointed to a chair. "Sit. Let's get this down. Start with height, weight, build."

"I thought you had that already." Trina glanced around. She'd been in Eve's office before, but not in eyewitness capacity. "How come you don't fix this place up, like the rest of the house?"

"It's not the rest of the house. Trina, concentrate."

"I just wondered why you'd want to work in the low rent section of the Taj Mahal or whatever."

"I'm a sentimental fool. Height."

"Okay, ummm. On the short side. Under five-eight. More than five-four. See, I was sitting at the counter at the bar, and he stood, and . . ." She pursed her lips, used the flat of her hand to measure the air. "Yeah. Like five-six or -seven? That's best guess."

"Weight."

"I don't know. When I do bodywork, people are naked. I don't gauge when they've got clothes on. I'm going to say he was, like, solid, but not the R-and-P type."

"R-and-P?"

"Roly and poly. He was . . ." She curved her hands over her stomach, rolled them up her chest. "Carrying it in the front, like some guys do. Not a waddler, but not Mr. Health and Fitness Club either. Poochy, like your uncle Carmine."

"If I had one. Okay. How about coloring?"

"He had this pewter brushback, thick on top and short on the sides. But that was the enhancer."

"Dark gray, short and thick."

"Dark gray's dull, you ask me. Pewter's got a soft gleam. But anyway, yeah. It was white when I saw him at the bar the other time. If it was him, which I pretty much think it was. Fluffy and white. Nice. Don't know why he'd go for pewter when he has the Snow Cap going."

"White hair. You're saying that wasn't a wig."

"It was a glimpse — a quick 'Oh, hey, I know that guy.' But yeah, at a glimpse it looked like his own topper. Not a hundred percent on that one."

"Eyes?"

"Jeez. Look, Dallas, I don't know for sure. I'm thinking light. On the light side, but I'm not sure if we're talking blue or green or gray, hazel. But I'm almost sure they weren't dark. You know, the hair enhancer looked off to me from the get, because it *was* dark, and the rest of him wasn't. He had really good skin."

"How so?"

"Pale, soft-looking. Some lines, sure, but not dug in. He takes care of his skin. No jowly stuff going on either, so he's maybe had a little work. He had a nice smooth texture to his skin."

"Pale," Eve mumbled. Pale hair, pale eyes, pale skin. A pale man. Maybe the Romanian psychic hadn't been completely full of shit.

"Yeah, yeah. He colored his eyebrows to match the enhancer. It was off, just a little. Mostly you wouldn't notice, but it's my business to notice. White in the bar when I was figuring to give this guy I was drinking with the ride of his life."

"You said he was a suit. Was that literal or just because he looked like a suit?"

"Both. He was wearing one — I think gray, like the hair and eyebrows. Probably. And he looked like the kind of guy who had a closetful of suits. Three-piece," she added. "Yeah, yeah, vest, pants, jacket. Little pocket accent and tie. Spiffed, you know? Same in the bar. Dark suit. Nice contrast with the white hair."

She paused, then rubbed the back of her neck. "It's just really hitting me. I'd've taken the gig. If he'd tagged me back, I'd've taken it. Personal day, a nice chunk of change. No harm."

Her breath trembled out as the color slid out of her cheeks. "He seemed so nice and . . . I want to say 'safe.' Some sweet older guy who wanted to do something special for his sick wife. I'd've charged him through the nose, but I'd have taken the job."

"You didn't take it," Eve reminded her. "And he made a mistake trying for you. You pay attention, you notice details and you remember. Listen to me."

She leaned forward because she could see it was, indeed, just hitting Trina. Not only had she lost color, she was beginning to shake a little. "Look at me and

213

listen to what I'm telling you. He took someone today. Another one today. She's got some time before he starts on her. He takes time. Are you hearing me?"

"Yeah." Trina moistened her lips. "Yeah."

"He made a mistake with you," Eve repeated. "And what you're telling me, what you're going to do tomorrow with the police artist is going to help us get to him. You're going to help us save her life, Trina. Maybe more than hers. You get that?"

Trina nodded. "Can I get some water, maybe? I just went so dry."

"Sure. Hold on a minute."

As Eve went into the kitchen, Roarke stepped into the room. "You're doing fine," he said to Trina.

"Got the shakes," Trina admitted. "Whacked, really. Here I am in the Fortress of Roarke in the Chamber of Dallas. Can't get any safer than that. And I've got the shakes. Mavis?"

"She's contacting Leonardo. You'll all stay here tonight, if that suits you."

"Right down to the ground. Classy place like Bliss. You just don't expect crazy killers to come in for a manicure. You know?"

"This one likes to work with tidy nails," Eve commented as she came back with a chilled bottle of water. "I'm going to need that appointment book," she said to Roarke.

"I'll see to it. And," he told Trina, "I'll make sure you're covered for tomorrow. Don't worry about it."

"Thanks." She gulped down water. "Okay."

Eve waited while Trina drank. "Tell me about his voice."

"Um . . . Soft, I guess. Quiet. Um . . . Refined? I think that's the word. Like somebody educated, and who had the money behind him for a really good one. Kind of culture but not poofy. It was another thing that made him seem nice and safe, now that I think about it."

"Any accent?"

"Not really. I mean, educated, yeah. Not like an accent though."

"Distinguishing marks, tats, scars."

"Nope." Her voice was steadying, her color coming back. "Not showing."

"Okay." It was enough, Eve thought. If she pushed too hard now, it could diminish what Yancy could draw out of Trina the next day. "Anything else you remember, you let me know. I'm going to need the names of everyone who was working the day he came in, who was working the counter where you talked to him, who might have tried to sell him anything in the retail section. I can get most of that from Roarke. I want you to try to get a good night's sleep."

"Yeah, so do I. I think I'll go down and stick with Mavis and Belle for a little while, till I smooth it out a little more."

"Summerset will show you where you'll stay tonight. If you need anything," Roarke added, "just ask."

"Will do. This is so . . . complete." Trina shook her head as she rose. "I'm just going to . . ." She started out, stopped. "He smelled good."

"How?"

"Good product — and not smothered in it. Some people don't know how to be subtle with a product. It was like . . ." She squeezed her eyes shut again. "Just a hint of rosemary, undertones of vanilla. Nice." She shrugged, then continued out of the room.

"Major break."

"For you." Roarke walked over to sit on the corner of her desk. "And, I'd say, for Trina."

"Yeah, being a hair-color slut paid off big-time for her. I need to get this description out. I want to run it through IRCCA. I don't think we'll hit there. I don't think he's been in the system, but it's worth the shot. You need to work it with the results from the unregistered. See if you've got a competitor who fits the bill."

"All right."

"Skipped over Trina, went for York instead."

"Christ. Don't tell her that."

Eve arrowed a glare at him. "Give me some credit."

"Sorry. Of course. I'll take another look at the real estate, focusing below Fiftieth. Check in when I'm done."

"Good enough. Odds are shifting. Tide's turning."

"I believe you." He reached out, rubbed a thumb along the shadows under her eye. "Try not to drink too much coffee."

She decided that trying didn't mean she had to succeed. Besides, how much coffee was, in actuality,

216

too much? She sent out the description, then keyed it into IRCCA.

She'd get countless hits with a description that general, and have to take a great deal of time to cull through them. But she couldn't leave out the step.

She began to run various probabilities. The suspect lived, worked, had ties to downtown Manhattan. The suspect frequented shops, restaurants, businesses in that sector in order to scout out targets. The suspect used various enhancements to alter his appearance during his meets with potential victims.

She ran a search of public and private parking lots and garages downtown, then began to contact owners, managers, attendants on duty.

She fought her way through a search of buildings — still standing or subsequently razed, that had housed bodies or had been used as clinics during the Urbans.

When it came through she read Newkirk's report on the first canvass of Greenfeld's apartment building.

Zip.

Still, she had to give Newkirk a nod for being thorough. She had names, addresses, and a detailed rundown of every conversation.

And thinking he may have come by it naturally, she flipped through her files and came up with Gil Newkirk's contact number.

He answered swiftly, on full alert, and with a blocked video that reminded her, abruptly, of the time.

"Officer Newkirk, Lieutenant Dallas. I apologize for disturbing you so late."

"No problem, Lieutenant. One minute."

She waited on blue-screen hold for thirty seconds less than that. Video popped on, and she saw a square-jawed, slightly grizzled version of the young cop she'd first met on scene. "What can I do for you?"

"I'm pursuing a new line, and should tell you beforehand that your son is a solid asset to the task force. You must be proud."

"Every day," he agreed. "Thank you, Lieutenant."

"I wonder if you can stretch your memory back, over your canvasses during the investigation nine years ago. I'm interested in a specific individual."

She related the description.

"Nine years ago."

"I know it's a stretch. He may be carrying some extra weight now, and we may be looking for darker hair. But I think the white may be consistent. He may have lived or worked or had a business in the area of one or more of the incidents."

"Talked to a lot of people back then, Lieutenant. And I wasn't pulled in until the second murder. But if you'll give me some time, I can look through my notes."

"Your notes are as concise and detailed as your son's reports?"

Gil grinned. "Taught him, didn't I?"

"Then I'd appreciate any time you can give me on this. I'll be at Central by oh-seven-hundred. You can reach me there, or any of my 'links, anytime. I'll give you my contact numbers."

He nodded. "Go ahead." When he had them down, he nodded again. "I've been going over some of my notes anyway. Captain Feeney and I have had some conversations about this."

"Yeah, I know. Feel free to contact him in lieu of me on this. Sorry to wake you."

"Been a cop thirty-three years. Used to it."

Another long shot, Eve thought when she ended transmission. But they were starting to pay off.

When Roarke walked in she had to struggle to focus. Her eyes wanted to give up. "Anything?"

"Nothing on the competitor search, nothing that fits cleanly."

"How about messily?"

"A handful of men who somewhat fit the description who are, in some way, involved in the upper echelons of competitors. No real hits. And a portion of those are out of the country, or off planet. When I take them through the other locations and times, none of them coordinates. I've gone down a few levels — supposing one of the lower-rung employees has a hard-on against me or my organization. I'm not finding anything there. And while I was running that, I realized that's chasing the wild goose."

"You gotta chase it to catch it."

"Eve, it's not my business. It's not even me that's the root. It's you."

She blinked twice. "I —"

"No, I can see it in your face." Temper whipped out in the words. "You're too damn tired to pull it off. This is no surprise to you. Goddamn it to bloody hell. You've had this in mind for some time now, and you've been fobbing me off with busywork."

"Whoa. Wait."

He simply strode over, lifted her right out of the chair. "You've no right. None. You know or you believe that he's using me because I'm connected to you. You, who connect to him, his first spree, the first investigation."

"Ease off."

"I damn well won't."

His wrath, hot or cold, was dangerous at the best of times. Add emotional turmoil and brittle fatigue and it was deadly.

"You'd be a target. The biggest jewel in his bloody crown. You've had that in your head, and never said, never gave me the courtesy of telling me."

"Don't. I've had about enough of people telling me I didn't give them courtesy. This is a murder investigation and I left my etiquette disc at the office. Ease off!"

He just drew her up until she was on her toes. "If I hadn't been so guilty and distracted, thinking it was something I did, or was, or had that was causing him to take my people, I'd have come to this myself long before. You let me think it."

"I don't know if it's me or if it's you, but I did know — and boy are you proving it out — that if I told you this possibility, you'd go off."

"So you lied to me."

Her fury bloomed, so ripe and real at the accusation she had to fight, viciously, to stop herself from punching him. "I did not lie to you."

"By omission." He dropped her back on her feet. "I thought we trusted each other more than this."

220

"Fuck it. Just fuck it." She sat down, pressed her hands to her head. "Maybe I'm screwing up, right, left, back, forth. Feeney, you. I *do* trust you, and if I haven't shown you that by now with every goddamn thing I have, I don't know how else to do it."

"Mentioning this bloody business might've done the job."

"I needed to think it through. It never really occurred to me until Mira brought it up. And that was just today. I haven't had time to *think*, goddamn it. I haven't even run the probability yet."

"Run it now."

She dropped her hands, looked up at him. Her own temper had fizzled like a wet fuse, and all that was left were the soggy dregs.

"I can't take it. You've got to know, however spineless it is, I can't take it if you slap me back, too. I can't take it from both of you in one day. I wasn't trying to hurt either of you. I was just doing my job the best I know how. I wasn't keeping this from you, I just hadn't . . . assimilated it yet."

"Or figured out how to use it, if your assimilation indicated it had merit."

"Yes. If it has merit, I will use it. You know that if you know me."

"I know that, yes." He turned away, walked to her windows.

"There was a time I wouldn't have had anyone to consult on a decision. There was a time," she continued, "I wouldn't have considered it necessary to take anyone's thoughts or feelings into account in any

221

decision I made. That's not true anymore. When I'd thought it through, when I'd come up with ideas or options, I would have told you. I wouldn't have moved forward without telling you."

True enough, he told himself as he mastered his own fury and fear. That was all true enough, for both of them. And small, hard comfort.

"Still, you'll move forward, if you believe you must, regardless of my thoughts and feelings."

"Yes."

He turned back. "I probably wouldn't love you so much it all but chokes me if you were otherwise."

She let out a breath. "I probably wouldn't love you, et cetera, et cetera, if you didn't understand I can't be otherwise."

"Well, then."

"I'm sorry. I know it's hard for you."

"You do." He crossed back. "Aye, you do, but you don't understand the whole of it. How could you? Why should you?" He touched her cheek. "I wouldn't have been so angry if it hadn't taken me so bloody long to realize it wasn't about me, but about you."

"Not everything's about you, ace."

He smiled, as she'd meant him to, but his eyes stayed intense. "We'll talk through, thoroughly, any plans you make to try to use this angle. To use yourself as bait."

"Yes. My word on that."

"All right, then. We need to go to bed. I'll have my way on that, Lieutenant. It's nearly two in the morning, and you'll want to be up around five, I'd guess."

"Yeah, okay. We'll catch some sleep."

222

She walked with him, but couldn't stop the ball he'd launched from bouncing around in her mind. "It was shuffling around in my head," she began. "The idea of me being a target. A lot of information and supposition was shuffling around in my head."

"As I've marched along with you on this one for the past two days and three nights, I have a good understanding of how much is crowded in your head on this."

"Yeah, but see — God, I'm becoming a woman even before the words come out of my mouth."

"Please, you must be stopped."

"I'm serious." Mildly embarrassed by it, she shoved her hands in her pockets. "The way women just nibble and gnaw at something, just can't let it alone. Any minute I'm going to start wondering which color lip dye works best with my complexion. Or my shoes."

He laughed, shook his head. "I think we're safe from that."

"If I ever start going that way, put me down. Okay?"

"My pleasure."

"But what I have to say, which is annoying, is that I don't even know if it's a viable angle. I'm not going to drop over to some guy's house to plan a party for him or teach him the samba."

"You often go to strangers' houses to interview them or take statements."

"Okay, yeah." She pushed at her hair as they entered the bedroom. "But I'm rarely solo, and I'm logged, and Jesus, Roarke, I'm a cop. It wouldn't be a snap for some old guy to get the drop on me."

"Which makes you quite the challenge. That would be an added appeal."

"And that's shuffling around, too. But —"

"He might have targeted you instead of Ariel Greenfeld. If you've been in his sights the last few days — weeks, come to that — it could've been you he took today."

"No, it couldn't." And this, she realized as she undressed, was why she was gnawing at this. He had to see, accept, and relax. "Think about it. I've barely had an hour alone in my own office since Friday night. Outside this house or Central, I've been with you or Peabody. Maybe you think he can get the drop on me, but is he going to get the drop on both of us, or on two cops?"

He stopped, studied her. The clenched fist in his gut relaxed fractionally. "You have a point. But you're considering changing that."

"Considering. If we go that route, and that's still a major *if*, I'll be wired, I'll be protected. I'll be armed."

"I want a homing beacon on your vehicle."

"There will be."

"No, I want one on before we leave the grounds in the morning. I'll see to it."

Give and take, she reminded herself. Even when — maybe especially when — give and take was a pain in the ass. "Okay. But there go my plans to slip off and meet Pablo the pool boy for an hour of hot, sticky sex."

"We all have to make sacrifices. Myself, I've had to reschedule my liaison with Vivien the French maid three times in the last couple of days."

"Blows," Eve said as they slipped into bed.

"She certainly does."

She snorted, jabbed her elbow back lightly as he drew her back against him. "Perv."

"There you go, stirring me up when we need our sleep." His fingers brushed lightly over her breast, trailed down her torso, teased, trailed lightly up again.

On a sigh, she laid her hand over his, encouraging the caress. This was better, she thought, this was the way to end a long, hard day. Body to body, sliding away in the dark.

When his lips found the nape of her neck, she stretched like a lazy cat. "Sleep's only one way to recharge."

"So it seems. Just as it seems I can't keep my hands off you."

She felt him harden against her, and heat. "Funny place for a hand. You ought to see a doctor about that. It could . . . Oh." She shuddered, seemed to shimmer when he slipped into her.

"There's a better place." Now his hand glided down, pressed against her as he pleasured them both with long, slow strokes.

She went soft, breath catching, body fluid as wine. His hands were free to touch, to take, to tease. Breasts, torso, belly, that glorious heat where they joined.

He could feel every quiver and quake that passed through her even as she surrounded him.

She breathed out his name as she rolled up and over, rolled through the climax. In the utter dark he knew all of her: body, heart, mind. Steeped in the moment, he murmured to her in the language of his shattered childhood. With her, he was complete.

So easy, so exquisite and simple, this merging, this melding. No empty spaces when he was with her, no haunting images of blood and death. Just peace, she knew only peace and pleasure. Those hands, so skilled, so patient. The whispers she knew were love dipped from a deep and turbulent well.

Here she could be pliant, here she could yield. So she rose up, and up, trembling as she clung, one moment, just one moment more to that breathless peak. Holding as she felt him climb with her, hold with her.

And so she slid down again, wrapped with him.

In the dark, she smiled, clutched his hand to bring it between her breasts. "*Buenas noches*, Pablo."

"*Bonne nuit*, Vivien."

She dropped, grinning, into sleep.

It was a shame. A true shame. But he could do nothing more with Gia. Nothing in his research of her had indicated she would have a mind so easily broken. Honestly, he felt as if they'd barely begun, and now he had to end it.

He'd risen early, hoping against hope that she'd revived sometime in the night. He'd given her dopamine, tried lorazepam — which weren't easy to come by, but he felt the trouble he'd gone to was necessary.

He'd tried electric shock, and that he could admit had been very interesting. But nothing — not music, not pain, not drugs, not the systemic jolts — had been able to reach in and find the lock to the door her mind had hidden behind.

After the truly rousing success with Sarifina, this was a crushing disappointment. But still, he reminded himself, it took two to make a partnership.

"I don't want you to blame yourself, Gia." He laid her arms in the channels that ran the length of the table so the blood would drain. "Perhaps I rushed things with you, approached the process poorly. After all, we each have our own unique tolerance for pain, for stress, for fear. Our minds and bodies are built to withstand only so much. Now, it's true," he continued as he made the first cut on her wrist, "that training, exercise, diet, education can and do increase those levels. But I want you to know I understand you did your very best."

When he'd opened the veins on her right wrist, he walked around the table, took her left. "I've enjoyed our time together, even though it was brief. It's simply your time, that's all. As my grandfather taught me, every living thing is merely a clock that begins winding down with the very first breath. It's how we use that time that counts, isn't it?"

When he was done, he moved away to wash and sterilize the scalpel, to scrub the blood off his hands. He dried them thoroughly under the warm air of his blower.

"Well now," he said cheerfully, "we'll have some music. I often play 'Celeste Aida' for my girls when it's time for them to go. It's exquisite. I know you'll enjoy it."

He ordered the aria and, as the music filled the room, sat, eyes dreamy, his memory stretching back decades, to her.

And watched the last moments of Gia Rossi's life drain away.

CHAPTER
THIRTEEN

Eve shuffled into the shower as Roarke was drying off from his. Her voice was rusty when she ordered the jets on, and her eyes felt as if someone had coated a thin adhesive inside her lids during the night.

The hot blast helped, but she knew it was going to take considerably more to get all engines firing. She considered the departmentally approved energy pill, then opted to hold that in reserve. It would boost her, no question, and it would leave her feeling overwired and jumpy all day.

She'd stick with caffeine. Lots and lots of caffeine.

When she came out, Roarke was wearing trousers. Just trousers, she noted — all bare-chested, bare-footed, with all that gorgeous black hair still a little damp from the shower.

There were other things that gave the system a good jolt, and he was certainly top of her personal list.

And when he crossed to her, offering a mug of black coffee, her love knew no bounds.

The sound she made was as much in appreciation of him as that first life-giving gulp.

"Thanks."

"Food's next. We didn't quite make it through dinner, and you're not going through the day on coffee and attitude."

"I like my attitude." But she went to the closet, pulled out what looked warm and comfortable. "How come you can look sexy and rested after a couple hours' sleep, and I feel like my brain's been used for Arena Ball practice?"

"Enormous strength of will and lucky metabolism." He selected a shirt, slipped it on, but didn't bother to button it. He studied her as she pulled on stone gray trousers. "I could order up an energy drink."

"No. They always have a crappy aftertaste and make me feel like my eyes are crossing and uncrossing. Weirds me." She pulled on a long-sleeved white tee, dragged a black sweater over it. "I'm just going to —"

She stopped, frowned at the knock on the bedroom door. "Who else in their right mind would be up at this hour?"

"Let's find out." Roarke walked to the door, and opened it to Mavis and Belle.

"I saw the light under the door."

"Is something wrong with the baby?" Roarke asked. "Is she sick?"

"Belle? No, she's trip T's — Totally Tip-Top. Just needed her morning change and snuggle. But I peeked out, saw the light. Okay if we come in a minute?"

"Of course. I was just about to deal with breakfast. Would you like something?"

"No, just too early for me to fuel up. Well, maybe some juice. Papaya maybe?"

"Have a seat."

"Everything okay?" Eve asked her.

"Yeah, well, you know. When Belle sent out the morning call, I just didn't want to cuddle in. Restless."

Mavis stood, in red-and-white-striped pajamas Summerset must have unearthed from somewhere. They were too big for her, and way too conservative.

They made her look, to Eve's eyes, tiny and fragile.

"Everything's fine, going to be fine. You've got nothing to worry about."

"I guess I just wanted to see if you were okay, and if there was something I could do."

"It's under control." Since Mavis was standing, swaying gently side to side in a way that was making Eve vaguely seasick, Eve gestured to a chair in the sitting area. "Sit down."

"I was thinking Trina and I could look over the appointment books, and maybe we could try to find the hair enhancement." Mavis shrugged. "And Trina was telling me she thinks the guy was using one of a couple of product lines — face and body creams and lotions. I could maybe track down where they're available, and — I don't know. Maybe it would help."

"Maybe it would."

Roarke set down a tall glass of juice, some fresh fruit, and a basket of muffins. Mavis glanced at them, then up at Roarke. "If I wasn't gone squared over my huggie bear, I'd fight Dallas for you."

"I'd squash you like a bug," Eve told her.

"Yeah, but you'd limp awhile after. Would it be all right if we stayed here — Belle and me — until . . .

Leonardo's going to be back this afternoon. I thought —"

"You can stay as long as you like," Roarke told her as he brought over two plates from the AutoChef.

"Thanks. He's just worried. He started thinking what if Belle and I had been with Trina, and this guy had made a move on her. I know it's fetched, but you have a kid and you start winding through the crazed meadow."

"All meadows are crazed," Eve commented. "You and Belle relax and hang."

On cue, Belle began to fuss and whimper. Mavis shifted, smoothly unbuttoning the pajama top. "I thought maybe if Trina was finished before —"

"Sure, sure." Instinctively Eve averted her eyes, grabbed her coffee. "I'll have her brought back here when she's done. No problem."

"Mag. Big relief. So —"

"Oh, well then." Roarke pushed to his feet as Mavis's breast popped out and Belle's eager mouth popped on. "I'll just . . ." Go anywhere else.

His reaction had Mavis's face clearing, and her laughter bubbling. "She wants her breakfast, too. Mostly everyone's seen my boobies before."

"And, as I believe I've said, they're absolutely charming. I wonder if I shouldn't —"

"No, sit." Giggling now, Mavis picked up the juice, rose, easily balancing the glass and the baby at her breast. "You'll get used to it before long, but right now, we'll go on back. Usually we both want a little nap after

232

breakfast. If I find anything on the hair enhancement, the products, I'll tag you."

"Do that."

When they were alone again, Roarke stared down at his plate. "Why do you suppose I chose this morning to want my eggs sunny-side up?"

"They do look like a pair of nice, shiny yellow breasts." Grinning, Eve plucked up a piece of bacon. "And Mavis has been known to paint hers yellow on occasion."

"Every time she feeds the baby, I feel so . . . rude."

"I thought it was freaked."

"A bit of that, but more intrusive. It seems so intimate."

"I'd say we're both going to have to get over it. We've got to get moving. Eat your boobies."

They separated at Central, Eve leading Trina through to where Yancy would work on the composite.

"You know, if cops put more thought and creativity into fashion and grooming, it might improve public relations."

Eve hopped on an up glide and watched a trio she recognized from Illegals troop onto a down. Stubbled faces, scarred shoes, and a sag at the side of each jacket where the sidearm rested.

They looked fine to her.

"Yeah, we're putting together a seminar on that. Defensive Fashion."

"That's not out there," Trina insisted. "Clothes can be like a defense, or an offense —"

"Tell me."

"Or a statement or a reflection. Yours say you're not only in charge but more than willing to kick ass."

"My pants say I'm in charge?" Eve didn't need Mira's various degrees to recognize babbling nerves.

"The whole deal. Dark colors, but not somber. Good fabrics, clean lines. Could power things up now and again, strong reds or greens, sharp blues."

"I'll keep that in mind."

"You should wear sunshades."

"I lose them."

"Well, stop. What are you, twelve? Sunshades would totally complete the package. Is this going to take long? Do you think this is going to take long? What if I can't do it? What if I get it wrong? What if —"

"Stop. What are you, twelve?" At Trina's nervous laugh, Eve stepped off the glide. "It takes as long as it takes. You need to stop, you stop. Yancy's the best I've got, best I've worked with. And if you get it wrong we'll just toss you in a cage for a few hours, until you get it right."

"You're rocking on this."

"Some." She pushed through doors.

Yancy was already there, setting up at his workstation. He rose, shot out his quick, easy smile. "Lieutenant."

"Detective. Appreciate you coming in early for this."

"No big. Trina?" He offered a hand. "How you doing?"

"A little tipped, I guess. I never did this before."

234

"Just relax. I'll steer you through it. How about something to drink? Something cold?"

"Uh, maybe. Maybe like a lemon fizz? Diet."

"I'll get that for you. Just have a seat."

Trina watched him walk out. "Whoa, daddy. He's a yummy one."

"You're not here to nibble on him."

"He's got to go off-duty sometime." Trina craned her neck to get a better view of Yancy's ass before he rounded the corner. "Did you ever bump with that?"

"No. Jesus, Trina."

"Bet that was your loss. Build like that, I bet he can hammer it all night."

"Thank you. Thanks so much for putting that into my head. It'll certainly enhance my working relationship with Detective Yancy."

"I'd like to enhance his working relationship." Trina blew out a breath. "Hey, thinking about sex makes me feel not so nervous. Good to know. Plus, it won't be a hardship to work with Detective Hot Ass."

"Don't screw around." Eve raked a hand through her hair as Yancy came back with Trina's drink and one for himself. "You know how to reach me," she told him.

"Yep. Trina and I . . ." He sent Trina a wink. "We'll get this guy's face for you. So, Trina, how long have you been in the business of beauty?"

Eve knew that was the way he worked, getting the witness to relax, talking small, easing them in. She fought back the need to tell him to push it, and simply stepped back. Walked away.

She had enough time to get to her office, organize the data — and her own thoughts — for the briefing. Pull in Peabody, Eve mused, as she aimed for Homicide. Get said data set up.

Do the briefing, then move out for the stupid, annoying morning media briefing. She needed to run the probabilities on herself as a target, work in some time during the day to discuss that with Mira. But she needed to get out in the field, needed to be out on the streets.

If this bastard was watching her, she might spot the tag.

She beelined for her office, then pulled up short when she saw Feeney sitting in her visitor's chair, brooding over a mug of her coffee.

He got to his feet. Worse for wear, she thought. That's how he looked, a hell of a lot worse for wear. Her back went up even as her stomach churned.

His eyes, baggy and shadowed, stayed on hers. "Got a minute?"

"Yeah." She stepped in, closed the door. And for once wished her office was bigger. There wasn't enough room for them to maneuver around each other, she thought, or to give each other enough space for whatever was coming.

Then it popped out of her, simply popped out without thought or plan. "I want to apologize for —"

"Stop." He tossed it out so quickly her head nearly snapped back as from a blow. "Just stop right there. Bad enough, this is bad enough without that. I was off. Out of line. You're primary of this investigation, and

236

you're heading up this task force. I was off, questioning you and your authority. And I was out of line with what I said to you. So." He paused, took a good slug of coffee. "That's it."

"That's it," she repeated. "That's how it's going to be?"

"It's your call on how it's going to be. You want me off the team, you got cause. You got my notes, and I'll get you a replacement."

At that moment she wished he had popped her one instead of handed her these hurtful insults. "Why would you say that to me? Why would you think I'd want you off?"

"In your shoes, I'd think about it. Seriously."

"Bullshit. That's bullshit." She didn't kick her desk. Instead she kicked the desk chair, sending it careening into the visitor's chair, then bouncing off to slam against the wall. "And you're not in my shoes. Stupid son of a bitch."

His droopy eyes went huge. "What did you say to me?"

"You heard me. You're too tight-assed, too stubborn, too *stupid* to put your hurt feelings aside and do the job with me, you're going to have to get the fuck over it. I can't afford to lose a key member at this stage of the investigation. You know that. You *know* that, so don't come in here and tell me I've got cause to boot you."

"You're the one who's going to get a boot, right straight up your ass."

"You couldn't take me ten years ago," she shot back, "you sure as hell can't take me now."

"Want to test that out, kid?"

"You want a round, you got one. When this case is closed. And if you're still carrying that stick up your ass, I'll yank it out and knock you cold with it. What the hell's wrong with you?"

Her voice broke, just a little, making them both miserable. "You come in here, stiff and snarly, and won't even let me apologize. You start spouting off, won't even let me apologize for fucking up."

"You didn't, goddamn it. *I* fucked up."

"Great. Fine. We're a couple of fuckups."

He sank down in the chair as if the wind had gone out of him. "Maybe we are, but I got more years at it than you."

"Now you want to pull rank on fuckup status? Great. Fine," she repeated. "You get the salute. Feel better?"

"No, I don't feel any goddamn better." He let out a tired sigh that smothered the leading edge of her temper.

"What do you want, Feeney? What do you want me to say?"

"I want you to listen. I let it eat at me. This one got away from me and I let it eat at me. Taught you, didn't I, that you can't get them all, and you can't beat yourself up when you can't put the pieces together, not when you gave it your best."

"Yeah, you taught me."

"Didn't listen to myself this time. And that bile just kept rising up out of my belly into my throat over it." His lips tightened as he shook his head. "You find a fresh angle, and instead of jumping on that, grabbing hold and pushing on that, I jump on you. Part of me's

238

thinking, 'Did I miss that? Did I miss that before, and did all those women die hard because I did?'"

"You know better than that, Feeney. And yeah, I get knowing better isn't always enough. How good was I nine years ago?"

"Needed seasoning."

"That wasn't the question. How good was I?"

He drank again, then looked up at her. "You were the best I ever worked with, even then."

"And I worked that case with you, minute by minute, step by step. We didn't miss it, Feeney. It wasn't *there*. The evidence, the statements, the pattern. If he got them that way, or some of them that way, the evidence wasn't there to show us."

"I spent a lot of time yesterday going over the files. I know what you're saying. What I'm saying is that's the reason I jumped on you."

He thought of what his wife had said the night before. That he'd railed at Dallas because she was his family. That she'd let him rail because he was her family. Nobody, according to his Sheila, beat each other up as regularly or as thoughtlessly as family.

"Didn't like you telling me I needed a break either," he muttered. "Basically telling me I needed a damn nap, like somebody's grandfather."

"You are somebody's grandfather."

His eyes flashed at her, but there was some amusement in the heat. "Watch your step, kid."

"I should've run the new angle by you before the briefing. No, I should have," she insisted when he shook his head. "Like you should've known I would have if everything hadn't been moving so fast. There's nobody on the job, nobody with a badge I respect more than you."

It took him a moment to clear his throat. "Same goes. I got one more thing, then this is closed." He rose again. "I didn't put you here. You never were a rookie," he told her in a voice roughened with emotion. "So I saw good, solid cop the minute I laid eyes on you. I gave you a hell of a foundation, kid, a lot of seasoning and pushed you hard because I knew you could take it. But I didn't put you here, and saying that, well, that was stupid. You put yourself here. And I'm proud. So that's it."

She only nodded. Neither of them would handle it well if she blubbered.

As he went out, he gave her two awkward pats on the shoulder, then closed the door behind him.

She had to stand where she was a minute until she was sure she had herself under control. After a few steadying breaths she turned, started to sit at her desk. Someone knocked on the door.

"What?" She wanted to snarl, then did just that when Nadine poked a head in. "Media conference at nine."

"I know. Are you okay?"

"Peachy. Go away."

Nadine just sidled in, shut the door at her back. "I came by a little while ago, and . . . well, let's say overheard a few choice words in raised voices. The reporter in me fought with the reasonably well-mannered individual. It was a pitched battle, and did take a couple of minutes. Then I wandered off until I thought the coast was clear. So again, are you okay?"

"That was a private conversation."

"You shouldn't have private conversations in public facilities at the top of your lungs."

Point well taken, Eve was forced to admit. "I'm fine. We're fine. Just something we had to work out."

"It made me think it might be interesting to do a segment on tension in the workplace, and how cops handle it."

"You're going to want to leave this one alone."

"This particular one, yes. Price of friendship."

"If that's all —"

"It's not. I know you didn't think much of the Romanian psychic, but —"

"Actually, there may have been a nugget there. Got another?"

"Really? I expect to be fully filled in on that. And, yes, I may just." In her slim-skirted suit the color of raspberry jam, Nadine managed to ease a hip down on the corner of Eve's desk.

"Bolivia," she began. "We've been digging through the tabloids. You'd be surprised what nuggets can be found there that you cops disdain."

"Yeah, those alien babies are a menace to society."

"A classic for a reason. But we found an interesting story about the Moor of Venice."

"Last time I checked, Venice was in Italy."

"No, Othello — Shakespeare? And Verdi. Othello was this black dude, important guy, married to a gorgeous white women — mixed race marriages were not common back then in . . . whenever the hell it was."

"Nine years ago?"

"No." Nadine laughed. "More like centuries. Anyway, Othello ends up being manipulated by this other guy into believing his wife's been cheating on him. Othello strangles her. And ends up in song and story."

"I'm not following this, Nadine."

"Just giving you some background. There was a big costume ball at the opera house in —"

"Opera?"

"Yeah." Nadine's eyes narrowed. "That means something."

"Just keep going."

"A woman in La Paz claimed she was attacked by a guy dressed like Othello. Black mask, cape, gloves. Claimed he tried to drag her off, tried to rape her. Since she didn't have a mark on her, and witnesses stated that she was seen chatting amiably with a guy in that costume earlier in the evening, and she was skunk drunk when she started shrieking, her claims were dismissed by the police. But the tabs played it up. She was thirty-one, brunette, and the alleged incident occurred between the discovery of the second and third bodies. Had The Groom tried to claim another bride? Was the Moor of Venice seeking Desdemona? She played it up, too."

Nadine shifted on the desk. "Or maybe she was giving some of it straight. She claimed he spoke exceptional Spanish, but with an American accent, was knowledgeable about music and literature, and was well-traveled. Now, with a little more research we learned she was a party girl — and that several were peppered through the guests to . . . entertain."

"An LC?" Eve pursed her lips thoughtfully. "He hasn't targeted any pros. Doesn't fit his profile."

"The party girls at functions like this don't advertise. They're frosting."

"Okay, so it's possible he didn't make her as a pro."

"Exactly, and you can read between the lines and assume she smelled money and played it up with this guy. He suggested they go out for some air, which they did. Then that they go for a drive — which she couldn't do or lose her event fee. In any case, she said she started feeling off — dizzy, woozy. She also claimed she hadn't been drinking, which, of course, she had. But I'm betting she knew her limit when she was working, and they mistook drugged for skunk drunk."

"Could be." Eve nodded. "Yeah, that could be."

"When she realized he was leading her away from the opera house, she resisted. Here's where I think she embellished or there would have been marks, tears, something. Figure when she started to struggle, to scream, he cut his losses. She tears back to the party. He slides off."

"You gotta have more than that."

"Yeah, I do. The third victim was a waitress, worked for the caterer who did this party. She worked the party. And a week later, she's dead. So —"

"He cherry-picks potentials at the event," Eve concluded. "Weeds it down to two. The first doesn't work out for him. So he goes for the second. Where was she last seen?" Eve turned to boot up the file.

"Leaving her apartment four days before her body was found. She'd been scheduled to work that evening, called in sick. She wasn't reported missing for two days because —"

"She's the one who took an overnight bag, clothes. Good clothes."

"Good memory. Yeah. It was assumed she'd gone off with some guy. Which, I guess she did. First woman said Othello had a voice like silk — soft and smooth. Wore heeled boots and a high headdress — compensating."

"Short guy, we got that."

Nadine's brows lifted. "Oh, do you?"

"You'll get everything when you get it. Anything else?"

"She said he talked about music — opera particularly — like it was a god. She said a lot of bullshit, actually. His eyes were burning red, his hands like steel as they closed around her throat. Blah, blah. But there was one more interesting thing that sounded true. She said she asked about his work, and he said he studied life and death. In a twisted way, that could be what he's doing, or thinks he's doing."

"Okay. That's okay."

"Worth any inside info?"

"I leak anything at this point, it's my ass. Don't bother with the media briefing. Send a drone. When I'm clear, you'll get it all."

"Off the record. Are you close?"

"Off the record. I'm getting closer."

Since the two conversations had eaten away her prep time, Eve just gathered everything up. She'd organize on the fly. Lining it up in her head, she headed out,

244

reminding herself there was now — courtesy of Roarke — decent coffee in the conference room.

She glanced over at raised voices, saw one of her detectives and a couple of uniforms dwarfed by a man about the size of the vending machine they'd gathered in front of.

"I want to see my brother!" the giant shouted. "Now!"

Carmichael, generally unflappable in Eve's estimation, kept her voice low and soothing. "Now, Billy, we explained that your brother's giving a statement. As soon as he's done —"

"You've got him in a cage! You're beating him up!"

"No, Billy. Jerry's helping us. We're trying to find the bad man who hurt his boss. Remember how somebody hurt Mr. Kolbecki?"

"They killed him dead. Now you're going to kill Jerry. Where's Jerry?"

"Let's go sit over —"

Billy screamed his brother's name loudly enough that cops stopped, turned, slipped out of doorways.

Eve changed direction, headed toward the trouble. "Problem here?"

"Lieutenant." The unflappable Carmichael sent Eve a look of utter frustration. "Billy's upset. Somebody killed the nice man he and his brother work for. We're talking to Billy's brother now. We're just going to get Billy a nice drink before we talk to him, too. Mr. Kolbecki was your boss, too, right, Billy? You liked Mr. Kolbecki."

"I sweep the floors and wash the windows. I can have a soda when I'm thirsty."

"Yeah, Mr. Kolbecki let you have sodas. This is Lieutenant Dallas. She's my boss. So now I have to do my job, and we're all going to sit down and —"

"You'd better not hurt my brother." Going for the top of the authority ladder, Billy plucked Eve right off her feet, shook her like a rag doll. "You'll be sorry if you hurt Jerry."

Cops grabbed for stunners. Shouts rang in Eve's ears as her bones knocked together. She judged her mark, estimated the ratio of his face and her fist. Then spared her knuckles and kicked him solidly in the balls.

She was airborne. She had a split second to think: *Oh, shit.*

She landed hard on her ass, skidded, then her head rapped hard enough against a vending machine to have a few stars dancing in front of her eyes.

Warning! Warning! the machine announced.

As Eve reached for her weapon, someone took her arm. Roarke managed to block the fist aimed at his face before it landed. "Easy," he soothed. "He's down. And how are you?"

"He rang my bell. Damn it." She reached around, rubbed the back of her head as she glared at the huge man now sitting on the floor, holding his crotch and sobbing. "Carmichael!"

"Sir." Carmichael clipped over, leaving the uniforms to restrain Billy. "Lieutenant. Jesus, Dallas, I'm sorry about that. You okay?"

"What the fuck?"

"Vic was found by this guy and his brother this morning when they reported for work. Vic owned a

246

little market on Washington. It appears the vic was attacked before closing last night, robbed and beaten to death. We brought the brothers in for questioning — we're looking for the night guy. We don't believe, at this time, the brothers here were involved, but that they may have pertinent information regarding the whereabouts of the night clerk."

Carmichael blew out a breath. "This guy, Billy? He was fine coming in. Crying a little about the dead guy. He's, you know, a little slow. The brother, Jerry, told him it was okay, to go on with us to get a drink, to talk to us. But he got worked up once we separated them. Man, Dallas, I never thought he'd go for you. You need an MT?"

"No, I don't need a damn MT." Eve shoved to her feet. "Take him into Observation. Let him see his brother's not being beaten with our vast supply of rubber hoses and saps."

"Yes, sir. Ah, you want us to slap Billy with assaulting an officer?"

"No. Forget it." Eve walked over, crouched down in front of the sobbing man. "Hey, Billy. Look at me. You're going to go see Jerry now."

He sniffled, swiped at his runny nose with the back of his hand. "Now?"

"Yeah."

"There was blood all over, and Mr. Kolbecki wouldn't wake up. It made Jerry cry, and he said I couldn't look, and couldn't touch. Then they took Jerry away. He takes care of me, and I take care of him. You can't take Jerry away. If somebody hurts him like Mr. Kolbecki —"

"Nobody's going to do that. What kind of soda does Jerry like best?"

"He likes cream soda. Mr. Kolbecki lets us have cream sodas."

"Why don't you get one for Jerry out of the machine? This officer will take it to him, and you can watch through the window, see Jerry talking to the detective. Then you can talk to the detective."

"I'm going to see Jerry now?"

"Yeah."

"Okay." He smiled, sweet as a baby. "My nuts sure are sore."

"I bet."

She straightened, stepped back. Roarke had retrieved her disc bag, and the discs that had gone flying as she had. He held it out now. "You're late for your briefing, Lieutenant."

She snatched the bag, suppressed a smirk. "Bite me."

CHAPTER
FOURTEEN

It was fascinating, Roarke thought, in so many ways to watch her work.

He'd wandered out of the conference room when he'd heard the commotion, in time to see the erupting mountain of a man lift her a foot off the ground. His instinct had been, naturally, to rush forward, to protect his wife. And he'd been quick.

She'd been quicker.

He'd actually seen her calculate in those bare seconds her head had been snapping back and forth on her neck. Punch, gouge, or kick, he remembered. Just as he'd seen more irritation than shock on her face when she'd gone flying.

Took a hell of a knock, he thought now, but temper had been riper than pain. He'd seen that, too. Just as he'd seen her compassion for the distress and confusion of a scared little boy inside a man's body.

And here she was, moments later, taking charge of the room, putting all that behind her.

It was hardly a wonder that it had been her, essentially from the first minute he'd seen her. That it would be her until his last breath. And very likely well beyond that.

She hadn't worn her jacket for the briefing, he noted. She looked lean and not a little dangerous with her weapon strapped over her sweater. He'd seen her drape the diamond he'd once given her over her neck before she'd put on the sweater that morning.

The priceless Giant's Tear and the police-issue. That combination, he thought, said something about their merging lives.

As he listened to her brisk update, he toyed with the gray button — her button — he always carried in his pocket.

"I expect to have a face within the next couple of hours," she continued. "Until that time, these are the lines we pursue. Urban Wars connection. Captain Feeney?"

"Slow going there," he said, "due to the lack of records. The Home Force did have documented billets and clinics in the city, and I'm working with those. But there were any number of unofficial locations used, and used temporarily. More that were destroyed or subsequently razed. I've interviewed and am set to interview individuals who were involved militarily, paramilitarily, or as civilians. I'm going to focus on body disposal."

"Do you need more men?"

"I've got a couple I can put on it."

"Do that. Knocking on doors. Newkirk, you and your team will recanvass this sector." She turned, aiming her laser pointer to highlight a five-block area around the bakery where Ariel Greenfeld worked. "Every apartment, every business, every street LC, sidewalk sleeper, and panhandler. Somebody saw

250

Greenfeld Sunday afternoon. Make them remember. Baxter, you and Trueheart take this sector around Greenfeld's residence. He watched her. From the street, from another building, from a vehicle. In order to familiarize himself with her routine, he staked her out more than once. Jenkinson and Powell, recanvass the area of York's and Rossi's residences. Peabody and I will take the gym and the club."

She paused, and Roarke could see her going through her mental checklist. "The real estate angle. Roarke."

"There are a significant number of private residences," he began, "and businesses with residences on site that have been owned and operated by the same individual or individuals for the time frame. Even reducing this search area to below Fiftieth in Manhattan, the number is considerable. I believe, if I cross with Feeney, do a search for private buildings that were in existence during the Urbans, whether as residences or otherwise, we'll cut that down."

"Good." She thought a moment. "That's good. Do that. Connecting cases. McNab."

"It's been like trying to pick the right flea off a gorilla."

"My line," Callendar muttered beside him, and he grinned.

"Her line, but I think we may have a good possible. First vic in Florida, housekeeper at a swank resort, last seen after leaving the Sunshine Casino at approximately oh-one-hundred. She habitually spent a few hours on her night off playing the poker slots. Going on the theory that her killer had made earlier contact, may have been known by her, I did a run on the resort's register for the thirty days prior to her death. Investigators at that time took a pass through it after the second body was discovered, but as it appeared the vic had been grabbed outside the casino, focused their efforts there. But a copy of the register was in the case file. Tits here and I went though it."

"And you got lucky," Callendar mumbled.

"And I'm so good," McNab said smoothly, "that I hit on a guest registered three weeks before the vic was snatched, with a four-day stay. Name of Cicero Edwards. Resort requires an address, to which Edwards listed one in London. I ran the name with said address and came up with zip. No Edwards, Cicero, at that address at that time. And better, the address was bogus. It's the address for —"

"An opera house," Eve said and had McNab's pretty face moving into a pout.

"Wind, sails, sucked out," he commented. "The Royal Opera House, to be exact. Leading your crack e-team to deduce this was our guy, and that our guy has a thing for fat women singing in really high voices."

"I have information that may add further weight to that." She encapsulated Nadine's information. "Good work." She nodded at McNab and Callendar. "Find more. Roarke, see if you can dig up any buildings that were used as opera houses or theaters that held operas during the Urbans. And —"

"He'll have season tickets," Roarke said. "If he's a serious buff, and is able to afford the luxury, he'd indulge it. Box seats, most likely. Here at the Met, very likely at the Royal and other opera houses of repute."

"We can work that," she replied. "Dig, cross-check. He likes to vary his name. Punch on any variation of Edward." She glanced at her wrist unit, cursed. "I'm late for the damn media. Get started."

She turned, studied the name she'd added to the white board. Ariel Greenfeld.

"Let's find her," she said, and went out.

She got through the media without actually grinding her teeth down to nubs. She considered that progress. Whitney was waiting for her outside the briefing room.

"I'd hoped to make it to your morning briefing," he told her. "I was detained."

"We do have some new leads since my report. Sir, I'd like to check on Detective Yancy's progress with the witness if I could update you on the way."

He nodded, fell into step beside her.

"An opera lover," he said when she'd brought him up to speed. "My wife enjoys the opera."

"Yes, sir."

He smiled a little. "I actually enjoy some opera myself. He may have gotten too clever with his fake addresses, using opera houses."

"Houses may be one of the keys, Commander. I don't know much about opera, but I take it they deal with death a lot of the time. The psychic in Romania talked about his house of death. Psychics are often cryptic or their visions symbolic."

"And we should consider he might have, or have had, some more direct connection with opera. A performer, or backer, a crew member, musician."

"It's a possibility."

"*Phantom of the Opera*. A story about a disfigured man who haunts an opera house, and kills," Whitney explained. "His killing place may be a former opera house or theater."

"We're pursuing that. There are other areas we may pursue. I'd like to discuss them with you and Mira at some point, if those areas seem relevant."

"We'll work around you."

He went with her to Yancy's division. Eve wondered if he registered the fact that wherever he passed, cops came to attention . . . or if it was something he no longer noticed.

Eve saw first that Yancy was alone at his workstation, and second that his eyes were closed, and he was wearing a headset. Though she'd have preferred the commander had been elsewhere when she was forced to berate a detective, it didn't stop her from giving Yancy's desk chair a good, solid kick.

He jerked up. "Hey, watch where you're — Lieutenant." Annoyance cleared when he saw Eve, then shifted over into something closer to anxiety when he spotted Whitney. "Commander."

He came out of the chair.

"Where the hell is my witness?" Eve demanded. "And just how often do you take a little nap on the department's time?"

"I wasn't napping. Sir. It's a ten-minute meditation program," he explained as he pulled off the headset. "Trina needed a break, so I suggested she go down to the Eatery or take a short walk around. At this point in the work, it's easy to stop guiding and start directing. Meditating for a few minutes clears my head."

"Your methods generally produce results," Whitney commented. "But in this case, ten minutes is an indulgence we can't afford."

"Understood, sir, but, respectfully, I know when a wit needs a breather. She's good." Yancy glanced at Dallas. "She's really good. She knows faces because it's her business to evaluate them. She's already given me more than most wits manage, and in my opinion, after this break she's going to nail it solid. Take a look."

He'd used both a sketch pad and the computer. Eve stepped around to get a closer look at both. "That's good," she agreed.

"It'll be better. She keeps changing the eyes and the mouth, and that's because she's second- and third-guessing. She can't pull out the eye color, but the shape? The shape of the eyes, the face, even the way the ears lie, she doesn't deviate."

The face was rounded, the ears lying neatly, and on the small side. The eyes were slightly hooded and held a pleasant expression. The mouth, a little thin on top, was curved in a hint of a smile. Short-necked, Eve noted, so that the head sat low on the shoulders.

All in all, it struck her as a bland, nondescript kind of face. The sort that would be easily overlooked. "Nothing stands out about him," she commented. "Except his absolute ordinariness."

"Exactly. And that makes it harder for the wit. Harder to remember details about somebody who doesn't really have anything about him that catches the eye. She was more into how he dressed, how he spoke, how he smelled, that sort of thing. They made the impression. Took her a while to start building the face beyond that. But she's good."

"So are you," Eve complimented. "Give me a copy of this for now. Get me the finished when you have it."

"Some of these details are going to change." Still, Yancy ordered a print. "I think the nose is going to be shorter, and —" He held up a hand as if signaling himself to stop. "And that's why we needed a break from each other. I'm projecting."

"This gives us a base. When you're done with Trina, I'd like you to arrange for her to be taken back to my residence. She's expected."

"Will do."

"Nice work, Detective."

"Thank you, Commander."

As they left, Whitney glanced at Eve. "Check with him in an hour. If there isn't any change, we'll release this image. We need it made public as soon as possible."

"Yes, sir."

"Contact me when you want to meet with me and Dr. Mira," he added, then peeled off to go his own way.

Eve didn't care how cold it was, it was good to be back on the street. She'd had enough, for the time being, of desk work and comp work and briefings. It was true enough she needed some thinking time, just her and her murder board, but right now, she needed to move.

"It's hard to believe we've only been on this since Friday night." Peabody hunched her shoulders as they walked to BodyWorks. "It feels like we've been working this one for a month."

"Time's relative." Ariel Greenfeld, Eve thought, missing for approximately eighteen hours.

"McNab humped on this until nearly three this morning. I fizzled just past midnight, but he was revved. Something about e-juice, I guess. Of course, when he's really humping the comp, he doesn't have any left to, you know, hump yours truly. This is the longest we've gone since cohabbing not using the bed — or some other surface — for recreational purposes."

"One day," Eve said as she cast her eyes to heaven, "one fine day you'll be able to go a full week without inserting an image of you and McNab having sex into my head."

"Well, see, that's what I'm worried about." They passed into the lobby of the center, flashed badges on the way to the elevator. "You think maybe the bloom's wearing off? That we're losing the spark? It's actually been since Wednesday night that we —"

"Go no further with that sentence." Eve ordered the elevator to take them to the main gym. "You can't go, what, four days without worrying about blooms and sparks?"

"I don't know. I guess. Well, no," Peabody decided, "because four days is basically a work week if you're not a cop. If you and Roarke went a week, wouldn't you wonder?"

Eve wasn't sure this had ever been an issue. She only shook her head and stepped off the elevator.

"So you and Roarke haven't gotten snuggly since we caught this?"

Eve stopped, turned. Stared. "Detective Peabody, are you actually standing there asking me if I've had sex in the last few days?"

"Well. Yes."

"Pull yourself together, Peabody."

"You *have!*" Peabody trotted after Eve. "I knew it. I *knew* it! You're practically working around the clock, and you still get laid. And we're younger. I mean, not that you're old," Peabody said quickly when Eve shifted very cool eyes in her direction. "You're young and fit, the picture of youth and vitality. I'm just going to stop talking now."

"That would be best." Eve went straight to the manager's office.

Pi got up from his desk. "You have news."

"We're pursuing a number of leads. We'd like to talk to the staff again, and make inquiries among some of your members."

"Whatever you need."

Though Yancy had a little time left on his clock, Eve drew out the sketch. "Take a look at this, tell me if you know this man, or have seen him."

Pi took the sketch, studied it carefully. "He doesn't look familiar. We have a lot of members, a lot of them casual, others who are transient, using this facility while they're in town for business or pleasure. I know a lot of the regulars on sight, but I don't recognize him."

He lowered this sketch. "Is this the man who has Gia?"

"At this time, he's a person of interest."

They spent an hour at it, without a single hit. As they stepped outside, Eve's 'link signaled. "Dallas."

"Yancy. Got it. Good as it's going to get."

"Show me."

He flipped the image on screen. Eve saw it was a bit more defined than the sketch she was carrying. The eyebrows were slightly higher, the mouth less sharply shaped. And the nose was, in fact, a little shorter. "Good. Let's get it out. Notify Whitney, and tell him I requested Nadine Furst get a five-minute bump over the rest of the media."

"Got that."

"Good work, Yancy."

"He looks like somebody's nice, comfortable grandfather," Peabody commented. "The kind that passes out peppermint candy to all the kids. I don't know why that makes it worse."

Safe, Trina had said. She'd said he looked safe. "He's going to see himself on screen. He'll see it at some point in the next few hours, the next day. And he'll know we're closer than we've ever been before."

"That worries you." Peabody nodded. "He might kill Rossi and Greenfeld out of panic and preservation, and go under again."

"He might. But we've got to air the image. If he's targeted another woman, if he's contacted her, and she sees it, it's not only going to save her life, it may lead us right to his door. No choice. Got no choice."

But she thought of Rossi. Eighty-six hours missing, and counting.

Considering the sketch she had was closer than most, Eve used it while they talked to other businesses, to residences, to a couple of panhandlers and the glide-cart operators on the corners.

"He's, like, invisible." Peabody rubbed her chilled hands together as they headed toward the club. "We know he's been around there, been inside the gym, but nobody sees him."

"Nobody pays attention to him and maybe that's part of his pathology. He's been ignored or overlooked. This is his way of being important. The women he takes, tortures, kills, they won't forget him."

"Yeah, but dead."

"Not the point. They see him. When you give somebody pain, when you restrain them, hold them captive and isolated, hurt them, you're their world." It had been that way for her, she remembered. Her father had been the world, the terrifying and brutal world the first eight years of her life.

His face, his voice, every detail of him was exact and indelible in her mind. In her nightmares.

"He's the last thing they see," she added. "That must give him a hell of a rush."

Inside Starlight it was colored lights and dreamy music. Couples circled the dance floor while Zela, in a waist-cinching red suit Eve had to assume was retro, stood on the sidelines.

"Very smooth, Mr. Harrow. Ms. Yo, relax your shoulders. That's the way."

260

"Dance class," Peabody said as Zela continued to call out instructions or encouragement. "They're pretty good. Oops," she added when one of the men wearing a natty bow tie stepped on his partner's foot. "Kinda cute, too."

"Adorable, especially considering one of them might dance on home after class and torture his latest brunette."

"You think . . . one of them." Peabody eyed Natty Bow Tie suspiciously.

"No. He's done with this place. He's never been known to fish from the same pool twice. But I'm damn sure he fox-trotted or whatever on that floor within the last few weeks."

"Why do they call it a fox-trot?" Peabody wondered. "Foxes do trot, but it doesn't look like dancing."

"I'll put an investigative team right on that. Let's go."

They headed down the silver stairs, catching Zela's eye. She nodded, then applauded when the music ended. "That was terrific! Now that you're warmed up, Loni's going to take you through the rhumba."

Zela gestured Eve and Peabody over to the bar while the young redhead led Natty Bow Tie to the center of the floor. The redhead beamed enthusiastically. "All right! Positions, everyone."

There was a single bartender. He wore black-tie, and set a glass of bubbly water with a slice of lemon in front of Zela without asking her preference. "What can I get you, ladies?"

"Could I have a virgin cherry foam?" Peabody asked before Eve could glare at her.

"I'm good," Eve told him, then drew out the sketch, laid it on the counter. "Do you recognize this man?"

Zela stared at it. "Is this . . ." She shook her head. She lifted her water, drank deeply, set it down again. Then, picking up the sketch, she angled it toward the lights. "I'm sorry. He just doesn't look familiar. We get so many men of a certain age through here. I think if I'd worked with him — in a class — I'd remember."

"How about you?" Eve took the sketch, nudged it across the bar.

The bartender stopped mixing Peabody's drink to frown over the sketch. "Is this the fucker — sorry, Zela." She only shook her head, waved the obscenity away. "This the one who killed Sari?"

"He's a guy we want to talk to."

"I'm good with faces, part of the trade. I don't remember him sitting at my bar."

"You work days?"

"Yeah. We — me and my lady — had a kid six months ago. Sari switched me to days so I could be home with my family at night. She was good about things like that. Her memorial's tomorrow." He looked over at Zela. "It's not right."

"No." Zela laid a hand over his for a moment. "It's not right."

There was grief in his eyes when he moved away to finish mixing the drink.

"We're all taking it pretty hard," Zela said quietly. "Trying to work through it, because what can you do? But it's hard, like trying to swallow past something that's stuck in your throat."

262

"It says a lot about her," Peabody offered, "that she mattered to so many people."

"Yeah. Yeah, it does. I talked to Sari's sister yesterday," Zela continued. "She asked if I'd pick the music. What Sari liked. It's hard. Harder than anything I imagined."

"I'm sure it is. What about her?" Eve glanced toward the redhead. "Did she work with Sari on any of the classes?"

"No. Actually, this is Loni's first class. We've had to do some . . . well, some internal shuffling. Loni worked coat check and revolving hostessing. I just bumped her up to hostess/instructor."

"I'd like to talk to her."

"Sure, I'll send her over." Zela rose, smiled wanly. "Pity my feet. Mr. Buttons is as cute as, well, a button, but he's a complete klutz."

The dancers made the switch with Loni giving her klutzy partner a quick peck on the cheek before she dashed over to the bar on three-inch heels.

"Hi! I'm Loni."

"Lieutenant Dallas, Detective Peabody."

Peabody swallowed her slurp of cherry foam and tried to look more official.

"I talked to those other detectives? I have to say *mmmm* on both. I guess they're not coming back?"

"Couldn't say. Do you recognize this man?"

Loni looked at the sketch as the bartender set down beside her something pink and fizzy with a cherry garnish. "I don't know. Hmmm. Not really. Sort of. I don't know."

"Which is it, Loni? Sort of or not really?"

"He kind of looks like this one guy, but that guy had dark hair, slicked back dark hair and a really thin mustache."

"Short, tall, average? This one guy."

"Ummm, let me think. On the short side. 'Cause Sari had an inch or two on him. Of course, she was wearing heels, so —"

"Hold on. You saw this man with Sari?"

"This one guy, yeah. Well, lots of the men liked to dance with Sari when she was working the floor. It's probably not this guy because —"

"Hold on." Eve pulled out her 'link, tagged Yancy. "I need you to alter the sketch. Give him dark hair, slicked back, a thin mustache. Send it to this 'link."

"Give me a minute."

"When did you see this man with Sari?" Eve asked Loni.

"I'm not sure. A few weeks ago, I guess. It's hard to remember exactly. I only remember at all because I was working the floor, and I asked this guy to dance. We're supposed to ask the singles to dance. He was sort of shy and sweet, and said how he'd just come in for the music, but thank you. Then just a little while later, I saw him dancing with Sari. It sort of frosted me, you know? Silly." She shrugged. "But I was, like, I guess he goes for brunettes instead of . . . Oh." She went a little pale. "Oh, God. *This* guy?"

"You tell me." Eve turned her 'link around so that Loni could view the screen with the adjusted sketch.

"Oh God, oh God. I think, I really think that's the guy. Brett."

"It's okay." The bartender took her hand. "Take it easy." He angled his head to look at the screen. Shook his head. "He didn't come to the bar. I don't remember him sitting at the bar."

"Where was he sitting, Loni?"

"Okay. Okay." She took long breaths as she swiveled around to study the club. "Second tier — I'm pretty sure — toward the back over there."

"I need to talk to whoever waits tables in that section. Can you pinpoint the night, Loni?"

"I don't know. It was a couple weeks ago. Maybe three? You know, I checked his coat once. I remember checking his coat, and that's why I zeroed on him that night. I'd checked his coat before, and he'd been alone. So when I was working the floor, I spotted him and thought, 'Oh yeah, that guy's a solo.' But he didn't want to dance with me."

A single tear slid down her cheek. "He wanted Sari."

CHAPTER
FIFTEEN

"Unobtrusive," Eve said, pushing her way through traffic as a thick, heavy snow began to fall. "Limits contact with anyone other than the target."

"None of the waitstaff could make him, none of the valets. Could live or work within walking distance of the club," Peabody ventured.

"Yeah, or he parks elsewhere on his own. Or he's using public transportation for this part of his game. What cabbie's going to remember picking up or dropping off a fare days later, or in this case weeks? We're spitting into the wind there. Loni only remembered him because he'd spanked her vanity. Otherwise he'd have just been another forgotten face. He'd have been smarter to dance with her. She wouldn't have remembered him for five minutes after."

Eve glanced in the sideview, changed lanes. "He comes in, slides into the crowd, stays out of the main play, keeps to the back. Probably tips the waiter smack on the going percentage. Later, they don't think, 'Oh yeah, this guy stiffed me,' or 'This guy seriously flashed me.' Just ordinary and average. Steady as she goes."

"The confirmation's good to have. Loni verifying he'd been in the club, made contact there with York. But it doesn't tell us much."

"It tells us he likes to alter his appearance. Slight alterations, nothing flashy. Dark hair, little mustache, gray wig. It tells us it's unlikely he frequents or revisits the point of contact after he's got the target. We know that he doesn't lose control, that he can and does maintain whatever role he's chosen to play during the stalking phase."

She turned, headed west for a block, then veered south. "He danced with York, had his hands on her. They're eye to eye, talking. It would be part of her job to talk to her partner. Everything we know about her says she was smart, self-aware, and knew how to deal with people. But she doesn't get any signals, nothing that puts a hitch in her step, that this guy is trouble.

"Check the side view," Eve told Peabody. "See that black sedan, six cars back?"

Peabody shifted, trained her gaze on the mirror. "Yeah. Barely. This snow is pretty thick. Why?"

"He's been tailing us. Five, six, seven back, since we left the club. Not close enough for me to make out the plate. Since, as was recently pointed out, you're younger than me, maybe your eyes are sharper."

Peabody hunched her shoulders. "No. Can't make it. He's too close to the car in front of him. Maybe if he drops back a little, or comes around."

"Let's see what we can do about that." Eve gauged an opening, started to switch lanes.

The blast of a horn, the wet squeal of brakes on sloppy pavement had her tapping her own. One lane over a limo fishtailed wildly in an attempt to miss hitting some idiot who dashed into the street.

She heard the thud, saw the boy fall and roll. There was a nasty crunch as the limo laid into the massive all-terrain in front of her.

"Son of a bitch."

Even as she flipped on her On Duty light, she looked in the rearview again. The sedan was gone.

She slammed out of her vehicle in time to see the boy scramble up, start a limping run. And to hear the scream of: "Stop him! He's got my bag!" over the urban symphony of horns and curses.

"Son of a bitch," she said again. "Handle it, Peabody." And set off in pursuit of the street thief.

He got his rhythm back quickly, proving — she supposed — someone else was younger than she. He dashed, darted, skidded, all but flew across the street, down the sidewalk.

He may have been younger, but her legs were longer, and she began to close the distance. He glanced back over his shoulder, his eyes showing both alarm and annoyance. As he ran he yanked the big brown bag out from under his bulky coat and began to swing it like a stylish pendulum.

He knocked over pedestrians like bowling pins so that Eve had to leap, dodge, swerve.

When he spun, swung the bag at her head, she ducked, snagged the strap, and simply yanked it to send him tumbling to the sidewalk.

Annoyed, she crouched. "You're just stupid," she muttered, and shoved him over on his back.

"Hey! Hey!" Some good Samaritan stopped. "What are you doing to that boy? What's the matter with you?"

Eve planted her boot on the boy's chest to keep him down, flipped out her badge. "You want to keep moving, pal?"

"Bitch," the boy said as the Samaritan frowned at Eve's badge. Then, like an angry terrier, bit her.

"Human bites are more dangerous than animal bites." Peabody had the wheel now as Eve sat in the passenger seat dragging up her pants leg to see the damage. "And he broke the skin," Peabody noted with a sympathetic wince. "Gee, he really clamped down on you."

"Little bastard son of a bitch. Let's see how he likes the assaulting-an-officer strike on top of the robberies. Biting Boy had a dozen wallets in his coat pockets."

"You need to disinfect that."

"Made me lose the sedan. Could've kicked him bloody for that." Setting her teeth, Eve used the clean rag Peabody had unearthed from somewhere to staunch the wound. "Turned on the cross street as soon as there was a commotion. That's what he did, that's what he does. Avoids crowds and confrontations. Fucking fucker."

"Bet that really hurts. You're sure it was the guy?"

"I know a tail when I see one."

"No question. I'm just wondering why he'd tail us. Trying to find out what we know, I guess. But what's the point? All he can get is where we go — and where we've gone is pretty standard for an investigation."

"He's trying to get my rhythm, my pace, my moves. Trying to find a routine."

"Why would . . ." It hit, and had Peabody jerking in her seat. "Holy shit. He's stalking you."

"Thinks I won't make a tail?" She jerked her pants leg back down because looking at the teeth marks only made it hurt more. "Thinks he can figure me. Fat chance. He doesn't know his target this time, he — ha — bit off more than he's going to be able to chew."

"How long have you known he was looking at you?"

"Known? Since about a half hour ago. Toyed with the possibility for a while, but having him tail us pretty much nailed it down."

"You could have mentioned the idea to your partner."

"Don't start. It was one of God knows how many possibles. Now I'm giving it a high probable, and you're the first to know. Black sedan, nothing flashy — which fits right in — round headlights, no hood ornamentation. It looked like a five-bar grill. We should be able to get a model from that."

She all but sighed with relief when Peabody turned into the garage at Central. She wanted to ice down the damn leg. "New York plate was all I could make. Just a quick glimpse on the plate color. Too much distance, too much snow to get any number."

"You need to take standard precautions with that injury."

"Yeah, yeah."

"One of them should be an hour in the crib. You're wiped out."

"I hate the crib." Eve climbed, somewhat achily, out of the car. "If I need to shut down for an hour, I'll use the floor in my office. It works for me. Do me a favor," she added as she hobbled to the elevator. "Set up a meet with Whitney and Mira, asap. I'm going to go steal some disinfectant and a bandage from the infirmary."

"You don't have to steal it. They'll fix you up."

"I don't want them to fix me up," Eve grumbled. "I hate them. I'll just palm what I need and take care of it myself."

Eve swung through the infirmary, committed — if you wanted to be absolutely technical — some basic shoplifting by pocketing what she needed without logging it in.

But if she logged it, they'd insist on seeing the wound. If she showed them the wound, they'd start badgering her to have it treated there. She just needed to clean it up, slap a bandage on it. And, okay, maybe take a blocker.

When she stepped into her office, Roarke was already there.

"Let's see it."

"See what?"

He merely lifted his eyebrows.

"Damn Peabody. She's got a mouth on her." Eve pulled the lifted items out of her coat pocket, tossed them on her desk. She hung her coat on the rack, then sat and propped her injured leg on the desk.

Roarke studied the wound when she tugged up her pants leg, and hissed a little. "Bit nasty, that."

"I've had worse than a nip from some half-assed sissy street thief."

"True enough." Still, he cleaned, treated, and bandaged the bite himself. Then leaned over and pressed a quick kiss to the neat white square. "There, that's better."

"He tailed me."

Roarke straightened now, and the quiet amusement in his eyes faded. "We're not talking about the half-assed sissy street thief."

"I made him — black sedan, couldn't get the plate, but I think we can pop on the model, maybe the year. I might've been able to get more, maybe even have managed to box him in if that asshole hadn't run out in the street. I had to control the vehicle or else crash into the limo that bumped the asshole and crashed into an ATV in front of me. A few seconds, and he was gone."

"He wouldn't know you made him."

"Don't see how, no. He's just cautious. There's trouble up ahead, so he slithers off and avoids it. If he's been out and about shadowing me, he might not have seen the media reports with his face on them. But he will."

She shifted to try to ease the throbbing in her calf. "Be a pal, would you? Get me coffee."

He went to her AutoChef. "And your next step?"

"Meet with Whitney and Mira to discuss the possibilities of baiting a trap. Check in with the team members, input any new data. At some point I need an hour or two just to think. I need to work it through in my head, play with it."

He brought the coffee back to her. "As a party with vested interest in the bait, I'd like to attend this meeting."

"Just can't get enough of meetings, can you? You'll have to leave your buttons outside the room."

"Sorry?"

"If your buttons aren't there, they can't be pushed." She let her head lean back for just a minute, let the coffee work its magic on her system. "And to remember I'm not just bait, I'm an experienced and kick-ass cop."

"With a sissy bite on her tightly muscled calf."

"Well . . . yeah."

"Dallas." Peabody stepped to the door. "How's the leg?"

"Fine, and as of now, removed from all discussion."

"The commander and Dr. Mira will take us in the commander's office in twenty."

"Good enough."

"Meanwhile, Officer Gil Newkirk's come in. He's in the war room."

"On my way."

Gil Newkirk wore his uniform well. He had a rock-solid look about him, indicating to Eve he knew how to handle himself on the street. His face bore the same sort of toughness, what she supposed Feeney might call "seasoning."

She'd met him a handful of times over the years, and considered him to be sensible and straightforward.

"Officer Newkirk."

"Lieutenant." He took the hand she offered with a firm, brisk shake. "Looks like you've got an efficient setup here."

"It's a good team. We're narrowing the field."

"I'm glad to hear it, and wish I'd brought you something substantial. If you've got some time . . ."

"Have a seat." She gestured, joined him at the conference table.

"You've got his face." Newkirk nodded to the sketch pinned to one of the four case boards. "I've been studying that face, trying to put it in front of me nine years back during one of the knock-on-doors. There were so many of them, Lieutenant. That face isn't coming up for me."

"It was a long shot."

"I went through my notes again, and I went over to Ken Colby's place, he was on this. He went down five years ago."

"I'm sorry."

"He was a good man. His widow, she let me dig out his files and notes on the old investigation. I brought them in." He tapped the box he'd carried in with him. "Thought they might add something."

"I appreciate that."

"There were a couple of guys that popped for me when I was going through it again this morning — going off what you gave me last night. But the face, it doesn't match."

"What popped about them?"

"The body type and coloring. And my boy and I, we've talked this through some." He cocked a brow.

"I've got no problem with that."

"I know you're working the Urban Wars angle, and I remembered one of these guys told us he used to ride along in a dead wagon in the Urbans, with his old man. Pick up bodies. Worked as an MT, then kicked that when he went to some convention in Vegas and hit a jackpot. I remember him because it was a hell of a story. The other was this rich guy, third-generation money. He did taxidermy for a hobby. Place was full of dead animals.

"I pulled them out." He passed her a disc. "In case you wanted to check them out again."

"We'll do that. Are you on duty, Officer Newkirk?"

"Day off," he said.

"If you got the time and the interest, maybe you could run these through with Feeney, for current data. I'd be grateful."

"No problem. I'm happy to assist in any way."

Eve got to her feet, offered her hand again. "Thanks. I've got a meeting. I'll check back as soon as I can. Peabody, Roarke, with me."

She had to concentrate not to limp, and giving into her throbbing leg, headed for the small and often odorous confines of the elevator.

"Remember," she said to Roarke, "you're a civilian, and this is a NYPSD op."

"That's expert civilian to you, copper."

She didn't smirk — very much — then squeezed herself onto an elevator. "And don't call the commander Jack. It negates the serious and official tone, and . . . it's just wrong."

"Yo, Dallas!"

She turned her head to see one of the detectives from Anti-Crime grinning at her. "Renicki."

"Heard some mope took a chunk out of you, and now he's got himself a case of rabies."

"Yeah? I heard some LC got a taste of you, and now she's got herself a case of the clap."

"And that," Roarke murmured as a number of cops hooted, "is serious and official."

In his office, Whitney stood behind his desk, and Mira beside a visitor's chair. "Lieutenant," he said. "Detective. Roarke."

"Sir, as I believe the expert consultant may be able to assist with the content of this meeting, I've asked him to be included."

"Your call. Please, sit."

While Roarke, Peabody, and Mira took seats, Eve remained standing. "With permission, Commander, to first update you and Dr. Mira."

She ran it through, quick and spare.

"You were shadowed?" Whitney didn't question her statement. "Any thoughts on why?"

"Yes, sir. Dr. Mira broached the possibility that I may be a target. That rather than the springboard for these particular women being Roarke, the springboard for any connection with Roarke may be me."

"You didn't mention this theory to me, Doctor."

"I asked Dr. Mira to give me time to evaluate," Eve said before Mira could speak. "To consider, and to run probabilities before we shifted the focus on this area of the investigation. Having done so, I believe it's a viable theory. I was a detective on the first investigation, partner to the primary. I fall within the parameters of his choice of victim. I may have crossed paths with him nine years ago, or walked a parallel line.

"I think he came back to New York for specific reasons. And I think one of them is his intention to bag me."

"He'll be disappointed," Whitney commented.

"Yes, sir, he will."

"How strongly do you support this theory, Mira?"

"I've run my own probabilities, and I believe, given his pathology, he would consider capturing the lieutenant, a woman with considerable training and authority, a woman married to a man with considerable power, to be his finest achievement. However, it leads me to another question. How will he top it?"

"He can't," Roarke stated. "And knows that he won't. She's the last, isn't she? The best, the most challenging, his ultimate."

"Yes." Mira nodded. "I agree. He's willing to alter, even slightly, his victim profile. This is not a woman who can be pinned to a specific routine, to a pattern of habits and haunts. Nor one he could approach, face-to-face, as we believe he has with many if not all in the past, and lure her. It must be worth it to him to take this great risk, to devise a way to pull her in. He's

277

circled back," Mira continued. "Come back to what we could call his roots. Because this will finish his work."

"He's stopped before," Peabody put in. "A year or two. But how can he just decide he's finished? This kind of killer doesn't stop unless he's captured or killed."

"No, he doesn't."

"You think he's dying," Eve said to Mira. "Or that he's decided to self-terminate after he finishes me."

"I do. Yes, I believe exactly that. I also believe he doesn't fear it. Death is an accomplishment to him, and a timed cycle, which he has, for nearly a decade we know of, controlled. He doesn't fear his own death, and that only makes him more dangerous."

"We need to give him an opening." Eve narrowed her eyes. "And soon."

"If it's too easy, he won't bite." Roarke met Eve's gaze when she turned. "I know something about challenges. If it comes too easy, it's not worth the trouble. He'll want to work for it. At the very least he'll want to believe that he outwitted you. And he's had much longer to plan, to devise and study the problem than you have."

"I agree." Mira leaned forward. "If what we believe is true, you're the finish to his work. You complete it. The fact that you're pursuing him even as he pursues you not only ups the stakes but adds a particular shine. You would be, quite literally, his masterpiece. With his need for control, he must feel he's manipulated the outcome. Lured you, despite your training and advantages, as he's lured the others."

278

"So we let him believe it," Eve said, "right up to the moment we take him down. He has to be aware by now that we know his face. My take, from the profile, from what we know, is that it will only add to his excitement, his enjoyment. No one's ever gotten this close before. And while he's never overtly sought attention from the killing, his method indicates pride in it. In the end, if that's what this is, won't he want to be known?"

"And remembered," Mira confirmed.

"We don't know where or when, but we know who the target is, and we know why. Big advantages. We have his face, body type, age range. We know more about him than we did nine years ago."

She wanted to pace, to move while she talked it through, but Eve considered that inappropriate in Whitney's office. "He probably has a connection with the Urban Wars, he likes opera, rather than physical means, he uses manipulation and deceit to obtain his victims, and often makes personal contact with them before the abduction. Unlike nine years ago, his victims lived or worked from midtown down. That's purposeful."

"He wanted us to get closer this time." Whitney nodded. "And by using Roarke's people, he made it personal."

"But he doesn't know how much we know," Peabody put in. "He doesn't know we've concluded Dallas is his end game. That's another advantage. As long as he thinks she's looking ahead — I mean that she's focused on the pursuit, he'll think he can ease around behind her, bag the prize."

"Back to an opening. One he can believe he helped make," Eve said to Roarke. "You're going to need to go back to work."

"Back to?"

"To the buying-controlling-interest-of-the-known-universe-one-sector-at-a-time work. He's not going to move on me if I'm in lockstep with you, or you," she said to Peabody, "or anyone else. We have to give him a little room. If he knows my routines, then he knows I generally travel to and from Central solo, that I might do a follow-up after shift on my own. We need to crack the window for him."

"Giving the appearance I've gone back to business, so to speak, is easy enough," Roarke replied. His tone was even, almost casual. But Eve heard the steel under it. "But as long as that window's cracked I'll be an active member of this team. This is not," he continued, and addressed himself to the commander now, "simply a matter of me insisting on having some part in protecting the lieutenant. This man has taken three of my people, and one is already dead. It won't be back to business for me until he's apprehended — or as dead as Sarifina York."

"Understood. Lieutenant, it was your choice to bring the civilian on board. Unless you feel his particular talents and expertise are no longer useful, I believe he should remain active."

"You can't stick too close," Eve began. "If he senses you're concerned for my safety, he could pull back. So make the appearance a good one."

"Not a problem."

280

"We keep working it, no dramatic shifts in the routine. But we split some of the legwork and interviews."

"And you go, wherever you go," Whitney ordered, "wired."

"Yes, sir. I'm going to set that up with Feeney. I'll need a homer for my vehicle, and —"

"Already done," Roarke said, then smiled serenely when she turned on him. "You agreed to that action earlier."

True, she thought, but she hadn't expected him to take it on himself before she'd officially cleared it. Which, she had to admit, was stupid. That's exactly what she should've expected. "Yeah, I did."

"You'll wear a vest," Mira told her.

"A woman after my own heart," Roarke murmured, and his smile spread at the annoyance on Eve's face.

"A vest's overkill. His pattern —"

"He's breaking pattern with you," Mira reminded her. "A vest ensures your safety and success, should he try to stun or injure you in order to incapacitate you. He's intelligent enough to know he needs a physical advantage with you."

"Wear the vest." Whitney's voice was clipped. "Set up the electronics with Feeney. I want to know where you are, from this point on, at all times. When you're in the field, in your vehicle, on the street for any reason, so is a shadow team. It's not just a matter of keeping one of my people safe, Lieutenant," he told her, "it's a matter of slamming that window shut, the minute he comes through it. Work it out, relay the details."

"Yes, sir."

"Dismissed."

Roarke ran his fingers down her arm as they headed for the glide down. "A vest isn't a punishment, darling."

"You wear one for a couple hours, then say that. And no 'darling' on shift."

"You can call me darling anytime," Peabody told him, and made him grin.

"I've a few arrangements to make. I'll see you back in the war room." He started to split off from them. "Later, darling. I was talking to Peabody," he said when Eve bared her teeth.

CHAPTER
SIXTEEN

It didn't take long for Roarke to make arrangements. In the end, however, it would be more than the appearance he was tending to his own organization. He'd have to put in some time on just that, once he could get to his home office, juggling deals and finance with murder.

But for now he headed back to the war room to keep the various balls of his e-work in the air. He caught sight of Eve coming from the direction of her office. With a few yards between them, he watched her — long, quick strides. Places to go, he thought, murderers to catch.

He stopped off, grabbing a bottle of water for both of them, then walked in.

She'd gone to Feeney's station. The cop Feeney was working with — the detail-minded young Newkirk's father, Roarke remembered — nodded, and gathering a few discs, shifted to another area.

So she wanted a direct with Feeney, Roarke concluded. He went to his own station to work on a problem, and to study their dynamics.

He could see Feeney absorb the information, see Feeney's eyes narrow in consideration. And the faintest frown of concern. There was some back-and-forth, rapid-fire on Feeney's part, then he scratched his ear, dipped into his pocket. Out came a bag.

It would be nuts, Roarke knew, as Feeney dipped into it, then held it out to Eve.

Taking that as a signal they were now at the thinking through and strategy stage, Roarke rose to walk over and join them.

"Raised his sights considerably," Feeney said to Roarke.

"So it would seem."

Feeney swiveled idly left to right, right to left, in his chair as he spoke. "We can wire her up, no problem there. Could put a camera on her, too. Give us eyes if and when we need them."

"I don't want him spotting a camera," Eve began.

"I have something." Roarke looked at Feeney. "The new generation of the HD Mole. XT-Micro. Most often used lapel-style, but as she's not known for accessorizing it can be easily reconfigured into a button — shirt or jacket. Voice print option. She can activate or deactivate it with any choice of keyword or phrase."

"She's standing right here," Eve pointed out.

"There were a couple bugs in the last generation," Feeney pointed out, easily ignoring Eve.

"Exterminated," Roarke assured him. "It would take care of audio and video, and with the XT model — unless she's going up against top-level security — it wouldn't be detected."

Feeney nodded and munched. "We can go with that. Like to have a look at it first."

284

"I've got one coming in now. I used a multitrack homer on her vehicle, military grade."

In appreciation of the high-level equipment, Feeney let out a low whistle, along with a quick grin. "We sure as hell won't lose her, even if she decides to drive down to Argentina. We'll set up receivers here, and in the mobile. Shadow team can give her five or six blocks."

"What about air?"

"We can mobilize if we have to."

"It's not a bloody coup," Eve muttered. "It's one homicidal old man."

"Who's captured, tortured, and killed twenty-four women."

Eve merely scowled at Roarke. "I think if he goes through the goddamn window, I can take him. You two go ahead and set up all the e-toys you want. But let's remember, it's not just smoking him out. It's getting in. For Rossi and Greenfeld to have a chance, we have to get to them. I have to get inside, let him think he's lured me in. We take him outside his place, there's no guarantee we'll nail down where he's keeping them."

She had their attention now, waited a beat. "I'm not having these two women bleed or starve to death because we're so worried about keeping my skin in place we take him down or put him down before we know where they are. Their safety is paramount. That's a directive from the primary."

Feeney rattled his bag of nuts, held it out to Roarke. "Gil and I boxed in a few locations and individuals worth checking out."

"Peabody and I will take that. That's SOP if he's watching. Give me what you've got. How long before your shiny new toy gets here?" she asked Roarke.

"Should be along in ten or fifteen minutes now."

"Good enough. I'll go dig out the stupid vests." She signaled to Peabody. "Roarke, you're going to have to arrange your own transpo home."

"Understood. Lieutenant, a moment." Roarke walked with her to the door. "I want those women back, safe, as much as you. I also like your skin exactly where it is. We're going to find a way to make all of that work. And that's a directive from the man who loves you. So watch your ass, or I'll be first in line to kick it."

He knew she wouldn't like it, but he needed it, so caught her chin in his hand and kissed her, hard and brief, before walking away.

"Awww." Peabody sighed a little as she hustled out of the war room behind Eve. "That's so sweet."

"Yeah, ass-kickings are sugar in our house. Locker room. Vests."

"Vests? That would be more than one?"

"I wear one, you wear one."

"Aw," Peabody repeated, but it an entirely different tone.

In under forty minutes they were in the garage, vested and wired. Peabody tugged on her jacket. "This makes me look fat, doesn't it? I know it makes me look fat, and I'm still carrying a couple pounds of winter weight."

"We're not trying to distract the son of a bitch with your frosty figure, Peabody."

"Easy for you to say." Shifting, she tried to get a look at her reflection in a side-view mirror. "This damn thing thickens my entire middle, which doesn't need any help in that area. I look like a stump. A tree stump."

"Stumps don't have arms and legs."

"They have branches. But I guess if they have branches, they aren't technically stumps. So what I look like is a stunted tree." She dropped into the passenger seat. "I now have extra motivation for taking this bastard down. He's made me look like a stunted tree."

"Yeah, we're going to fry his ass for that one." Eve pulled out. "Watch for a tail. Activate, Dallas," she said to test the recorder. "You copy?"

"Eyes and ears five-by-five," Feeney responded. "Shadow will hang back, minimum of three blocks."

"Copy that, remaining open while in the field."

They took the former dead wagon rider first. He'd done well for himself, Eve mused. Had a dignified old brownstone all to himself in a quiet West Village neighborhood.

A droid answered the door — a stupendously designed female Eve would have gauged as more usual in the sexual gratification department than the domestic. Smoky eyes, smoky voice, smoky hair, all in a snug black skin-suit.

"If you'd like to wait in the foyer, I'll tell Mr. Dobbins you're here." She walked off — more slinked off, Eve thought, like a lithe and predatory feline.

"If all she does is vacuum around here," Peabody commented, "I'm a size two."

"She may vacuum, after she polishes the old man's brass."

"Women are so crude," Roarke said in her ear.

"Mute the chatter." Eve studied the foyer.

More of a wide hallway, she noted, with the light coming in through the front door's ornate glass panel. Doors on either side, kitchen area probably in the back. Bedrooms upstairs.

A lot of room for a man to shuffle around in.

He did just that, shuffled in on bunged-up slippers. He wore baggy sweats, and had his near-shoulder-length hair combed back and dyed a hard and improbable black.

His face was too thin, his mouth too full, his body too slight to be the man both Trina and Loni had spoken with.

"Mr. Dobbins."

"That's right. I want to see some identification, or you're both turning right back around."

He studied Eve's badge, then Peabody's, his mouth moving silently as he read. "All right then, what's this about?"

"We're investigating the murder of a woman in Chelsea," Eve began.

"That Groom business." Dobbins wagged a finger. "I read the papers, I watch the news, don't I? If you people did your jobs and protected people you wouldn't have to come around here asking me questions. Cops come around here years ago when that girl across the street was murdered."

"Did you know her, Mr. Dobbins? The girl who was murdered nine years ago?"

"Saw her coming and going, didn't I? Never spoke to her. Saw this new one's picture on screen. Never spoke to her, either."

"Did you ever see this new girl?" Eve asked.

"On the screen, didn't I just say? Don't get up to Chelsea. Got what I need right here, don't I?"

"I'm sure you do. Mr. Dobbins, your father drove a morgue truck during the Urban Wars?"

"Dead wagon. I rode with him most days. Loaded up corpses right, left, and sideways. Got a live one now and again somebody took for dead. I want to sit down."

He simply turned around and shuffled through the doorway to the right. After exchanging glances, Eve and Peabody followed.

The living area was stuffed with worn furniture. The walls might once have been some variation of white, but were now the dingy yellow of bad teeth.

Dobbins sat, took a cigarette from a tarnished silver tray, and lighted it. "A man can still smoke in his own damn house. You people haven't taken that away. A man's home is his damn castle."

"You have a lovely home, Mr. Dobbins," Peabody commented. "I love the brownstones in this area. We're lucky so many of them survived the Urbans. That must've been a terrible time."

"Not so bad. Got through it. Toughened me up, too." He jabbed the air with the cigarette as if to prove it. "Seen more by the time I was twenty than most see in a hundred twenty."

"I can't even imagine. Is it true that there were so many dead in some areas, the only way to keep a record of them was to write an identification number right on the bodies?"

"That's the way it was." He blew out a stream of smoke, shook his finger. "Looters get to them first, they'd take everything, strip them right down. I'd write the sector we found them on the body so we could keep track. Haul them in, and the dead house doc would write the number after that, record it in a book. Waste of time mostly. Just meat by then anyway."

"Do you keep in touch with anybody from back then? People who worked like you did, or the doctors, the medics?"

"What for? They find out you've got a little money, they just want a handout." He shrugged it off. "Saw Earl Wallace a few years back. He'd ride shotgun on the wagon sometimes. Stirred myself to go to Doc Yumecki's funeral, I guess five, six years back. Paid my respects. He was worth respecting, and there aren't many. Gave him a nice send-off. Grandson did it. Waked him in the parlor instead of the main house, but it was a nice send-off all the same."

"Would you know how to reach Mr. Wallace, or Dr. Yumecki's grandson?"

"How the hell should I know? I check the obits. I see somebody I know who's worth the time, I go to their send-off. Said we would back then, so I do."

"What did you say back then?" Eve prompted.

"Dead everywhere." His eyes blurred, and Eve imagined he could see it — still see it. "No send-off. Ya burned them up, or you buried them, and mostly with company, you could say. So, those of us that carted them in, ID'd and disposed, we said how when it was our time, we'd have a send-off, and those of us still living and able would come. So that's what I do."

"Who else does it? From the Urbans?"

Dobbins took one more drag. "Don't remember names. See a few now and again."

"How about this one?" Eve took out the sketch. "Have you seen this man?"

"No. Looks a little bit like Taker maybe. A little."

"Taker?"

"We picked up the bodies, dropped them off. He took them, so he was Taker. Went to his send-off twenty years back, maybe more. Big one for Taker." He sucked wetly on the cigarette. "Good food. Long time dead."

Out in the car again, Eve sat a moment to think. "Could be an act — bitter, slightly tipped old man. But that's reaching."

"He could've worn a disguise when Trina saw him."

"Could've," Eve agreed, "but I'd say Trina would have spotted any major face work. It's what she does. Let's run down the two names he remembered."

Her next stop was a Hugh Klok off Washington Square Park. The victim Dobbins had seen "coming and going" had been dumped there. Gil Newkirk's notes stated that Klok had been questioned, as were the other neighbors. Klok was listed as an antiquities dealer who had purchased and renovated the property several years before the murders.

He was listed as cooperative and unilluminating.

Antiquities turned a good profit if you knew what you were doing. Eve assumed Klok did as the property was impressive. What had originally been a pair of town houses had been merged into one large home, set back from the street by a wide courtyard.

"Pretty spruce," Peabody commented as they approached the courtyard's ornamental iron gate.

Eve pressed the button on the gate and was momentarily ordered by a computerized voice to state her business.

"Police. We'd like to speak with Mr. Hugh Klok." She held up her badge for scanning.

Mr. Klok is not in residence at this time. You may leave your message at this security point or — if you choose — pass through and leave same with a member of the household staff.

"Option two. Might as well get a closer look," she said to Peabody.

The gate chinked open. They crossed the bricked courtyard, climbed a short flight of steps to the main level. The door opened immediately. This, too, was a droid, but fashioned to represent a dignified middle-aged man.

"I'm authorized to take your message for Mr. Klok."

"Where's Mr. Klok?"

"Mr. Klok is away on business."

"Where?"

"I'm not authorized to relay that information. If this is an emergency or the business you have with him of great import, I will contact Mr. Klok immediately so that he can, in turn, contact you. He is, however, expected home within the next day or two."

Behind the dignified droid was a large, dignified entrance hall. And surrounding it Eve sensed a great deal of uninhabited space. "Tell Mr. Klok to contact Lieutenant Eve Dallas, NYPSD, Cop Central, upon his return."

"Of course."

"How long has he been gone?"

"Mr. Klok has been out of residence these past two weeks."

"Does Mr. Klok live alone?"

"He does."

"Any houseguests in his absence?"

"There are no guests in residence."

"Okay." She'd have preferred to get inside, snoop around a little. But without warrant or cause, there was no legal way past the threshold.

She left the Klok house for a bustling section of Little Italy.

One of the victims had been a waitress in a restaurant owned by Tomas Pella. Pella had served on the Home Force during the Urbans, and in them had lost a brother, a sister, and his bride of two months. His young, doomed wife had served as a medic.

He'd never remarried, had instead opened and owned three successful restaurants before selling out eight years before.

"Reclusive, according to Newkirk's notes," Eve said. "Also listed as hot-tempered and angry."

293

He lived in a trim whitewashed home within shouting distance of bakeries, markets, cafés.

When she was greeted for the third time by a droid — female again, but of the comfortable domestic style — Eve concluded that men of that generation preferred electronic to human.

"Lieutenant Dallas, Detective Peabody. We'd like to speak to Mr. Tomas Pella."

"I'm sorry, Mr. Pella is very ill."

"Oh, yeah? How's that?"

"I'm afraid I can't discuss his medical condition with you without his authorization. Is there any other way I can be of help?"

"Is he lucid? Conscious? Able to speak?"

"Yes, but he requires rest and quiet."

Droids were tougher than humans on some levels, but could still be bullied and intimidated. "I require an interview with him." Eve tapped her badge, kept her eyes keen and level. "I think it would disturb his rest and quiet a great deal more if I had to get a warrant and bring police medicals in here to evaluate his condition. Is there a medical with him?"

"Yes. There's a medical with him at all times."

"Then inform the medical that if Mr. Pella is awake and lucid, we need to speak with him. Got that?"

"Yes, of course." She stepped back, shutting the door behind them before going to a house 'link. "If Mr. Pella is able, there are two police officers here who insist on speaking to him. Yes, I'll wait."

The domestic glanced back at Eve and looked as intimidated as a droid could manage.

The entrance boasted soaring ceilings, and was elegantly if sparely furnished. The staircase was directly to the left, a straight, sleek line, the treads were highly polished wood with a faded red runner climbing their center. The chandelier was three tiers of blown glass in shades of pale, delicate blue.

She wandered a few feet farther to glance to the right, into a formal parlor. Photographs lined the creamy white mantel, and from the style of dress worn in them, she judged them to be a gallery of Pella's dead. Parents, siblings, the pretty and forever young face of his wife.

Third man on the list, she thought, and it could be said — in this case — that Pella occupied a house of the dead.

"If you'd come with me?" The droid folded her hands neatly at her waist. "Mr. Pella will see you, but his medical requests you make your visit as brief as possible."

When Eve didn't answer, the droid simply turned and started up the steps. They creaked softly, Eve noted. Little moans and groans of age. At the top was a landing, which split right and left. The droid walked to the right, and stopped at the first door.

It would, Eve thought, overlook the street and the bustle of life outside.

It wasn't life she sensed when they stepped inside. If this was a house of the dead, this was its master chamber.

The bed was enormous, canopied, with head- and footboards deeply carved with what she supposed were cherubs on the wing. The light was dim, drapes drawn fully across the tall windows.

The man in bed was ghostly pale, propped against white pillows. An oxygen breather was fixed over his face, and above it his eyes were almost colorless and full of bitter rage.

"What do you want?"

For a sick man, his voice was strong enough, though the breather made it raspy. Fueled, perhaps, by what Eve saw in his eyes.

"Sir." The medical was female, sturdy and competent. "You mustn't upset yourself."

"Go to hell." He tossed it off like a shrug. "And get out."

"Sir."

"Out. I'm still in charge around here. You get out. And you." He pointed a finger that shook slightly at Eve. "What do you want?"

"We're investigating the murder of a woman whose body was found in East River Park."

"The Groom. Back again. I was a groom once."

"So I hear." She stepped closer to the bed. She couldn't insist he remove the breather, and with that and the poor light, his features were difficult to distinguish. But she saw his hair was white, his face round. She would have said somewhat doughy — and thought: steroids. "You're aware she was killed in the same way Anise Waters, who worked for you, was killed nine years ago."

"Nine years. A fingersnap of time, or a life sentence. Depends, doesn't it?"

296

"Time's relative?" she asked, watching those eyes.

"Time's a son of a bitch. You'll find out."

"Eventually."

"You cops looked me over nine years ago. Now you're back to do the same? Well, take a look."

"When's the last time you were out of bed?"

"I can get up whenever I damn well please." There was frustrated insult in his voice as he shifted to sit up straighter. "Can't get very far, but I can damn well get up. You thinking I got up and killed that girl. Grabbed myself a couple others?"

"You're well informed, Mr. Pella."

"What the hell else do I have to do all damn day but watch the screen." He jerked his chin toward the one on the wall opposite the bed. "I know who you are. Roarke's cop."

"Is that a problem for you?"

He grinned, his teeth showing through the breather.

"How about him." Eve pulled out the sketch. "Do you know who he is?"

He glanced toward the sketch in a way that told Eve he was ready to dismiss it all. Then she saw something come into his eyes, saw something pass in and out in that beat where he really looked at the face. "Who is he?"

"Guy who likes to kill women, be my guess." That hard resistance was back on his face, the *screw you* expression. "From where I'm sitting, that would be your problem, not mine."

"I can do a lot to make it your problem, too. Do you like brunettes, Mr. Pella?"

"I don't have time for women. They don't listen to you. Die on you."

"You served on the Home Force during the Urbans."

"Killed men, women, too. But they called it heroic. She was busy saving lives when they killed her. Somebody probably said that was heroic. None of it was. Killing's killing, and you never get it out of your head."

"Did you identify her body?"

"I'm not talking about that anymore. You don't talk about Therese anymore."

"Are you dying, Mr. Pella?"

"Everyone's dying." He grinned again. "Some of us are just closer to finishing it than others."

"What's finishing you?"

"Tumor. Beat it back, been beating it back for ten years. This time they say it's going to beat me. We'll see about that."

"Any objection to my partner and me looking around while we're here?"

"You want to run tame in my house?" He pushed himself up a little. "This isn't the Urbans, Roarke's Cop, where your kind can do as they damn please. And this is still the United States of goddamn America. You want to search my house? You get a warrant. Now get out."

Eve stood outside, hands on hips, studying Pella's house. In moments she saw the bedroom drapes twitch, then quickly settle.

"Tough son of a bitch," Eve commented.

298

"Yeah, but is he tough enough?"

"I bet he is. If killing's what he wanted, killing's what he'd do. There's the groom angle, the lost love. Why should these women live, be happy, young, when he lost his wife? Soldier during the Urbans. Knows how to kill, and he strikes me as a man with plenty of anger, and a lot of control — when he wants to use it."

"The sick room, the breather," Peabody considered. "Could be an act."

"Could be, but he has to know we could find that out. Of course, if he is dying, that's just one more check in the plus column. And no judge is going to give us a warrant with what we have to search the home of a dying, bedridden old man.

"Dallas, mute off. Feeney, you copy?"

"Read you."

"Let's put a couple of uniforms on this place. Surveillance goggles. Pella doesn't give me the full buzz, but there's a minor tingle happening. He knows something about something, and the face in that sketch triggered it."

"Done."

"Shadow pick up on any tail?"

"Nada."

"Yeah, me either. I'm going to drop Peabody by her place, head home myself. I'll be working from there. Dallas out."

"Home sweet home?"

"Home where you can start digging up data on Pella's dead wife. Details, all you can find. I can wrangle clearance to search his medicals. Take a closer look at Dobbins, too."

"Looks like I'm not getting laid again tonight."

Eve ignored her. "I'll take another glance at the currently unavailable Hugh Klok. Guy's into antiquities and that says travel to me. Let's see if any of these guys frequents the opera. Roarke can take a closer look at their real estate. Maybe the houses mean something. I want blueprints in any case."

She pulled away from the curb, hoping to sense someone watching, someone sliding through the traffic behind her. But all she felt was the crowded streets, and the sluggish push of vehicles that had turned the earlier snow into dismal mush.

CHAPTER
SEVENTEEN

"Locked in," Eve said when the gates of home closed behind her. "Eyes and ears off. Dallas out." No ugly mush and slush here, she thought. The snow spread, pure and pristine, over the grounds, draped heavy as wet fur on the trees so that the great house rose like the powerful focal point of a winter painting. And like a painting, now that the frigid March wind had died, it all stood utterly still.

She left the car, and even moving through winter's irritable bite, she had the thought that maybe Peabody was right. Maybe spring was edging closer.

As she entered the house Summerset oozed into the foyer with the fat Galahad shadowing him.

"I'm to tell you that Roarke will be somewhat late. It seems he has considerable business of his own to deal with as he's been spending so much of his time entrenched in yours."

"His choice, Scarecrow." She tossed her coat over the newel.

"There's blood on your pants."

She glanced down. She'd nearly forgotten the bite. Little thieving bastard. "It's dry."

301

"Then you won't drip on the floor," he said equably. "Mavis wishes you to know she wasn't able to pinpoint the hairpiece, but she and Trina believe they may have narrowed the brand of body cream down to three choices. The information is on your desk."

Eve climbed two steps, partly because she just wanted to get the hell upstairs, and partly because it allowed her to look down on him. "They're gone?"

"Since midday. Leonardo returned. I arranged for their transportation home, where Trina will be staying with them until this matter is resolved."

"Good. Fine." She went up two more stairs, then stopped. He was a righteous pain in her ass most of the time, but she'd heard the concern in his voice. Whatever his numerous flaws — and don't get her started — he had a big, gooey soft spot for Mavis.

"They've got nothing to worry about," she said, looking straight into his eyes. "They're clear of this."

He only nodded, and Eve continued upstairs. Galahad trotted up after her.

She went to the bedroom, but only glanced at the big, gorgeous bed. If she went down, she knew she'd stay down, and that wasn't the answer. Instead, she stripped, placing her weapon — and the clutch piece she'd strapped onto her ankle that afternoon — her badge, electronics on the dresser, then pulled on a tank and shorts.

She started to pick at the bandage on her calf, then ordered herself to stop. If she looked at the wound, the stupid thing would start hurting again.

302

What she needed was a good, strong workout where she could empty her mind and push her body awake.

Galahad obviously had other ideas on how to use his time and was already curled up dead center of the bed. "See, that's why you're fat," she told him. "Eat, sleep, maybe prowl around a little, then eat and sleep some more. I oughta get Roarke to put a pet treadmill downstairs. Work some of that pudge off you."

To show his opinion of the suggestion, Galahad yawned hugely, then closed his eyes.

"Sure, go ahead. Ignore me." She stepped into the elevator, went down to the gym.

She did a two-mile run, using her favored shoreline setting. She had the texture of sand under her feet, the smell of the sea around her, the sight and sound of waves rolling, receding.

Between the effort and the ambiance, she finished the run in a kind of trance, then switched to weights. Sweaty, satisfied, she ended the session with some flexibility training before she hit the shower.

Okay, maybe the bite on her leg throbbed a little in protest, but it was still better than a nap, she assured herself. Though she had to admit the cat snoring on the bed looked pretty damn happy. She pulled on loose pants, a black sweatshirt she noticed with baffled surprise was cashmere, thick socks. With her file bag in tow, she went from bedroom to office.

She programmed a full pot of coffee, and drank the first cup while updating, then circling and studying her murder boards. She paused, looked into the eyes of the killer Yancy had sketched.

"Did you come home to die? Ted, Ed, Edward, Edwin? Is it all about timing and circles and death? Has it all been your own personal opera?"

She circled again, studying each victim's face. "You chose them, used them. Cast them away. But they all represent someone. Who is that? Who was she to you? Mother, lover, sister, daughter? Did she betray you? Leave you? Reject you?"

She remembered something Pella had said, and frowned.

"Die on you? More than that? Was she taken, killed? Is this a recreation of her death?"

She studied her own face, the ID print she'd pinned up. And what did he see when he looked at it? she wondered. Not just another victim this time, but an opponent. That was new, wasn't it? Hunting the hunter.

The grand finale. Yes, Mira could be right about that. The twist at the end of the show. Applause, applause, and curtain.

She poured out a second cup of coffee, sat to prop her feet on her desk. Maybe not just an opera fan. A performer? Frustrated performer or composer . . .

The performer didn't fit profile, she decided. It would involve a lot of training, a lot of teamwork. Taking direction. No, that wasn't his style.

A composer, could be. Most people who wrote anything worked alone a lot of the time. Taking charge of the words or the music.

"Computer, working with all current data, run probability series as follows. What is the probability the perpetrator has returned to New York, has targeted

304

Dallas, Lieutenant Eve, in a desire to complete what he may consider his work?

"What is the probability that desire is fostered by his knowledge of his own death, or plans to self-terminate?

"What is the probability, given his use of opera houses for false addresses, he is or was involved in opera as a profession?

"What is the probability, given the timelines of the perpetrator's sprees and subsequent rest periods, he utilizes chemicals to suppress or release his urge to kill?"

Acknowledged.

"Hold it. I'm still thinking. What is the probability the victims represent a person connected to the perpetrator who was, at some time, tortured and killed by methods he now employs? Begin run."

Acknowledged. Working . . .

"You do that." Leaning back, Eve sipped coffee, closed her eyes.

She let it filter in, chewed on it awhile, used the results to formulate other runs. Then she simply sat and let it all simmer in her head.

When Roarke stepped in, she had her boots on the desk, ankles crossed. There was a coffee mug in her hand. Her eyes were closed, her face blank. The cat padded in behind him and arrowed straight for the sleep chair, lest someone get there first. Then he sprawled out, as if exhausted by the walk from nap to nap.

Roarke started across the room, then stopped dead in front of the murder board. If someone had slammed a steel bat into his chest it would've been less of a jolt than seeing Eve's face on that board, among the dead and missing.

He lost his breath. It simply left his body as he imagined life would if he lost her. Then it came back, blown through him by sheer rage. His hands clenched at his sides, hard balls of violence. He could see them punching through the face of the man who saw Eve as a victim, as some sort of grand prize in his collection. What he felt, literally, was the connection of those fists to flesh, to bone and blood, not to empty paper and ink.

And he reveled in the raw phantom pain in his knuckles.

She didn't belong there. Would never belong there, in that hideous gallery of death.

Yet she had put herself there, he realized. Had put her image among the others. Steely-minded, he thought now. His cop, his wife, his world. Coolheadedly, cool-bloodedly aligning the facts and data, even when her own life was part of them.

He ordered himself to calm, to understand why she'd put herself there. She needed to see the whole picture, and seeing the whole picture would shut it down.

He looked away from the board and over to her. She was exactly as she'd been when he entered. Kicked back, still — and safe.

He went to her, realized some of the rage and fear was still with him when he wanted to simply pluck her up, wrap himself around her, and hold on. And on.

Instead he reached down to take the mug out of her hand.

"Get your own coffee," she muttered, and opened her eyes.

Not asleep, he realized, but in the zone. "My mistake. I thought you were sleeping on the job."

"Thinking time, pal. Didn't hear you come in. How's it going?"

"Well enough. I grabbed a swim and a shower to delude myself that I was still feeling human."

"Yeah, I went the beach run and iron pumping route. Mostly works. I've been doing probabilities and some data juggling. I need to write up a report, then do some runs. When —"

"I want ten minutes," he interrupted.

"Huh?"

"Ten minutes." He took the coffee now, set it aside, then captured her hand to pull her out of the chair. "Where it's just you, just me."

She cocked up her eyebrows as he drew her away from the desk. "Ten minutes isn't anything to brag about, ace."

"I'm not meaning sex." He slid his arms around her, kept moving in what she now understood was a slow and easy dance. "Or not precisely that. I want ten minutes of you," he repeated, lowering his brow to hers. "Just that, without anything or anyone."

She drew in a breath, and smelled the shower on him. That lingering scent of soap on his skin. "It already feels good." She touched her lips to his, angled her head. "Tastes good, too."

He skimmed a finger down the dent in her chin, brushed his lips on hers. "So it does. And there's this spot I know." He used his finger to turn her head slightly, then laid his lips along her jawline, just below her ear. "Just exactly there. It's perfect."

"That one spot?"

"Well now, there are others, but that's a particular favorite of mine."

She smiled, then rested her head on his shoulder — a favorite spot of hers — and let him guide her through the easy dance. "Roarke."

"Mmm?"

"Nothing. It just feels good to say it."

His hand stroked up and down her back. "Eve," he said. "You're right again. It does. I love you. There's nothing that feels more perfect than that."

"Hearing it's not bad. Knowing it's the best." She lifted her head, met his lips again. "I love you."

They held on, and they ended the dance as they'd begun. With his brow resting against hers. "There, now," he murmured. "That's better." He drew back, then lifted her hands to his lips.

He had a way, just that way, of making her insides curl. His lips warm on her skin, and those wild blue eyes looking over their joined hands into hers made her wish she had a hundred ten minutes just to be. As long as he could just be along with her.

"It's pretty damn good," she told him.

"Why don't I get us a meal," he suggested, "and you can tell me about those probabilities."

"I'll get it. It's got to be my turn by now. You can go ahead and look them over if you want."

She stepped back, turned. And saw, as she realized now he would have seen, her photo on the board. "Oh, Jesus. Jesus." Appalled, she gripped a handful of her own hair and tugged. "Listen, this was stupid. I'm stupid. I only put this up there to —"

"Don't call yourself stupid, for you're far from it most of the time." His tone was cool and even. "I'm more than happy to let you know when you are stupid. It's not a problem for me."

"Yeah, you've made that clear in the past. But this was just so —"

She broke off again when he held up a hand. "You put yourself there because you have to be objective, and more — you have to be able to see yourself as he does. Not only as you are, but as he sees you. If you don't, you may be careless."

"Okay, yeah." She slid her hands into her pockets. "Got it in one. Are you okay with this?"

"Does it help you if I'm not okay with it? Obviously not. So I'll deal with it. And I'll kill him if he hurts you."

"Hey, hey."

"I'm not meaning the garden variety of bumps, bruises, and occasional bites," he added with a glance at her leg, "you seem to incur on an alarmingly regular basis."

"I hold my own," she snapped back, oddly insulted. "And you've taken some hits yourself, pal." Her eyes

309

narrowed when he held up a finger. "Oh, I really hate when you do that."

"Pity. If he manages to get past your guard, past me, and all the rest, and causes you real harm, I'll do him with my own hands and in my own way. You'll have to be okay with that, as that's as much who and what I am and it's who and what you are that put your own face up there."

"He won't get past my guard."

"Then we won't have a problem, will we? What's for dinner?"

She wanted to argue, but she couldn't find any room to maneuver. So she shrugged and stalked off toward the kitchen. "I want carbs."

The man was exasperating. One minute he was kissing her hand in the sort of quietly romantic gesture that turned her to putty, and the next he was telling her he'd do murder in that calm, cool voice that was scarier than a blaster to the temple.

And the hell of it was, she thought as the cat bumped his head against her leg, he meant both those things absolutely. Hell, he *was* both of those things absolutely.

She ordered spaghetti and meatballs, leaned back on the counter, and sighed. He might be exasperating, complicated, dangerous, and difficult, but she loved every piece of the puzzle that made him.

She gave the now desperate Galahad a portion from each plate — fair was fair — before carrying them back into the office. She saw he'd correctly interpreted her carbs as spaghetti, and had opened a bottle of red. He sat, sipping, and scanning her comp screen.

310

"Maybe he'll cause you real harm." Eve set the plates on her desk. "Then I'll kill him."

"Works for me. Interesting questions posed here, Lieutenant." As if it were any casual meal — and for them perhaps it was — Roarke expertly wound noodles around his fork. "Interesting percentages."

"Probability's high Mira hit it with the reasons he's come back to New York, and the reason he's targeted me. Also in the high range he's connected to opera professionally. I'm not sure I agree."

"Why?"

"Has to be a lot of work, right? Focus, energy, dedication. And in most cases, a lot of interaction with others. Factor it in, sure," she said, studying the display on-screen, "but when I rolled it around during my thinking time, it doesn't fit for me. He's no team player. My gauge is he likes his quiet time. You could, on some level, call his killings performances, but that's not how I see them. They're more intimate. Just between him and the vic until he's done."

"A duet."

"A duet. Hmm." She rolled that around, too. "Yeah, okay, a duet, I can see that. One man, one woman, the dynamics there, extremely personal. A performance, okay, without an audience, too intimate to share. Because, I think, at some time he was intimately connected to the woman all the rest represent. Yeah. They were a duet."

"And his partner was killed."

"Derailed his train. That's why I think he uses chemicals to rein himself in for long periods — or conversely to free himself for short ones. There, the computer and I agree. So, I look for types of medications that can suppress homicidal urges. And if he's sick, as we're theorizing, he may be taking meds for whatever his condition might be. Do you know Tomas Pella?"

"The name's not familiar, no."

"He seemed to know you."

"I know a great many people."

"And a great many more know you, I get that. He used to own some restaurants in Little Italy. Sold them shortly after the time all this started nine years ago."

"I might have bought them, or one of them. I'll check the records."

"How about Hugh Klok, antiquities dealer. You buy a lot of old stuff."

"Doesn't ring."

"I'll do a run on him. One of the others Newkirk remembered from the prior was this guy who did taxidermy. You know, stuffed dead animals."

"Which always begs the question: Why in the bloody hell?"

"Yeah, what's with that?" Eve slanted her gaze over to Galahad, who'd wandered back in to sit and wash up after his meal. "I mean, would you want . . . you know, when he uses up his nine?"

"Good God, no. Not only, well, creepy would be the word, wouldn't it, for us, but bloody humiliating for him."

"Yeah, that's what I think. I liked the idea of the taxidermy guy for the symbolism. House of death and blah. But he's clear. Lives on Vegas II, and has for four years. Checked out. So anyway, you want the background on these other two, and the third I questioned today, Dobbins?"

"I'm sure it's as much sparkling dinner conversation as the philosophy of taxidermy and dead cats. Go ahead."

Downtown in their apartment, Peabody and McNab worked on dueling computers. Because he worked better with noise and she didn't care, the air blasted with trash rock and revisionist rap. She sat, hunched over, tuning most of it out and picking her way through a complicated search.

He was up and down like a restless puppy, alternately snapping out directives and singing lyrics. She didn't know how anyone could get any work done that way. But she also knew he not only could, he had to.

The remnants of the Chinese delivery they'd ordered were scattered around both their workstations. Peabody was already wishing she'd resisted that last egg roll.

When she finally found the data she was after, tears blurred her eyes. The hot prick of tears warned her she was overtired and her resistance was bottoming out.

"Hey, hey, She-Body!" McNab caught the look on her face. "Music off. Computer, save and pause. What's wrong, honey?"

"It's so sad. It just makes me so sad."

"What does?" He'd already come behind her to pat and rub her shoulders.

It was a pretty good deal, she thought, to have somebody there to pet you when you were shaky. "I found Therese — Therese Di Vecchio Pella. Tomas Pella's wife, one of the guys Dallas and I talked to today."

"Yeah, from Old Newkirk's notes, from the first go-round."

"They got married in April. They were with the Home Force. He was a corporal, she was a medic. And see, look." She tapped the comp screen. "In July she was dispatched to this area, on the edge of SoHo and Tribeca. An explosion, mostly civilian casualties. There was still firing in the sector, but she went in. She was wearing the red cross — the medic symbol. But she got hit by sniper fire when she tried to reach the wounded. She was only twenty. She was trying to help wounded civilians, and they killed her."

She sat back, knuckled away the tears. "I don't know. It just rips me, I guess. You've got to have hope, right, to stop long enough to get married in the middle of all that. And then, you're gone. Trying to help people, and you're gone. She was only twenty."

McNab leaned down, pressed a kiss to the top of her head. "Want me to take this for a while?"

"No. We talked to that old man today. Well, not that old, really, but it seemed like he was older than Moses in that bed, with the breather on. And then I read this, and think how he'd been so young, and he'd loved this girl. Then . . . she's too young."

"I know it's tough, baby, but —"

"No, no. I mean, yeah, it's tough, but she's too young to be the source of the pattern." Tears — and some still clung to her lashes — were forgotten. "She was only twenty, and the youngest vic was twenty-eight. Twenty-eight to thirty-three, that's been his span. So Therese Pella died too young, it most likely eliminates Pella as a suspect."

"You were seriously looking at this guy?"

"He's the right age, the basic type, connection with the Urbans, private home — and can you spell bitter? Got a tumor — or he says — Dallas is checking that. Lost his bride — bride and groom — who was a pretty brunette. But after that it doesn't follow."

Peabody sat back, shaking her head at the data on screen. "Doesn't follow pattern. She's hit by sniper fire, not tortured. She's eight years younger than his youngest vic when she was killed. Misses the profile. But there was something. A tingle, Dallas called it. There was a tingle when we talked to him."

"Maybe he knows something. Maybe he's connected."

"Yeah, maybe. I need to get this to Dallas, then try for deeper data on Pella."

"I'll give you a hand." McNab gave her shoulders another rub, then toyed with the ends of her hair. "Okay now?"

"Yeah. I guess it's not enough sleep and too much on the brain."

"You need to take a break."

"Maybe I do." She knuckled her eyes again, but this time to clear fatigue instead of tears. "If it wasn't so cold out, I'd take a walk, get some air, some exercise."

"I don't know about the air," he said as she rose. "But I can help with the exercise." Grinning, he laid a hand on her ass, gave it a squeeze.

"Yeah?" Her eyes danced; her libido boogied. "You wanna?"

"Let me answer that question by ripping your clothes off."

She let out a laughing squeal as they tumbled to the floor. "I thought, you know, you weren't feeling the bloom and spark."

"Something's blooming just fine," he said as he dragged off her sweater.

She tugged his pants down over his hips to check for herself. Looking down, she said, "I'll say."

"And as for sparkage." He crushed his mouth to hers in a kiss hot enough she envisioned smoke coming out of her ears. "Any more, and we'd torch the place."

She saw his eyes go dreamy when his hand cupped her breast, felt her stomach muscles tighten in response.

"Mmmm, She-body, the most female of females. Let's see what we can light up."

Later, considerably later, Eve studied the data Peabody had sent to her office unit. "She's right," Eve mumbled. "Too young, wrong method. Dobbins hits me as just too sloppy, just too disinterested. Klok's coming across as straight and narrow. But there's something here. I just can't see it yet."

"Maybe you would if you got a decent night's sleep."

Instead, she walked around her boards again. "Opera. What about the opera-tickets angle?"

"I've got the list for season ticket holders for the Met. Nothing on the first cross-check. I'll try others."

"He jumps names, jumps names and ID data. Covert stuff. Smooth, under radar. Where'd he learn how? Torture methods. Covert operations have been known to employ torture methods."

"I can tell you my sources on the matter of torturers isn't popping anyone of this generation still living and in business, or anyone who moonlights by targeting young brunettes."

"It was worth a shot," Eve mused. "Covert might change that. Someone who was in military ops, or paramilitary at one time. He learned the methods somewhere, and developed the skill to manipulate his data."

"Or has the connections or the funds to hire someone to manipulate it," Roarke reminded her.

"Yeah, there's that. So. Why do we torture someone?"

"For information."

"Yeah, at least ostensibly. Why else do you torture? Kicks, sexual deviation, ritual sacrifice."

"Experimentation. Another tried and true rationale for inflicting pain."

She looked at him. "We eliminate the need or desire for information, and the sexual deviation. No doubt in my mind he gets personal gratification from inflicting pain, but it has to be more. Ritual's part of it, but this isn't some sick religious deal or cult. So, experimentation," she repeated. "Fits. Factor in that he's very good at it. Torture skills are specialized. He isn't messy about it, he's precise. Again, where did he learn?"

"And you're back to the Urbans."

"It keeps crossing there. Someone taught him, or he studied. Experimented before the experimentation. But not here, not in New York."

Circling her board, she studied, considered angles. "We ran searches for others before. I did a Missing Persons run on the victim type. But what if he experimented elsewhere? If he purposefully mutilated the bodies to eliminate the correlation, or disposed of them altogether?"

"You're going to do a global search on mutilations and missing persons involving the victim type."

"He might not have been as careful. If we find something . . . he might have left something behind." She stopped, stared at the sketch of the man she hunted. "Still honing his craft, still finding his way. We did globals, but maybe we didn't go back far enough."

"I'll set it up. I can do it faster," he said before she could argue. "Then it'll take a good long while for any results you can actually work with. I'll set it up, then we're getting some sleep."

"All right. Okay."

The dreams came in blurry spurts, as if she were swimming through fog that tore and re-formed, tore and re-formed. The clock ticked incessantly.

Over that endless, echoing tick, she heard the sounds of a battle raging. A firefight, she thought. Blasts and bullets and the wild shouts and calls of the men and women who fought.

She could smell the blood, the smoke, the burning flesh before she could see it. Carnage carried a sickly sweet aroma.

As vision cleared, focused, she saw the battle was on a stage, and the stage was dressed to depict the city in a strange, stylized form. Buildings, all black and silver, were tipped and tilted above hard white streets that jagged into impossible angles or inexplicable dead ends.

And the players on stage were dressed in bright, elaborate costumes that flowed through bloody pools and swirled in dirty smoke as they murdered each other.

She looked down on it all with interest, from her gilded box seat. Below, in a pit where bodies lay twisted, she could see the orchestra madly playing their instruments. Their fingers ran with blood from razor-sharp strings.

On stage, the shouts and calls were songs, she realized, fierce, violent. Vicious.

War could never be otherwise.

"The third act is nearly over."

She turned, looked into the face of the killer as he took a huge stopwatch out of the pocket of his formal black.

"I don't understand. It's all death. Who writes these things?"

"Death, yes. Passion and strength and life. Everything leads to death, doesn't it? Who would know that better than you?"

"Murder's different."

"Oh, yes, it's artful and it's deliberate. It takes it out of the hands of fate and puts the power into the one who creates death. Who makes a gift of it."

"What gift? How is murder a gift?"

"This . . ." He gestured to the stage as a woman, brown hair bloody, face and body battered, was borne in on a stretcher. "This is about immortality."

"Immortality's for the dead. Who was she when she was alive?"

He only smiled. "Time's up." He clicked the stopwatch, and the stage went black.

Eve came rearing up in bed, sucking for air. Caught between the dream and reality, she closed her hands over her ears to muffle the ticking. "Why won't it stop?"

"Eve. Eve. It's your 'link." Roarke curled his fingers over her wrists, gently tugged her hands down. "It's your 'link."

"Jesus. Wait." She shook her head, pulled herself into the now. "Block video," she ordered, then answered. "Dallas."

Dispatch, Dallas, Lieutenant Eve. Report to Union Square Park off Park Avenue. Body of unidentified female, evidence of torture.

Eve turned her head, met Roarke's eyes. "Acknowledged. Notify Peabody, Detective Delia, request Medical Examiner Morris. As per procedure on this matter, relay notification to Commander Whitney and Dr. Mira. I'm on my way. Dallas out."

"I'll be going with you. I know," Roarke said as he rose, "you don't make prime bait with me along, but that'll be Gia Rossi left on the ground. And I'm going with you."

"I'm sorry."

"Ah, Eve." His tone changed, softened. "So am I."

CHAPTER
EIGHTEEN

As Eve had seen their home in its snowy landscape as a painting, Roarke saw the crime scene as a play. A dark play with constant movement and great noise, all centered around the single focal character.

The white sheet on the white snow, the white body laid over it, with deep brown hair shining in the hard lights. He thought the wounds stood out against the pale flesh like screams.

And there his wife stood in her long black coat, gloveless, of course. They'd both forgotten her gloves this time around. Hatless and hard-eyed. The stage manager, he thought, and a major player as well. Director and author of this final act.

There would be pity in her, this he knew, and there would be anger, a ribbon of guilt to tie them all together. But that complicated emotional package was tucked deep inside, walled in behind that cool, calculating mind.

He watched her speak to the sweepers, to the uniforms, to the others who walked on and off that winter stage. Then Peabody, the dependable, in her turtle-shell of a coat and colorful scarf, crossed the stage on cue. Together, she and Eve lowered to that lifeless focal point that held the dispassionate spotlight of center stage.

"Not close enough," McNab said from beside him.

Roarke shifted his attention, very briefly, from the scene to McNab. "What?"

"Just couldn't get close enough." McNab's hands were deep in two of the many pockets of his bright green coat, with the long tails of a boldly striped scarf fluttering down his back. "Moving in on a dozen roads from a dozen damn directions. Moving in, you can feel we're getting closer. But not close enough to help Gia Rossi. It's hard. This one hits hard."

"It does."

Had he really believed, Roarke wondered, a lifetime ago, had he honestly assumed that the nature of the cop was to feel nothing? He'd learned different since Eve. He'd learned very different. And now, he stood silent, listening to the lines as the players played their parts.

"TOD oh-one-thirty. Early Monday morning," Peabody said. "She's been dead a little over twenty-six hours."

"He kept her for a day." Eve studied the carving in the torso. Thirty-nine hours, eight minutes, forty-five seconds. "Kept her a day after he was finished. She didn't last for him. The wounds are less severe, less plentiful than on York. Something went wrong for him this time. He wasn't able to sustain the work."

Less severe, yes, Peabody could see that was true. And still the cuts, the burns and bruising spoke of terrible suffering. "Maybe he got impatient this time. Maybe he needed to go for the kill."

"I don't think so." With her sealed fingers, Eve picked up the victim's arm, turned it to study the ligature marks from the binding. Then turned it back to examine more closely the killing wounds on the wrist. "She didn't fight like York, not as much damage from the ropes, wrists and ankles. And the killing strokes here? Just as clean and precise as all the others. He's still in control. And he still wants them to last."

She laid the arm down again, on the white, white sheet. "It's a matter of pride in his skill — torture, create the pain, but keep them alive. Increasing the level of pain, fear, injury, all while keeping them breathing. But Rossi, she wound down on him ahead of his schedule, ahead of his goal."

"Before he'd have been able to see the media bulletins with his image," Peabody pointed out. "It's not because he panicked, or took his anger out on her."

Eve glanced up. "No. But if he had, she'd still be dead. If he had, we still did what we had to do. Put that away. He started on her Saturday morning, finished early Monday. York Friday night. So he had a little celebration, maybe, or just gets a good night's sleep before he rewinds the clock for Rossi."

Takes time out to shadow me, Eve thought. Another tried and true torture method. Rest and revisit. Time out again to lure and secure Greenfeld. Need your next vic in the goddamn bullpen.

"Cleans her up, takes his time. No rush, no hurry. Already got the dump spot picked out, already surveyed the area. Set up a canvass."

From her crouched position, Eve surveyed the area. "This kind of weather, there aren't going to be a lot of people hanging out in the park. Bides his time," she continued. "Loads her up, transports her here. Carries her in."

"Sweepers have a lot of footprints to work with. The snow was pretty fresh and soft. They'll make the treads, give us a size, a brand."

"Yeah. But he's not worried about that. Smart enough, he's smart enough to wear something oversized, try to throw us off. To wear something common that's next to impossible to pin. When we get him, we'll find them, help hang him with them, but they won't lead us to him."

As dispassionate now as those harsh crime scene lights, Eve examined the body. "She was strong, in top shape." Good specimen? she wondered. Had he thought he'd had a prime candidate for his nasty duet? "She struggled, but not as much as York. Not nearly as hard as York, not as long. Gave out, that's what she did. Physically strong, but something in her shut down. Must've been a big disappointment to him."

"I'm glad she didn't suffer as much. I know," Peabody said when Eve lifted her head. "But if we couldn't save her, I'm glad she didn't suffer as much."

"If she could've held out longer, maybe we could've saved her. And either way you look at it, Peabody, doesn't mean a fucking thing."

She straightened as she spotted Morris coming toward them. In his eyes she saw something that was in her, some of what was in Peabody. She would, Eve thought, see that same complicated mix of anger, despair, guilt, and sorrow in the eyes of every cop involved.

"Gia Rossi," was all Morris said.

"Yes. She's been dead a little more than twenty-six hours by our gauge. A group of kids cutting through the park found her. Mucked up the scene some, but for the most part then just cut and ran. One of them called it in.

"Something went wrong for him with her." Eve looked down at the body again. "He didn't get a lot of time out of her. Maybe she just shut down, or maybe he used something — experimenting — some chemical that shut her down."

"I'll flag the tox as priority. She isn't as damaged as the others."

"No."

"Can she be moved yet?"

"I was about to roll her."

With a nod, he bent to help, and together they rolled the body.

"No injuries on her back," Morris said.

"Most of them don't. He likes face-to-face. It has to be personal. It has to be intimate."

"Some bruising, lacerations, burns, punctures on the back of the shoulders, the calves. Less than the others." Gently, he brushed the hair aside, examined the back of the neck, the scalp, the ears. "In comparison, I'd say he barely got to stage two in this case. Yes, yes, something went wrong. I'll take her in now."

He straightened, met Eve's eyes. "Will there be family?"

He never asked, or so rarely she'd never registered it. "She has a mother in Queens, a father and stepmother out in Illinois. We'll be contacting them."

"Let me know if and when they want to see her. I'll take them through it personally."

"All right."

He looked away, past the lights into the cold dark. "I wish it were spring," he said.

"Yeah, people still end up dead, but it's a nicer atmosphere for the rest of us. And, you know, flowers. They're a nice touch."

He grinned, and some of the shadows around him seemed to lift. "I like daffodils myself. I always think of the trumpet as a really long mouth, and imagine they chatter away at each other in a language we can't hear."

"That's a little scary," she decided.

"Then you don't want to get me started on pansies."

"Really don't. I'll check in with you later. Peabody, get that canvass started." She left Morris, heard him murmur, *All right now, Gia,* then stepped up to Roarke.

"I'm nearly done here," she began. "You should —"

"I won't be going home," Roarke told her. "I'll go in, start working in the war room. I'll take care of getting myself there."

"I'll go on in with you." McNab looked at Eve. "If that's all right with you, Lieutenant."

"Go ahead, and contact the rest of the team. No reason for them to lay around in bed when we're not.

This is a twenty-four/seven op now. I'll work out subteams, twelve-hour shifts. The clock's about to start on Ariel Greenfeld. We're not going to find her like this."

She looked back. "I'm goddamned if we're going to find her like this."

It was still shy of dawn when she got to Central. Before she went to her office, she walked into the war room. As the lights flicked on she looked around. It was quiet now, empty of people. It wouldn't be so again, she thought. Not until they'd closed this down.

She was adding more men, more eyes, ears, legs, hands. More to work the streets, flash the killer's picture, talk to neighbors, street people, cabbies, chemi-heads. More to knock on the doors of the far too numerous buildings Roarke had thus far listed in his search.

More people to push, push, push, to track down every thread no matter how thin and knotted.

Until this was done there was only one investigation, only one killer, only one purpose for her and every cop under her.

She walked to the whiteboard and in her own hand wrote out the time it had taken for Gia Rossi to die after Rossi's name.

Then she looked down at the next name she'd written. Ariel Greenfeld.

"You hold the hell on. It's not over, and it's not going to be over, so you hold the hell on."

She turned, saw Roarke watching her from the doorway. "You made good time," he told her. "McNab and I detoured up to EDD, to requisition more equipment. Feeney's on his way in."

"Good."

He crossed over to stand, as she was, in front of the whiteboard. "It depends, on some level, on her now. On you, on us, certainly on him, but on some level, on her."

"Every hour she holds on, we get closer."

"And every hour she holds on, is another hour he may move on you. You want that. You'd will it to happen if you could."

No bullshit, she decided. No evasions. "That's right."

"When they killed Marlena, all those years ago, broke her to pieces to prove a point to me, I wanted them to come at me."

Eve thought of Summerset's daughter, how she'd been taken, tortured, and killed by rivals of the young, enterprising criminal Roarke had been. "If they had, the whole of them, you'd have ended up in the ground with her."

"That may be. That very likely may be." He shifted his gaze from the board to meet hers. "But I wanted it, and would have willed it if I could have. But since that wasn't to be, I found another way to end every one of them."

"He's only one man. And there may not be another way."

Thinking of those who were lost, he looked at the board again. Only one man, and perhaps only one way.

"That's all very true. Here's what I know, here's what I understood out there in the cold and the dark with you tending to what he'd made of Gia Rossi. He thinks he knows you."

He turned his head now, and those brilliant blue eyes fired into hers. "He thinks he understands what you are, knows who you are. But he's wrong. He doesn't know or understand the likes of you. If it comes to the two of you, even for a moment, if it comes to the two of you, he may get a glimmer of who and what you are. And if he does, he'll know something of fear."

"Well." A little shaken, a little mystified, she blew out a breath. "That's not what I was expecting out of you."

"When I looked at her, at what he'd done to her, I thought I would envision you there. Your face with her face, as it is on your board."

"Roarke —"

"But I didn't," he continued, and lifted his hand to brush his fingers to her cheek. "Couldn't. Not, I think, because it was more than I could stand. Not because of that, but because he'll never have that power or control over you. You won't allow it. And that, Darling Eve, is of considerable comfort to me."

"It's a nice bolster for me, too." She aimed a glance toward the door, just to make sure they were still alone. Then she leaned in, kissed him. "Thanks. I've got to go."

"And if he kills you," Roarke added as she strode to the door, "I'm going to be extremely pissed off."

"Who could blame you?"

330

She started back to her office, stopped when Peabody hailed her. "Baxter and Trueheart are notifying the mother, as ordered. I just spoke with the father."

"All right. When Baxter reports in, we'll clear it for her name to be released to the media."

"Speaking of the media, I poked into your office in case you were there. There's about a half a million messages from various reporters."

"I'll take care of it. Let me know when everyone's in the house. We'll do the briefing asap."

"Will do. Dallas, do you want me to update the boards?"

"I've already done it." She turned away to go to her office.

She flicked through the source readout on the messages, transferring them to the liaison. Only when she came to one from Nadine did she pause, then order playback.

"Dallas, the lines are buzzing you've got another one. It's going to get ugly, so this is a heads up. The spit's already flying and most of it's going to splatter on you and the NYPSD. If you've got anything I can use, get back to me."

Eve considered, then ordered the callback. Nadine picked up on the first beep.

"I thought media darlings slept till noon."

"Sure, just like cops. I'm already in my office," Nadine told her. "Working on some copy. I'm going on at eight. Special report. If you've got anything, now's the time to share."

"A source from the NYPSD stated this morning that new and salient information regarding the individual the media has dubbed The Groom has come to light."

"What new and salient information?"

"However, the source would not divulge any details of this information due to the need to confine any and all such data within the investigation. It was also stated by the same source that the task force formed to pursue the investigation is working around the clock to identify and apprehend the individual responsible for the deaths of Sarifina York and Gia Rossi. As well as to seek justice for them and for the twenty-three other women whose deaths are attributed to this same individual."

"Nice, but there's a lot of spin in there. The media's going to come at you hard. You're going to take hits."

"You really think I give a rat's ass about a few publicity bruises right now, Nadine? Air the statement. What I want is for him to know we're coming, and to worry about what we might have. Don't release Rossi's name until the eight o'clock airing."

"How about this? Will the NYPSD source confirm or deny that the investigation is focused on a specific suspect?"

"The source won't confirm or deny, but stated that members of the task force are seeking or have located and interviewed persons of interest."

"Okay." Nadine nodded as she scribbled. "Still doesn't really say anything, but it sounds like it says something."

"Do you still have your researchers on tap?"

"Sure."

"I may have something for them to play with later. That's it, Nadine. You want the official department statement, go to the liaison."

Eve clicked off, got coffee. Though it annoyed her, she used it to chase an energy pill. Better jumpy than sluggish, she decided, then called up the results from the global search she'd done from home.

As the names began rolling on, she sat back, closed her eyes. Thousands, she thought. Well, what had she expected given the search elements she'd had Roarke input.

So she had to narrow them, refine it.

Her 'link beeped. "Yeah, yeah."

"Team's in the house," Peabody told her.

"I'll be there."

Tired cops, Eve thought when she stepped into the war room. Her team now consisted of tired, frustrated, and pissed off cops. Sometimes, she thought, cops did their best work that way. They'd be running on adrenaline and irritation — and in a lot of cases the boost of energy pills.

No bullshit, she thought again. No evasions.

"We lost her." The room fell instantly silent. "We've got the full resources of the top police and security departments in the country behind us. We've got the experience, the brains, the bullheadedness of every cop in this room. But we lost her. You've got thirty seconds to brood about that, to feel crappy about it, to shoulder the guilt. Then that's done."

She set down her file bag, walked over to get more coffee. When she came back, she took out the copy she'd made of Ariel Greenfeld's photo, pinned it in the center of a fresh board.

"We're not losing her. As of now we're round the clock for the duration. As of now, she's the only victim in this city. As of now, she is the single most important person in our lives. Officer Newkirk?"

"Sir."

"You and the officers you've been working with will take this first twelve-hour shift. You'll be relieved by officers I've assigned at . . ." She checked her wrist unit. "Nineteen hundred. Captain Feeney, I'll use your recommendation for another pair of e-men to take the second shift. Field detectives, I'll have your relief lined up shortly."

"Lieutenant." Trueheart cleared his throat, and Eve could see him fighting the urge to raise his hand. "Detective Baxter and I have worked out a crib rotation. I mean to say we discussed same on the way back from notifying next of kin. With your permission, we'd prefer not to be relieved, but to handle the twenty-four-hour cycle ourselves."

"You need more men," Baxter added, "you get more men. But we don't go off the clock. How about you, Sick Bastard?" He used Jenkinson's nickname.

"We'll sleep when we get him."

"All right," Eve agreed. "We'll try it that way. I've done a global search for mutilations, murders, and missings meeting the targets' descriptions. We concluded in the first investigation that it was likely the killer had killed before, practiced before. I widened the search," she told Feeney, "went global and back five years, and netted thousands of results."

She held up the disc copy of the run, tossed it to Feeney. "We need to whittle it down, refine it. And we need to find one or more that could be his — and find his mistakes.

"Item second," she continued, and worked through her list.

As Eve briefed her team, listened to their reports and coordinated the duties, Ariel Greenfeld came awake. She'd surfaced twice before, barely registering her surroundings before he'd come in. Small room, glass walls, medical equipment? Was she in the hospital?

She struggled to see him clearly, but everything was so blurry. As if her eyes, and her mind, had been smeared with oil. She thought she heard music, high trilling voices. Angels? Was she dead?

Then she'd gone under again, sliding down and down to nothing.

This time when she awoke, the room was larger. It seemed larger to her. The lights were very bright, almost painful to her eyes. She felt weak and queasy, as though she'd been sick a very long time, and again thought, "Hospital."

Had she been in an accident? She couldn't remember, and as she lay still to take stock, felt no pain. She ordered herself to think back, to think back to the last thing she *could* remember.

"Wedding cakes," she murmured.

Mr. Gaines. Mr. Gaines's granddaughter's wedding. She had a chance for the job, a good job, designing and baking the cake, standing as dessert chef for the reception.

Mr. Gaines's house — big, beautiful old house, pretty parlor with a fireplace. Warm and cozy. Yes! She remembered. He'd picked her up, driven her to his house for a meeting with his granddaughter. And then . . .

It wanted to fade on her, but she pushed the fog away. When it cleared, her heart began to hammer. Tea and cookies. The tea, something in the tea. Something in his eyes when she'd tried to stand.

Not the hospital. God, oh God no, she wasn't in the hospital. He'd drugged her tea, and he'd taken her somewhere. She had to get away, had to get away now.

She tried to sit up, but her arms, her legs were pinned. Panicked, sucking back a scream, she pushed up as far as she could. And felt terror run through her like a river.

She was naked, tied, hands and feet, to a table. Some sort of metal table with rope restraints that looped through openings and bit into her skin when she strained against them. As her eyes wheeled around the room she saw monitors, screens, cameras, and tables holding metal trays.

There were sharp things on the trays. Sharp, terrifying things.

As her body began to shake, her mind wanted to deny, to reject. Tears leaked when she twisted and writhed in a desperate attempt to free herself.

The woman in the park. Another woman missing. She'd seen the media reports. Horrible, that's what she'd thought. Isn't that horrible. But then she'd gone off to work without another thought. It didn't have anything to do with her. Just another horrible thing that happened to someone else.

It always happened to someone else.

Until now.

She dragged in her breath, let it out in a scream. She screamed for help until her lungs burned and her throat felt scorched. Then she screamed some more.

Someone had to hear, someone had to come.

But when someone heard, when someone came, fear choked off her screams like a throttling hand.

"Ah, you're awake," he said, and smiled at her.

Eve input the names on the list Roarke had generated of season ticket holders. Her first search requested highlighting males between sixty and eighty years of age.

She'd expand that, if necessary, she thought. He may have created a bogus company for this particular purpose, or any type of persona.

No guarantee he sprang for season tickets, she mused. He could cherry pick the performances that appealed to him rather than just blanket the whole season.

When the amended list came up, she followed through with a standard run on each name.

She was over three-quarters through when she zeroed in.

"There you are," she murmured. "There you are, you bastard. Stewart E. Pierpont this time? 'E' for some form of Edward. Who's Edward to you?"

His hair was salt-and-pepper in the ID photo, worn in a long, dramatic mane. He claimed to be a British citizen, with residences in London, New York, and Monte Carlo. And a widower this time around, Eve noted. That was new.

The deceased wife was listed as Carmen DeWinter, also British, who died at the age of thirty-two.

Eve narrowed her eyes at the date of death. "Urban War era. Maybe you got too damn clever this time, Eddie."

She did a run on DeWinter, Carmen, but found none who matched the data given on the Pierpont ID. "Okay, okay. But there was a woman, wasn't there? She died, was killed, or hey, you took her out yourself. But she existed."

She went back to Pierpont, checked the listed addresses. An opera house in Monte Carlo, a concert hall in London, and Carnegie Hall in New York.

Sticks with his pattern, she thought. But the season tickets were either delivered somewhere, or were picked up.

She grabbed what she had, hustled to the war room, and Roarke's station. "Who do you know at the Metropolitan Opera, and how much grease can you use to clear the way for me?"

"I know a few people. What do you need?"

"Anything and everything on him." She tossed down the printout on Pierpont. "That's him, season-ticket-holder style. Nice call on that, by the way."

"We do what we can."

"Do more. There isn't time for bureaucracy and red tape. I want a clear path to whoever can give me the juice on this guy."

"Give me five minutes," he said, and pulled out his personal 'link.

She stepped away to give him room as her own 'link signaled. "Dallas."

"Might have something," Baxter announced. "On the rings. We've been working it, and I think we've nailed where he bought them. Tiffany's — gotta go with the classic."

"I thought we checked there before."

"Did, nobody remembered, no rings of that specific style carried. We decided to give it another push. Classic style, classic store. And while they're not flashy, they are sterling. We're trolling the clerks, batting zero, then this woman overhears. A customer. She remembers being in there right before Christmas and noticing this guy buying four sterling bands. Commented on it, and the guy gives her a line about his four granddaughters. She thought it was charming, so she remembers it. Turns out, when we get the manager to dig a little, they carried a limited supply of that style late last year."

"Record of the sale."

"Cash, four sterling accent bands, purchased December eighteenth. The wit's a peach, Dallas. Said she 'engaged him in conversation.' I get the feeling she was trying to hit on him, and she said she complimented him on his scent, asked what it was. Alimar Botanicals."

"Trina's got a damn good nose. That's one of her picks."

"Better yet, he mentioned he'd first discovered it in Paris, and had been pleased to find it was carried here in New York, in a spa boutique on Madison, with a downtown branch. Place called Bliss. He scoped Trina in the downtown salon."

"Yeah, that's the spot. See if your wit will work with Yancy."

"Already asked and answered. She'd be, quote, 'tickled pink.' A peach, Dallas, with eyes like a hawk. She saw a photo in his wallet when he took out the cash. She said it was an old photo, took her back to her own youth. A lovely brunette. She thinks she can give Yancy something to work with there, too."

"That's good work, Baxter. That's damn good work. Bring your peach in. Dallas out. It's moving for us." Her eyes were hard and bright as she turned back to Roarke. "It's moving now."

"Jessica Forman Rice Abercrombie Charters." Roarke tossed Eve a memo cube. "Chairman of the Board. She'll be happy to speak with you. She's at home this morning. If she can't help you, she'll find the person who can."

"You're a handy guy."

"In many, many ways."

The smile felt good on her face. It felt powerful. "Peabody, with me."

CHAPTER
NINETEEN

Jessica with the many last names lived in a three-story apartment the size of Hoboken. The sprawling living area was highlighted by a window wall that afforded a panoramic view of the East River.

On a clear day, Eve calculated, you could stand at the clear wall and see clear to Rikers.

The lady had furnished the place to suit herself, mixing the very old with the ultra-new, with the result an eclectic and surprisingly appealing style. Eve and Peabody sat on the thick cushions of a sofa done in murderous red while their hostess poured tea from a white pot scattered with pink rosebuds into distressingly delicate cups.

The tea and a plate of paper-thin cookies had been brought in by a smartly dressed woman with the build of a toothpick.

"We have met a time or two," Jessica began.

"Yes, I remember." Now that she had the face, Eve did remember. The woman was a trim and carefully turned-out eighty-something with short, softly waved hair of deep gold around a sharp-featured face. Her mouth, long and animated, was painted petal pink, and her eyes — thickly lashed — a deep river green.

"You wear Leonardo."

"Only if he washes up first."

Jessica giggled, an appealing sound of eternal youth. "One of my granddaughters is mad for his designs. Won't wear anyone else. He suits her, as he does you. I believe people should always choose what suits them."

When she passed Eve the tea, Eve had to resist commenting that coffee in a good, sturdy mug suited her.

"We appreciate you giving us your time, Ms. Charters."

"Jessica, please." She offered Peabody a cup and a flashing smile. "Indulge me just one moment. Could I ask, when the two of you interrogate — oh, wait, the term's 'interview' these days — when you interview a suspect, do you ever rough them up?"

"We don't have to," Peabody told her. "The lieutenant scares confessions out of them."

The giggle rang again. "What I wouldn't give to watch that! I just love police dramas. I'm always trying to imagine myself the culprit, and how I'd stand up under interviews. I desperately wanted to kill my third husband, you see."

"It's a good impulse to resist," Eve commented.

"Yes." Jessica smiled her flower petal smile. "It would've been satisfying, but messy. Then again, divorce is rarely much tidier. Now, I'm wasting your time. How can I help you?"

"Stewart E. Pierpont."

Jessica's eyebrows quirked. "Yes, yes, I know that name. Has he done something murderous?"

"We're very interested in speaking to him. We're having a little trouble locating him."

Though mild confusion was evident on Jessica's face, her tone remained absolutely pleasant. "His address would be on file. I'll have Lyle look it up for you."

"The address he's listed doesn't jibe. Unless they're taking tenants at the Royal Opera House or Carnegie Hall."

"*Really?*" Jessica drew out the word, and now came a quick and avid light to her eyes. "Well, well, well. I should have known."

"How and what should you have known?"

"A very odd duck, Mr. Pierpont. He's attended a few galas and events over the years. Not particularly sociable and not at all philanthropic. I could never wheedle donations out of him, and I am the world record holder for wheedling."

"Galas and events are by invitation, aren't they?"

"Of course. It's important to — Ah! I see. How did he receive invitations if his address is not his address? Give me one moment."

She rose, crossed the polished tiles, the thick Turkish rug, and went out of the room.

"I like her." Peabody helped herself to a cookie. "She kind of reminds me of my grandmother. Not the way she looks, or lives," Peabody continued with a glance around the room. "But she's got that snap to her. Not just that she knows what's what, but like she's *always* known.

"Hey, these cookies are mag. And so thin you can practically see through them." She took another.

"See-through food can't have many calories. Eat one, or I'm going to feel like an oinker."

Absently, Eve took a cookie. "He doesn't donate to the Met. Goes to a function now and then, but doesn't lay out any real bucks. Tickets cost, events cost, but he's getting something out of those. There's the control again. If you donate, you can't direct, not precisely, where your scratch is going."

She looked over as Jessica returned.

"The mystery's solved, but remains mysterious. Lyle reports that our Mr. Pierpont requested all tickets, all correspondence, invitations, begging letters, and so on, be held for him at the box office."

"Is that usual?" Eve asked.

"It's not." Jessica sat, picked up her tea. "In fact, it's very unusual. But we try to accommodate our patrons, even those we have to squeeze funds out of."

"When was the last time you saw or spoke with him?"

"Let me see. Oh, yes, he attended our winter gala. Second Saturday in December. I remember I tried, again, to convince him to join the Guild. It's a hefty membership fee, but has lovely benefits. He's the type who enjoys the opera, who knows and appreciates it, but isn't interested in funding. Tight-fisted. I've seen him come or go to performances over time. Always on foot. Doesn't even spring for a car. And always alone."

"Did he ever speak to you at all about his personal life?"

"Let me think." Crossing her legs, she swung one foot back and forth. "Drawing on the personal is an

344

essential tool of the wheedle. A longtime widower, travels a great deal. He claims to have attended performances in all the great opera houses of the world. Prefers Italian operas. Oh!"

She held up a finger, closed her eyes just a moment as if to pull together a thought. "I remember, some years ago, pumping him a bit — as he'd had a couple of glasses of wine, I thought I might slide that membership fee out of him. I had him discussing whether true appreciation for art and music is inherent or learned. He told me he'd learned his appreciation from his mother when he was a boy. I said that was, arguably, inherent. But no, he said, though she had been the only mother he'd known, she had been his father's second wife. She had been a soprano."

"A performer."

"I asked him just that. What did he say? It was a bit odd. She had been, but circumstances had denied her, and time had run out. I'm sure that's what he said. I asked him what had happened, but he excused himself and abruptly walked away."

"Would Lyle know when Pierpont last picked up anything from the box office?"

"He would, and I asked him, anticipating you. Just last week."

"How does he pay?"

"Cash, Lyle tells me. Always, and yes, that's unusual. But we don't quibble about eccentricities. He always wears black-tie to the theater, which is also a bit eccentric, I suppose. So do his guests."

"You said he's always alone."

"Yes. I meant whenever he gives his performance ticket to a guest." An obliging hostess, she lifted the pot to pour more tea into Peabody's cup. "I've occasionally seen other men in his box. In fact, there was a guest in his seat at the opening of *Rigoletto* last week."

"Can you describe him?"

"Ah, black and white. That's how I thought of him, actually. Black-tie — very formal — white hair, white skin. I remember wondering if he might be a relation of Mr. Pierpont. There was a resemblance, or it seemed to me there was. I didn't see him before or after the performance, or at intermission. Or I didn't notice."

"Can you dig up the names of those who have been in the same box with Pierpont?"

"There never is anyone when Pierpont or one of his guests attend." Jessica smiled as she held out the plate of cookies. "That's rather odd, isn't it?"

"Buys up the other tickets in the box," Eve said when they were in the car. "Doesn't want anyone else nearby, disturbing him, or getting too close."

"We'll stake out the opera." Peabody pulled out her book to key in some notes. "Maybe he'll need another fix."

"Yeah, we'll set that up. His stepmother. That's who the women represent. That's whose picture he carries in his wallet. Idealizes and demonizes her at the same time."

"You sound like Mira."

"It's what plays. He kills her, again and again — probably re-creating her actual death. Then he washes

346

her, lays her on white linen. Her time ran out, so he sees that time runs out for the ones he picks to represent her. That's the core of it, with the cross in the Urbans. She clocked out in the Urbans, and I'm betting on the date he's used for his fake wife in the Pierpont data."

"The wife thing — the wedding band. His stepmother, but also his fantasy woman," Peabody theorized. "His bride. He doesn't rape her, that would shatter the fantasy. Not sexual, but romantic. Pathologically romantic."

"Now who's Mira? We start searching for women of her description who died on or about the date in the Pierpont data."

"A lot of deaths weren't recorded during the Urbans."

"Hers will be." Eve whipped the wheel to change lanes and shoehorn herself into a minute opening in the clog of traffic. "He'd have seen to it. It would've been here in New York. New York's the beginning and the end for him. We find her, and she'll lead us to him."

Eve heard the internal clock in her head ticking, ticking, ticking away the time. And thought of Ariel Greenfeld.

She didn't know it was possible to experience such pain, to survive it. Even when he stopped — she'd thought he would never stop — her body burned and bled.

She'd wept and she'd screamed. In some part of Ariel's mind, she'd understood he'd enjoyed that. He'd

347

been entertained by her helpless shrieks, wild sobs, and desperate struggles.

She lay now, shivering in shock while voices twined through the air in a language she didn't understand. Italian? she wondered, fighting to focus, to stay conscious. It was probably Italian. He'd played music while he'd hurt her, and her screams had cut through the voices then as his nasty little knives had cut through her flesh.

Ariel imagined using them on him. She'd never been violent. In fact, she'd been a pitiful failure in the basic defense classes she'd taken with a couple friends. *Weakfeld*, they'd called her, she remembered. And they'd all laughed because they'd never believed, not really, that any of them would ever have to use the punches and kicks they'd tried to learn.

She was a baker, that's all. She liked to cook and create cakes and cookies and pastries that made people smile. She was a good person, wasn't she? She couldn't remember ever hurting anyone.

Maybe she'd toked a little Zoner in her teens, and that was wrong. Technically. But she hadn't caused anyone any harm.

But she found the idea of causing him harm dulled the pain. When she imagined herself breaking free, grabbing one of the knives and just plunging it into his soft belly, she didn't feel so cold.

She didn't want to die this way, this horrible way. Someone would come, she told herself. She had to hold on, had to survive until someone came and saved her.

But when he came back, everything inside her cringed. Tears flooded her throat and her eyes so that even her whimpers were drowned.

"That was a nice break, wasn't it?" he said in that hideously pleasant voice. "But we have to get back to work. Now then, let's see. What's it to be?"

"Mr. Gaines?" Don't scream, she ordered herself. Don't beg. He likes that.

"Yes, my dear?"

"Why did you pick me?"

"You have a pleasing face and lovely hair. Good muscle tone in your arms and legs." He picked up a small torch. She had to bite back a moan as he turned it on with a low hiss, narrowed the flame to a pinpoint.

"Is that all? I mean, did I do anything?"

"Do?" he said absently.

"Did I do something to upset you, or make you mad at me?"

"Not at all." He turned, smiled kindly as the narrow flame hissed.

"It's just, Mr. Gaines, I know you're going to hurt me. I can't stop you. But can you tell me why? I just want to understand why you're going to hurt me."

"Isn't this interesting?" He cocked his head and studied her. "She asks, always she asks why. But she screams it. She doesn't ever ask so politely."

"She only wants to understand."

"Well. Well, well, well." He turned the torch off, and Ariel's chest heaved with relief. "This is different. I enjoy variety. She was lovely, you know."

"Was she?" Ariel moistened her lips as he pulled up a stool and sat so he could speak face-to-face. How could he look so *ordinary*? she wondered. How could he look so nice, and be so vicious?

"You're very pretty, but she was almost exquisite. And when she sang, she was glorious."

"What . . . what did she sing?"

"Soprano. She had a multiple voice."

"I . . . I don't know what that means."

"Her brilliance was so bright. She was *allegra* — those high, clear notes seeming to simply lift out of her. And the color, the texture of *lirica* with the intensity and depth of the *drammatica*. Her range . . ."

Moisture sheened his eyes as he pressed his fingers to his lips, kissed the tips. "I could, and did, listen to her for hours. She would accompany herself on the piano when at home. She tried to teach me, but . . ." He smiled wistfully as he held up his hands. "I had no talent for music, only a vast appreciation for it."

If he was talking he wasn't hurting her, Ariel thought. She had to keep him talking. "Is it opera? I don't know anything about opera."

"You think it's stuffy, boring, old-fashioned."

"I think it's beautiful," she said carefully. "I've just never really listened to it before. She sang opera?" Questions, Ariel thought desperately. Ask questions so he'll spend time answering. "And — and was a soprano? With, um, multiple voice like — like ranges?"

"Indeed, yes, indeed, that's very good. I have many of her recordings. I don't play them here." He glanced around the room. "It wouldn't be appropriate."

350

"I'd love to hear her sing. I'd love to hear her multiple voice."

"Would you?" His eyes turned sly. "Aren't you clever? She was clever, too." He rose now, picked up the torch.

"Wait! Wait! Couldn't I hear her sing? Maybe I'd understand if I could hear her sing? Who was she? Who was — Oh, God, God, *please!*" She tried to shrink away from the tip of the flame he traced, almost teasingly, along her arm.

"We'll have to chat later. We really must get to work."

Eve went directly to Feeney when she reached Central. "Female brunettes between the ages of twenty-eight and thirty-three who died on this date in New York. We need names, last known addresses, cause of death."

"Records around that time are sketchy," he told her. "A lot of deaths went unrecorded, a lot of people were unidentified, or misidentified."

"Dig. She's what's going to open locks on this. I'm going to check with Yancy, see if he's got any sort of an image on the wallet photo."

To give Yancy more time, she went first to Whitney and asked for more men to form a stakeout team at the Met.

"Done. I need you for a media briefing at noon."

"Commander —"

"If you think I don't know how pressed and pressured you are, you're mistaken." And he looked just as irritated as she did. "Thirty minutes. I'll cut it off at thirty, but unless you're on your way to arrest this son

351

of a bitch, I need you there. We have to hold back the flood."

"Yes, sir."

"Confirm the new and salient you fed Nadine this morning, and the twenty-four-hour shifts. I want you to express confidence that Ariel Greenfeld will be found alive."

"I will, Commander. I believe she will be."

"Let them see you do. Dismissed. Oh, Lieutenant, if I learn you've stepped foot outside this building without your vest or your wires, I'll skin you. Personally."

"Understood."

It was a little annoying to realize he'd sensed she was considering *forgetting* the vest. She hated the damn thing. But she had to respect a man who knew his subordinates.

She strode into Yancy's section and saw him working with Baxter's peach. He caught Eve's eye before she wound her way through the stations. He rose, smiled, and said something to the witness before heading Eve off.

"I think we're making progress here. She's got him nailed, but she only got a quick look at the photo. We're working on it, Dallas. You've got to give me more time, more room."

"Can you give me him?"

"Already sent it to your office unit. Subtle differences in the facial structure from Trina's image, different hair, eyebrows. My eye says same guy."

"Your eye's good enough for me. When you get the woman's image, send it to me, and to Feeney. Make it work, Yancy. This one could be the money shot."

By the time Eve reached her own division, Peabody was heading out of the war room. "Tried Morris, as ordered. He's on his way here with the tox results. Jenkinson and Powell reported in. They're at the spa boutique. There's a clerk who thinks maybe she saw our guy in there sometime."

"There's a fresh image on my unit. Send it to them, have them show it around the store and the salon."

"Got it."

"Lieutenant Dallas?"

Both she and Peabody turned. Ariel's hungover neighbor, Eve realized. "Erik, right?"

"Yeah. I have to talk to you. I have to find out what's going on. That woman, Gia Rossi, she's dead. Ariel . . ."

"I'll take him," Peabody told Eve.

"No, I got it. Get the image to Jenkinson. Let's sit down, Erik." She didn't have time to take him to the lounge, didn't have the heart to boot him out. Instead, she led him to one of the benches outside her own bullpen.

"You're worried and you're upset," Eve began.

"Worried? Upset? I'm scared out of my goddamn mind. He's got her. That maniac has Ariel. They said he tortures them. He's hurting her, and we're just sitting here."

"No, we're not. Every cop assigned to this case is working it."

"She's not a *case!*" His voice rose, threatened to crack. "Goddamn it, she's a human being. She's Ariel."

"You want this prettied up for you?" Her voice was sharp, deliberately so to cut off any risk of hysteria. "You want pats and strokes, you've come to the wrong place, and you've come to the wrong person. I'm telling you that everything I've got is on this, is in this, just like every cop working it. If you think we don't know who she is, you're wrong. If you think her face isn't in everyone's head, you're wrong."

"I don't know what to do." His hands fisted on his thighs, pounded against them. "I can't stand not knowing what to do, how to help. She must be so scared."

"Yeah, she must be scared. I'm not going to bullshit you, Erik. She's scared, and she's probably hurting. But we're going to find her. When we do, I'll make sure you're contacted. I'll make sure you know we've got her safe."

"I love her. I never told her. Never told me either," he managed on a long, shaky breath. "I'm in love with her, and she doesn't know."

"You can tell her when we've got her back. Go home. Better, go be with a friend."

When she'd nudged him along, she went back to the war room, straight to Roarke's station. She picked up his bottle of water and guzzled.

"Help yourself," he commented.

"Popped a buzz a couple hours ago. Always makes me thirsty. And . . ." She rolled her shoulders. "Wired.

Location, location, location," she added and made him smile.

"I have some others for you, and I'm working on trimming the number of them down. Any help on the opera connection?"

"Pieces, bits and pieces of him — and I'm getting a handle on the women he's re-creating, we'll say. Once we ID her, we're going to have more data on him. I've got to go flap lips with the media."

She started out, nearly ran headlong into Morris. "Sorry. Sorry." The damn booster made her feel as if she were jumping out of her own skin. "What have you got? Tell me while we walk. I've got to get to the media room."

"Energy pill?"

"It shows?"

"Generally, on you. He used dopamine and lorazepam on her. We haven't detected those substances before."

"What do they do?" She wished she'd copped Roarke's water. "Would they have turned her off?"

"I'd say he was hoping for the opposite result. They're sometimes used on catatonics."

"Okay, so she turned off on him, and he tried to bring her around, keep the clock going."

"I agree. Still, if she went into true and deep catatonia, he could have, potentially, kept that clock going for hours more. If not days."

"But what fun is that?" Eve countered. "Not getting any reaction. She's not participating."

"Yes, again I agree. It holds with the fact she didn't sustain as many injuries as the others. He couldn't bring her around, so he gave up."

"I don't imagine you can pick up dopamine or whatzit?"

"Lorazepam."

"Yeah, those. Probably didn't pick them up at his local drug store."

"No. And a doctor isn't going to prescribe either for home use. It's something that would be administered, by a licensed professional, under controlled conditions."

"Maybe he's a doctor, or some sort of medical. Or managed to pose as one." Good at posing, she thought. Good at his roles. "Could be he scored it from a hospital or medical facility. But he's never used it before, so why would he have had it on hand? Wouldn't," she said before Morris could speak. "If he scored it, he scored it over the weekend, and in New York."

"Psychiatrics, primarily, would be the most logical source."

"Give this to Peabody, okay? I want a search on facilities in New York that carry those meds. Tell her to use Mira if she needs grease or an expert. Meds like that have to be, by law, under lock and fully accounted for."

"By law," Morris agreed, "but not always strictly by practice."

"We track it down. Start by getting full accountings from those facilities of these drugs. Any deviation, we take another push."

"I can do this. A doctor for the dead's still a doctor," he added when she frowned at him. "I think I could help on this."

"Take it to Peabody," Eve repeated. "Work with her. I'll check back with you when I'm done in here."

In the war room Roarke saved, copied, and printed out the real estate list. Curious, he took out his PPC to access the last few minutes of Eve's briefing while he wandered out for another bottle of water. She looked, he thought, rough and tough — and if you knew her as he did, a little ragged around the edges.

She'd make herself ill if this wasn't over soon, he concluded. Push herself until she, very literally, collapsed.

There was absolutely no point in nagging or browbeating her this time as he was in it too deeply himself. He switched off as she was finishing up, then shifted to communications.

He thought if he ordered a dozen pizzas, she'd at least end up eating something. And he could damn well do with some food himself at this point.

After returning to his station, he took a fresh look at his list. Lowell's Funeral Home, Lower East location, he mused. Sarifina York's memorial was being held there. Today, he remembered. He should go, pay his respects.

He called up the funeral home on his comp to check the time of the service. If he couldn't get away from the work — and the living took precedence over the dead — he could and would at least send flowers.

He noted down the time, the address, the specific room where the memorial was scheduled to be held. Cleverly, he thought, the page linked to a local florist. Handy and quick, he decided, but he preferred to trust Caro for the floral tribute.

Thoughtfully, he glanced at the link labeled "History," and tapped it. It might tell him more than the standard data he'd already unearthed from the records.

Moments later his eyes went cool, his blood went hot. Roarke glanced over at Feeney, who was pushing at his own search.

"Feeney. I believe I have something."

CHAPTER
TWENTY

Eve stood, hands fisted on her hips, studying the data Roarke ordered on wall screen.

"The property didn't pop in the initial searches as it's been retitled a number of times, and not officially owned by the same person, persons, or company for the time period you asked I check. But with a deeper search, the ownership is — buried under some clever cover — held by the Lowell Family Trust."

"Funeral parlor. Death house."

"Indeed. As you see from the website history, the building first belonged to the Lowell family in the early nineteen-twenties, used both as a residence and as a funeral home. James Lowell established his business there, and lived in residence with his wife, two sons, and one daughter. The older son was killed in the Second World War, and the younger, Robert Lowell, joined the business, taking it over at his father's death. He expanded, opening other locations in New York and New Jersey."

"Death's a profitable business," Eve commented.

"So it is. And more so during wartime. Robert Lowell's eldest son, another James, joined in the business, residing in their Lower West Side location —

they had a second by that time. During the Urbans, this location, the original, was used as a clinic and base camp for the Home Force. Many of the dead were brought there, and tended to by the Lowells, who were reputed to be staunch supporters of the HF."

"The second James Lowell is too old." With her hands on her hips, Eve studied the data. "There are some spry centurians, but not spry enough for this."

"Agreed. But he, in turn, had a son. Only one child, from his first marriage. He was widowed when his wife died from complications in childbirth. And he subsequently remarried six years later."

"Pop," Eve said quietly. "Have we got the second wife? The son?"

"There's no record of the second wife that we've found as yet. A lot of records were destroyed during the Urbans. And the databases were far from complete in any case."

"It's one of the reasons these clowns — the Lowells," Feeney said, "were able to manipulate the records."

"Likely for tax purposes at one time," Roarke continued. "Changed the name from Lowell's to Manhattan Mortuary during the Urbans — with a bogus sale of the building. Then to Sunset Bereavement Center, another sale, roughly twenty years ago, with a return — five years ago — to the original name, with another deed transfer in the officials."

"Just kept switching."

"With a bit of creative bookkeeping, I imagine," Roarke confirmed. "It caught my interest when I read that a Lowell has been at the helm of the business for four generations. Interested enough, I scraped away a bit."

"The man's got a golden e-shovel," Feeney commented, and gave Roarke a slap on the back.

"Well, digging in, it turns out that the Lowell Family Trust owned companies that owned companies, and so on, which included the ones who ostensibly purchased the building."

"Meaning they've been there all along."

"Exactly so. And on the last generation, Robert — named for his grandfather — we have this."

He pulled up the ID shot and data. Eve stepped closer to the screen, frowned. "He doesn't look like Yancy's sketch. The eyes, yes, maybe the mouth, but he doesn't look like the sketch. Age is right, professional data, okay. Address in London."

"Which is the English National Opera," Feeney put in. "We ran it." He tapped the image on screen. "Could Yancy have been this far off?"

"Never known him to be. And we have two wits verifying. That's not him." Eve shoved her fingers through her hair. Time to move. "Print it out. I want a team of five: Feeney, Roarke, Peabody, McNab, Newkirk. We'll pay a visit to a funeral home. I want the team ten minutes behind me."

"Ten?" Roarke repeated.

"That's right. It's time to open that window a little wider. Time's moving for Ariel Greenfeld. And this might be when he makes his move on me, either en route to this place or when I'm inside it."

She held up a hand as Yancy came in. "Feeney, get us a warrant. I don't want any trouble going through that building. Yancy, give me a face."

"Here she is."

A strong face, Eve thought. Strong and very feminine, almond-shaped eyes, slim nose, a wide, full mouth, and a cascade of dark hair. She was smiling, looking directly out. Her shoulders were bare but for two slim, sparkling straps. Around her neck was a glittering chain holding a pendant in the shape of a tree.

Tree of Life, Eve remembered. "Well, son of a bitch." Another point for the Romanian psychic.

"Callendar, get a copy of this face. Find her. Run a data match for her picture. Search the newspapers, the magazines, the media reports from 1980 through 2015. Cross-check her with opera."

"Yes, sir."

"Yancy." Eve jerked her chin at the image still on screen. "That's what his official ID has him looking like."

"No." Yancy just shook his head. "No way. Trina had him. This is a relative, maybe. Brother, cousin. But that's not the guy Trina gave me, or the one Ms. Pruitt described from Tiffany's."

"Okay. Morris, you all right working on the meds alone?"

"I can handle it."

"You get a hit, I get the buzz. Let's move it, people. Ten minutes at my back. And nobody comes inside until I give the signal."

"Sarifina York's memorial is being held there," Roarke reminded her. "It would be completely appropriate for me to pay my respects."

Eve gave it a moment's thought. "Ten minutes at my back," she repeated. "Unless I signal sooner, you come on in to pay your respects. Get us that warrant, Feeney."

"Vest and wire," Roarke said, firmly.

"Yeah, yeah. In the garage. In five." She strode out to prep.

When she pulled out of the garage, Eve's instincts were tuned for a tail. And her mind was on Ariel.

She prayed to pass out, but the pain wouldn't allow the escape. Even when he stopped, finally stopped, agony kept her above the surface. She tried to think of her friends, her family, of the life she'd led before, but it all seemed so distant, so separate. Nothing that had been would come clearly into focus.

There was only now, only the pain, only him.

And the time ticking away on the wall screen. Seven hours, twenty-three minutes, and the seconds clicking by.

So Ariel thought of how she would make him pay for taking away everything she had. Her life, her sense of order, her pleasures, her hopes. If only she could get free, she would make him pay for stripping her bare.

Talk, she reminded herself. Find a way to make him talk again.

Make him talk, and live.

★ ★ ★

Eve didn't spot a tail, and found that it pissed her off. What if he'd changed his mind about trying for her? If she'd somehow scared him off, and even now he was moving in on another innocent woman?

"At location," she said. "And heading in. Feeney, make me smile."

"Warrant's coming through."

"All right. Keep the chatter down. Ten minutes, on the mark."

Studying the building, she crossed the sidewalk. Three floors, including basement. Riot bars, solid security. Solid, if faded, red brick. Two entrances in the front, and two in the back, with emergency exits front and back, top floor.

If Ariel was inside, odds were on the basement. Main level was public, third level public and staff.

She climbed the steps, pressed the buzzer.

The door was opened moments later by a dark-skinned woman in dignified black. "Good afternoon. How can I help you?"

Eve held up her badge. "Sarifina York."

"Yes, we're gathering in the Tranquility Room. Please come in."

Eve stepped in, scanned the area. The wide central hallway split the main floor in two parts. The air smelled of flowers and polish. She could see through the open double pocket doors to her left that several people had already arrived to memorialize Sarifina.

"I'll need to speak to whoever's in charge."

"Of the service?"

"Of the business."

"Oh. Of course. Mr. Travers is with a client just at the moment, but —"

"What about Mr. Lowell?"

"Mr. Lowell isn't in residence. He lives in Europe. But Mr. Travers is head of operations."

"When's the last time Mr. Lowell's been here?"

"I couldn't really say. I've been with Lowell's for two years, and haven't met him. I believe you could say he's essentially retired. Would you like to speak with Mr. Travers?"

"Yeah. You'll have to interrupt him. This is official police business."

"Of course." As if she heard the phrase "official police business" every day, the woman smiled serenely as she gestured. "If you'll come with me, I'll take you to one of the waiting rooms upstairs."

Eve looked into the Tranquility Room as she passed. There were photographs of Sarifina, the flowers were plentiful, and the music was the retro big band sound the deceased had loved.

"What's in the basement?" Eve asked as they went upstairs.

"It's a work area. Preparation areas. Many of the bereaved request or require viewings of those they've lost."

"Embalming? Cosmetics?"

"Yes."

"How many work down there, routinely?"

"We have a mortician, a technician, and a stylist on staff."

Stylist, Eve thought. No point in being unfashionably dead.

The woman led her to a small waiting room full of quiet, flowers, and soft-cushioned furniture. "I'll tell Mr. Travers you're waiting. Please be comfortable."

Alone, Eve wandered the room. Not here, she thought. It didn't make sense for him to have brought Ariel and the others here, where work went on throughout the building. Too many people. Too much business.

He wasn't part of a troupe, but a solo act.

But this was a conduit, she was sure of it. Just as she was damn sure Robert Lowell, or whatever he was currently calling himself, wasn't in London.

Travers came in. He was tall, reed thin, with a comfortable if somber face. If Eve had been casting funeral directors, he'd have been her top pick.

"Officer?"

"Lieutenant. Dallas."

"Kenneth Travers." Since he offered his hand as he crossed to her, Eve took it. "I'm director here. How may I help you?"

"I'm looking for Robert Lowell."

"Yes, so Marlee indicated. Mr. Lowell lives in Europe, and has for some years now. While he retains ownership of the organization, he has very little actual involvement with the day-to-day operations."

"How do you get in touch with him?"

"Through his solicitors in London."

"I'll need the name of the firm, and a contact number."

"Yes, of course." Travers folded his hands at his waist. "I'm sorry, may I ask what this is in reference to?"

"We believe he's connected to an ongoing investigation."

"You're investigating the murders of the two women who were found recently. Is that correct?"

"That would be right."

"But Mr. Lowell is in London." He repeated the information slowly, and with what seemed to be a wealth of patience. "Or traveling. He travels quite extensively, I understand."

"When did you see him last?"

"Five, perhaps six years ago. Yes, I believe it would be six."

Eve pulled out the ID print. "Is this Robert Lowell?"

"Why yes, yes it is. I'm very confused, Lieutenant. This is Robert Lowell, the first. He's been dead for, my goodness, nearly forty years. His portrait hangs in my office."

"Is that so?" Smart, Eve decided. Some smart son of a bitch. "How about this man?" She took out Yancy's sketch.

"Yes, that's the current Mr. Lowell, or a close likeness." His color receded a bit as he looked from the sketch to Eve. "I saw this displayed on screen, on media reports. I honestly never connected it. I — as I said — I haven't seen Mr. Lowell in several years, and I never . . . I simply didn't see him in this until you asked just now.

"But you see, there has to be some mistake. Mr. Lowell is a very quiet and solitary man. He couldn't possibly —"

"That's what they all say. I have a team arriving momentarily, with a warrant. We need to go through this building."

"But Lieutenant Dallas, I assure you he's not here."

"It happens I believe you, but we still go through the building. Where does he stay when he comes to New York?"

"I don't honestly know. It's so rare . . . and it wasn't my place to ask." Travers's fingers moved up to the knot of his somber tie, brushed there twice.

"There was a second location on the Lower West Side during the Urbans."

"Yes, yes, I believe so. But we've been the only location downtown for as long as I've been associated with the company."

"How long would that be?"

"Lieutenant, I've been director here for almost fifteen years. I've only had direct contact with Mr. Lowell a handful of times at best. He's made it clear he doesn't like to be disturbed."

"I bet. I need the lawyers, Mr. Travers, and any other information on Robert Lowell you have. What do you know about his stepmother?"

"His . . . I think she was killed during the Urban Wars. As she wasn't, to my knowledge, involved with the business, the information I have on her is very minimal."

"Name?"

"I'm so sorry, I don't know it offhand. It might be in our records. Well, this is — this is all very disturbing."

"Yeah," Eve said dryly. "Murder can just ruin a perfectly good funeral."

"I only meant —" Color came into his cheeks, then died away. "I understand you must do your job. But, Lieutenant, we have a memorial in progress for one of the women who was killed. I have to ask you and your men to be discreet. This is an extremely difficult and delicate time for Ms. York's friends and family."

"I'm going to make sure Ariel Greenfeld's friends and family don't end up in your Tranquility Room anytime soon."

They were as discreet as a half a dozen cops could be, with Feeney and McNab tackling the electronics for any data. Eve stood in the basement prep room with Roarke.

"Not much different from the morgue. Smaller," she noted, scanning the steel worktables, the gullies on the sides, the hoses and tubes and tools. "I guess he got some of his knowledge of anatomy working here. Might have had some of his early practice sessions on corpses."

"Charming thought."

"Yeah, well, being as they were already dead — hopefully — it probably didn't upset them too much. Oh, and FYI? When my time comes, I don't want the preservatives and the stylist. You can just build a big fire, slide me in. Then you can throw yourself on the pyre to show your wild grief and constant devotion."

"I'll make a note of it."

"Nothing down here for us. I want the second location that was up and running during the Urbans. Any other properties owned by Lowell, in any of his guises or fronts."

"I'll get to it," Roarke told her.

She drew out her communicator, scowled at the buzzing static. "Reception's crappy down here. Let's go up. I want to see if Callendar had any luck with the stepmother.

"She could have had property in her name," Eve continued as they started out. "Maybe he uses that. Lawyers are dragging their feet, as the breed's prone to do. Between Whitney and Tibble they'll cut through that bullshit quickly enough."

"If he continues to be smart," Roarke commented, "the lawyers would only lead you to a numbered account and message service. He covers himself well."

"Then we'll tackle the account and the service. Fucker's in New York. He has a bolt-hole here, a work space, transportation. And one of these lines we're yanking is going to bring us down on him."

Eve had no more than reached the main level when her communicator beeped. "Dallas."

"Found her!" Callendar all but sang it. "Edwina Spring. Found her in the music and entertainment section of an old *Times*. Opera sensation, if you believe the hype. Prodigy. Barely eighteen when she bowled over New York at the Met. I've got more coming up now that I've got her name."

"Run a multitask. See if you can find any property in the city listed under her name."

"On it."

"Get it all together, Callendar. I've got a stop to make, then I'm heading in."

"What stop?" Roarke wanted to know.

"Pella. He knows something. His medicals confirm he's clocking out, and is barely able to walk across the room. But he knows something, and I'm not dicking around with him."

"You weren't tailed here."

"That's right."

"Then it's unlikely you'll be tailed from here. As Peabody's busy, I'll go with you to see this Pella."

"I can handle myself."

"You certainly can. But do you want to pull any part of the team here off to run your wire? Simpler, quicker, if I go with you, then the rest of them meet us back at Central."

"Maybe." And for the sake of expediency, she shrugged. "Fine."

When they arrived at Pella's, there was a great deal of objecting and hand-fluttering from both the housekeeping and medical droids. Eve just pushed through it.

"If you've got a complaint, report it to the chief of police. Or the mayor. Yeah, the mayor loves to get complaints from droids."

"We're obliged to look after Mr. Pella, to see to his health and comfort."

Obviously, some joker had programmed the housekeeping droid to whine. "None of you are going to feel very healthy or comfortable if I haul you into Central. So move aside or I'll cite you for obstructing justice."

Eve elbowed the medical away, shoved open the bedroom door. "Stay back, out of eyeline," she said quietly to Roarke. "He might not talk if he sees I've brought company."

It was dim, as it had been before, and she could hear the steady rasps of Pella sucking air through the breather.

"I said I didn't want to be disturbed until I called for you." His voice was testy, and sounded years older than it had the day before. "I'll have you broken down into circuits and limbs if you don't give me some damn *peace*."

"That would be tough to manage from where you are," Eve commented.

He stirred, his eyes opened to latch on to hers. "What do you want? I don't have to talk to you. I spoke with my lawyer."

"Fine, speak with him again and tell him to meet you at Central. He'll explain that I can hold you there for twenty-four hours as a material witness to homicide."

"What kind of bullshit is this! I haven't witnessed anything but those damn droids hovering like vultures for the past six months."

"You're going to tell me what you know, Pella, or a good chunk of the time you've got left is going to be spent with me. Robert Lowell. Edwina Spring. Tell me."

He shifted restlessly in the bed, plucked at the sheet. "If you know so much, why do you need me?"

"Look, you son of a bitch." She leaned over him. "Twenty-five women are dead, and another is in dire straits. She may be dying."

"I *am* dying! I fought for this city. I bled for it. I lost the only thing in the world that mattered, and nothing has mattered since. What do I care about some woman?"

"Her name's Ariel. She bakes for a living. She has a neighbor across the hall from her pretty little apartment. Seems like a nice guy. She doesn't know he's in love with her, doesn't know he came to me today desperate and scared, pleading with me to find her. Her name is Ariel, and you're going to tell me what you know."

Pella turned his head away, stared toward the draped windows. "I don't know anything."

"You lying fucker." She grabbed hold of his breather, saw his eyes go wide. She wouldn't actually rip it off — probably wouldn't — but he didn't know that. "You want to take another breath?"

"The droids know you're in here. If anything happens to me —"

"What? Like you just — oops — fall over dead when I happen to be talking to you? An officer of the law, sworn to protect and serve. And with a witness to back me up?"

"What witness?"

Eve glanced over, jerked her head so that Roarke stepped into Pella's view. "If this fucker just happened

373

to kick it when I was duly questioning him about his knowledge of a suspect, it would be an accident, right?"

"Absolutely." Roarke smiled, cold and calm. "An unforeseen event."

"You know who he is," Eve said when Pella's eyes wheeled. "And who I am. Roarke's cop, that's what you called me. Believe me when I tell you if you happen to stop breathing, and I lie about how that might've happened, he'll swear to it."

"On a bloody stack of Bibles," Roarke confirmed.

"But you're not ready to die yet, are you, Pella?" Her hand stayed firm on the breather when he batted at it. "It shows in the eyes when someone's not ready to die yet. So, if you want that next breath, then the one that comes after, you tell me the goddamn truth. You know Robert Lowell. You knew Edwina Spring."

"Let go of it." He wheezed in air. "I'll have you up on charges."

"You'll be dead, and the dead don't scare me. You knew them. Next breath, Pella, say yes."

"Yes, yes." He shoved his hand at Eve's, and the harsh sound of his labored breath eased when she lifted it. "Yes, I knew them. But not to speak to. They were the elite. I was only a soldier. Get the hell away from me."

"Not a chance. Tell me what you know."

Pella's eyes ticked over to Roarke, back to Eve. Then, for a moment, he simply closed them. "He was about my age — a few years younger — but he didn't serve. Soft." Pella's hand trembled a little as it came up, stroked over the breather to be sure it was in the correct position. "Soft look about him, and he had his family money at his back, of course. His type never got dirty, never risked their own skin. She . . . I need water."

Eve glanced over, saw the cup with a straw on the bedside table. She picked it up, held it out.

"I can't hold the damn thing. It's bad today. Worse since you got here."

Saying nothing, she angled it down so he could guide the straw with a trembling hand to the opening in the breather.

"What about her?"

"Beautiful. Young, elegant, a voice like an angel. She would come to the base sometimes, sing for us. Opera, almost always Italian opera. She'd break your heart with every note."

"You have a thing for her, Pella?"

"Bitch," he muttered. "What would you know of real love? Therese was everything. But I loved what Edwina was, what she brought us. Hope and beauty."

"She came to the base on Broome?"

"Yes, on Broome."

"They lived there, didn't they?"

"No. Before I think, but not during the fighting, not while soldiers were based there. After, who the hell knows, who the hell cares? But when I was assigned there, they didn't live in the base on Broome. They had another place, another place on the West Side."

"Where?"

"It was a long time ago. I was never there, not a foot soldier like me. Some of the others went, officers, and you heard things. Yeah, some of the officers, and the Stealths."

She felt the next click. "The coverts?"

"Yes. You'd hear things. I heard things." He closed his eyes. "It hurts to go back there." For the first time, his voice sounded weak. "And I can't stop going back there."

"I'm sorry for all you lost, Mr. Pella." And in that moment she was. "But Ariel Greenfeld is alive, and she needs help. What did you hear back then that might help her?"

"How the hell do I know?"

"It would have to do with her, with Edwina Spring. She died, did she?"

"Everyone dies." But his hand came to his breather again, and his eyes watched Eve warily over it. "I heard her — Edwina — talking to a soldier I knew. Young first lieutenant, sent down from upstate. Can't remember his name. They'd slip off when she'd come to sing. Or you could see the way they looked at each other. The way Therese and I looked at each other."

"They were lovers?"

"Probably. Or wanted to be. She was young, a lot younger than Taker."

"Who? Taker?"

"That's what they called Lowell — James Lowell."

"Because he took the bodies the dead wagon brought in," Eve said, remembering Dobbins's comment.

"That's right. She was half his age, vital, beautiful. He was too damn old for her, and . . . and there was something in his eyes. In the old man's, too, his father.

376

Something in their eyes that brought the hair up on the back of the neck."

"They found out about her and the soldier."

"Yes. I think they were going to run away. He wouldn't have been the first to desert, or the last. It was summer. We had the sector secured, temporarily in any case. I went out, just to walk, to remind myself what we were fighting for. I heard them talking, behind one of the supply tents. Her voice, you couldn't mistake it for anyone else's. They were talking about going north, up into the mountains. A lot of people had fled the city for the mountains, the country, and he still had family up that way."

"She was going to leave her husband, run off with this soldier." And Robert Lowell, Eve calculated, would have been around twenty.

"I didn't let them know I was there. I wouldn't have turned him in. I knew what it was to love someone, and be afraid for her.

"I backtracked a little, then crossed the street so they wouldn't know I'd been close. Give them privacy, you know. Fucking little privacy back then. And I saw him, on the other side of the tent, listening to them."

"Lowell," Eve realized. "The younger one."

"He looked like he was in a trance. I'd heard he had a mental condition. There were whispers, but I thought it was just the excuse they used to keep him out of the fight. But when I looked across the street, when I looked at him, there was something not right. No, not right at all. I need water."

Once again, Eve lifted the cup and straw to his mouth.

"He turned them in."

"He must have. There was nothing I could do, not with him there. I was going to warn them later, warn the lieutenant about the kid. But I never got the chance. I went up the block, debating with myself on what I should or shouldn't do — wanted to talk to Therese about it first. They were gone when I came back. The soldier off on assignment, and Edwina back home. I never saw either of them alive again."

"What happened to them?"

"It was more than a week later." His voice was tiring, genuinely, she judged. She wouldn't get much more. "The soldier was listed as AWOL, and she hadn't been back. I thought they'd gotten away. Then one night, I went out for sentry duty. She was on the sidewalk. No one would ever say how whoever had tossed her there had gotten through the posts. She was dead."

A tear slid out of his eye, tracked around the side of the breather. "I'd seen bodies like that before, I knew how they came to be like that."

"Torture?"

"They'd done despicable things to her, then tossed her, naked and mangled, on the street like garbage. They'd shorn off her hair, and had ripped up her face, but I knew who she was. They'd left her wearing the Tree of Life necklace she always wore. As if to make certain there would be no mistake."

"You thought the Lowells did it? Her husband, father-in-law, stepson."

"They said she'd been taken and tortured by the enemy, but it was a lie. I'd seen that kind of work before, and it had been on the enemy. The old man was a torturer. Everyone knew it, and everyone was careful not to speak of it too loudly. If they believed a prisoner had information, they took him to Robert Lowell — the old one.

"When they came to get her, he wept like a baby, the one you're looking for now." Pella's eyes opened, and they were fierce despite his flagging voice. "When he saw her under the sheet we covered her with, he wept like a woman. Two days later, I lost Therese. Nothing mattered after that."

"Why didn't you tell the police this nine years ago when these murders started?"

"I didn't think of a dead woman from a lifetime ago. I never thought of it, nor of her. Why would I? Then, I saw that sketch. A long time ago, but I thought there was something familiar. When you came yesterday, I knew who he was."

"If you'd given me this yesterday, given me his name, you might have spared Ariel twenty-four hours of pain."

Pella just turned his head away and closed his eyes. "We all have pain."

Riding on disgust, Eve stormed out of Pella's town house. "Miserable bastard. I need any and all properties owned by the Lowells, or Edwina Spring, during the Urbans. Get out that damn golden shovel and dig."

"You drive, and you'll have it," Roarke told her, already working with his PPC.

She got behind the wheel, then tagged Callendar at Central. "Any more data?"

"Data, yes, property, no. I can tell you Spring retired — with great lamentations from opera buffs, at the age of twenty when she married the wealthy and prominent James Lowell. There's society stuff after that. This gala, that party, then interest in her seemed to fade out some.

"But I found her death record. She's listed as Edwina Roberti. Data reads opera singer, and that she was survived by her spouse, Lowell, Robert. COD is listed as suicide. There's no image, Lieutenant, but it's got to be her."

"It's her."

"And, Lieutenant, Morris has something."

"Put me through."

"Dallas, the Manhattan Family Center on First. There's a children's psychiatric wing that was funded by the Lowells in the late twentieth. Endowment continues through a trust. I've spoken with the chief of staff. Saturday they received an unexpected visit from the Lowell Family Trust's representative. A Mr. Edward Singer. At his request, he was taken through the facility. Their drug count's off."

She calculated the distance. "I'll send somebody over to get a statement."

"Dallas, they keep their security discs, in full, for seven days. They have him on disc."

"We'll pick 'em up. We'll have sweepers go over the drug cabinet. Maybe we'll keep getting lucky. Nice going, Morris."

380

"Felt good."

"Know what you mean. Out." She clicked off, looked over at Roarke as she switched over to Peabody's communicator. "We're building the cage. All we have to do is throw the bastard in it."

CHAPTER
TWENTY-ONE

She was building a good case, lining up her connections, her motives, her pathology. She had no doubt that when they found and arrested Robert Lowell, they'd be handing the prosecuting attorney a slam dunk.

But that didn't help Ariel Greenfeld.

"Get me something," she said to Roarke as they stepped into the elevator at Central's garage.

"Do you know what the records are like from that era?" he snapped. "What there are of them? I'm putting together a puzzle where half the major pieces are missing or scattered about. And I need better equipment than my bloody PPC."

"Okay, all right." She pressed her fingers to the center of her forehead. The damn energy pill was wearing off, and she could feel the system crash waiting to happen. "Let me think."

"I don't know how you can at this stage. You're going to fall flat on your face, Eve, if you don't take a bit of downtime."

"Ariel Greenfeld doesn't have any downtime." She swept out of the elevator. "We need the locations of all Lowell's businesses and documented properties — worldwide. Anything current's going to pop straight out, and we work from there. Talk to the director, put the strong arm on these damn Brit lawyers, the financial institutions where he has his numbered accounts."

"I can tell you it would take weeks — at the very best — to pry anything out of the financials. Their lawyers will have lawyers, who will run you around. And if he was careful, and I imagine he was, in setting these up, those accounts would simply feed into others, and so on. I could cut through that, at home, but it would take considerable time."

Would it help find Ariel? Eve asked herself. "I can't spare you for that. We'll push on the properties and the lawyers first. Got to have a bank box, too. Or boxes. Uses cash, so why wouldn't he store cash in a bank box at the different locations where he has homes, or plans to work? Downtown bank's best bet."

She walked into the war room, and up to Callendar. "Search for downtown banks. I want you to send every one of them every sketch and description we have on Robert Lowell, along with the various known aliases. And I want a search for any and all relations on Lowell, living or dead. Names, last known locations, property deeded in their name.

"Roarke, if you need any help on the property search, pull in any of the EDD team. Heads up," she said, boosting her voice over the chatter and clacking. "When Captain Feeney isn't in the house, and I'm not in the war room, the civilian's in charge of electronics. Questions on that? Go to him."

"Lieutenant's pet," Callendar said just loud enough for Roarke to hear, and in a mock sulk that made him smile a little.

"I'll wager ten I hit on the property before you hit on the banks."

"You're on, Prime Buns."

Eve left them for her office to update her notes, to take another pass through them. While she worked she tried Feeney.

"Anything for me?"

"There's nothing on the records here. The business passed to our guy when his old man died. These records list the same bogus London address. Director said there were some paper records, some disc files in storage, but Lowell took them years ago. Sorry, kid."

"Tidy son of a bitch. Anyone still working there who was employed when Lowell was still in residence?"

"No, checked that. I'm bringing in what records there are. We'll pick through them. On my way in now."

"I'll see you in the war room."

She pushed up, wanting to be on her feet. Her system was bottoming out, she could feel it, and if she didn't keep moving, she'd drop.

He was in New York, she thought. And wherever he lived and worked, wherever he was holding Ariel would be in New York, in a building that survived, or at least partially survived, the Urbans. It would have a connection to him, to her, to that time.

Nothing else would do for him, she was sure of it.

384

Death was his business. Body preparation or disposal, echoes of the Urban Wars, profit and science. He lived by death.

By killing he re-created the death of one woman, over and over again, while feeding his own need to control, to give pain. To study pain and death.

The torture devices were, in the opinions of the ME and the lab, tools and implements used during the Urbans with a few modern devices worked in. Same with the drugs found in the victims. He had to keep the connection.

Opera. The drama, the scope, the tragedy, and again the connection to Edwina Spring. The disguises were really costumes, the aliases simply roles to play.

Weren't the victims the same? Just another element of his role-playing.

How much longer before he gave Eve her cue to come onstage? And why the hell was she waiting?

She got herself some coffee, took out another energy pill. Technically she wasn't supposed to take a second one within the same twenty-four-hour period. But if she was going to push for her entrance in the play, she wasn't going out so blurry she couldn't remember her lines.

She popped it, and with the coffee in hand went back to the war room.

She opened communications so anyone in the field could hear and participate. "Updates. EDD first. Feeney?"

"We're about to run searches through the discs taken from Lowell's Funeral Home. We'll go through the paper records as well, looking for any pertinent data on Robert Lowell and/or Edwina Spring. Secondary unit has a list of prior open homicides and Missings that may be his earlier work. We're requesting case files, moving from the highest probability down."

"Anything sing for you?"

"Two. Both in Italy, one fifteen years back, one twelve. Both missing females that bull's-eye our vic profile. One from Florence, one from Milan."

"Roarke, does Lowell have business operations in Italy, either of those cities?"

"Milan, established just prior to Lowell's inheriting the business."

"I want every detail of the Milan case first. Baxter, I want you to reach out to the investigating officer or his superior. Get a translator if necessary. Roarke, put the other Lowell operation locations on screen.

"We hit these," she said as he complied. "Blanket warrant — Feeney, make that happen. Three-man teams at each location, communication open throughout. Hit private and/or employee-only areas first. Get statements, get data, get every fucking thing."

"I have two prior business locations," Roarke put in. "Buildings that were sold. One was severely damaged during the war, torn down and rebuilt as an apartment building. The second was intact, but sold by this Lowell's father twenty-three years ago. He bought it shortly after the Urbans."

"I'll take those two. Fire up my eyes and ears, Feeney. Peabody and two uniforms can shadow me. Ten-block minimum. I move out in five."

Roarke got up to follow her out, and after scratching his head, Feeney went after both.

"Three-man teams," Roarke commented. "Except for you."

"You know why."

"I don't have to like it. You can spare a uniform. I'll shadow with Peabody."

She shook her head. "I need you here. Out there, you're just weight. In here, you may make the difference."

"That's a hell of a thing."

"Can't be helped." She swung into her office for her coat, spotted Feeney when she started to pull it on.

"Let's check you out, kid."

"Oh. Right." She depressed and turned the button on her jacket to activate. "System's a go?"

He glanced at his hand monitor. "That's affirmative." Then he looked up at her. "We're closing in. You get that, too?"

"Yeah. Another twenty-four, maybe thirty-six, we'll pin him. I don't want it to go that long, Feeney. He probably started on her this morning, bright and fucking early this morning. Been at her now ten or twelve hours, I'd say. Maybe she can make another twenty-four or thirty-six. Maybe she can't. I can't make him go for me, but I'm going to be out there the next few hours, giving him the chance to try."

Feeney's glance drifted to Roarke, then back to her. "Not enough for him to try."

"No. I've got to get inside, got to get him to take me where she is. I know how to handle it. I know how to handle it," she repeated, looking directly at Roarke. "If he gives me the chance. If he doesn't, I need the two of you here, digging out the next piece that brings us to him. If we had this much nine years ago, if we believed he might move on me then, Feeney, what would you have done?"

He puffed out his cheeks. "I'd've sent you out."

"Then I'd better get going."

Roarke watched her go, and when he was back at his station, split his work screen with her camera. He could see what she saw, hear through his ear bud what she heard.

That would have to be enough.

She took the second location he'd given her first. Private home, higher probability. While his searches ran he focused all his attention on the building she approached. Urban and attractive, he decided, tucked in among other urban and attractive buildings.

When the door was opened by a woman with a dog yapping at her feet and a toddler on her hip, he relaxed. The probability had just dipped very low.

Still he kept her on split screen as she went inside, sidestepping the dog the woman shooed away.

He let bits of the conversation wind through his head as he put the bulk of his concentration on the work. Everything the woman said to Eve confirmed the official data on the property. A family home owned by a junior exec and his wife, professional mother, who lived there with their two children and a very irritable terrier.

"Nothing here," Eve said as she moved back outside toward her vehicle. "Heading to second location. No tails spotted."

She was cold. She was so awfully cold. It was probably shock, Ariel told herself. In vids when somebody went into shock, they put a blanket over them. Didn't they?

Parts of her had gone numb, and she didn't know if that was a blessing or if it meant those pieces of her had died. She knew she'd lost consciousness the second — or had it been the third? — time he'd hurt her.

But then he'd done something, something that had shot her back into the nightmare. Something that had jolted her like a hot blue electric current.

Sooner or later, he wouldn't be able to bring her back. A part of her wanted to pray for that, so she buried that part, that weeping, yielding part.

Someone would come. She would stay alive, then someone would come.

When he came back, she wanted to scream. She wanted to scream and scream until the force of the sound shattered all those glass walls. Until it shattered him. She could imagine it, how that kind and quiet face of his would shatter into pieces like the walls of glass.

"Could I . . . May I please have some water?"

"I'm sorry, but that's not allowed. You're getting fluids through the IV."

"But my throat's so dry, and I was hoping we could talk some more."

"Were you?" He wandered over to his tray. She wouldn't let herself look, didn't dare look at what he picked up this time.

"Yes. About music. What's the music that's playing now?"

"Ah, that would be Verdi. *La Traviata*."

He closed his eyes a moment, and his hands began to move like a conductor's. "Brilliant, isn't it? Stirring and passionate."

"Did — did your mother sing this one?"

"Yes, of course. It was a favorite of hers."

"It must have been so hard for you when she died. I had a friend whose mother self-terminated. It was terrible for her. It's . . . it's hard to understand how anyone could be so sad or so lost that it seems to them death is the answer."

"But of course, it is, just that. It's the answer for all of us in the end." He stepped closer. "It's what we all ask for when our time comes. She did. You will."

"I don't want to die."

"You will," he said again. "Just as she did. But don't worry, I'll give you that answer, and that gift, just as I did for her."

Other chatter came and went as teams reported in from their destinations. Roarke drank coffee and painstakingly scraped layers off old records, pried out ragged bits of data, and tried to sew them together into answers.

The second building had a basement. Though Eve knew the chances were small, she did a walk-through.

Not his kind of place, she decided. Too modern, too ugly, too crowded, and with too much security. A guy couldn't comfortably drag a terrified or unconscious woman inside without annoying the neighbors.

Still she questioned a few, showed Lowell's picture.

What if she was off, she wondered, about him working out of the city? Maybe he'd bought a damn house in the suburbs, and used Manhattan for hunting and dumping. How much time would she have wasted looking for the right building among thousands if he was killing women in some ranch in White Plains or Newark?

She got back in the car. She'd go back to the bakery, back to Greenfeld's apartment. Maybe she'd missed something. Maybe they all had. She'd do another sweep of each victim's home and place of employment.

Swinging out into traffic, she relayed her intentions back to base. "It'll keep me out on the street a couple more hours, keep me in the open. And it'll look like what it is. Like I'm chasing my goddamn tail."

"I've got another possibility," Roarke told her. "It was a sewing machine factory, regentrified into lofts in SoHo late in the twentieth. I've got a bit about it being used for barracks during the Urbans, taking some considerable hits. It was repaired and sold for lofts again in the early thirties."

"Okay, I'll check that one. Give me the location." She pursed her lips when he gave her the address. She'd gone from west to east, and now would cross west again, head north. "Peabody, you copy that?"

"Affirmative."

"Heading west."

She made her turn, then answered the signal of her in-dash 'link. "Dallas."

"Lieutenant Dallas? I'm calling for Mr. Klok. You requested that he contact you when he returned home.

He arrived today, and would be happy to speak with you if you still wish it."

"Yeah, I still wish it."

"Mr. Klok is able to meet with you at your convenience. However, it would be helpful if you could come to his residence as he's injured himself in a fall. His doctors prefer he remain at home for the next forty-eight hours."

"Yeah? What happened?"

"Mr. Klok slipped on some ice on the sidewalk upon his return. He suffered a mild concussion and a wrenched knee. If it's not convenient for you, Mr. Klok wishes for me to relate to you that he will come to your office as soon as his doctors allow."

"I can come to him. Actually, I'm in the area now. I can be there in a few minutes."

"Very well. I'll inform Mr. Klok."

Eve ended the transmission, and said, "Hmmm."

"Got a smell to it," Feeney commented in her ear.

"Yeah, awfully well timed and convenient. It's also pretty stupid for our guy to invite me into his home to make his move. No tail on me. As far as he knows I've got my partner here."

She tapped her fingers on the wheel as she thought it through. "Klok ran clean — and no, I'm not discounting that could be another fabrication. Either way, I want to talk to him. And if this actually turns out to be his move on me, he's giving me free entry."

"Into a trap," Roarke pointed out.

"It's only a trap if I let him spring it. I've got three men at my back, I've got eyes and ears. I'm going in, and you can dig deeper on his house while I'm in transit. If I see or feel anything off, you'll know it. Peabody move in, secure the van three blocks from destination."

"Copy," Peabody acknowledged. "We're about ten blocks back now, got a little snag in traffic. We'll route around it and move in."

"Go ahead and do another run on Klok. Let's see if he arrived in New York today as advertised. Search public and private shuttles and transports. If you get those results while I'm in, relay. Otherwise, cut all chatter now. I'm only a couple blocks away."

Jumpy, Eve thought, rolling her shoulders. Damn chemicals from the energy pills were bouncing around inside her like little springy balls.

"Transmission's going a little fuzzy on the homer," Feeney commented, then glanced over at Roarke. "You getting that?"

"I am. A little interference. Could be some stray transmission that bled onto the frequency. Can you clean it up?"

"Working on that. Peabody, you still have her?"

"Yeah. McNab says the beacon's jumping a little."

"It's interference," Roarke repeated as the signal went in and out. "It's another transmission, crossing ours. Bloody hell." He shoved back from his station. "It's another homer. Another homer on her vehicle. It's crossed ours now because she's near or at the base point. He's tracked her, that's how he knew to call her in. He knew she was close."

"Dallas, Dallas, you copy?" Feeney shouted into the receiver. "Dallas, goddamn it. Peabody, move in, move the fuck in." He leaped up, rushed after Roarke as Roarke ran out of the room. "She knows what she's doing," Feeney said as they shoved onto an elevator.

"So does he."

Eve parked, then moved across the sidewalk. The courtyard gate opened for her. Awfully damn accommodating, she mused, and shifted her shoulders just to feel the weight of her weapon.

"At the door," she murmured into her receiver and pressed the bell.

The droid opened it. "Lieutenant, thank you for coming. Mr. Klok is in the parlor. May I take your coat?"

"No. Lead the way."

She'd keep the droid where she could see him, just in case.

The curtains were drawn, the lights low. She could see the figure of a man in a chair near a quiet fire, his foot wrapped with a soft cast and resting on a padded stool.

He had a short brown beard, short brown hair, some bruising around his left eye. "Corpulent" would have been the polite word for him, Eve supposed. Hers would have been "really fat."

"Lieutenant Dallas?" He had the slightest Germanic accent. "Please pardon me for not getting up. I was clumsy, banged myself up a bit this morning. Please sit down. Can I offer you something? Tea? Coffee?"

"No."

He offered his hand as he spoke. She moved in to take it. The common gesture would bring her closer, close enough, she judged for her to determine if he was Robert Lowell.

And as she angled herself to look into his eyes, she knew. She shifted, pulling her right hand back to reach for her weapon. "Hello, Bob."

He only smiled. "No one has ever called me Bob. You saw right through me."

"Get up. You." She gestured toward the hovering droid. "If you don't want your circuits fried, stay exactly where you are."

"I'm a little hampered," Lowell said pleasantly. "All this padding, and the cast."

Eve kicked the footstool away, so his foot thudded on the floor. "On the floor, on your face, hands behind your back. Now."

"I'll do my best." He slid and humped his way off the chair, huffing as he struggled to roll onto his belly.

When she reached down to grab his wrist, to pull his arm behind his back, he turned his hand, closed it over hers.

She felt the prick, cursed. "Son of a bitch tranq'd me." She aimed her weapon mid-body, fired a stream. Then her legs buckled and sent her to her knees.

"An old method," Lowell said as he effortfully rolled over. "Often used in assassinations at one time. Just a tranquilizer now, as you said." He smiled as she slid the rest of the way to the floor. "Very quick acting, of course."

He sat where he was until he'd unbuttoned the padded suit, pulled it aside. Underneath he wore standard body armor. "I thought, as you're very skilled, you might fire your weapon. It's always wise to take precautions. Carry her down to my workroom," he ordered the droid.

His duplicate droid was already taking her car away, very far away.

"Yes, sir."

Plenty of time, Lowell thought. When he was certain all was well, he'd call the droid home, replace his hard drive as he would replace this house droid's memory. As he'd done many times before.

Clean slate.

For now, he gathered the suit, the cast, picked up the weapon Eve had dropped. It was possible she'd called in her intention to stop there. Someone would come, be that the case. But there would be no sign she'd been there.

Her vehicle would be found miles away.

He would have all her communication devices, and all would be shut down.

He would have her, Lowell thought as he started down the steps to his work area. And complete his life's work.

Outside the house, Peabody stood sick with frustration and dread. She'd called for a battering ram for the door they couldn't budge, and for laser torches to cut through the riot bars on every window.

Eve was inside, and she couldn't find a way in.

"You've got to override the security."

"I'm working on it," McNab said between his teeth as he pulled out every trick he knew. "It's got backups on its backups. I've never seen anything like it."

They both whirled as a car squealed to a halt in the street. Some of her dread lessened when she saw Roarke and Feeney jump out.

"We can't get past the system. The place is locked down like a fort."

"Move aside." Roarke shoved McNab away, pulled out his own tools.

"Tried the master, tried the override, got my comp to spit out codes. But when you input, they shift to another sequence."

"It was a Stealth base during the Urbans," Feeney told Peabody as sweat rolled down his back. "The minute she walked in, all comms were useless. We got the data on the way over. First Robert Lowell had it titled in his wife's maiden name, ran a branch of the business out of here. More a front during the Urbans.

"Get that damn system down," he ordered Roarke.

"Quiet and let me work."

"You don't get that down, get us inside before he puts hands on her, I'll be kicking your ass for the rest of my natural life."

Ariel's eyes tracked to him as he came in behind the droid. "Who is she? Who is she?"

"You could say the last of her breed." He leaned over the table where the droid laid Eve, went through her pockets for her 'link, her communicator, her PPC. He removed her wrist unit. "Take these and put them into the recycler. Go upstairs, shut down," he told the droid.

"Well, now." Gently Lowell brushed a hand through Eve's hair. "You'll need to be washed and prepared. Best to do that while you're sleeping. We're going to spend some time together, you and I. I've been looking forward to it."

"Are you going to kill me now?" Ariel asked.

"No, no, indeed, your time's still running. But I am going to do something very special." He turned to Ariel as if pleased to be able to discuss it. "I've never taken the opportunity to work with two partners at the same time. And you're proving to be so much more than I anticipated. I really believe you're going to exceed most, if not all who came before you. But she?" He glanced back at Eve. "I've set the bar very high for her. The last Eve."

"She . . . she looks familiar."

"Hmm?" Absently, he looked at Ariel again. "Yes, I suppose you might have seen her on some of the media reports. Now —"

"Mr. Gaines!"

He stopped his pivot back to Eve, frowned down at Ariel. "Yes, yes? What's so urgent? I have work."

"What . . . what is the most time? I mean, how long is the longest anyone — any of the women you've brought here — has lasted?"

His eyes brightened. "You're such a delightful surprise to me! Are you challenged? Have I tapped your competitive streak?"

398

"I can't . . . if I don't know how long, I can't try to last longer. Will you tell me how long?"

"I can." With her clutch piece in her hand, Eve sat up on the steel table. "Eighty-five hours, twelve minutes, thirty-eight seconds."

"No." He looked baffled first, then red-faced and furious. "No, no. This is *not* allowed."

"You don't like that, you're going to hate this."

Eve shot out a stun, on a setting a little higher than was considered proper procedure, and dropped him like a stone. "Fuckhead," she muttered, and prayed she wasn't going to pass out or vomit.

"I knew you'd come." Tears swam in Ariel's eyes. "I knew someone would come, and when I saw them bring you in, I knew it was going to be okay."

"Yeah, hold on." She had to slide to her feet, give herself a moment to balance. "You did good. You did real good keeping his attention on you so I could get to my piece."

"I wanted to kill him. I imagined killing him. It helped."

"I bet it did. Listen, I'm a little off center. I don't think I'd better try cutting those ropes just yet. You've got to hang in there a little bit longer. I know you hurt, but you've got to hang in."

"I'm so cold."

"Okay." Eve managed to pull off her coat, then draped it over Ariel's bleeding and battered body. "I'm going to secure him, okay? I'm going to secure him, then go call for backup."

"Would you bring me back some water?"

Eve laid a hand on Ariel's cheek. "Sure."

"And maybe a whole bunch of drugs." While the tears spilled out, Ariel struggled to smile. "This is a really nice coat."

"Yeah. I like it."

CHAPTER
TWENTY-TWO

Two energy boosts with a tranq chaser, Eve thought. The combination had her feeling stupid, shaky, and not a little sick. But she not only had to stay on her feet, she had to do the job.

Reaching around, she fumbled at her back for her restraints. Either they weren't there, or she'd lost all sensation in her left hand. "Crap. I've got to restrain this son of a bitch, but my cuffs . . . I must've dropped them upstairs when he tranq'd me. Let me just . . . okay."

She turned, saw the ropes looped through the side holes in the table. "Here we go. Okay."

"You don't look so good," Ariel commented. "I probably look a whole lot worse, but you don't look so good."

"Been putting in a lot of hours looking for you, Ariel." Eve fought the knots on the rope, cursing under her breath as her fingers felt as agile as limp soy dogs.

"Thanks."

"No problem. Bloody buggering hell! Was this son of a bitch a Youth Guide or something?"

"I always thought they were little psychos."

Unsteady fingers slick with sweat, Eve tugged and dragged. "Almost got this bitch. Just hold on."

"I'm not going anywhere."

Eve muscled one rope free, then bent over from the waist, blowing out breath as her stomach tried to heave. "Little sick to my stomach. Don't be alarmed if I boot."

Ariel managed a smile through gritted teeth. "If you do, boot on him. Bastard."

On an appreciative and slightly drunk laugh, Eve crouched down to tie Lowell's hands. "You're a stand-up, Ariel. A goddamn Amazon. I can see why Erik's in love with you."

"What? Erik? Erik loves me?"

Eve swiped at her sweaty brow, glanced up and over at Ariel's pale face. "That was probably something I was supposed to keep to myself. Crossed the line. Blame the tranq. But listen," she continued as she tied the rope around Lowell's wrists just a little tighter than strictly necessary. "If you don't go for him, you know? If you don't, take it easy on him, okay? 'Cause he's really gone over you."

Eve stood, ignoring the way her head swam, to release the second rope for Lowell's feet. And saw tears sliding down Ariel's cheeks. "Oh, man, I know you're hurt. I know this sucks out loud, but just hang on a few minutes more."

"I've loved that dumbass almost since he moved in across the hall. Dumbass never made one move."

"Oh." God, people were strange, Eve thought. The woman had stood up under unspeakable pain, but she was leaking because some guy was soft on her. "He probably will now. Jesus, music off!" she ordered as she bound Lowell's feet. But the voices continued to soar. "You know how he shut that shit off?"

"Not really. I've been kind of tied up since I got here."

Eve plopped down on her ass and laughed like a loon. "You ever think of giving up baking and going into police work, Ariel — I swear you've got the spine and the nasty streak for it."

"I like baking. I'm going to bake you the most incredible cake. It's going to be a goddamn work of art. Oh, God, God, do you think someone's coming with drugs soon?"

"It won't be long. I'm going to see if I can get the doors open, or break the glass."

"But . . . don't leave me."

"Listen." Eve gained her feet, stepped over so she and Ariel were face-to-face. "I'm not going anywhere without you. On my word."

"What's your name? I'm sorry, did you tell me your name already?"

"It's Dallas. Eve Dallas."

"If I give Erik a break and we get married, I'm naming the first kid after you."

"There's a lot of that going around."

"Get us the hell out of here, Dallas."

Eve moved to the door, yanked, shoved, pulled, kicked, rammed. Cursed. Turning again, she pulled the coat over Ariel's face. "Just for a minute, in case the glass flies around." And taking out her weapon again, she upped the stream and blasted at the door.

The glass held, but she saw it shake. She hit it again, aiming for the same spot, then a third time. On the forth, the glass erupted into a wild spiderweb of cracks.

"Nearly through, Ariel." Eve holstered her weapon, picked up the stool and slammed it into the damaged door. She beat at it until the ground sparkled and the opening was clear.

After heaving the stool aside, Eve went back to uncover Ariel's face. Paler now, Eve noted, shaking a little more. Had to get moving, had to get gone. "Found a way out. I'm going to cut these ropes now."

"Try not to let the knife slip. I'm pretty tired of getting cut."

Eve picked up one of Lowell's tools, nudged the coat away from Ariel's arm. It was patterned with cuts, punctures, burns. Eve set the blade on the rope, looked up into Ariel's eyes. "He's going to pay. He's going to pay for every minute you spent in here. I swear it."

She had to saw through the rope, leaving bracelets of it around Ariel's abraded wrists. And she had to turn her mind, her rage away from the wounds she saw.

As she freed Ariel's feet, she heard Lowell give a soft groan.

"He's waking up, he's waking up." Voice pitched in panic and pain, Ariel struggled to sit. "He can't get loose, can he?"

"No. He's not getting up on his own. And look, if he tries, we have this." Eve drew her weapon again.

"Why don't you stun him again? While I watch."

"Appreciate the sentiment, but I think it's time to get you out of here. Here, let's get this coat on you." As Eve slid the sleeves on, Ariel hissed. "Sorry."

"It's okay." She kept her eyes trained on Lowell. "I'm okay. Can you help me down so I can kick him? In the

404

face. That's what I imagined doing. I want to kick him in the face."

"Again, kudos on the sentiment. But here's what we're going to do. I want you to wrap your arms around my neck. Glass everywhere, and I don't have a spare pair of shoes on me. I just need you to hold onto me, and I'm going to carry you out. You hold onto me, Ariel. I'll get you out."

"Like . . . Like piggyback," Ariel managed between shaky breaths when Eve backed up to the table.

"Yeah, that's the way. You get a little piggyback ride, and I'm hoping you don't sample a lot of your products."

Ariel managed a watery laugh, then collapsed against Eve's neck and shoulders.

"Ready? Here we go." With her own legs wobbly from the drugs, Eve bent to take the weight. She focused on the door. Five feet to get through, she calculated as she put one foot in front of the other. Another two, maybe three to get past the broken glass on the floor.

There was communication equipment out there, she reminded herself as sweat slid over her skin and Ariel bit back whimpers. She'd tag her backup, the MTs.

She heard something crash, then the rush of feet. And tightened her grip on the weapon in her hand. She let out the breath she was holding when she heard Roarke shout her name.

"Back here! Call the MTs! That's the cavalry, Ariel."

"No." Ariel's head slumped on Eve's shoulder. "You are."

Roarke flew through the maze of the basement toward the echo of Eve's voice. The sound of it had stabbed through the music, blown through him like breath.

He saw her, pale, face gleaming with sweat, her weapon in her hand, and a quietly weeping woman on her back.

He lowered his own weapon, let the tremor in his belly come and go. "We've come to save you."

She worked up a grin for him. "About damn time."

He was to her in the single beat of a heart, and despite the flood of cops pouring down, gripped her exhausted face in his hands and kissed her.

"Here." He shifted to lift Ariel from Eve's back. "Let me help you."

"Is he yours?" Ariel asked.

"Yeah. He's mine."

Ariel stared up into Roarke's face. "Wow." She let out a deep, deep breath, then just closed her eyes.

"MTs, now." Eve bent, bracing her hands on her knees. "Peabody, you here?"

"Present and accounted for."

"I want this place secured. I want a team of sweepers in here, going over every inch, documenting everything."

"Dallas, you look a little green."

"Tranq'd me. Fucker got by me for a half a second. Energy pills, tranqs, I'm a chemical stew." She stayed as she was, snorting out a laugh. "Damn it. All electronics seized. Droid somewhere upstairs deactivated. And Jesus, somebody get that music off before my head explodes."

406

She pushed herself up, swayed, and might have tumbled if Feeney hadn't gripped her arm. "Head rush. I'm okay, just a little queasy. Lowell's in there, secured. You need to haul his ass in. Your collar."

"No, it's not." Feeney gave her arm a squeeze. "But I'll haul his ass in for you. McNab, help the lieutenant upstairs, then get your butt back down here and start on the electronics."

"I don't need help," Eve protested.

"You fall on your face," Feeney murmured in her ear, "you'll ruin your exit."

"Yeah. Yeah."

"Just lean on me, Lieutenant." McNab wrapped an arm around her waist.

"You try to cop a feel, I can still put you down."

"Whatever your condition, Dallas, you still scare me."

"Aw." Touched, she slung an arm around his shoulders. "That's so sweet."

Taking her weight, he led her through the maze of rooms, up the stairs. "We couldn't get in," he told her. "We were maybe ten minutes behind you — traffic snarl — then we couldn't get in the damn house. Your car wasn't there, but we knew you'd gone in. I couldn't get through the security. Roarke did. We had battering rams and laser torches coming, but he got through."

"Nothing much keeps him out."

"It took time, even for him. Place is like the frigging Pentagon or something. Then we had to get through the next level on the basement."

"How long was I in there?"

"Twenty minutes, half an hour, maybe."

"Not too bad."

"I'll take her from here," Roarke said.

"Don't — aw, no picking me up." But she was already cradled in his arms.

"I have to, for a minute anyway." He simply buried his face against the side of her neck as cops and techs swarmed by. "I couldn't get to you."

"Yeah, you did. Besides, I told you I could handle myself."

"So you did, so you always do. Are you hurt?"

"No. Feel like I guzzled a bottle of wine, and not the good stuff. But it's passing some. Gee, your hair smells good." She sniffed at it, caught herself, and winced. "Damn tranqs. You gotta put me down. This is undermining my rep and authority."

He eased her onto her feet, but kept his arm around her waist for support. "You need to lie down."

"Really don't. You lie down and everything starts spinning around. Just need to walk it off."

"Lieutenant?" Newkirk walked up with her coat. "Ms. Greenfeld asked that this get back to you."

"Thanks. Where is she?"

"MTs are working on her, in the hall — the foyer, I guess it is."

"All right. Officer Newkirk? You did good work."

"Thank you, Lieutenant. Right now it feels like good work."

"I want to take a look at her before they transport her," Eve said to Roarke, and let him help her to the foyer.

Ariel was on a stretcher, covered with a blanket, a pair of MTs preparing to roll her out.

"Give me a minute. Hey," she said to Ariel, "how you doing?"

"They gave me some really mag drugs. I feel *sooooo* good. You saved my life." Ariel reached up to grip Eve's hand.

"I had a part in it. So did the cops crowding into this place, and this civilian here, too. But mostly, Ariel? You saved yourself. We're going to need to talk to you some more, when you're feeling a little better."

"So he pays."

"That's right."

"Anytime, anyplace."

"Okay. One more second," she told the MTs, and held out a hand to Roarke. "Let me have your pocket 'link." She took it, keyed in a number. "Hey, Erik. Hey," she repeated when he began to spew out questions. "Quiet down. I've got someone here who wants to talk to you." She put the 'link into Ariel's hand. "Say hi, Ariel."

"Erik? Erik?" She began to cry, to laugh, and beamed up at Eve with drug-hazed eyes. "He's crying. Don't cry, Erik. I'm okay now. Everything's okay."

"Go ahead," Eve said to the MTs, "and tell the guy on the 'link where you're taking her. He'll want to be there."

"Nice job, Lieutenant," Roarke murmured as they wheeled Ariel out.

"Yeah. And you can always get another 'link. I have to go in, finish this up."

"We have to go in, finish this up," Roarke corrected.

★ ★ ★

She was steadier when she got to Central, and forced down some of the Eatery's fake eggs in the hopes of smoothing out her system. She forked them up in the war room, chasing them with all the water she could stand.

She wanted a shower, she wanted a bed. But more than she wanted anything, she wanted a turn with Lowell in the box.

She set the food aside, rose, and walked over to stare at all the names on the board. "For all of them," she said quietly. "What we did, what we do now, it's for all of them. That's the point that has to be made. In the box, in the courts, in the media. It's important."

"No one who worked in this room these last days will forget them," Roarke told her.

She nodded. "This is going to take some time. I know you're not leaving until it's done, so I won't bother suggesting it. You can stand in Observation, or be more comfortable and watch from one of the monitors."

"I like Observation."

"Okay then. I'm going to have him brought up, so go pick your spot. I need to talk to Peabody."

She headed toward the bullpen. It was buzzing, and as she stepped inside, applause broke out. Eve held up a hand. "Save it," she ordered. "It's not done yet. Peabody."

Peabody shoved up from her desk, turned, and took a quick bow before going out after Eve. "We're pumped."

410

"Yeah, I know. Peabody, I have to ask you for a solid."

"Sure."

"You earned a turn in Interview with this bastard, and you're secondary on the investigation. It's your right. I need to ask you to step aside for Feeney on this."

"Can I stand in Observation and give Lowell the finger?"

"Absolutely. I owe you."

"No. Not on this one. Nobody owes anybody on this one."

"Okay. Bring him up for us, will you? Interview A."

"Oh, my sincere pleasure. Dallas? I've just gotta dance." And she did so, a kind of tap/shuffle as she walked away.

Eve went into her office, tagged Feeney. "Interview A, he's coming up."

"Burn his ass."

"Then get yours down here and help me fry him, ace."

"Peabody —"

"Is observing, like half the cops in this place. Come on, Feeney, this one's ours. Let's wrap it up."

"I'm on my way."

When it was time, she walked into Interview A with Feeney. Lowell sat quietly alone, an ordinary-looking man past middle age with a pleasant if somewhat quizzical smile on his face.

"Lieutenant Dallas, this is very unexpected."

"Record on, Dallas, Lieutenant Eve, and Feeney, Captain Ryan, in interview with subject Lowell, Robert." She fed in the case numbers — all of them, then read off the Revised Miranda. "Robert Lowell do you understand your rights and obligations in this matter?"

"Of course. You were very clear."

"You understand you're being charged with the abductions, assaults, forced imprisonments, and murders of six women, the abduction and forced imprisonment of Ariel Greenfeld, and will subsequently be questioned by Global authorities on the abductions, assaults, illegal captivity, and murders of others."

"Yes, I do." He continued to smile genially, folded his plump hands. "Should we save time by my acknowledging all those charges. Confessing to them? Or would that be anticlimactic?"

"You're awful damn chipper," Feeney commented, "for a man who's going to spend the rest of his miserable, murdering life in a cement cage."

"Well, actually, I won't be. I will be quietly ending my time within the next twenty-four hours as per my requested and granted self-termination contract. It will stand," he said pleasantly, "as my doctors have certified my terminal condition and my application. My lawyers have assured me that the certification will override even criminal charges. Neither the State nor Global will supersede an individual's right to die. And, of course, it saves considerable expense. So . . ." He lifted his shoulders.

"You think you can get off, get out, by swallowing a few pills?" Feeney demanded.

"Indeed I do. It's not what I hoped for, believe me. I haven't finished my work, not completely. You were to be my ultimate," he said to Eve. "The culmination of everything. When you were finished, then I would have approached my own death with all fully realized. Still, I have accomplished a great deal."

"Well." Eve leaned back in her chair, nodded. "You sure covered the bases. I have to say — Bob — you thought of everything. I admire that. It's not nearly as satisfying to pull in a sloppy killer."

"Order is one of my bywords."

"Yeah, I noticed. I appreciate you saving us time by being willing to confess to everything, but after all the work we put in, we'd really like the details. You could call it our culmination. So . . . this is going to take a while," she said with an easy smile. "You want something to drink? I'm still a little off from the tranq you got into me. I'm going to go get myself some cold caffeine. You want?"

"That's very nice of you. I wouldn't mind a soft drink."

"You got it. Feeney, why don't you step out while I hit Vending. Pause record."

"What the hell," Feeney began when they were outside Interview.

Everything about her hardened: face, eyes, voice. "I've got a way around this. I don't want you to ask me about it. Ever. When we go back in, we play along. We

413

get the details, and we sew him up. Give me your 'link, will you? I haven't replaced mine yet. And wait for me."

She took Feeney's 'link, wandered down to Vending. And beeped Peabody on privacy mode. "Tell Roarke — quietly — to step out for a minute. Don't say anything to me. We haven't spoken." She clicked off, then stared at the machine.

Moments later, Roarke walked up behind her. "Lieutenant?"

"Get me a Pepsi, a ginger ale, and a cream soda. I need you to make this go away," she said under her breath. "Can you make his self-termination clearance disappear? No trace of it, anywhere?"

"Yes," he said simply as he ordered the tubes.

"It crosses the line, what I'm asking you. I gave her my word he'd pay. And in the war room before I came out, I gave them all my word. So I'm crossing the line."

He retrieved the tubes, passed them to her. His eyes, meeting hers, spoke volumes. "I have to get on," he said in a clear voice. "I wish I could stay, wait for you, but I'm expecting some calls and transmissions, and you gave Ariel my 'link. I'll try to come back once I've taken care of this. Otherwise, I'll see you at home."

"Yeah. Okay. Thanks."

They parted ways with her heading back to Feeney. "I got you cream soda."

"For Christ's sake —"

"Hey, if you wanted something else you should've said so. It's going away," she whispered. "Don't ask me about it, just take my word. He's not going out the way he wants. We'll let him think he is, until we have everything we need."

Feeney stared into her eyes for a long moment, then nodded. "Okay, let's get it down."

It took hours, but Lowell never requested a break. He was, Eve realized, basking. After all the time, all the effort, he was finally able to share his obsession.

He gave them meticulous details on every murder.

Eve and Feeney worked in tandem, an old and easy rhythm.

"You got yourself a good memory," Feeney commented.

"I do. You'll find every project documented — keeping records, and we could say *amending* them, was one of my tasks during the wars. I'm sure you've collected all the records from my lab and office. I'd hoped, before I learned I was dying, to arrange for my work to be published. It will have to be posthumously, but I believe that's appropriate."

"So, your work," Eve began, "what got you started? We understand the women —"

"Partners. I considered them partners."

"I bet they didn't see it your way, but fine. Your partners represented to you your stepmother."

"They *became* her, which is entirely different. She was the first, you see. The Eve." He smiled brilliantly. "So you can see why I knew you were to be the last."

"Yeah, too bad about your luck on that."

"I always knew I could fail, but if I succeeded it would have been perfection. As she was. She was magnificent. You'll also find many recording discs of her performances. She gave up a great career for me."

"For you?"

"Yes. We were, well, the term would be 'soul mates.' While I could never play — she was an accomplished pianist — nor did I have a voice to offer, it was through her I gained my great love and admiration for music. It was by her I was saved."

"How so?"

"My father considered me imperfect. Some difficulties with my birth, which caused, well, you could call it a defect. I had some trouble with controlling my impulses, and there were mood swings. He institutionalized me briefly, over my grandfather's objections, when I was quite young. Then Edwina came into my life. She was patient and loving, and used music to help me remain calm or entertained. She was my mother and my partner, and my great love."

"She was killed during the Urbans," Eve prompted.

"Her time came during the Urbans. The human cycle is about time, you see, and will and individual acceptance."

"But you turned her in," Eve said. "You heard her talking with the man, the soldier she was in love with. Heard that she was planning to leave you. You couldn't let her go, could you?"

Irritation flickered over his face. "How do you know anything about that?"

"You're a smart guy, Bob. We're smart guys, too. What did you do when you found out she was going to leave you?"

416

"She couldn't leave me, she had no right. We belonged together. It was a terrible betrayal, unforgivable. There was no choice, none at all, in what had to be done."

"What had to be done?" Feeney asked him.

"I had to go to my father, and my grandfather, and tell them that she'd betrayed us. That I'd overheard her planning betrayals with one of the men. That she was a traitor."

"You made them think she was a spy. Betraying the cause."

He spread his hands, all reason. "It was all the same, and a great tragedy for us all. She was taken, as the soldier was, down to my grandfather's laboratory."

"In the house where you took the women, here in New York. Down where you worked, where your grandfather tortured prisoners during the Urbans."

"I learned a great deal from my grandfather. I watched as he worked with Edwina — he insisted on it. I understood so much as I watched. It made me strong and aware. Days, it took. Longer than it took for the soldier."

He moistened his lips, took a small, tidy drink. "Men are weaker, my grandfather taught me. So often weaker than women. In the end, she asked for death. I looked into her eyes, and I saw all the answers, all the love, all the beauty that comes when the body and mind are stripped down to the core. I stopped time for her myself, my gift to her. She was my first, and all who've come after have only been reflections of her."

"Why did you wait so long to look for those reflections?"

"The medication. My father was very insistent about my medication, and monitored me quite closely. The understanding, the clarity of mind needed for the work dulls with the medication."

"But Corrine Dagby, here in New York nine years ago, she wasn't your first." Eve shook her head. "Not nearly. You had to practice, to perfect. How many were there before Corrine?"

"I learned from my grandfather, continued my education, and worked in the family business. I practiced on the dead under my grandfather's tutelage. And I traveled. I first began serious practice nearly twenty years ago, after my father's death. I had a great deal to learn and experience first. It took me another decade before I felt ready to begin the projects. I did document all the others, the failures, the near successes. You'll find all that in my records."

"Handy." Eve glanced over at the knock on the door. Peabody poked her head in.

"Excuse me, Lieutenant. Can I see you just for a minute?"

"Yeah. Keep going," she said to Feeney, then stepped outside.

"Roarke just tagged me. He asked if I'd tell you that he was able to finish the work he needed to deal with, and since it's cleaned up, he was heading back down. He said he hoped to see you finish the interview."

"Okay. I need you and McNab to check on this bastard's ST. No point in taking his word that he's got

418

the go to clock out. Check all his personal data taken from the scene, wake up his lawyers in London. His doctors, if you find their data. I want confirmation he's not stringing us on it."

"Why would he —"

"Just get me confirmation, Peabody."

"Yes, sir."

Eve went back in, slid into a chair as Feeney pried more details out of Lowell.

"I meant to ask you," she inserted, "how long Edwina Spring lasted. Her time."

"My grandfather employed different methods, with longer rest periods than I've found necessary. Regardless, she was very strong, and had a high survival instinct. It was ninety-seven hours, forty-one minutes, and eight seconds. No one has ever reached her capacity. I believe you may have done so, which is why I wanted to end with you as I'd begun with her."

"I wonder how long you'd last," Eve commented, and rose as Peabody appeared at the door again.

Eve stepped out and eased the door closed behind them. "And?"

"I don't get it. There's no documentation supporting his claim. Nothing in his records, nothing in the official data banks, and McNab searched through them twice. I contacted the London lawyer — head of the firm, who was not pleased to be disturbed at home."

"Aw."

"Yeah. He did the privacy dance. I explained that his client was under arrest for multiple murders, and hauling out this ST claim to avoid trial and incarceration. Pulled the commander into it. Legal guy claimed Lowell had secured certification, but he couldn't produce the documentation either. Went a little nuts about it. He's spouting about holding interviews and so on, but he doesn't have any pull in the U.S. of A."

"That's all I need."

"But —"

"Going to wrap this up now, Peabody. Good job."

Eve walked back in, closed the door in Peabody's face. "Just to summarize," Eve began. "You have confessed, with full understanding of your rights and obligations, having waived any counsel or representation, to the crimes heretofore documented?"

"'Crimes' is your word, but yes, I have."

"How long did the medicals estimate you had left?"

"No more than two years, with the last several months extremely painful, unpleasant, and demeaning even with medication. I prefer a quiet and controlled end to my time."

"I bet you do. But you know, you're not going to get it. You don't have any ST certification on record. Bob."

"I certainly do."

"Nope — and your fancy Brit lawyers can't produce one either." She laid her palms on the table, leaned over into his face. "No record means we're under no obligation to take your word for it, under no obligation to accommodate your easy out. A couple of years isn't as much as I'd like, but you'll be spending it in a box. You'll be spending some of it in pain, in distress, in despair."

"No." He shook his head slowly. "I have certification."

"You've got nothing. And you are no longer free to apply for ST. You've been charged and you have willingly confessed to multiple homicides. Your out just slammed shut."

"You're lying." His lips trembled. "You're trying to upset me, to trick me."

"You go ahead and think that. You go on thinking that for the next two years. You get to live, and every second you get to live, you're going to suffer."

"I want . . . I want my lawyers."

"Sure. You can have an army of goddamn lawyers. They're not going to help you." Her eyes were fierce now, not the flat, objective eyes of the cop, but the fierce, burning eyes of justice. "You're going to know pain. You're going to choke out your last breath in pain."

"No. No. It's my time, it's all worked out. I need my music, my pills."

"Bob, you need to die a long, slow, agonizing death." She straightened. "Why don't you haul him down, Feeney. He can go cry to his lawyers before he starts learning what it's like to live in a cage."

"I've been waiting for nine years to do this." Feeney hauled Lowell to his feet. "I'm betting on medical science," he said as he dragged Lowell to the door. "Couple of years? They might find a fix. That would be sweet." He glanced over his shoulder, sent Eve a strong smile. "That would be goddamn sweet."

EPILOGUE

When Eve stepped out, cops poured out of Observation, out of the conference room where the monitors had been set up. She saw Roarke with them before Baxter elbowed through, and shocked her speechless by hauling her off her feet and planting a noisy kiss on her mouth.

"Jesus Christ, are you out of your tiny mind?"

"Somebody had to do it, and he always gets to." He jerked his thumb at Roarke. "I'm already punchy so don't hit me. You either," he said to Eve as he dropped her back on her feet. "Call me a sucker, but I get emotional at happy endings."

"I'm going to be calling you in the nearest hospital if you try anything like that again. All of you who aren't on regular shift, go home. Dismissed, get the hell . . . Commander."

"Excellent job, all of you. I suggest you follow the lieutenant's orders. Go home, get some sleep. The department is goddamn proud of every one of you. Lieutenant."

"Sir. I'll have the paperwork finished and filed within the hour."

"No, you'll get the hell out. You'll go home. I'll see the paperwork is dealt with."

"Sir —"

"That's an order." He took her hand, shook it. "And consider that I'm going to give you a very large break and handle the media."

"Yes, sir."

She didn't object when Roarke slung an arm around her shoulders. "Why don't I drive you home, Lieutenant."

"Yeah, you could do that. Peabody, I don't want to see you here before ten tomorrow."

"I am so all over that. Dallas —"

"Don't even think about hugging me. Is there no end to the humiliation my men dole out?"

"Aw," Peabody said, but was grinning as Eve walked away.

She dropped off like a stone the minute she was in the car. Roarke drove with one hand on the wheel, one hand over hers. Halfway home, he switched to auto and let his own exhausted mind rest.

The lights of home were like stars, shining. He took his hand from hers to press his own fingers to his eyes, then climbed out to go around and open her door. But when he reached down to lift her, she batted a hand at his arm.

"No. I can walk."

"Thank Christ, because I think trying to haul you up at this point would have both of us on our asses in the bloody driveway. Here." He gripped her hand, gave her

423

a tug. And the two of them stood a moment in the cold, bleary with fatigue.

"We just have to get inside, get upstairs, and fall into bed," she decided. "We can do that."

"All right then. Here we go."

They wrapped arms around each other's waists, held each other up as they walked to the front door, and through.

"Look at the pair of you." Summerset stood like a black cloud in the foyer. "Stumbling in like drunks, and I'd say in need of a good wash and a decent meal."

"Up yours, fuckface."

"As always, such a command of the language."

"Have to stand with my wife on this one," Roarke said. "Or fall, as may very well be the case any moment. Though the fuckface was a bit harsh. Let's take the elevator, darling. I'm too bleeding tired for the stairs."

Summerset shook his finger at Galahad, who stood up to follow as they passed. "I think not," he said quietly to the cat. "Let's leave it just the two of them, shall we? And now that the children are home safe and sound, we'll have a little snack before bed."

"Bed," Eve said as they stumbled out of the elevator. "I think I can actually smell bed — but in a good way." She began to let things fall — her coat, then her jacket, her weapon — on her way to the bed, as Roarke did exactly the same.

"I have something to say."

"Better make it quick," she warned, "because I think I'm already asleep."

"I've worked with you before, watched, understood — to some extent — what you do. But I haven't really gone the gamut, as with this time. Beginning to end, and most of the steps between." He fell into bed with her. "You're an amazing woman, Lieutenant, my darling Eve."

"You're not so shabby yourself." She turned to him, and with the lights still on looked into his eyes. "I'm not going to ask how you pulled off what I asked you to pull off."

"It's a bit complicated to explain at the moment in any case."

"We had him, we stopped him, and Ariel Greenfeld's safe. But there wouldn't have been justice, not even a shadow of real justice, if you hadn't done it." She laid her hand on his cheek. "We did good work."

"So we did." Their lips pressed together briefly. "Now let's have ourselves an eight-hour vacation."

"To quote Peabody," she said, voice already slurring, " 'I'm so all over that.' "

"Lights off," he ordered.

In the dark, with her hand on his cheek, they slid into sleep.

J